# TINY GLITCHES

REBECCA CHASTAIN

www.rebeccachastain.com



Mind Your Muse Books
PO Box 374
Rocklin, CA 95677

ISBN: 978-0-9906031-6-0

# ALSO BY REBECCA CHASTAIN

## NOVELS OF TERRA HAVEN

### GARGOYLE GUARDIAN CHRONICLES

*Magic of the Gargoyles*

*Curse of the Gargoyles*

*Secret of the Gargoyles*

*Lured**

### TERRA HAVEN CHRONICLES

*Deadlines & Dryads*

*Leads & Lynxes*

*Headlines & Hydras*

*Muckrakers & Minotaurs*

## MADISON FOX ADVENTURES

*A Fistful of Evil*

*A Fistful of Fire*

*A Fistful of Flirtation**

*A Fistful of Frost*

*Madison Fox Novella Box Set*

## STAND ALONE

*Tiny Glitches*

*Exclusive to newsletter subscribers

*To Cody,*
*for never complaining about all the bulbs that burned out and lamps that broke*
*every time I worked on this novel.*

*I promise I'll be more careful with my next plot idea so future instances of my*
*fiction shaping our reality are more enjoyable.*

# ONE

THIS WASN'T ABOUT ME, and as satisfying as it'd be to embrace the anger simmering in my blood, it wouldn't help Sofie. If I didn't want to be forced to leave, I needed to find tranquility.

*I'm floating on a cloud of coffee cake. A fluffy brown sugar and cinnamon cake dense enough to choke the bastards—*

I pried my teeth apart to ask the gallery owner, "What did the police say?"

Gabriel slammed the back door of the gallery's storage room as the patrol car pulled out of the alley. His ruffled purple shirt fluttered in the back draft. "Best guess, they think it was a mistake, that the thief took the wrong art. Like *that's* helpful."

"The wrong art?" My nails curled into my palms.

In the middle of the night, some pea-brained imbecile had burgled Galileo Gallery, swiping every S. Sterling piece waiting in storage for next week's show. S. Sterling—my aunt Sofie—wasn't due back from San Francisco until this afternoon, which was why I stood in front of a ripped-open crate practicing deep-breathing exercises in a futile attempt to rein in my anger and dampen my curse. The stuttering fluorescent light above me mocked my ineffectual control.

"Sterling's art is . . . well, it's not the most expensive or the most coveted. Or sophisticated. Or—" Gabriel met my scowl and rushed to clutch my hands, smoothing them straight. "But what do the police know? Your aunt's paintings are exquisite and *always* sell, which is the point, right, Eva?"

I pretended I didn't see the sheepskin sleeves pop into existence around his arms. Rescuing my hands from Gabriel's enthusiastic soothing, I examined the art in the boxes to either side of Sofie's. Those on the left sold for double my aunt's asking price. Across the storage room, uncovered, rested a painting worth more than all my aunt's stolen artwork combined. The police's theory was logical. It was also infuriating and insulting. If some moron had to steal Sofie's artwork, he should steal it because he wanted it, not because he couldn't read the labels on the boxes.

The light above me popped, darkening half the room. Gabriel squinted at the burned-out bulb, then spun away with a toss of his glossy black hair to prop open the back door. Sunlight spilled in from the alley.

*I am floating on a coffee cake cloud.* I crossed my arms and thrummed my fingertips against my forearm.

"I have been *violated*. I feel like Frida Kahlo after the trolley car," Gabriel said. His sheepskin sleeves disappeared and an ankle-high, insubstantial plastic pink flamingo materialized beside his left foot, then another by his right. The apparitions floated back and forth with his pacing feet. "How dare someone invade our *sanctuary*. Never again! We'll be locked as tight as the Louvre before sundown." The flamingos multiplied into a wall of identical arched pink necks and crooked right legs that marched with him like one long, tasteless yard-art army.

Grimacing, I took a deep breath and sought tranquility. My curse was gaining momentum, and calming exercises were barely taking the edge off my anger.

"What about Sofie's art? What are the police doing?"

"Nothing useful. Checking pawnshops, notifying auction houses. That sort of thing." A white, 1950s-style, full-coverage bra engulfed his chest, obscuring the bulk of his shirt. The bra spontaneously combusted. "I've got a broken lock and a *slew* of missing art, and they inferred *I* am at fault for not having video surveillance."

The burning bra tested my hard-won ability to ignore these unasked-for apparitions. Flames licked up the straps and the cups disintegrated, exposing Gabriel's ruffle-front shirt through the blackened holes.

Like all the women in my family, I was privy to apparitions others couldn't see. At least Sofie, my mother, and Nana Nevie saw useful visions. I suffered through a barrage of people's emotions, represented by intangible images that floated around their bodies. The apparitions were unique to each person, following no rhyme or rule—and definitely no logic. In other words, I was privy to divination gibberish. Case in point: What the hell did a burning bra on a middle-aged man mean?

In my twenty-six years of apparition bombardment, I had learned it was easier to judge a person's emotions by their expressions and actions than by using my questionable "gift." If I could have turned off the visions, I would have flipped the switch years ago.

The bra's embers drifted toward Gabriel's feet, disappearing at his knees. I sucked in a deep breath and held it for a count of five, only half listening to Gabriel's ongoing rant.

". . . swap my testicles for turnips if they remember to check—"

Gabriel's teeth clicked shut as a shadow darkened the door. I followed his gaze. The man peering into the storage room from the alley had a dusty-blond five o'clock shadow and striking blue eyes that warranted a double take. His tousled dirty-blond hair said *surfer* but his posture and physique said *military*. I approved of both, especially how the sun outlined his broad shoulders and trim hips.

My pent-up breath eased out. The gallery owner's burning brassiere melted away, and he stood on the deck of a colorful gondola. It bobbed in the concrete beneath his shoes, extending three feet in front and behind him, the prow and stern severed by the sharp lines of reality.

Gabriel floated to the handsome stranger, hand extended. "Gabriel Galileo. May I help you?"

"Hudson Keyes. We spoke on the phone this morning about upgrading your security." A dimple flashed in Hudson's five o'clock shadow, and a layer of my morning's tension lifted at the sight, making it almost easy to ignore the heavy, wide-brimmed blue sombrero dwarfing Hudson's head. Enormous gold shells circled the base of the sombrero's barrel, and golden pom-poms clustered the brim. When he spoke, a matching poncho draped his chest.

"Yes, of course." Gabriel shook Hudson's hand. The pom-poms swayed.

Hudson turned his smile to me, and Gabriel released him to make the introduction. "This is Eva Parker, niece of S. Sterling, the artist whose collection was abducted last night."

Hudson's large, warm hand enclosed mine, and the contact zinged through my body. For the first time since I'd learned of the theft earlier that morning, I smiled.

The three remaining fluorescent lights sputtered out, drowning the storage room in shadows.

"If it's not one thing, it's another," Gabriel exclaimed. In the glow of the sunlight slanting through the open back door, I watched Gabriel test the light switches, then throw up his hands. "What else could go wrong?"

"I'm sorry for your family's misfortune," Hudson said to me, unfazed by the lighting issues.

"Aren't we all," Gabriel said. "Simply awful. Sterling's pieces are amazing. Definitely worth stealing. Not that someone should have stolen them. Not that *anyone* should ever steal *anything*. Oh, dear, I'm babbling." He clapped both hands over his mouth, then shrugged, dropped his hands with a smile, and barreled through the space between Hudson and me. "At least the lights are still on in the gallery."

Gabriel flung open the interior door, and Hudson and I threaded through the cramped, gloomy storage room into the spacious gallery. Hudson glanced around, his eyes on the ceiling rather than the art. My gaze slid down Hudson's backside to appreciate the fit of his jeans.

"I didn't see a camera out back and I don't see any video surveillance in here—"

"First the officers, and now you! I'm starting to feel like *I'm* the criminal." Gabriel thrust his wrists toward Hudson. "Okay, I confess. I don't have any cameras. Lock me up."

"I don't think that'll be necessary." Hudson didn't hold back his grin, and Gabriel swooned toward him. "What about an alarm?"

I eased away from the men. I wouldn't have minded ogling Hudson Keyes a bit longer. I could use a dose of handsome to counterbalance the frustrations of the morning, but I should have left the moment I saw the gondola.

Shoving familiar bitterness back into its mental box and wedging the lid shut, I strode down the hallway to Gabriel's immaculate office. I closed the door behind me and leaned against it. Picturing a placid lake, I dumped my emotions into it, letting the anger and frustration sink beneath the surface. As my emotions calmed, I restored the barriers around my curse and did my best to smother it.

Technically, I wasn't cursed; my gift simply required fuel. Unlike my body, which ran on water, food, sunlight, and good sex, the nonstop apparitions ran on electricity. What little control I'd mastered over my body's passive consumption of electricity deteriorated in proportion to my emotional distress; the stronger my emotions, the faster I sucked in electricity and the more numerous and elaborate my divinations.

Pushing from the door, I thumbed through the leather satchel on my shoulder. Organized inside its plethora of pockets and pouches were the tools of my trade as a feng shui consultant. The bag also contained the flotsam of a woman who never knew where her curse would strand her next.

It was a big bag.

I pulled out a packet containing photographs and information on all the stolen paintings and placed it in the center of Gabriel's spotless desk. The police had already received their own copy. Sadly, hand-delivering the paperwork was the extent of my usefulness.

I reached for the door but paused before opening it. Seeing Hudson had done wonders for restoring some of my calm. A little light flirting was just what I needed to shake my lingering irritation before the bus ride home. I pulled my mussed hair back into a high ponytail and applied a fresh layer of pink lip gloss. Some redheads are summery and freckled. I'm pale. A kind ex had called my skin alabaster. It sounded better than fish-belly white. With the right makeup, I could pull off exotic; without makeup, I looked like a ghost in a wig.

I emerged from the hallway in time to see Hudson bustle into the back room carrying a ladder and a tool pack. The door closed behind him and I sighed. So much for this morning's silver lining.

"Please let your aunt know I'm taking every precaution to make sure this doesn't happen again," Gabriel said, wringing his hands. Iridescent peacock feathers were braided through his hair, and a comfy green armchair trailed his heels like a puppy. "Ms. Sterling's work is so uplifting. People are going to be *terribly* disappointed. Our Twitter feed has been flooded with fans tweeting about her show, and the click-through rate on our ads featuring her work was phenomenal."

He spoke a form of gibberish I'd heard often enough to grasp the gist of, but I wasn't fluent enough to attempt to respond in kind. As a computer's archnemesis, I possessed only peripheral awareness of all things Internet.

I left without promising anything on my aunt's behalf. I wasn't sure I could—or wanted to. Sofie wasn't going to be pleased Gabriel was only now making efforts to protect his gallery from thieves.

The bright midmorning Los Angeles sun warmed my legs when I stepped outside. Sundress weather in April—I lived in the perfect city. The light breeze carried the smell of hot asphalt and exhaust, and the only clouds in the sky were plane contrails.

With the sun's rays soaking into my skin, my frustration evaporated to genuine calm. Sofie's plane would touch down in a few hours, so I had time to burn. I turned right, following the delicious cinnamon smell wafting from a nearby café. If the café sold cinnamon rolls, maybe they also sold coffee cake.

Behind me, the gallery doors jingled open and someone called my name. I turned to see Hudson rush out, wearing a ship captain's hat this time. My stomach fluttered. I pivoted to face him, fighting to keep my eyes on his face and not scanning down his body as he jogged toward me. The breeze pushed his blue company T-shirt against his chest, and my fingers tightened around the strap of my bag.

"Hey, Eva, I wanted to assure you that after I get done today, no one will be able to steal from Galileo Gallery again," he said when he caught up to me. "Not that it's much of a consolation, I guess."

"It's good news for the rest of the artists, but I won't be happy until the bastards who did this are caught."

The conversation stalled, but Hudson's dimple rooted me in place, and his heavy eye contact suggested he hadn't chased me out of the gallery just to brag about his job skills. Plus, while I didn't understand the emotional significance of his changing hats, I thought I could accurately read the butterfly-size sharks circling through his midriff as nerves. I smiled and felt only a smidge guilty to capitalize, however remotely, on my aunt's misfortune.

"Would you like to get lunch with me sometime? I've got this thing." Hudson gestured back toward the gallery with a boyish grin. "Otherwise I'd suggest right now."

"I like your enthusiasm."

"Wait, you don't have a boyfriend, do you?"

"Nope."

The sharks disappeared and formal navy dress whites covered his jeans and T-shirt. The captain's hat tucked under his arm didn't move when Hudson reached into his back pocket and pulled out his phone. "So that's a yes, right?"

Gravity got a little lighter as we grinned at each other. "Yes, when—"

A hand clamped on my arm and spun me around. I yelped in surprise.

"Eva? Eva Parker? What a surprise to find you here."

I leaned away from the short black woman who squeezed my arm in a vise grip. Her large eyes showed too much white around the brown irises and focused on me with an unnerving intensity. She smiled a quick flash of teeth behind full lips. Racehorse blinders sprouted next to her temples, intensifying her stare.

"It's Jenny," she said. "Jenny Winters. From Santa Monica High."

"High school?" I couldn't remember any high school friend or acquaintance named Jenny. I tried to gently extract my arm, but she dragged me forward a step.

"We had a class together. Honors English. Junior year."

"Right. Overachievers unite. Look, it's great to see you again—"

"Yes, how the years have flown by. Isn't it amazing? Can you believe it?" Jenny recited the platitudes in a flat voice, the words fast.

"I really can't." I dug in my heels and yanked my arm free, wondering if she'd left bruises. Jenny glanced behind us, then peered into a nearby narrow alley. A warning tingled in my spine, and I eased back a few steps. "Are you okay?"

"Perfectly fine."

The dark circles under her eyes, the dirt-smeared khaki pants, and the waist-length jacket on the balmy day all gave lie to her claim.

"I've been looking for you, Eva. You're a hard woman to find. I wouldn't have known where to look if I hadn't remembered Arianna da Via."

Dirty Coke-bottle glasses dropped onto her face, obscuring her eyes. She lunged for my arm again, and I stumbled out of her reach and into Hudson. He steadied me with a hand on my hip, and the heat of his palm rushed through me. I glanced up at him; then my gaze dropped to his full bottom lip.

Wait, Jenny had been looking for *me*? And she had tracked me down through my best friend Ari?

"What does Ari have to do with anything?" I straightened, focusing on Jenny. Ari would have mentioned chatting with a crazy woman from our past, and she definitely wouldn't have told her where to find me.

Jenny clamped a light brown fist around my wrist and jerked me between two parked cars and into the road. "I need to show you something. It's urgent. We need to cross." Jenny yanked, and my arm strained in its socket. A car horn blared and I jumped half a foot, planting my free hand on the car's bumper to steady myself. Crap! She'd almost gotten me run over.

"Let go of me!" My skin burned when I attempted to twist out of her grip.

"Hurry!"

"Let me go!"

Jenny wrenched me forward, and against my will, I ran across the remaining three lanes of traffic, opting to extricate myself from the safety of the opposite sidewalk. Heavy footsteps followed, then Hudson caught up to us.

"Who are you?" Jenny demanded, glaring at Hudson.

Hudson draped a warm, muscular arm across my shoulder, trapping my free hand against his side when he squeezed me to him. "Eva's boyfriend." His fake possessive maneuver forced Jenny to release me.

She eyed him up and down. "Fine. Actually, that's better. We're going right in here."

Jenny popped open the latch on the back of a horse trailer parked next to the curb. Hudson kept his arm around me like he belonged there. Jenny leaned around the side of the trailer to check up the sidewalk, then behind us, before scanning the rooftops.

I remained frozen in place. For a second, when Hudson had made his ridiculous statement, a straitjacket had engulfed Jenny's torso. It vanished just as fast, replaced by a bundle of arrows piercing her rib cage directly through her heart. Not good. Definitely not good.

"Come on," Jenny said. She pulled the trailer door open and slipped inside.

"Any idea what's in there?" Hudson whispered, dropping his arm.

I shook my head and examined the trailer. It was large and dark gray, with suspicious stains smeared across the bumper beneath the swinging door. And it smelled. Bad.

My imagination conjured up plenty of graphic possibilities of what an insane woman would stash in a trailer: an injured horse, a sick person, a dead horse. A dead person?

I shivered, missing the warmth of Hudson's arm despite the

eighty-degree heat and the sun on my shoulders. I couldn't walk away and leave some creature—human or otherwise—at this crazy lady's mercy. Gingerly, I pulled the door open wider. My heart pattered in my chest, and I tensed to run as I peeked inside.

"You have an *elephant!*"

Hudson yanked the door wider and stared over my shoulder.

"Shh, keep your voice down." Jenny stretched to her tiptoes to peer out the high windows on the side of the trailer. "Come inside and close the door."

Against my better judgment, I stepped into the trailer. Hudson eased in behind me and pulled the door shut.

The elephant was small, no taller than my waist. Its wrinkled gray skin was crusted with dried mud and peppered with long wiry hairs. A stubby trunk the length of my arm curled back over its head. I amended my statement. "You have a *baby* elephant?"

"Basically. Her name is Kyoko," Jenny said.

The elephant didn't look injured. It looked perfectly healthy, if wildly out of place in a horse trailer in the middle of Los Angeles. The stench had to be emanating from the greenish brown piles splattered against the edge of the trailer. I craned to look up and down the side-walk through the tall windows on the side of the trailer. "Do you have its mother around here somewhere?"

"No. Listen up. I need you to keep Kyoko for a few days."

"What!"

The elephant shifted, and the entire trailer shuddered.

"For optimum success, here are the parameters," Jenny said, her earlier agitation gone, replaced by a calm, almost clinical tone. She ticked points off on her fingers as she spoke. "Kyoko doesn't like loud noises, so no more yelling. She needs company; you can't abandon her by herself. You will go to prison if you're caught transporting or possessing an endangered species." She flipped her hand to point at the elephant. Its long eyelashes blinked over large, golden-brown eyes. "Don't get caught."

Rapid-fire, the arrows shot from Jenny's chest and studded the floor in a straight line from her feet to mine. Even knowing they were insubstantial apparitions, I flinched and swallowed a scream. The remaining arrows burst from her chest and peppered the trailer's walls. Had they been real, Hudson would have been dead.

"Hold up. *I'm* not getting caught, because *I'm* not in possession of an elephant." I waved my hands in front of me in the universal this-isn't-my-problem gesture. "I don't know what you're involved in, Jenny, or why you think I would help—"

"I chose you because of your"—her eyes flicked to Hudson, then back to me—"special relationship with power. It makes you unpredictable. I noticed it in high school. I watched you, studied you." Hard brown eyes met mine. "I know several people in the government who'd be interested in my observations."

"I don't know what you're talking about," I said through numb lips. Hudson's curiosity bore into my flesh. His eyes darted between Jenny, me, and the elephant. I should have already been walking—running—away, but my feet had welded to the trailer.

"Five computer lab crashes," Jenny said, ticking off points on her fingers again. "Byron Davy's spate of dead car batteries after prom—"

He'd deserved every single one of them, the two-timing bastard, but I couldn't summon my usual vindictive satisfaction. Each finger tick doubled my heart rate.

"Twenty-two classes with no power. Three school brownouts—"

"What are you saying? That you think . . . That you'd . . ." I couldn't finish the sentence, but I needed to make her stop talking in front of Hudson. Somehow, this woman I didn't know or remember had figured out my curse. She'd freaking *studied* me. The thought of one stranger knowing about my curse limned my veins with icy foreboding. Her threat to tell other people, to make me a helpless lab rat, overwhelmed rational thought.

"All I need is for you to take care of Kyoko for a few days."

"I can't." I lifted a feeble hand in protest. Jenny snapped something cold and hard around my wrist. Metal clanged on metal, and I was handcuffed to a steel brace on the side of the trailer.

"If you don't help her, they'll kill her," Jenny said. She darted out of the trailer.

"Wait! You can't do this!"

"Hey!" Hudson rushed to my side and gave the handcuff attached to the trailer a quick yank. It held firm.

Jenny peeked around the back of the trailer. "It's only for a few days. I need to get organized." Pieces of black and white sheets like mutated Scantron forms coated her shirt. "It's imperative you keep Kyoko's existence a secret, for her and you. If you go to the police, I go to the papers, Eva. And don't bother with the feds. The government can't help you, and they'll— Listen: Don't trust the government and don't tell them about Kyoko. If you do, we'll all be dead." Jenny ducked out of sight.

"Are you crazy?" I shouted.

The baby elephant trumpeted. I jumped. The handcuff snapped against my wrist.

"Ow!"

"What the hell?" Hudson asked.

"Stop her!"

With eyes as round as saucers, Hudson leapt after Jenny. I stretched to look out the side of the trailer. He sprinted down the sidewalk, only to slow a few car lengths later. He pushed his hands through his thick hair and jogged back to me.

"She got away," he said.

Peachy. Jenny was on the loose with my secret and I was shackled in a trailer with a baby elephant.

I examined my imprisoned wrist, then the illegal, endangered animal. The elephant wasn't tethered to anything. It snaked its trunk back and forth, a savage gleam in its eye.

"Easy there, little elepha—"

It charged.

# TWO

THE TRAILER ROCKED, the heavy metal frame groaning in protest. The trailer wasn't wide, and before the elephant could stampede more than four steps, it mashed against me, pinning me to the wall. I scrunched my toes in my open sandals and braced for a mauling. The elephant flapped her ears and the hem of my skirt fluttered. My eyes popped open.

"Good elephant, you don't want to hurt me," I said, wriggling to the side. "Please don't eat me."

"I think elephants are vegetarians," Hudson said, coming into view at the open back of the trailer. He stepped inside and pulled the door shut behind him.

"It looks hungry. Maybe it's starved beyond reason. And look at those feet. It could cripple me with a single step. Oh God, what are you doing?"

The elephant snuffled me with her trunk. I backed up as far as my bound arm would allow. She followed. The moist tip of the trunk prodded my knee below the line of my skirt and beelined for third base. Dirty sandpaper skin scraped up my naked thigh.

"No! No, no, no, no. Bad elephant!" I twisted and thrust my butt away from the elephant, the tendons in my shackled arm radiating fiery pain from my bruised wrist to my shoulder. Doubled over as I was, if the wild elephant charged, she'd slam into my solar plexus and rip my arm clean off.

The elephant's trunk reversed direction and constricted around my ankle. I squeaked. Bright brown eyes lifted to my face. The trunk tip released me to molest the straps of my sandals. I shimmied to the side, easing the pressure on my arm.

"That's a good elephant. Keep your trunk to yourself and—eep!"

The elephant swung her head to look at Hudson, pivoting on a back foot, rocking the trailer. It took me a moment to recognize the incongruous sound.

"You're laughing? Now?" With my ass in the air and my body contorted painfully around an unpredictable killing machine, he had the audacity to laugh? Shooting Hudson a glare, I squeezed between the elephant and the wall of the trailer and straightened, sidling closer to the bar I was handcuffed to. The man had great crow's-feet when he grinned, the bastard.

Hudson stifled his laughter down to a smile. "She's just checking you out."

"This isn't funny. I'm trapped"—I rattled my handcuff—"in a death box with a wild animal who could crush me with its head."

"She hardly seems wild. Just curious."

"Then it can be curious somewhere else." I fluttered my free hand at the elephant. "Shoo. Attack him."

The elephant tilted her head to look at me, then turned her attention to my satchel.

"Oh, no you don't." I couldn't stop her from crushing me, or eating me, but that didn't mean I had to let her rifle through my oversize purse. I twisted my bag behind me and used my thumb and forefinger to tug the questing trunk away from the top flap. It was like trying to lift an anaconda with my pinky. The elephant's trunk disappeared into my bag.

"Out," I said without an ounce of authority. The trunk slid deeper.

"No. Bad elephant. Out." I tugged on the trunk with three fingers. The elephant shifted closer and pulled the satchel toward her mouth. Her large round teeth looked like they could crush my forearm. I stepped back. The elephant followed.

Gritting my teeth, I grabbed the trunk and pulled it free of my bag. I released it immediately and waited for the elephant to flatten me, curling my toes up again for good measure. The trunk slid around my free arm, hot but not as rough as it had felt against my inner thigh. It flexed and I froze, bombarded by visions of being dismembered. The elephant released me and veered toward the bag again. I took a deep breath.

"A little help?" I asked Hudson.

"Do you have food in there?"

"Uh, some crackers, I think. And carrots."

"Maybe Kyoko wants them."

"I am *not* letting an elephant rummage through my bag!" I took a firm grip on the trunk and lifted it free of the bag. Again.

"Give it here." Hudson held out his hand.

I slid the shoulder strap over my head, thankful Jenny hadn't cuffed my other hand, and held my precious satchel out to a perfect stranger. Hudson took it and the elephant pivoted toward him. He took a step back, and the elephant followed him.

"Oh, shit."

"Yeah, who's laughing now?"

Hudson darted out of the trailer and banged the latch home. Trumpeting, Kyoko body-slammed the back door. The whole trailer's frame shrieked in protest, and the elephant trumpeted again. I staggered into the wall, clutching one ear with my free hand.

"Oh crap, oh crap, oh crap," I chanted. I was going to die. *Killed by Elephant Tantrum*, my headstone would read. Future generations would assume I was a circus performer. *Oh, hell no.*

I slid the handcuff up the metal pole for a closer look. It was the real deal—solid metal with a single keyhole at each loop. I squeezed my thumb to my palm and made a point with my fingers, but my hand was still too thick to escape the steel band. The other cuff circled a bar welded at both ends to the trailer's wall. I swiped at sweat on my forehead.

The trailer bounced, and I spun to check the elephant. She prodded the seam of the door with her trunk.

"You want out of there?"

I jumped at Hudson's voice and banged my head against the side of the trailer. I jerked my hand to rub my head, wincing when the handcuff snapped my wrist. Snarling, I turned toward the sound of his voice.

Hudson stood on the outside ledge of the trailer, peering in.

"What do you think?"

"Hey, I'm just trying to help."

"Do you happen to have a handcuff key on you?"

"Nope."

I didn't know whether to be relieved or not. A yes would have been creepy, but it would have meant I was free. A no was less creepy but unhelpful.

I eyed the elephant again. She didn't look perturbed anymore. She looked relaxed. She looked . . .

"Don't you dare. Not with me right he—"

The elephant lifted her tail and pooped. Noxious fumes blasted me, searing my nostrils.

"Oh God!" I gagged and covered my mouth with my free hand.

"Whew," Hudson said, his voice muffled as he dropped back from the trailer.

The elephant turned large liquid eyes toward me and batted long eyelashes. She stepped back, landing a foot square in the pile, then started for me.

"Hudson. Hudson!"

"Right here. Oh, man, it's making my eyes water."

"Get me out of here!" The elephant stopped next to me, and I clamped my hand tighter over my nose and mouth, but it didn't stop tears from forming. The elephant nudged my knee with her trunk, then dropped it to lay curled atop my foot. When I shifted my blurred vision, those large eyes stared at me.

Nothing malicious gleamed in the elephant's gaze. The way she pressed against me seemed almost like she was comforting me. Or herself. Trying not to breathe, I lowered my hand and reached for her head. The elephant didn't move when I ran light fingers across the grooved crown of her skull. Leather and wiry hair stretched across a cast-iron forehead. I slid my hand over the divot in the middle, and one of her ears flapped.

"Hang on. I'll be right back," Hudson said.

I wanted to give him a snarky response—shackled as I was, I wasn't going anywhere—but that would have meant opening my mouth.

It took an hour for Hudson to return. Or maybe it was only minutes. The lack of oxygen made the passage of time foggy. He was on the phone. Miraculously, the tiny gadget had withstood being brushed up against me.

"You'll have to send Matvei." Hudson paused, then said, "Wade, I wouldn't be calling if it were anything other than an emergency." Pause. "Yes." Pause. "Of course. I'll let you— Hello? Wade?" This time the pause was followed by cussing.

Ah, the familiar sound of someone too long in my company. The phone had died. It had been inevitable, especially since Hudson had stopped just outside the trailer.

"I'm coming in," Hudson announced.

Kyoko perked up and trotted toward the back door.

"Wait!" I yelled over the cacophony of the abused trailer. Hudson popped up beside me. "I think she's planning on making a break for it."

"Nah. I think I know what she wants. I hope you don't mind I went through your bag. Damn, it's *stinky* in there."

Hell, yes, I minded. "You went through my—"

Hudson thrust his hand through the slats. He dropped a cracker to the floor. Kyoko eyed it, then turned back to the door.

"You could have asked first, you know," I said.

"Would you have said no?"

"That's not the point."

Hudson barked a laugh and stuck his other hand through the slats. This one held carrots. When he dropped one of them, Kyoko ambled over to investigate. Hudson disappeared, then the latch creaked before he slipped inside. Kyoko turned eagerly to him, and he tossed the remaining carrots to the front of the trailer. The baby elephant dashed after them. Hudson grabbed the side of the trailer and I braced my feet wide in the ensuing earthquake.

"Now what?" I asked.

Hudson approached, covering his nose in the crook of his elbow. I was ninety-nine percent sure that the hilt of a broadsword clearing his shoulder was an apparition. He wiped his palm on his pants, then pulled a slender packet from his back pocket. "Now we see if I can pick a cuff lock." His voice was muffled behind his arm.

"You're serious?"

"You have a better idea?"

I shifted to give him access to the handcuff.

"Hold your hand out. No, the free one."

I held out my free hand, palm up. He rested the open packet on it and selected a slender tool from a dozen similar-looking flat instruments. Bending close, he began to prod the lock. I stared at the top of his head. Yep, the broadsword was an apparition. The hilt was silver and black, with an engraving of a running horse. Rust covered the scabbard, doing little to bolster my confidence.

I went over what I knew of my would-be rescuer. Name: Hudson Keyes. Profession: security installation. Drove a company van; masqueraded as the boyfriend of women he just met; carried picklock tools; was unfazed by a baby elephant; went through women's purses without asking. It wasn't much to go on.

"Uh, thank you for your help," I said.

He looked up, his bottom lip caught between his teeth. I added *sexy as hell* to my list. The scales tipped in his favor.

"You're welcome." He wiggled the tool in the handcuff hole. "You've got some strange friends."

"Jenny is *not* my friend. I'm not even sure we really did go to school together."

"Yet she left you an elephant."

"I don't think she's sane."

Hudson snorted. The lock clicked and the handcuff dropped away.

"Holy crap, it feels good to be free. Thank you." I shook my wrist, then impulsively kissed his cheek, barely registering his stubble before pulling back. He smiled, the tips of his lips curling up and a flush staining his cheeks as he put away the picklock tool. The rust disappeared from the scabbard. The moment he took the tool set back, I rubbed my bruised wrist.

"What now?" he asked.

"Now I get out of here."

We slipped out the back before Kyoko noticed, but when the elephant heard the latch click, she bugled her displeasure and the trailer bounced against the curb. I didn't stop moving until I was across the sidewalk and leaning against a storefront, breathing fresh air. I flapped my dress's bodice to dry my sweat. Dirt streaked across the hem of the purple skirt, and my legs were smeared with trunk trails. My hand smelled like elephant.

"I meant in a larger sense," Hudson said, coming to stand beside me.

I had been doing a pretty good job of not thinking about the larger picture. The one in which an insane baby elephant kidnapper threatened to expose my most closely guarded secret to the world. Despite what I'd told Hudson, I was positive we *had* gone to school together. The facts Jenny had cited were too specific. Anyone could have looked up the power problems that plagued Santa Monica High during my four-year attendance, but Jenny had known about Byron's car battery, too.

To my knowledge, no one had ever connected the dots between me and the electrical destruction left in my curse's wake. Not good friends, not boyfriends, not clients or landlords or teachers. It was just my luck the one person who had figured it out was a whacko. Ironically, it didn't matter if she was insane or a criminal or had a whole menagerie of endangered animals she planned to deposit around LA; if she convinced just one person to do tests on me, my life would be over.

With the accuracy of a sniper, Jenny had hit the bull's-eye of my single greatest fear: becoming a lab rat. I'd had years to map every possibility of being exposed, and the topography always spelled doom. At best, scientists would study me. It wasn't a matter of giving my consent. I couldn't turn my visions off, which meant I couldn't stop my curse from draining electricity. Anyone spending extended time in my vicinity would see it work. If by some miracle I wasn't turned into a lab rat, it wouldn't stop people from talking. My secret would spread. I'd end up on the cover of newspapers or, worse, tabloids— "Los Angeles Woman Eats Electricity for Breakfast, Electrocutes People for Lunch" or "Electricity-Eating Woman Threatens to Cripple Civilization to Stone Age" or "Eva Parker: Sign of the Apocalypse or Antichrist?" The source wouldn't matter: eventually strangers would know about my curse, refuse to do business with me, treat me like a pariah, and run in fear, clutching their beloved phones, laptops, and tablets.

The darker scenarios involved government agencies detaining me in some underground bunker for the rest of my life, dissecting my brain for clues on how to re-create my curse, using me or my ability as a weapon—

Sofie said I had an overactive imagination, but I'd watched this country's reactions to scientific discoveries long enough to know I wasn't far off base. I loved my life. I'd found my niche in the sprawling landscape of Los Angeles, learned to adapt my activities to hide my curse, and had created a little slice of almost normal for myself. The thought of all that crashing down on me because some woman I went to high school with could expose my secret brought me close to hyperventilating. Her bargain—keeping my secret in exchange for me hiding her stolen baby elephant—was no bargain at all. It was blackmail.

And it was going to work.

"I don't know," I said, finally answering Hudson's question.

A couple walking by stopped to examine their shoes. I sniffed my dress. *Pee-yew.*

"If Jenny thinks telling the world you had the elephant is going to hold up in court, she's wrong. All we have to do is tell them what happened today. She's got nothing on you."

I blinked at Hudson's earnest, confused expression and tried to process the conversation from his point of view. He was right. If we went immediately to the authorities, we could convince the police (or a jury, if it came to that) of our complete innocence in the abduction of Kyoko from wherever she had been taken. Logically, we should be rushing to the nearest police station and telling them everything we knew.

*Doom.*

"You know, this isn't really your problem," I said.

"You want me to walk away? Pretend I didn't see anything?"

Yes, damn it. The fewer people who knew of even the hint of my curse, the better. Jenny had practically spelled it out for him, and after the shock of the elephant wore off, he would—consciously or subconsciously—make the connection.

"You got swept up in this," I said. I met Hudson's deep sapphire eyes. He really did seem like a good guy. "This is crazy and you should have—"

"Let that insane woman kidnap you? Because that's what it looked like she was doing."

"No. You're right. Thank you for getting me out of there." I wriggled my bruised wrist.

"Do you really think I *could* walk away from this?" Hudson asked. "A baby elephant mysteriously dropped off in a trailer in downtown Culver City. An attractive woman I rescued from handcuffs who smells like elephant poop. How could I resist?"

My heart sank. The broadsword glowed bright enough to halo Hudson. He thought this was some grand adventure. He thought he was going to rescue me.

"Look," he said when I didn't respond with the enthusiasm he had expected. "I've got a laptop in the van. Let's figure out where this elephant was taken from, drive her back, and sort this all out with the police once that baby is reunited with her mother. Hopefully we can get Jenny some mental help in the process."

Well, crap. He really was going to rescue me. I was doomed.

# THREE

I ORDERED us both drinks from a nearby café, scrambling furiously
for a plan. One that wouldn't involve Hudson putting Jenny in a position to expose my secret to the world. Hudson hunched over his
laptop at one of the outside tables, engrossed in his grand rescue
strategy.

"Nothing. Can you believe it? At least not on the major news sites.
I'll check more locally . . ."

I excused myself to go to the bathroom. I wiped the dirty trunk
marks from my legs with wet paper towels, then stared at myself in
the mirror. My cheeks were paler than normal, and my slate-blue eyes
looked haunted.

"This won't do," I told myself. I fixed my ponytail, reapplied lip
gloss, and patted some color into my cheeks. I've never been
impressed by white knights or their co-conspirators, the damsels in
distress. Their whole relationship was predicated on the belief that the
white knight could intuit the damsel's needs, but I had yet to meet a
man with telepathy. Like Hudson, the knights bumbled along, using
logic based on only half the facts. Left alone, my white knight would
mess everything up in his endeavor to be the hero. So, like women
throughout history before me, I had to rescue myself from my

problem *and* from the "help" of the hero. Only, I didn't have logic on my side, and I couldn't explain my reasoning without revealing my secret. I'd have to get creative, and as much as I didn't want to, I'd also have to trade on the attraction that had drawn Hudson to me and this mess in the first place.

"Any luck?" I asked when I sat down at the table.

"Nothing. You'd think it'd be a top story, at least locally. How often are elephants stolen?"

"What if Jenny was on to something?"

Bright blue eyes lifted to my face. "Meaning?"

"She seemed to think Kyoko is in danger. What if she's right? What if we were to return her to wherever she came from, and they were torturing her?" I nibbled at my bottom lip, giving him Bambi eyes.

"Ah, well, I hadn't considered that. We could take her to an animal rescue facility."

Damn. Another good solution. Was he trying to ruin my life? I consciously mirrored the position of his arms on the table, then crossed my leg in his direction. Using flirtatious body language in such a calculated manner felt sleazy, but desperation helmed this train wreck. "If we did, then what about Jenny?"

"You think she'd steal another elephant?"

Okay, it sounded pretty far-fetched to me, too. "She could be an extremist. If we keep the elephant a day or two, when Jenny comes back for Kyoko, we could turn her *and* the elephant over to the police."

"Or we could track her down first. Damn it, I thought this thing was fully charged." Hudson tapped at the black screen of his laptop. When it didn't respond, he shoved it aside. "What about the Byron guy with all the dead batteries? What was that about? Would he know where she is?"

I shook my head and sipped my drink to give myself a moment to compose my expression. "I think we have a better shot at finding Jenny than some guy she remembered from high school." Not that I thought we'd have a lot of luck finding Jenny. I couldn't remember meeting her once in high school, and now Hudson thought we could find her in the middle of twelve million people living in and around Los Angeles?

Hudson studied my face, then my hands, which I relaxed from their white-knuckle grip on my drink. "You sure this is what you want to do? Keeping Kyoko isn't legal, like Jenny said. We don't have any idea why she targeted you." He paused, the unspoken question in his sentence clear, and I shook my head. "We don't even know how she found you. Do you come by the gallery every Thursday morning?"

"I was here only because of the burglary. Maybe she followed me." How *had* she known where I'd be? I didn't exactly have a normal routine, but she would have been far more likely to find me at home than at the gallery. If Sofie hadn't been out of town, I wouldn't have been at the gallery at all. I pushed the unanswerable question into the bundle of others I'd set aside, like "Why me?" and "Where did Jenny get an elephant?" and "Was Jenny insane?" I met Hudson's gaze and did my best to look like I had a plan. "I want to keep Kyoko at least for a day."

Thick black-rimmed glasses settled on his face. They didn't give me any insight into the emotions behind his closed-off expression, but the nerd look worked for him. Combined with the sombrero and a slender metal tie constricting his throat, it was easy to guess Hudson's feelings were mixed.

I suppressed a sigh, leaned forward to clutch Hudson's hand, and said, "I would really appreciate your help."

The broadsword glowed iridescent. The tie disappeared. "Then we better get moving, or someone's going to investigate why that trailer keeps trumpeting. But to where?"

Guilt and relief sloshed nauseatingly in my stomach when I stood. "I have an idea."

———

HUDSON CHECKED the latch on the trailer, then fiddled with the wires and chain around the hitch. I didn't ask if he knew what he was doing. I didn't want to hear a no.

I checked on Kyoko. She looked a great deal smaller now that I wasn't caged in the trailer with her. Not so much frightening as pitiful. I stretched a hand through the high slats of the trailer and tentatively rubbed the top of the trunk she stretched toward me. She ran the firm tip up my arm, then lowered her trunk and shuffled to the middle of the trailer.

"The keys are in the truck," Hudson said from behind me. He'd retrieved sunglasses from somewhere. They were sporty and mirrored to hide his eyes. "Can I borrow your cell phone? Mine died and I need to check in with my boss."

"I lost it." The lie rolled off my tongue, primed and ready from regular use. I'd found people accepted a lost cell phone lie more readily than a confession of never having owned a cell phone.

"Seriously? Never mind. That fits with today's luck."

The truck's interior emanated the sweet chemical odor of new seats, new plastic, and new carpet. I tossed my dusty bag on the immaculate floorboards and hopped inside, straightening my skirt before pulling on the seat belt. A rigid Scottish terrier stood on Hudson's lap, made completely out of shiny silver. It faced the window, like it was ready to put its head out. If it were real.

I pulled my eyes from Hudson's crotch just when he looked at me.

"Where to?"

"Santa Monica." I plucked my starlet-style sunglasses from my bag and slid them on, hoping I wasn't blushing as bright as it felt.

Hudson pulled out into traffic and headed for the 10. I'd never been in a truck pulling a trailer, but it was a lot like riding the bus: slow off the line, slow around the corners, and slow to stop. Every so often, the whole vehicle and trailer lurched—I assumed it corresponded with Kyoko's movements—and since Hudson made no comment, I hoped it was normal.

"What's in Santa Monica?" Hudson asked.

"My aunt."

"S. Sterling?"

"Aunt Sofie to me. She's got a house with a yard. Very private." I glanced at the clock. Her plane landed in forty minutes. We might beat her home.

"And she'll be okay with you showing up unannounced with an elephant?"

I smiled. "Yeah."

"She sounds a lot cooler than my relatives."

Hudson merged onto the 10, easing into speeding traffic with skill. I'd powered the window halfway down while we were on the surface streets to air out the stench embedded in my clothing, and when I attempted to power it up, the glass moved half an inch, the mechanism in the door fired off three rounds, and the door lock snapped home. I eased my arm onto the window ledge and pretended the gap pleased me.

The interior electronics were always the first to go. They were the most sensitive part of a vehicle. The entire truck was delicate, no matter what the manufacturers wanted you to believe in their ads. Cut a vehicle's electricity, and it became little more than a lump of aluminum, steel, and plastic. Given the rate of electrical deterioration, it seemed my terror in the trailer had shortened the truck's life span by half the normal Eva-passenger time. Our brief interlude at the café hadn't given it the recovery boost I'd hoped for. The knot in my stomach fisted tighter.

"What do you know about Jenny?" Hudson asked. "Anything at all?"

"Nothing." I didn't even remember my Honors English teacher's name junior year. "I guess she was nerdy. I have a vague memory of a skinny girl with glasses, but I could be making that up. I'm shocked she remembered *me*."

"She said she tracked you down."

"I don't know what to do with that, either."

"Where'd you say you went to school?"

"Santa Monica High."

"And you live in Santa Monica now, too?"

"I moved to Mid-Wilshire after I graduated."

The truck's clock light faded in a slow death. Hudson didn't seem to notice. Dread sank into my spleen, and I reined it in along with the rest of my emotions. Any agitation on my part would kill the truck faster. Substitute agitation with fear, spike it with confusion, and spritz it with sexual attraction, and I was the perfect cocktail for vehicular destruction.

"You remember anything else?" Hudson asked.

I shook my head.

Hudson darted his gaze to mine, then back to the road. He'd gained a silver top hat to match the terrier. The man liked to accessorize with his apparitions.

"What was she talking about, all those brownouts? What does that have to do with the elephant?"

Adrenaline spiked, and I squashed it. "I don't know. Maybe she was trying to prove we went to school together. She seemed skittish. Paranoid. Oh, crap. Do you think she's on drugs?" Why hadn't that occurred to me before?

"If she is, they're pharmaceutical, not recreational. I'd guess she's *off* her drugs."

I dropped my head in my hands and took deep breaths. My life teetered in the hands of a mental patient.

"Huh." Hudson tapped the dashboard. The lights had died there, too, and it no longer displayed our current speed. "You'd think a new truck like this wouldn't have any problems."

"You'd think." A brand-new horrible thought popped into my head. "Is it possible this truck is stolen?"

Hudson grimaced. The silver Scottish terrier in his lap grew to Labrador size, its insubstantial body engulfing Hudson's arms. "Probably. Trailer, too. I've been keeping my eye out for cops just in case."

Traffic slowed to stop and go. It was midmorning on a weekday, but traffic in LA didn't need a reason to turn into a parking lot. Hudson slipped into the slow lane behind a semi. The truck stuttered; then the gas caught again and it smoothed out.

"What's that all about?" Hudson asked the truck.

I could have answered, but the truck did it for me in the form of a grinding squeal under the hood.

"Uh . . ." I said.

"Shit."

Hudson steered toward the off-ramp we were approaching at a crawl. The truck lurched, then lurched again on the echoing jerk of the trailer. I felt like a bobblehead.

"Hang on." Hudson pulled into the breakdown lane, but he didn't stop. Moving barely faster than the traffic, he drove straight for the off-ramp. Pings and clangs of debris hit the undercarriage of the truck, and behind us, Kyoko trumpeted her displeasure. "Hang in there," Hudson coaxed. I didn't know if he was talking to me, Kyoko, or the truck.

We coasted off the freeway and into the parking lot of a dilapidated strip mall, serenaded by the frantic metallic-chicken clucking of the engine.

"Something doesn't feel right," Hudson said.

I refrained from commenting on the obvious.

Hudson cut the engine and the truck shuddered like a dog shaking off water. I trotted back to the trailer and saw what Hudson meant. One of the two tires on the trailer's passenger side was shredded. The trailer canted at an angle, the back corner dipping toward the pavement.

I hopped onto the step and peered inside. Kyoko bugled, not moving from where she quivered against the front of the trailer. White showed around her dark eyes, and she swung her head and trunk back and forth in agitation.

"Shh, it's okay. It's over. You're safe."

"It's definitely over," Hudson said from behind me.

I turned and fought a grin. The silver top hat sat at a rakish angle. The round barrel was mirror smooth and just as shiny; the sunlight reflecting off it would have blinded me if it were real. Maybe President Lincoln could have pulled the look off, but not Hudson, especially not in a short-sleeve T-shirt. The silver terrier stood on point at his side, as large as a Great Dane now. Beneath its feet lay a recognizable square of a Monopoly game board with a green bar across the top: Pennsylvania Avenue. I looked around for a silver iron or boot or wheelbarrow, or better yet, the horse and rider, but it appeared Hudson's emotions were linked to only these two pieces.

Hudson scowled at the ruined tire and ran his hand through his short hair—and the metal hat. The reality of the situation punctured my momentary humor.

"Now what?" Hudson asked. "Where are we supposed to find another trailer in this town?"

The trailer wasn't our only problem. "Uh, how's the truck?" I asked, eyeing the worn cowboy boots engulfing Hudson's shoes. Perhaps he fancied himself a cowboy? We did have a horse trailer, after all.

Hudson swung his gaze to mine. "Okay, where are we supposed to find another trailer *and truck* in this town?"

"I don't know. I've never had the need."

"Me, neither." He pulled out his cell phone and glared at it, mashed at the black screen, then shoved it back in his jeans' pocket. "I can't even access my contacts list."

I surveyed our location. The strip mall looked like a thousand others in the greater LA area, though this one fortunately had a large parking lot; the truck and trailer took up six spaces at an angle. A Thai restaurant, Laundromat, window blinds store, tattoo parlor, nail salon, and frozen yogurt shop filled the two-block strip. The dull roar of the freeway mixed with the revved engines and stereo sounds at the crossroads. This wasn't anywhere I recognized. It wasn't near a familiar bus route, and I'd never had a feng shui consultation in this neighborhood.

"I'm going to get a new phone, then figure something out," Hudson said. He pointed across the street at a hole-in-the-wall electronics store whose front window was crammed floor to ceiling with tiny doodads and gizmos.

"Okay. I'll stay here with Kyoko." It was the best solution for everyone, especially the proprietor of the claustrophobic shop.

Hudson waited for a break in traffic before running across the four-lane road. The statue-still, pony-size silver terrier gliding along on its Monopoly square wasn't what pulled my gaze from Kyoko to watch him go.

It took a few minutes of soothing babble before Kyoko calmed enough to mosey across the trailer to whuffle my hand and arm.

"I wish you could talk." That'd make everything a whole lot easier.

I was sitting on the step of the trailer, arms outstretched, ankles crossed, soaking in a little sun with my eyes closed when Hudson returned. He plopped down beside me, shifting the trailer fractionally. The top hat was gone, and the terrier was normal size again, minus the Monopoly square.

"There's good news and bad news. Good news: I have a phone, crappy as this burner is." He held up a small black flip phone. "The guy over there had a phone book, so I found us a car rental place. Bad news: No one around here rents horse trailers. That meant trucks were not an option since we're trying to keep Kyoko out of sight, and they didn't have any work vans, so I went with the next-best thing. A Suburban."

I knew cars like I knew HBO's fall lineup, which was to say, not at all. When you can't drive and every vehicle you get in breaks down after one use, what's the point of learning more about cars? "Remind me what a Suburban is."

"Big SUV. Hopefully, there'll be enough clearance to fit an elephant."

That'd make a great slogan for a billboard ad. A vehicle so big, it can fit an elephant.

"Thank you," I said.

"Hold off on the thanks until we see if she fits." He leaned back against the hot side of the trailer and closed his eyes, gripping the edge of the step with his hands. "What a day."

My gaze slid down the tanned column of his neck. His shirt had flattened against his pectorals and bunched across his stomach. He was lean, but I could see muscle definition under the contours of the thin cotton. Visions of six-pack abs had my mouth watering, and I forced myself to look away, but it wasn't long before my gaze drifted back. He looked like a model in repose, right down to the disgruntled expression.

Muffling a sigh, I forced my eyes closed and tried to think with my brain instead of my ovaries.

"How are we going to get the Suburban?"

"They bring it to you. Part of their shtick. We just have to drive the guy back to his office."

"Convenient."

I shifted my bag closer. I'd used some of the time Hudson had been gone to go through it, straightening what Kyoko and Hudson had messed up. Now I pulled out a water bottle and the remaining packet of crackers. These had peanut butter sandwiched between two tiny Ritz. I cracked open the plastic and offered one to Hudson. He took it, proving his eyes were open behind his shades.

"Do you always pretend to be the boyfriend of women you've just met?" I asked after I chewed my cracker sandwich.

"Only those with red hair. What about you? Do you always kidnap men who pretend to be your boyfriend?"

"Only the tall ones."

Hudson grinned and took another cracker.

"Is there anything important I should know about you?" I asked. "I mean, I know your name and that you work for a security company, but, well . . ."

"Am I a serial killer in my spare time?"

"Something like that."

"Let's see. I'm twenty-seven. I don't have any pets. I like football. And I have no desire to be in a movie."

"What? You live in LA and don't aspire to being an actor? I'm shocked."

"I'm the lone man left. What about you? Any plans for stardom?"

"No, thank you. I'm quite happy as a feng shui consultant."

"A what?"

"It's like a specialized form of interior design," I clarified, more than used to the question. "Basically feng shui is a practice of arranging your environment to suit, attract, and maintain the life you want."

"That sounds . . . New Agey."

"Ancient Chinese, actually, but I can see how you'd think that. There's a lot of chi flow and energy movement to what I do, but also a lot of organization and spatial arrangement."

"Huh. So you do what? Go into people's homes and fluff their chi?"

I recognized his attitude. I got it from about half the people I encountered. It seemed you were either a believer in energy outside yourself working to influence your life—the universe, chi, God—or you weren't. Typically, nonbelievers didn't believe in feng shui. I didn't take offense, and I wouldn't try to make him believe. I'd seen feng shui work a thousand times; I didn't have anything to prove to Hudson. "It's a little more complicated than that. Less fluffing and more heavy lifting and bell ringing."

"I wondered about the Christmas bells," he said.

I shook my bag, and it gave a faint jingle. Bells were a great cure for a multitude of feng shui problems, most commonly to get chi flowing in stagnant areas of a house.

"You do that full-time?"

I shrugged. "I work for myself, set my own hours. I don't have to work full-time to get by."

"That sounds nice. Nine-to-fivers suck the soul right out of you."

I nodded, though I'd never worked a nine-to-five job in my life. The closest I'd come was shortly after high school when I worked at a nursery where I could spend most of my time out with the plants and far away from the building's phones and lights and cash registers. It had been a peaceful job that built up my upper-body strength, but it didn't pay well and it ruined all my clothes. It also hadn't fulfilled any creative calling in my soul, something feng shui did in spades.

"So, a feng shui consultant with an artist aunt. That's all you're going to give me? If today's any judge, I'm going to have to do something spectacular to impress you on our first date, so help me out."

I lifted my glasses to my forehead, and he mirrored me. He looked sincere. "You still want a date after this?" I gestured behind us at Kyoko inside the trailer.

"This is a hiccup."

"A hiccup." My eyebrows met my hairline. "Does this sort of thing happen to you a lot?"

"It's a first, but I've got high hopes."

I looked away, but I couldn't suppress my grin. We were in the middle of an illegal scheme we were only peripherally aware of, poised for prison time if we didn't get this elephant back to a questionably sane woman, and he was flirting with me. I liked his style. "Okay, I'm twenty-six, like softball, play a mean game of Bunco, and don't have any pets either."

A few questions later and Hudson knew I could converse passingly in Spanish, had lived in LA for my entire life, and had attended UCLA. The last was a stretch. While I'd gone to UCLA for college classes, I couldn't enroll in a full graduate program. I couldn't use a computer to type the reports. I couldn't take the requisite lab classes. Instead, I'd taken extended education classes in interior design and feng shui, and I'd audited a few business management classes.

In turn, I learned Hudson had grown up in Austin, Texas, moved to Santa Barbara for college, was headhunted for a cushy electrical engineer position his senior year, and had been in LA ever since. He'd since found a new passion in designing custom high-end security systems for EliteGuard.

I envied how casually he mentioned relocating. Travel for any reason was out of the question for me. Cars couldn't get me out of LA without breaking down. Trains lasted longer, but I'd never stayed on one more than a half hour, afraid of what would happen if something that large and carrying that many people malfunctioned. Even sailboats had too much electronic navigational equipment to get me to Catalina Island and back. Planes were out of the question.

An enormous boxy black vehicle pulled into the parking lot. There wasn't a speck of dirt or a smudge of a fingerprint on the entire gleaming surface, and the black-wall tires glistened around silver rims. Hudson stood up, verifying the tank was our ride. I eyed the back end of the Suburban. It looked big enough to fit an elephant, at least a baby one.

"Are you sure you don't want to come with me while I drop the guy off?" Hudson asked.

"I'm sure. I don't want to leave Kyoko alone."

"Okay. I'll be back."

I fervently hoped so. Until I watched him stride away, admiring the view, I hadn't considered what I would do if he didn't return.

The shiny black SUV disappeared around a corner, and I turned back to the trailer. Kyoko dozed on her feet, trunk relaxed against the floor of the trailer. I sat back down. The fumes of her excrement had aired out while we were on the freeway, or else I'd become immune.

The sun warmed my skin, and the city sounds soothed my anxiety. It was tempting to turn my brain off, but I forced myself to review my bizarre day. Taking Kyoko to Sofie's was a temporary fix, and one I wasn't happy with. I didn't want to involve my aunt in anything illegal. *I* didn't want to be involved in anything illegal. But it would give us time to find Jenny—or for Jenny to find me again—and for us to force her to take Kyoko back.

*Us* was another topic to ponder. The superficial information Hudson and I had shared made great first-date material, but it didn't provide much to go on when forming an opinion about a partner in crime. Other than the obvious white-knight broadsword, the apparitions I'd seen had been predictably useless. A sombrero, a pair of well-worn cowboy boots, and a few Monopoly pieces told me nothing. Maybe Hudson liked Mexican cowboys. Maybe he'd played a lot of Monopoly as a child.

There had been nothing vague about his actions, though. He had a hero complex, he reacted quickly, and he hadn't flinched or backed down when he had a chance to extricate himself from this bizarre situation. All in all, pretty good qualities. Qualities I would have preferred to admire in a nice social setting, one that didn't involve crimes, cars, or crazy women.

Oh, yeah, or the pesky blackmail threat that could ruin my life.

# FOUR

"I DID some thinking on the drive back," Hudson said, taking a seat next to me on the trailer step and opening a container of Pad Kee Mao I'd set aside for him. When no brilliant solutions to Jenny's blackmail had surfaced, I'd decided to refuel at the Thai restaurant. My own box of Pad Thai sat empty by my feet. "This smells good. Thanks. How's Kyoko?"

"Sleeping."

"She didn't try to break out and trample you? Chew off an arm?"

"Until you've been shackled in there barefoot, you don't get to laugh."

"You've got to admit it was a teensy bit funny."

I arched an eyebrow at him. "You were about to prove you're more than just a pretty face," I prompted.

Hudson grinned. "Okay, here's a puzzle for you: How do we get Kyoko into the Suburban?"

I stared at the thigh-high back bumper of the Suburban, then down at the trailer, whose floor stood a foot and a half off the ground. A dog could make the jump easily, but not a stumpy-legged baby elephant.

"Well, crap." I glanced around for inspiration. No convenient loading dock, no steel-enforced plywood we could fashion into a ramp, no wheelchair lift.

"Exactly," Hudson agreed around a mouthful of food.

We brainstormed while he ate and came up with nothing.

"Where's a weightlifter when you need one," I joked, walking back from the trashcan.

"You know . . ." Hudson jumped up onto the step and peered at Kyoko. He turned to look at me over his shoulder. "That's not a bad idea. She can't weigh that much, right?"

"More than I can lift." She had to weigh at least twice as much as Hudson. "More than I can lift even half of, if that's what you're thinking."

"No. Even if she played along and didn't struggle, that would be too much for the two of us. But if we had help . . ."

"You have weightlifter friends in the area?"

"Not a single one. But I have cash."

Hudson's idea turned out to be two parts of horrible. First, he wanted to pay the thug-looking guys loitering around the tattoo shop to assist us. Second, he wanted me to enlist their help.

"Men are much more likely to assist a woman than they are a man," he explained.

"Or maybe that's just you."

"Trust me. You walk in there and ask them for help and they won't even need a cash incentive."

"And the fact that there will be a whole bunch of witnesses to us carting off an elephant?"

"That's where the money will come in."

"Just like that. I walk in and ask for some help."

"Unless you're afraid to."

I shot Hudson a look over the top of my sunglasses. He could have played the you-got-us-into-this-mess-you-deal-with-it card, but he hadn't. He'd pricked my pride instead. I smiled and tossed my bag into the Suburban. I pulled my hair free of its ponytail and finger combed it while checking myself in the side mirror. A quick reapplication of lip gloss, and I was ready.

The front window of the tattoo parlor mirrored the sun's glare, disguising the interior. Through the propped-open door, the bass of rap music pulsed beneath a mechanical whine I'd not heard outside a dentist's office. I could see two Hispanic guys through the doorway, both dressed in baggy jeans and work boots. One had a tank top under an open plaid shirt, and his long hair was pulled back into a tight, low ponytail. Tattoos covered his chest and arms. The other was younger, had a colorful sleeve that looked like a *Día de los Muertos* tribute, and wore a black ski mask apparition. Like the straitjacket I'd seen on Jenny, the ski mask didn't need sophisticated interpretive skills.

I took a deep breath and put some sway in my hips. My hair floated around my shoulders in scarlet waves, my own, personal neon sign for attracting attention when I worked it right, and I was working it. I sauntered through the open door and settled my glasses atop my head. Conversation stopped.

Two other men lounged in the dilapidated waiting room. The one seated near the register was the leader. He had direct line of sight on the door—always a power position, as any good feng shui consultant will tell you. He was Asian, his hair short and spiky and dyed blue on the tips. Colorful tattoos swirled underneath his thin white T-shirt, peeking through the V-neck and flowing down both arms to his wrists. A bright blue apron appeared with the words *Kiss the Chef* embroidered in black. I hadn't a clue what that meant, but it helped me relax enough to notice he was a few years younger than me and had a good jawline and sharp, tilted eyes. Definitely the most handsome man in the room. Or maybe it was his attire; I was a sucker for a man in jeans and a white T-shirt.

The final man was Samoan, big, and wearing a basketball jersey. His tattoos were black and tribal. Handsome in a giant sort of way, his arm muscles made the leader's look like spaghetti. Perfect. His pink-feathered princess tiara was a bonus.

"Please tell me you came in to get sleeves," the leader said. He strode over to me, hand extended. "I'm Mark Kim." I reached to shake hands, but he lifted my hand out in front of me, turning it back and forth as he examined my arm. "Luminescent. Flawless. The art I could ink on you, girl. Are you Canadian? Icelandic?"

"LA born and raised. This is the power of sunscreen." Vats and vats of it.

"A redhead without freckles. That's rare."

"It's a family blessing," I said. "But I'm not here for a tattoo."

"Are you sure? What about a half sleeve? Maybe a little something on your shoulder blade?" His eyes scanned down my body to my bare legs. "A little ankle adornment?"

I shook my head, smiling, and freed myself. He let me go easily and stepped back.

"I'd know if you were here for a homeboy," he said.

"You can be here for me, baby," Ski Mask said, shifting his belt buckle suggestively.

"Hmm. How much can you bench?"

"One fifty," he answered with a swagger.

"Kind of a lightweight, aren't you?"

"Oooh, snap," the older man beside him said. Ski Mask glared at the laughing men.

"But still stronger than me," I acknowledged. "And I've got a little problem that needs more muscle than I have."

It took surprisingly little to convince the men to follow me back to the trailer. I introduced Hudson as Tim and myself as April, something Hudson and I had agreed upon as a precaution.

"We need your help lifting a little cargo from the trailer to the Suburban," I said.

Mark shot me a sharp glance.

"Cargo?"

I gestured to the trailer. The men jumped onto the running board on either side of the wheels and peered inside. The trailer tilted alarmingly. Kyoko bugled.

"Holy shit! It's an elephant!" was the general sentiment.

"It needs to be an elephant in a Suburban," I said once they'd gotten over their shock and Kyoko had snuffled all their hands with her trunk.

"Dude, where did you get an elephant?" Plaid Shirt asked.

"Trade secret," I said. Hudson shrugged.

"That's not legal. I know that's not legal," the Samoan said.

"It flirts with the law a little," I conceded.

The big guy grinned at me.

Hudson backed the Suburban up to the trailer, and I swung the trailer's door wide, tossing some carrots Hudson had purchased toward the front of the trailer to distract Kyoko while we prepped. Mark popped the Suburban's hatch open. Since the hatch didn't clear the top of the trailer, we had to leave a three-foot gap between the trailer and the SUV. More than enough room for Kyoko to escape through. I pulled the trailer door flush with the Suburban to barricade my side, and the men did a pretty good job blocking the other side.

"What's that smell?" the Samoan asked.

I pointed to the pile.

"This is a fine ride," Mark said, running his fingers lightly over the Suburban's glossy paint. He peered into the pristine carpeted back. Hudson had lowered the back set of seats, and even the exposed cracks were lint-free. "Are you sure you want to do this?"

"Positive."

The men clustered around, rubbing chins and swinging their gazes from Kyoko to the Suburban and back.

"Whatever you do, don't let her escape," I said. I had a horrifying vision of Kyoko galloping off into traffic. Not only would that botch my agreement with Jenny and give her ample reason to follow through on her threat, but it would also endanger Kyoko. Blackmail or no blackmail, no animals were getting hurt on my watch.

I pulled a carrot from my pocket and stepped into the trailer. Kyoko finished the few I'd thrown in and eyed the open door. I skirted the offensive pile and looked up in time to see Kyoko trotting toward the opening. She barreled straight past my outspread arms and the offered carrot and tipped off the end of the trailer to the asphalt. It wasn't graceful, and she had to catch herself with her trunk, but the moment she recovered, she swung toward the nearest man, Mark, and jabbed her trunk straight into his crotch. He squeaked and doubled over, falling back a step. The big Samoan beside him shimmied to the side.

"Whoa there, Kyoko," Hudson said, stepping into the gap. "You okay, man?" he asked Mark over his shoulder.

The blue-haired man groaned through clenched teeth and nodded, clutching his crotch protectively.

"Okay, you step around her and get the other side," Hudson instructed the Samoan.

"No way. You didn't tell me it was a pervy elephant."

"She's not pervy," I said. "That was an accident."

"You afraid of a baby elephant?" Ski Mask taunted. He stepped to my side of the small opening. Of the four men, he was the one I wanted near me the least, but I held my ground. Kyoko prodded his calf, then ran her trunk up the inside of his leg. He jumped back just in time. "Shit, man. She *is* pervy!"

I sidestepped him and offered Kyoko a carrot, but she was more intrigued by the newcomers. Plaid Shirt scuttled backward when she reached for him. Kyoko followed. The Samoan, in his haste to avoid being felt up, hemmed Hudson against the trailer. Kyoko spied the open parking lot and freedom, and the men were forgotten. I lunged for Kyoko and grabbed her around the neck. The elephant dragged me two feet before she stopped, and then only because Hudson pushed in front of her.

We were almost beyond the side of the Suburban. Another step, and the world would see me hugging a baby elephant. Kyoko swung her head, agitated. Her trunk smacked me in the butt, and I yelped.

"She's pervy with women, too," Ski Mask said, snickering.

"Huh," the Samoan said.

"Any day now, guys," I said.

The Samoan *finally* stepped forward. "Hector, get your arms under her neck and front legs," he said, gesturing to Plaid Shirt. "Tim, you and Xavier get her right side. I'll take the left."

Behind him, Mark braced his hands on his knees and nodded when the others looked to him for affirmation. Hudson joined Ski Mask on my side, Hector squatted to grab Kyoko's neck, and the Samoan slid his arms under her belly. I let go, reaching for a carrot.

"On three," Hudson said. "One, two, three." They hoisted Kyoko a foot in the air.

Kyoko prodded Hector's back, questing beneath the waistband of his sagging shorts and straight down the center of his crack.

"Those aren't kiwis!" Hector shouted, springing away from Kyoko. Her trunk snapped free of Hector's waistband, and she loosed an ear-blasting trumpet, dangling front legs flailing. The Samoan lurched back a step, catching the brunt of Kyoko's squirming weight. In an awkward pyramid, the men tilted two steps back, then three forward.

I leapt for the Suburban, scrambling inside ahead of Kyoko, less concerned with flashing the men than I was with Kyoko's safety. The elephant poked the hatch door, hooking her trunk on the lip. I grabbed the curled tip of her trunk and pulled her head down, trying not to think about the agile appendage's most recent location.

"A little help," the Samoan said, teeth gritted.

"No way! That elephant molested me. It touched my cajones!"

"Man up." Mark shoved Hector behind Kyoko. They each braced against a cheek and pushed from behind. The moment Kyoko's front feet touched the carpeted Suburban, she bugled again and flailed with her back legs. Faces red with strain, the men shoved her the last two feet into the SUV. The tank-size vehicle tilted, groaning, before settling at a twenty-degree cant. Everyone staggered back and Hudson whisked shut the hatch, locking me inside with an irate elephant.

I threw myself over the row of seats in case Kyoko was in a trampling frame of mind. The roof cleared her head by less than a hand span. The sides weren't much wider than her rotund belly. She tried to turn around, knocking her butt, then her head against the plastic-wrapped metal bracings. She plastered her cheeks against the rear window, and through the tinted glass, I saw the Samoan point and laugh. All the men scuttled to the side when the glass gritted in its mooring. I grabbed the last of the carrots and dumped them onto the carpet.

"It's okay, girl. This won't be for long," I said, praying the

Suburban would make it to my aunt's. I didn't think Kyoko—or Hudson—would be up for doing this twice.

Kyoko slid the tip of her trunk along the window, then the back of the seat. I let her snuffle my hand and arm but leaned back when she went for my hair. There were limits to where I'd let her put that thing, especially since I knew her exploratory predilections.

She tilted her head back, trumpeted loud enough to rattle the windows, then reached for a carrot and stuffed it into her mouth.

I straightened my dress—how long had the top been that low?—then jumped out, ears ringing. I brushed hands down my body and winced at my knees rubbed red from the carpet and tender to the touch. Through the tinted windows, I could barely make out the hulking shape of Kyoko. Good. She shouldn't attract attention.

Hudson paid the men. Hector looked wild-eyed, and he rubbed surreptitiously at his crack. When Xavier tried to razz him, Hector punched the younger man hard on the arm.

"Redheads and trouble go hand in hand," Mark said, walking over to me after he pocketed Hudson's money. "That's what my father always said. But always worth it." He winked and pressed a business card into my palm. I'd guessed correctly: He was the owner of the tattoo parlor. "Anytime you want, I'll ink you wherever you want. On me."

The group sauntered back to the strip mall. Mark limped, and he unabashedly massaged himself through his pants.

"What was that about?" Hudson asked.

"Apparently I have perfect skin," I said. "And I can get free tattoos."

"See. What'd I tell you? You didn't see them offering me anything free. In fact, that cost me everything I had."

I winced. "I'll pay you back."

"Don't worry about it." He went to the driver's side and opened the passenger door. He pulled a bowl and a water bottle out of the plastic bag behind the seat, then crawled in and placed the bowl down on Kyoko's side. I climbed into the front seat while he filled the bowl. I was more than ready to leave this parking lot.

The Suburban purred when Hudson turned over the engine. A

trickle of cool air fed through the vents, circulating the smell of musty elephant. I adjusted the vents to angle back toward Kyoko.

"What about the truck?" I asked as we rolled past it. Even compared to the truck, the Suburban felt big—wide, long, and heavy. It fit a freaking elephant; that should say it all.

"The moment we find Jenny, we'll tell her where it is," Hudson said.

"And if it was stolen, what about evidence?" I'd read plenty of thrillers; I knew how forensics worked these days.

"I called work while I was driving back earlier. I had the same thought. They ran the plates for me. It's registered to Edmond Zambo. I'm hoping he was the driver of the car Jenny got away in."

"She had a getaway driver? How long has she been planning this?"

"You sure she doesn't hold a grudge against you for something stupid in high school?"

I shook my head. "If so, I'm clueless. Wait, how does a security installation company run a plate?"

"EliteGuard is on good terms with the police. Wade, my boss, free-lances for them sometimes."

I filed that information away. "What about finding information on Jenny? Can they do that, too?" Preferably in a careful, controlled way that wouldn't spook Jenny.

"Wade's already on it."

"What?" My heart jumped to my throat. If Hudson had told his boss about Kyoko, my life could already be over.

"I asked him to run a background check on her. I thought I'd better hold off on mentioning the elephant until we know what we're dealing with."

I eased out a breath and loosened my grip on the door handle. "Ah. Good thinking."

Hudson merged back onto the 10. I twisted in my seat to watch Kyoko. The stop-and-go traffic had cleared while we'd been sitting in the parking lot, and Kyoko appeared as unfazed by the traffic ebbing around us as she was by going seventy miles an hour. I faced forward and straightened my skirt.

"Do you ever do that?" I asked. A van full of teenagers whipped around us and passed in the slow lane. No one took a second look at the Suburban.

"What?"

"Freelance for the police."

"Not often. It's not really my specialty."

Water sloshed behind us. I twisted in time to see Kyoko lift a dripping trunk toward her mouth.

"Looks like she was thirsty. Good thinking on the bowl," I said.

"Thanks."

She reversed her trunk and curled it over her head. Water sprayed across the ceiling of the Suburban.

"Holy crap!"

Hudson yanked the rearview mirror into a new position. "Did she just . . . ?"

"Turn into a fountain? Yep."

Kyoko sprayed herself again, and it sounded like a hurricane swirled through the back of the Suburban. Most of the water soaked the ceiling above her head. The thin fabric sagged, then it started raining. Kyoko dunked her trunk again.

"No!" I cried. "No, no, no, no." I unbuckled my seat belt and twisted onto my knees. Hudson changed lanes, and I tipped into the center console. He grabbed for me, steadying me with a hand square on my ass. I clutched the back of the seat and shot him a look. His eyes remained glued to the road, but his hand lingered a fraction longer than necessary.

Kyoko doused the left side of the roof with water. She shifted, and the whole vehicle sagged to the right. Hudson compensated at the wheel. Water dripped to the carpet in soggy splats, and Kyoko bugled her delight. I clamped my hands over my ears. She ran her trunk along the roof, sending a spray of water across her face and leaving a furrow of mud.

I lunged over the center console again, but Hudson grabbed my arm.

"I need to get the water away from her," I said.

"There's no point now."

Kyoko swung her trunk, smacking into the window. It vibrated but held.

"What's the elephant safety rating of these windows?" I asked.

"Substandard, I'm guessing."

Kyoko dipped her trunk into the bowl but came up dry. She reached for the roof and plucked the loosened fabric with the tip of her trunk. Droplets splattered me, and I lurched back, half sitting on the dash. The stain of water on the roof bloated outward and tunneled in rivulets down the ceiling toward the back door. Fat drops hammered the carpet and drummed on the leather seats. Kyoko prodded the inky ceiling, turning in tight steps to chase the rivulets. Her rough hindquarters slid along the side of the Suburban. A seat belt caught on her back leg and stretched with ominous clicks. Another shuffled step, and it ricocheted back to the plastic panel with a loud crack. I winced.

At a turn in the freeway, Kyoko sat on the edge of the window frame. The door groaned. Hudson lurched for the electronic lock button and the locks slammed home in surround sound. Kyoko stood and shuffled until she had her back to us, her trunk pressed to the rear window, making slimy patterns in the trails of water.

I shared a horrified look with Hudson.

"Did that just happen?"

He sprouted a silver top hat; Baltic Avenue draped his chest.

I dropped my forehead to the headrest. Thanks to Hurricane Kyoko, I may have just purchased my first vehicle. My meager savings evaporated in my mind's eye.

A groan of leather brought my head up. Kyoko pressed her butt against the back of the second row of seats and leaned her weight into it, reaching for the ceiling again. Something popped deep in the seat.

"Shoo, Kyoko. Get up." I waved my arms halfheartedly.

Kyoko raised her stubby tail.

"Oh, shit!" My knee slipped, and I fell half to the floor. Something made the flapping sound of a Whoopee Cushion. "Did she just—"

The fumes of her fart hit me like a slap. I coughed and crumpled completely under the dash, burrowing my nose in my elbow.

"Was that you?" Hudson asked.

I gaped at his innocent expression, then clamped my mouth shut.

Hudson hit a button on his armrest and both our windows zipped down; then he cracked the next set of windows. Hot air swirled through the cabin, whipping my hair into my eyes. Car exhaust had never smelled so good.

When I glanced up at Hudson, his eyes were crinkled at the corners. The Monopoly board apparitions were gone, replaced by an enormous fluffy white cloud with false rays of sun shining through it, haloing Hudson's upper body.

"Are you laughing?" I shouted above the freeway noise. This wasn't funny. Kyoko had *ruined* this rental.

Hudson's lips twitched; then he broke into a full-faced grin. Panic leaked from my limbs and I became aware of my sprawl. I yanked my skirt down from my waist to cover my thighs and shoved myself back into my seat, glowered at everything, including the van of teenage boys who had slowed down to stare at me.

"Did I flash them, too?" I asked, not meeting Hudson's eyes.

"Only when you had your ass in the air. Since then, it's been just me."

"Like what you saw?" It was difficult to convey sarcasm while shouting over freeway noise.

"I was hoping for a thong."

———

THE SUBURBAN WAS GRINDING and sputtering when Hudson made the final turn onto my aunt's street. I pointed to her house, and we coasted into the private circular driveway.

The Suburban died with quiet dignity. It had lasted exactly twenty-seven minutes.

Not bad, considering my horror and acute embarrassment.

Hudson set the emergency brake. His scowl was back, along with the silver top hat and terrier, both situated on enormous Monopoly squares—Park Place and Boardwalk this time.

"What are the odds of two vehicles breaking down on us? I think this elephant is cursed. That's why Jenny foisted it off on you."

I let his grumblings wash over me. I had more pressing concerns. Aunt Sofie stood in her front doorway, staring at me through the windshield of the SUV, *that* smile on her face when she spotted Hudson in the driver's seat. Among the collection of content and happy-to-see-me apparitions, oversize finger puppets tipped the nails of her right hand—knit wolves, with leopard spots. She was about to meddle.

Sofie had the strongest gift our family had seen in five generations. It had been Sofie, not my mother, who had taught me about my unique ability, first to keep it a secret as a toddler and later how to live with it. As Sofie had explained it, layers of divinations flowed around everyone in a kaleidoscope of images. My gift gave me access to one wavelength of apparitions: a person's current emotional state. It was like seeing only one color in the spectrum. Sofie was privy to a modified rainbow. She had a weaker version of my gift, and she also saw critical emotional crossroads in someone's past and images of people and places strongly tied to each person. Occasionally, she caught glimpses of what a person wanted—an area my mother specialized in. Sofie never glimpsed apparitions related to relationships, like Nana Nevie, or so she claimed. Sofie's gift had limits, but one look at Hudson, and she probably knew more about him than I did.

I didn't stand a chance of hiding anything from her. Sofie raised me. She knew my apparitions better than I knew hers. There wasn't an emotion I felt that she didn't know by sight. While this had been a blessing when I was a child, we'd set ground rules when I became a teenager. The number-one rule was if I wasn't expressing the emotion verbally or through normal body language, she was to pretend she couldn't tell what I was feeling and vice versa. This complicated our interactions sometimes, but it also allowed me to feel like a normal teenager—and now a normal adult—with a private life, thoughts, and emotions.

When I hopped out of the Suburban, Sofie's eyes roved over me before meeting mine, and the finger puppets disappeared, replaced by a large wolf at her side, standing tall enough for her dangling fingers to rest in its insubstantial fur. She'd gone into protector mode. Add in some fear—a corset of ebony vines riddled with thorns piercing her flesh—and curiosity in the form of a beehive of sea shells, and I almost missed the castanet when she glanced at Hudson. Despite the apparitions she saw on me, a slice of meddling lurked in her.

A golden bundle shot through the door behind her and down the shallow steps. Salvador Dali, Sofie's Lab, bounced around me, sniffing and licking and making soft woofing noises of delight to see me. I rubbed his head and came away with slimed fingers. Hudson walked around the hood of the dead vehicle, and Dali darted to him with toenails scrabbling on the stone driveway in his enthusiasm. If Hudson's silver terrier had been real, it would have been bowled over.

"Hi, baby girl," Sofie said. She enfolded me in a hug. I breathed in the aroma of paint and perfume, and a tightness in my shoulders eased. Sometime in my teens, I had surpassed Sofie in height, but not by much. Our shared genetics were impossible to miss. We both had the family curves, though hers were more lush than mine. Our hair was nearly the same shade—Sofie's with a little help from a bottle these days. We shared mannerisms and our laugh was almost identical. But the subtle cleft in my chin, my blue eyes, and my long slender fingers were my mother's. My full, almost square lips must have come from my father's side.

"I didn't expect you to arrive in such style," Sofie said, pulling back. Her eyes held a hundred questions.

"Neither did I." I wanted to blurt out everything, but Hudson finally extricated himself from Dali's exuberant welcome. "I'd like you to meet Hudson Keyes. Hudson, this is my aunt Sofie. Hudson works for the company Gabriel hired to improve his security."

Hudson shook Sofie's hand.

"It's a pleasure to meet the famous S. Sterling," Hudson said. "I'm sorry your paintings were stolen. We'll do everything possible to make sure it never happens again."

"Why ever would you do that?" Sofie asked. "I think this is wonderful."

I gaped at her. Of all the reactions I'd expected, glowing cheer hadn't even made the list. "You're happy?" I asked.

"Happy? More like thrilled. Only the greats get stolen. I thought I'd have to wait until I was dead to see it happen. But we can talk about that later. You two look hungry"—her eyes dipped to the stains on my skirt and the dirt on Hudson's clothes—"and like you have a story to share. Why don't you—"

We all jumped when something hit the Suburban's back window with a loud pop. The SUV creaked on its shocks.

"Do you have something in there?" Sofie asked, squinting at the tinted windows.

"As a matter of fact, I do," I said. "It's, uh, well . . ."

Sofie pressed her face to the side window, shading her eyes with her hand. Her jaw dropped open and she eased back a few steps.

"An elephant?" she breathed. Wide brown eyes leapt from me to Hudson and back again. "Where? How?"

Muted pounding came from inside the vehicle. The oval tip of Kyoko's trunk flattened against the window closest to us.

"Explanations later, Sofie, I promise. We need to get her out of there before she does more damage," I said.

Sofie wasn't listening. She yanked open the back passenger door and popped her head into the vehicle. Dali, beside himself with curiosity, wriggled at her feet, barking excitedly. I saw the dim outline of Kyoko raising her head, and I clamped my hands over my ears in time to muffle her bugle. Sofie fell back, dazed, and shut the door.

"That explains the smell," Sofie said.

I snapped my fingers at Dali. "Hush. Sit," I ordered. The Lab swung his head to look at Sofie, then me. I took a step toward him. He sat, mouth closed.

"Where was that authority in the trailer with Kyoko?" Hudson asked.

"Stunted by the handcuffs."

"Handcuffs?" Sofie echoed. The wolf at Sofie's side bared its teeth. A locket around its neck bristled like a blowfish.

I shook my head. "Later. Right now, we need a ramp, because the three of us aren't lifting that beast out by ourselves."

Sofie nodded and strode toward the house. Surviving my childhood had fine-tuned Sofie's ability to prioritize in the face of unusual adversity. Or maybe she'd always been skilled at adapting, and that's why she'd been able to raise me while my mother hadn't.

My aunt had nothing strong enough to serve as a ramp, but we found two wide tables—one a worktable, the other a coffee table built to withstand a nuclear bomb—and we set them behind the Suburban to serve as steps.

"She didn't have a collar that I noticed," Sofie said. "How do you plan to get her to follow you?"

The open side gate to the backyard stood ten feet away. I lifted a plastic bag of baby carrots I'd raided out of Sofie's fridge when I'd locked Dali in the house. "Bait."

"Ready?" Hudson asked.

I nodded. An enormous great white shark loomed behind Hudson, maw agape, then disappeared to be replaced by the sombrero. The Monopoly pieces were gone. I glanced at Sofie. I would have really loved to confer with her about Hudson's images, but we didn't have the time. The elephant was restless.

When Hudson popped open the back door, Kyoko didn't hesitate. She tottered off the soggy carpet onto the table. The SUV squeaked; the table groaned. Kyoko plunged to the coffee table. It bore her weight silently. Then she had all four feet on solid ground and she swung straight toward Sofie.

"Watch out! She—"

"Whoa, there!" Sofie said, scooting back a step to avoid a trunk to the crotch.

"She really is a pervy elephant," Hudson said.

I shook the plastic bag of carrots and poured some into my hand. Kyoko trotted to me and snatched them from my palm, stuffing them into her mouth. Her attention wandered to the landscaped flower beds, and I grabbed for another carrot. Three more bribes, and she ambled through the gate. Hudson and Sofie closed the latch behind us, reinforcing it with a dead bolt. The wall to Sofie's yard was stucco, matching the Tuscan-style house. Only the gate was wooden. If Kyoko planned to escape, it'd be through there. Fortunately, the little elephant showed no interest in the way out. She trotted straight to the eggplant-shaped swath of lawn, dropped to her knees, flopped to her side, and rolled.

"Would you look at that," Sofie said.

Dali's whines pierced the back door of the house, where we'd shut him inside before releasing Kyoko. Seeing an elephant in his yard broke through the usually mannered dog's restraint, and his claws scrabbled at the sliding glass window.

"Uh-oh. I'd better—"

The glass door inched open and he shoved his nose through the gap, using his feet to widen the opening.

"Shoot. He just learned how to do that." Sofie rushed up the patio steps, but Dali was quicker. He wriggled through the opening and shot across the patio, clearing the five steps to the lawn in a single leap. Kyoko pushed to her feet and trumpeted. Skidding to a halt, Dali barked. Kyoko reached for him with her trunk, ears flapped forward.

"Should we stop them?" Hudson asked.

"Too late."

Dali sidled up to Kyoko, his whole body wriggling with happiness, and sniffed her trunk, her ear, her grass-stained stomach. She, in turn, prodded at him with the tip of her trunk, which he didn't seem to mind at all. Standing side by side, Dali came to the middle of Kyoko's barrel belly, yet he looked huge, being only a few feet shorter than an elephant.

Once the preliminary introductions were completed, Dali bounded away several yards, then raced back, ears and tongue flapping. Kyoko bugled and trotted after him. She followed him in circles while he did excited puppy pounces, lowering his front feet, leaving his hind end in the air, then darting away when she got too close.

I couldn't help but smile.

"Dali's a good host," Sofie said, coming back down the stairs. "I can't wait to hear the story behind . . . What did you say her name was again?"

"Kyoko."

"Ms. Sterling, can I—"

"My friends call me Sofie," Sofie interrupted.

"Ah, Sofie, can I use your phone? It seems the salesman lied about this burner's reliability." Hudson held the little flip phone open in his hand, its screen black.

"Of course." Sofie shot me an amused look. "Let me show you where it is."

Sofie led Hudson into the house. I settled into a lounge chair near the pool, well clear of the game of tag. The soft lawn wasn't made for safari animals, and Kyoko's feet gouged huge chunks every time she pivoted to confront Dali. I sighed. My next six months' worth of consultations were going to be spent paying for everything this elephant destroyed. Maybe Jenny would reimburse me.

Ha. That was about as likely as her forgetting about my curse.

Kyoko's attention was diverted by the pool. She slowed to a walk as she neared the edge, running her trunk along the hot flagstones and smacking the water.

Large, square, with a dark bottom and salt water instead of chlorine, the pool contained a wide shelf that spanned the width of one end, designed for lounging where the water rose only calf deep. The rest of the pool dropped to six feet deep for laps. Dali raced to the shallow shelf and plunged into the water. Kyoko followed, dropping into the pool beside the dog. Mud and feces and unidentifiable grime washed into the water. I added pool-cleaning services to my list of growing debt.

In doggy heaven, Dali romped around Kyoko, his tail a wet whip spraying water in arcs behind him. Kyoko slid her trunk into the water, then raised it over her head, spraying her back. Dali barked ecstatically. Kyoko did it again, only this time she angled her trunk to wash over Dali. He yipped and leapt out of blast range straight into the deep water, paddling to a step on the opposite side. The expression on his face made me laugh, and my shoulders loosened.

I was home. Safe. I was as far as I could get from anything electrical, situated where my curse could do the least damage. I relaxed the clamp I'd wrapped around my emotions. Mental knots of tension lifted, and I felt physically lighter.

I unbuckled my sandals and tossed them under the lounge chair, then padded to the shallow shelf.

"Are we friends?" I asked the elephant. She turned to watch Dali, who had climbed out of the pool at the opposite end and was now rolling in the grass. I stepped into the pool beside Kyoko and stretched a hand to touch her side. She twisted to look at me, and her trunk hit the water, the spray soaking my side. "Not cool, Kyoko."

Dali trotted to the edge of the pool, dropped a tennis ball into the water by my legs, and shook. I obediently tossed the ball across the lawn, then watched him tear out after it.

A blast of cold water hit the back of my head and drenched me. I spun to Kyoko, shoving strings of hair off my face. She blinked large brown eyes at me with false innocence.

"Fine. Let's see how you like it." I splashed an arc of water into Kyoko's face. She tilted her head back and opened her mouth to catch it. "Oh, you like that, do you? How about this?" I circled her, kicking and splashing and spraying her with as much water as I could. She blasted me with another trunkful. She looked so smug I burst out laughing. "You just wait," I said.

I was headed back to the pool with the hose when I noticed my audience. Sofie sat at the patio table with three glasses of water and snacks. She watched Hudson watch me, puppets the size of small mice coating her fingers. I narrowed my eyes at her, and she smiled serenely. Hudson stood at the railing, arms crossed over his chest, grinning like a fool. He unabashedly stared, and my body went hot when I realized my drenched dress clung to me like a second skin. A surreptitious glance confirmed my headlights were on. I blushed, then gave a mental shrug, seizing on my favorite embarrassment-coping strategy: pretend everything is normal.

"Want to join in?" I called to Hudson.

"Looks like you've got it covered." His gaze roamed down my body, and fire followed in its wake.

"Chicken." I put my thumb over the end of the hose and sprayed water in his direction. It fell well short of the patio. He backed up anyway, holding his hands up in surrender. Too bad. I wouldn't have minded seeing his shirt molded to his chest. He could even have taken it off, if he was worried about getting it wet. If Sofie hadn't been there, I would have suggested it.

I turned my attention back to Kyoko, who was splashing water at no one in particular.

"Okay, let's get you clean," I said, abandoning my original plan for payback. I detached the head of the pool brush from the pole and stepped into the pool beside Kyoko, brush in one hand, hose in the other. Kyoko had to examine the brush, then the end of the hose—which she shoved into her mouth for a drink—before allowing me to bathe her. The step was gritty under my feet by the time Kyoko moseyed over to the lawn and rolled. I glared as all my hard work was smeared with grass and dirt. At least she no longer smelled like a manure pile.

Hudson turned off the water to the hose and helped me coil it back up.

"That was nice of you," he said. "I think she liked it."

He stood close enough for my chilled, wet skin to feel his body's radiating heat. I looked a mess—wet hair stringy, arms splattered with mud, my dress clinging in wrinkled clusters on my thighs—but Hudson's expression said otherwise. I recognized the hunger on his face; it was mirrored on my own.

# FIVE



I FORCED MYSELF BACK A STEP. I didn't normally retreat from intense chemistry, but one of us needed to be rational. The bizarre circumstances of our tenuous acquaintance could have been skewing our reactions. What felt like lust could have been a byproduct of adrenaline and the psychological bond created by shared danger.

My gaze dipped to his lips. Okay, had we not been at my aunt's, and had she not been within shouting distance, I probably wouldn't have bothered with thinking. Hudson was hot, he was looking at me like he wanted to lick me dry, and I was eager to see under his clothes.

I nibbled my bottom lip and shuffled around him. "I, uh, I'm going to get cleaned up." His stare warmed my skin until I closed the pool house door behind me.

Twenty minutes later, I'd showered and dressed in soft, worn jeans and a T-shirt, thanks to a stocked dresser in the pool house.

When Sofie had first purchased this property, the pool house had been off-limits to me. It had been where she'd kept all the appliances, conducted her Internet transactions and phone conversations, and worked at night. The big house had been where we'd lived, and the distance between the pool house and main house stretched far enough to prevent me from killing all of Sofie's electronics.

Now the pool house had been stripped of appliances and converted into my oasis away from home, complete with my own decor. Given its location next to the pool and the view of the ocean, I'd balanced the interior with fire and earth elements. I'd selected minimalist but inviting furniture, and the light-colored, warm-hued walls drew in the outdoor light to compensate for the usual lack of electricity. The addition of candles throughout the bathroom, dinette, and bedroom added to the retreat vibe.

I ran my finger along the spines of books on the single slender bookcase while I towel-dried my hair. Sofie saved titles she thought I would like, and I snagged a copy of Bill Bryson's *I'm a Stranger Here Myself*, holding the book up to catch the setting sun's rays so I could read the back cover. I turned at the scrabble of nails on rock in time to see Dali race past the sliding glass doors and across the lawn after a ball. Kyoko trotted in his wake, trunk and tail up, sounding like . . . well, like a herd of elephants running past.

*Nope, only one*, I thought, then grinned. The whole situation was absurd, made no less so by my aunt's calm acceptance. She stood in the middle of the yard throwing the ball for Dali and Kyoko as if elephant visitors were an everyday occurrence. The sunset highlighted her auburn hair and glowed in her dark eyes. The soft light washed away a dozen years, and not for the first time, I wished she had been the pregnant teen to give birth to me.

Dali dropped the ball at her feet, but Sofie sidestepped when Kyoko barreled up behind him and snatched the ball with her trunk. Curling her trunk over her head, she flung the ball. It landed a few feet in front of her, but Dali tore after it like she'd launched it across the yard. He returned the ball to Kyoko this time, not Sofie, and my aunt burst out laughing. Seeing me watching, she came up to the pool house and let herself inside.

"I've been replaced."

"Who can compete with an elephant?" I said.

"Dali is going to be so upset when his new companion has to go."

"Yeah. About that. Thank you for being so easygoing about me showing up with a baby elephant."

She smiled. "That wasn't all you showed up with."

I flattened my lips and gave her a stern look, which she ignored.

"When are you going to stop dawdling and come over to the house so you can tell me how you met Hudson"—she raised her hands when I opened my mouth—"*and* how you got Kyoko?"

I rolled my eyes. Only my aunt would be more interested in Hudson than a baby elephant. Of course, she was right; I was stalling. I needed distance between myself and Hudson to see if I was reading my emotions correctly—and to cool my hormones. If we were going to figure out how to find Jenny and return Kyoko, I needed to think with my head, not my libido. Plus, I wanted to look nice when I emerged from the pool house. I'd frightened myself when I'd gotten a good look in the mirror before my shower. My pride needed a pick-me-up.

"I'll be right there," I said. Sofie arched a brow at me. When she turned to leave, paintbrushes stuck out of her back pocket. Paint covered the ends, so I knew they were a divination. Sofie was content. That wouldn't stop her from meddling, though.

I placed the book on the nightstand, then hung my towel in the bathroom. My hair had dried enough to have wave again. I fluffed it over my shoulder and stared at myself. I was pale, with pale auburn eyebrows and pale pink lips. Only my eyes were dark. I reached for my makeup bag, then returned it to my satchel. I wasn't going on a date or a consultation. I was going to sit in my aunt's house and have dinner and talk about my day's criminal activities. With a man who made my pulse race with one quirk of his sexy lips.

"Hopefully he likes pale redheads." The fact that I cared proved my dawdling hadn't lessened my attraction to Hudson.

Kyoko and Dali were back in the pool, splashing in the shallow end. I crossed the far side of the yard and darted up the patio steps and inside before Dali sprinted up the stairs behind me. I slammed the sliding glass door closed and stopped short.

The vision that was Hudson sitting at the kitchen bar, Sofie's laptop in front of him, shocked me motionless: Green, paint-stained sweats rode up his calves like cropped pants and a pink and blue Getty museum V-neck T-shirt strained across his shoulders and strangled his armpits.

"Are you wearing my aunt's clothes?" I asked.

Hudson looked up, and a blush tinted his cheeks. "She stole my clothes while I was in the shower."

"I didn't steal them. I put them in the laundry," Sofie said from where she stood at the stove. "They're almost done. Those sweats were the only pants I had that would fit you. I thought you'd prefer them to a wraparound skirt."

"*Fit* isn't the term I would have used," Hudson grumbled, tugging at the tight collar of the T-shirt.

I bit my lip to contain my laughter.

"Yeah, yeah. Yuck it up," Hudson said. His eyes snagged on my bare feet when I kicked off my flip-flops. I grinned and turned toward the living room.

The open floor plan of the living room, kitchen, and dining room made a large L, with the kitchen at the center, visible from both rooms. Sofie had a gas stove so we could cook together, but the refrigerator and microwave were both electric. I curled up on the sofa cushion farthest from the kitchen. If it had been just the two of us, I would have helped Sofie, neither of us concerned with the fridge shutting down for a few hours. Now I hated the useless feeling of sitting idle while my aunt did all the work, but it was that or explain yet another electronic malfunction to Hudson.

"It says here that baby elephants take up to ten years to be fully weaned," Hudson said, pointing at the laptop screen. Yet another good reason for me to be across the room. "Where are we going to get elephant milk?"

A rectangular object floated a few inches off his right bicep. It was green, with small black and silver and gold squares perched on it like a bizarre futuristic miniature city. I couldn't figure out what it was, let alone what to make of it, so I did what I usually did with apparitions: I ignored it.

"She seems to like carrots well enough," I said. "Maybe she's already partially weaned."

"What do they eat as adults?" Sofie asked.

"Grass, if she's an Asian elephant, which I think she is, judging from the size of her ears and the shape of her head."

I rose and walked to the floor-to-ceiling windows facing the back-yard, pool, and the ocean views beyond.

"Good guess."

Hudson came over to stand beside me. We watched Kyoko use the end of her trunk to twist hunks of grass out of Sofie's lawn and shove them into her mouth.

"Jenny somehow found a baby elephant who was already weaned," Hudson said.

"How old do you think she is?"

"She's barely larger than the site says elephants are when they're born."

I couldn't prevent my gaze from dropping to examine Hudson up close. The sweats were baggy, but not baggy enough to conceal that he was going commando. I jerked my eyes front and center again, turning my head so Hudson couldn't see the flush staining my cheeks. How old was I? Sixteen?

A muffled beep emanated from the hallway.

"Dryer's done," Sofie announced.

Hudson moved before she spoke. I turned to watch him, admiring the clench of his ass beneath the soft material and silently laughing at how gangly he looked in the too-short sweats. My laughter died when he peeled off the tight shirt. He waited until he was beyond the kitchen, in the gloomy hallway and out of Sofie's sight. Had I gone back to my seat on the couch, I would have missed the show, too. As it was, I wished he'd flipped the hallway light on. What the dim lighting revealed made my mouth water.

*And now let's see the front,* I thought, admiring the play of muscles across his back. As if he heard me, just before he slipped into the washroom, he turned his head and met my eyes. He gave me a slow grin as he looped his thumbs into the waistband of the sweats and tugged them down a tantalizing three inches to reveal the upper swell of his white ass before he stepped out of sight. I blinked and took a step in his direction.

"Close your mouth, dear," Sofie said, softly enough for only me to hear.

I clicked my mouth shut and blushed to the roots of my hair. Sofie cackled. I pretended acute interest in Kyoko.

———

HUDSON and I took turns telling Sofie our bizarre tale while we devoured several helpings of her famous enchiladas. By the end of dinner, we'd caught my aunt up on the entirety of our predicament.

"She claims to have gone to school with me, and she must have, because she remembered all those brownouts *and* Byron's car battery problems," I said.

Sofie's dark gaze pinned me. Thorny vines slithered around her midriff. She understood the unspoken importance of Jenny connecting those incidents to me.

"I didn't want to get you involved, too," I said, "but I couldn't think of anywhere else to take Kyoko."

"You did the right thing, Eva. But now what?"

"Our plan is pretty simple," Hudson said. Dressed again in his jeans and blue T-shirt, minus his socks and shoes, he relaxed against the back of his chair. Though we'd met only that morning, he didn't look out of place at my aunt's dinner table. "I didn't find a report of a missing elephant on any news feed. Somehow Jenny got her hands on an unclaimed baby elephant. So, we need to find Jenny and sort this out before anyone finds us with Kyoko."

"What if Jenny doesn't want her back?" Sofie asked as I topped off everyone's margarita glasses. None of us were eager to rush from the table.

"I don't think she intends to give Kyoko to me for good," I said. "She seemed nervous, like she thought she was being followed. I think she wants me to keep Kyoko safe for a while."

"And if that was only the insanity talking?" Sofie pressed.

"Then we contact the authorities and convince them of our innocence," I said. My stomach tightened at the thought.

"I'm more concerned right now about the bad luck that elephant carries with her," Hudson said.

"The cars breaking down?" Sofie guessed. I didn't say anything, and Sofie didn't look at me.

"Yeah. And the phones. It's more than a string of bad luck."

"You don't honestly believe that, do you?" I asked. "A cursed elephant?"

"Exactly. It's cursed." A foot-tall marble winged cherub flapped lazy stone wings off his left shoulder. I eyed it, then Sofie. If I could see the divination, she could, too, along with a whole lot more. But if she understood what it meant, she didn't clue me in.

"Plus we've got that trashed Suburban to fix." Hudson gestured toward the carport. "Normally I would call up the rental company and have them send us a new car, but I can't. Not with all the water damage. Somehow we've got to get it cleaned up before we can report that it broke down. That's going to take time I'd rather spend finding Jenny and getting ourselves out of this mess."

"Perhaps the car will be working by tomorrow," Sofie said, eyes innocently wide.

I calculated the distance from the pool house to the carport. Far enough. Ten hours was plenty of time for a vehicle to recover from my company.

Hudson shook his head. "I've never known a vehicle to spontaneously repair itself. Plus, I can't impose on you. I really should be getting home and working on finding Jenny."

"I thought you said your coworkers were doing that," Sofie said.

"They are, but this whole thing is a mess, and the sooner we can get it straightened out, the better. God, the back of that Suburban . . . I don't think we're ever going to get it clean."

"It will all look better in the morning," Sofie said. "There's no sense in you rushing home tonight when I've got a perfectly good spare bedroom. And Eva can stay in the guesthouse, like always." She raised a hand to cut Hudson off when he started to protest.

"Plus, tomorrow you can have a professional detailer tackle that mess."

Hudson looked at me, raising his eyebrows in silent question.

"I'm more than happy to spend the night and start fresh tomorrow. But I have a change of clothes here and you don't," I said, giving him an out.

He glanced at his wristwatch—thankfully mechanical, not digital—then at me. Finally, he shrugged. "Starting tomorrow does sound better. Today has been a massive string of bad luck. I'm afraid if I get into another car—Kyoko present or not—the damn thing will break down, too." The cherub disappeared. Twin bananas hung from his shoulders, each dripping rotten slices down his chest. I tried not to stare.

"Your day wasn't all bad, was it?" Sofie asked.

I did a mental eye roll. I didn't need to look to know her finger puppets were back. "The day did begin with your artwork being stolen," I said, hoping to distract her and bypass any awkwardness.

"Exactly! Isn't that fabulous?"

"No, it's not. Art you made—pieces you spent time and money on and were planning to sell—was taken by an imbecile. Where's the good in that?"

"I told you, Eva. Artists wait a lifetime to become famous enough to be forged or stolen and sold in some seedy black-market transaction. In my twenty-five-year career, this is *the best* thing that has ever happened to me." Sofie got up and grabbed a stack of papers from the edge of the kitchen island. "This is a list of people who called today to interview me for local papers and magazines," she said, handing me a paper with five names on it. "This is a list of the national presses picking up the story." Three more names. "Two art blogs and an auction house blog have requested interviews, too. And"—she paused before presenting the final paper with a flourish—"this is the list of sales I made online today." Twelve names and addresses filled the paper.

I fanned the pages. "Really? Just today?" A good month's online sales meant two prints or maybe an original. Most of Sofie's work was commission-based, with sales at gallery shows augmenting her income.

"Just today. And the hits on my site are . . . Well, I won't bore you with the details, but they've been fantastic. I also made two appointments for commissioned work, and one is an office that wants at least five pieces."

Grinning, Sofie plopped back into her seat. She raised her half-full glass to us. "A toast: To whoever stole my paintings, may they be as blessed as I am." We clinked glasses and I sipped my margarita.

People amazed me. My aunt oozed talent. Her artwork had shown around the world, a testament to her talent and her dedication to making a name for herself in the art community. But it took a thief to bring her to the attention of the general public. Some unknown individual had proclaimed they valued S. Sterling's artwork enough to risk imprisonment to obtain it, and now everyone else jumped on the same bandwagon, afraid to miss out.

Shaking my head, I began to clear the dishes. Hudson immediately rose to help. Together we filled the dishwasher and wiped down the kitchen. We worked together easily, like we'd shared domestic chores all our lives. He didn't talk, and I was content to say nothing. Even this camaraderie was seductive. Plus, what's not sexy about a man who pitches in with chores without hesitation? Hudson had the manners of a modern-day gentleman. The damn man was making it difficult to maintain my distance, even with Jenny's threat looming in the back of my mind.

Sofie swooped in as we finished, shooing us out of the kitchen before Hudson could attempt to start the dishwasher. It wouldn't have complied, having died over an hour earlier. She pulled frozen cream puffs from the freezer, arranged them on a platter, and drizzled stove-warmed hot fudge over the top. I uncorked a caramel-colored dessert wine and poured three slender glasses for us. Hudson made minimal protests about Sofie going to too much trouble, but she assured him it was no less than she would have done if she'd been home alone. It was the truth, too. My aunt had taught me early on to enjoy the simple pleasures in life.

We settled into cushy chairs in the living room, and Sofie switched on the gas fireplace to disguise the fact that the living room lights were out of commission. I sat with my feet tucked under me and savored a partially thawed cream puff.

"You have a beautiful home," Hudson said after the silence had settled around us. "It's very inviting."

"That's all Eva." A large wolf appeared at Sofie's feet, curled up against the front of the couch, but I eyed the fairy wand resting in her right hand with more trepidation. Black wood with a sculpted white quartz handle and tipped with blunt silver, the wand was one step up from finger puppets. Sofie had decided to influence Hudson based on the divinations she saw.

"She's positively gifted when it comes to interior design," my aunt continued. "And I've never met a more talented feng shui consultant. If I were left to my own devices, the walls would have art, but everything else would be a mishmash. And I know for a fact that Bernie wouldn't be in my life." Sofie pointed to a picture on the mantel of her and Bernie kissing.

Bernie was Sofie's boyfriend of eight months. They'd met after we'd removed the enormous watercolor of a lonely woman from Sofie's romance and relationship bagua and replaced it with a painting of two intertwined trees. I'd done a few enhancements in the relationship sections of each room—a matched pair of swan salt and pepper shakers for the kitchen, a candle with two wicks for the front room, a full-leafed plant in her studio—and Sofie had purchased new bedsheets with the intention of sharing them with someone special. A month later, Sofie met Bernie through a mutual friend, and they'd been dating happily since.

"So you think that because the things in your house were placed a certain way, it brought you romance?" Hudson asked. The bananas were back, rotten cores and all.

"Oh, definitely, though that's rather simplistic. You explain, Eva."

It had been at Sofie's urging that I'd tried my hand at feng shui as a teenager. We'd already discovered I had more decorating skills than Sofie, and I liked doing it a great deal more. Plus, Sofie's suggestion had been motivated as much by desperation as love. As graduation loomed ever closer, I'd grown increasingly despondent. While my friends raced toward futures of endless opportunity, I trudged toward adulthood, dread hobbling every step. Living and working in the "real world" meant battering myself against a culture in which my biological curse fated me to fail time after time. Traditional schooling had already set up the pattern, and the life beyond my seventeen-year-old tunnel vision had looked downright depressing.

"You only get one life, baby girl," Sofie had told me, rubbing my back while I sobbed my despair into a pillow. "If you don't make sure you're having fun while you live it, no one else will." She had placed a book on feng shui in my hands. "You're happiest when you're puttering around here. Start there."

It had been the best advice of my life. After reading the slim volume, I knew I'd found my calling. The ancient art form of feng shui originated before electricity and was largely based around energy movement and intention. Even better, unlike my gift, the invisible powers of feng shui could be channeled into a fulfilling career.

Nine years later, I had absorbed everything I could about feng shui, and I was still in love with it. I could talk feng shui for hours, but only to people who were interested.

"Hudson doesn't believe in feng shui, Sofie. It's okay."

"No, I'd like you to explain it," Hudson said.

I took a sip of wine to give myself a moment to collect my thoughts. Hudson was an electronics guy, which meant he was a science guy. I tried to put it in terms he would understand. "Everything you see is one of two things," I said, "energy or matter. Right?" Hudson nodded. "You interact with the objects, or matter, in your house daily, and these interactions can positively or negatively affect your energy. If your house isn't supporting you, you might feel depressed or apathetic instead of joyful or energized. Whether you intend to or not, you're going to carry this energy with you wherever you go. To follow the analogy, you're far less likely to find the love of your life if you're moping about. But if you change your energy by changing the objects in your home, then you can change the way you interact with the world and the way the world interacts with you."

"So, what, by putting a plant on my doorstep, I'll suddenly find the love of my life because it changed my energy?" Hudson asked.

"No. Not exactly. Just like there are rules to the way the world works—the laws of physics and all that—there are some guiding rules to feng shui. The plant would probably help your career more than anything." I had pamphlets to help my clients understand the principles of feng shui, but I didn't think Hudson wanted to read the literature. "I think the best way to understand it is this: Feng shui has strong roots in common sense. You'd be surprised how often people forget it when decorating. They don't have enough light in a room; they crowd furniture or plants near the door; they clutter their garages with so much junk they can't fit their vehicle. All these little and big annoyances add up. They block your chi, which—"

"Don't get too technical, Eva," Sofie interrupted. She turned to Hudson. "Eva does magic, my dear. She's trying to dress it down with science and mundane terminology, but it comes down to magic. She can enter a space and tell you what you need to change to make it feel better. She can walk through a person's house and know things about them their shrinks don't, just from their environment."

"You're making it sound too wishy-washy," I said, knowing she'd cost me whatever credence I'd gained with Hudson.

"I guess I'll have to take this house as proof that whatever you do with feng shui, it works," Hudson said diplomatically.

"You could always hire Eva to feng shui your home."

"I don't know about that. I rather like my bachelor pad. And my life."

———

I LEFT the light on when I went to bed. The lamp would last at least an hour in my relaxed state, but I knew I wouldn't have to wait that long. I had barely cracked open *I'm a Stranger Here Myself* when I heard the side door open. The door led directly to the bathroom along a tiled hallway, ideal for wet swimmers. I listened for the click of Dali's toenails, but it was only Sofie who peeked into the studio-style bedroom.

"Where's Dali?" I asked.

"Bunking down with his new best friend. They're curled together on his blanket, neither of them really fitting. I wanted to take a picture, but since we're not supposed to have Kyoko . . ."

I sat up and propped a pillow behind me. Sofie settled on top of the covers beside me and did the same. She had changed into lightweight flannel pants and a short-sleeve baggy shirt sporting a *Starry Night* print. Her feet were bare, and her toenails were adorned with lavender polish.

"Jenny knows about the curse?"

"She figured it out. She threatened to tell people—newspapers, scientists—if I didn't help her." My voice quavered. Saying it aloud made it sound even worse.

Sofie took my hand and squeezed it. "Does she really want Kyoko back?"

"Yes. Definitely. She seemed scared, but not scared about having Kyoko. I think something else had her spooked."

"Good."

"I don't know how we're going to find her," I said. "Hudson may have coworkers who can look, but . . . but what if they fail? What am I supposed to do?"

"Nothing. She found you once; she'll find you again. If you can't find her, patience will sort this all out."

"What's to stop her from telling people even if I do everything she asks?"

"Nothing." Sofie smiled. "But she's known for ten years, and she hasn't said anything, so I don't think she's going to go blabbing now. You did the right thing. It's not going to hurt anyone for us to watch Kyoko for a few days."

"And if we learn something awful about her and can't give Kyoko back, what then?"

"Then we face whatever happens. Between your mom, your nana, and me, we won't let anything happen to you."

But if Jenny convinced someone, anyone, to examine my curse seriously, I wouldn't be the only one under scrutiny. They'd want to know where I got this ability, and how. They'd check my family first. The thought of reporters or scientists nosing around Sofie or Nana Nevie made my head hurt. Around my mother—the thought sent a chill down my spine. If I ruined her career, I didn't think it'd matter if scientists commandeered my life; she would make it a living hell first.

"All the what-ifs in the world are not going to change a thing, so I suggest you spend your energy more wisely. Speaking of which, I got Hudson all tucked in."

I laughed even as I spied the finger puppets. I considered picking my book back up, but my curiosity about what she'd seen on Hudson stayed my hand.

"Spit it out. What did you see?"

"Oh, I saw lots. He's a good man. Very intriguing. He handled the cars breaking down well, don't you think?"

"About how most people would."

"And Kyoko and Jenny, he handled that about how most people would?"

"What are you trying to say, Sofie?"

"You know exactly what I'm saying. He's attractive. He's adaptable. He's—"

"A career electricity man."

Sofie shrugged. The finger puppets were replaced with the fairy godmother wand. "He's attracted to you. I'm just saying you shouldn't let little things get in the way of your happiness."

I twisted to look straight at Sofie. She knew I wasn't pining away for my Prince Charming, so why the campaign now? "You're pushing. Why?"

"I like Hudson. He's complex. He's nice. I like what I see when he looks at you."

"Like what?"

"Like the way he couldn't tear his eyes off you when you were bathing Kyoko and when you were sitting on the couch. Like the way you sneak glances at him when you think he and I aren't looking."

"Don't play games. What did you *see*? Did you see us together?"

"You know it doesn't work like that."

"Bull. You saw Nana Nevie with Theo the first time they met. A crossroads moment for them both." Nana Nevie and Theo's marriage had lasted two years and three months—a normal-length marriage for Nana. While they'd been together, you couldn't be in a room with them without knowing in your bones that they loved each other. When they'd divorced, it had been an amicable parting, and they were still friends, as Nana was with all her ex-husbands.

"Mom's a lot more open to love than you are," Sofie said softly.

I opened my mouth to protest, then closed it. I was open to love, but I didn't believe in the One True Love and it didn't believe in me. Men were wonderful in short doses, which was all my curse allowed. Lasting love was a myth. On some level, Sofie agreed with me. She had never married. She had long-term relationships, but they were always an afterthought, something tucked in around everything else she enjoyed. No man had ever shared her home.

The women in my family didn't experience fairy-tale, lifelong-monogamy love. Maybe we weren't capable of it. Even Nana Nevie, so open to love, didn't follow the traditional path. She had been married five times in my lifetime and three times before my birth. My mother had married once. It had lasted three months before the annulment. The man hadn't been my father. She hadn't married since, and as far as I knew, she'd never come close again.

"I want you to be happy, Eva."

"I *am* happy."

"You're content. Happy is different."

"Content feels like happy."

"Content is a bland cousin to happy."

"You think a man is going to make me happy?"

"No. *A* man isn't. But finding the right person to share your love with? Yes, that will make you happy." The wand disappeared. A plate of coffee cake sat on her lap. *Uh-oh.*

"Where's this going, Sofie?"

"The same place all your missed opportunities go, if you let the damn curse rule your life," Sofie said, her voice sharp.

"It doesn't rule my life. I have relationships."

"You're a serial dater. You play with men. You don't have relationships."

"Tell that to Antonio or Locke or Jordan."

"You just proved my point."

"I don't know what your point is. Did you or did you not see something on Hudson?"

"Yes." For a long moment, she stared at the cover of the book on my lap, or possibly at something else she saw there. "I saw danger represented—"

"Danger?"

"—and adventure and a puzzle that unlocked with a key you held."

I swallowed. "That could mean a lot of things."

"It does."

"How dangerous?" I asked.

She shrugged. The coffee cake still sat on her lap. Despite her vague air, she was laser focused on meddling in my life. The problem was, she knew exactly which of my buttons to push. If she'd told me Hudson was safe or reliable—chemistry be damned—I would have kept my distance. A dangerous puzzle, though . . .

She stood, kissed my forehead, and then headed for the door. "This is going to be fun," she said.

"Sofie . . ."

"Sleep tight, Eva."

"Sofie!"

The door clicked shut behind her. I flopped back against my pillow and glared at the empty room. "Great. Now I want coffee cake."

SIX



MY FIRST THOUGHT when I woke was of Hudson stripping in the hallway. The image had burned into my brain, right down to the tantalizing rise of his butt and that teasing grin. It wasn't a bad way to wake up.

I replayed last night's conversation with Sofie while I dressed. My aunt wouldn't lie to me, but she wasn't above omitting details that didn't suit her purpose. *Danger* and *adventure* and *puzzle* were flame-bright words to my inner moth, and she knew it. Conversely, Sofie's interest and her belief that Hudson might have long-term potential made me leery. I appreciated a short, hot relationship. No part of me wanted a lengthy romance.

I stuttered over the thought, then decided to pretend an infinitesimal part of me wasn't calling my bluff.

I pulled on a skirt and V-neck, saw myself in the mirror, and immediately took everything off. It looked like I was trying too hard. I grabbed a pair of jeans and a tank top. Much better. The jeans hugged my butt and the creamy tank top made my skin look golden and flashed a hint of cleavage. Sexy without being overt. By the light of a Coleman lantern, I brushed brown mascara over my lashes, darkened my eyebrows, and slathered on sunscreen. I left my hair down and wavy, but I tucked a hair band into my pocket for easy access.

The sun was hidden behind the Santa Monica hills, but it glinted off the ocean's waves. I paused on the pool house patio to take in the serenity of Sofie's home, hearing the silence as much as any sound. No traffic noises, no sirens, no music. Just the ocean's murmur scored by the cries of seagulls and the rustle of wind through the high fronds of the palm trees lining the property. I loved my apartment. I loved living in the city, where I could walk to everything I needed and buses circulated every few minutes. But I always missed this quiet.

Kyoko trumpeted, and a flock of pigeons burst from the eaves. Dali barked, circling Kyoko with a stick in his mouth. When he saw me, he galloped toward me, Kyoko thundering after him.

"Shoot!" I clutched my bag and sprinted across the yard to the main house. Dali thought it was a game, and he ran circles around me while I dodged the sharp end of the stick. Kyoko bugled again. In desperation, I grabbed the stick and threw. Both Dali and Kyoko spun and gave chase. I leapt the porch steps and burst through the back door, slamming it behind me. Hudson and Sofie laughed at me from their front-row seats on the couch.

"Thanks for the help," I said, tossing my bag down and gulping air.

Hudson was fully dressed. Not that I expected him to be lounging around my aunt's house without his shirt on, but a girl could hope. His gaze rested a fraction too long on my heaving chest before he looked down at his mug. Sofie smirked when she met my gaze. The wolf sat at her side, facing Hudson, its tongue lolling in a canine grin. A full moon floated above Hudson's head. I glanced from the wolf to the moon and back. Not even Sofie could project an apparition to coordinate with someone else's. It was a coincidental cultural association. And creepy.

"I've got pancake batter all ready to go," Sofie said, rising.

Hudson grinned. "I haven't eaten this good in years, Sofie."

"Stick around, Hudson. You haven't seen anything yet."

"Do you want some help?" I asked Sofie when she passed me.

"Oh, no. This won't take a moment. Sit. Relax."

I narrowed my eyes at her and she gave me a false innocent look. I sat, selecting a chair far from the kitchen and across from Hudson.

"Good news," he said. "I don't know how, but the Suburban works. I drove down to the gas station and back without a problem."

"Looks like your bad luck broke," Sofie said from the kitchen.

"That's great," I said. "How's it look?"

"Trashed." A silver terrier popped into the air at his feet.

We sat in silent commiseration until Sofie called us to set the table.

"I got Jenny's last known address," Hudson said after we all helped ourselves to fluffy pancakes from the tiered platter in the middle of the table. "It's in Arlington Heights, close to Koreatown. I thought we could drop by the gallery to pick up your car; then we'll have a vehicle when we drop the Suburban somewhere to get it detailed."

I stuffed a bite into my mouth and chewed while I thought of the best lie for this situation.

"Eva doesn't have a license," Sofie said baldly.

I bugged my eyes at her and swallowed too quickly. I gulped some orange juice and met Hudson's gaze. His expression flattened, and thick black-rimmed glasses perched on his nose.

"You don't have a license." It sounded like an accusation.

"Uh, not right now. It got, ah, revoked."

Sofie sighed.

"For what?"

"For . . ." I came up blank.

"For not paying her parking tickets," Sofie said. Hudson likely mistook the irritation in her voice to be disappointment over my supposedly delinquent payments, not my lie.

"Wow. You must have had a lot of tickets," Hudson said.

"Parking is limited near my apartment." That, at least, was the truth, according to Ari.

"Huh." Hudson leaned back in his chair. The glasses disappeared. He steepled his hands and a Rubik's Cube popped into existence above his fingers. "Well, we can work with that, I guess."

———

SOFIE SAW us off from the front porch, a wolf seated at her side. The wolf had a pipe in its mouth. I hadn't seen that one before.

"Come back anytime, Hudson," she said, giving him a hug before squeezing me tight. "Give him a chance, Eva," she whispered.

"Hopefully we'll be back later today with Jenny," Hudson said.

We drove with the windows down even though the cool morning air pebbled my skin. With the windows up, the stench would have suffocated us, and the wind helped dry the back. Hudson turned the heater on our feet, and for a while it worked. Noise from the wind and traffic made it difficult to hold a conversation, so I didn't try. I focused on keeping my emotions calm, which meant burying my guilt for involving my aunt. I had literally left my problem at her doorstep, and even though we had a plan, chances were it wouldn't work. Jenny would prove to be insane, and I would be responsible for my aunt being implicated in this illegal fiasco.

I focused on suppressing my curse and picturing lush fields of grass and sky, open and peaceful. Hudson's topless image overlaid it and my heart rate spiked. I pictured lounging in my bathtub, but then a naked Hudson was rubbing soapy hands down my body. The Suburban's electric locks protested with a *zit-zit* sound. I pounced on a mental image of Chatter, Ari's cat. As a Bengal breeding reject, Chatter couldn't decide if she wanted to be a wild cat, a lap cat, or a dog, and I loved her. As we cruised down the 10, I replayed some of my favorite memories of Chatter as a kitten. Hudson—half naked or otherwise—didn't intrude.

Miraculously, the Suburban survived over a half hour with me as a passenger. The electronic windows and locks, the dash displays and clock, and the heater didn't, but the engine was only just beginning to putter and clunk when we coasted into a business park and bounced over an endless line of speed bumps. Five-story concrete buildings loomed on all sides, with pockets of trees cowering in spindly group-ings. Hudson passed the parking garage and parked in one of the few empty spaces near double doors discreetly marked with EliteGuard's logo. He pulled out a new flip phone he'd picked up on his morning gas run. The black screen stared back at him. He crunched the power button. Nothing happened to the phone, but tiles of the weird metal city on green plastic sprouted around Hudson's torso like body armor.

"I guess I'll be calling the detailer from inside," Hudson said. "You want to come?"

Hmm, let me think. The headquarters of Hudson's security company. A building full of computers and cameras. It even had an electronic security panel next to the door. "No. I'll wait here."

I hopped out and slung my bag over my shoulder once Hudson disappeared inside, trailed by a man-size winged marble cherub. Hudson joined me after a few minutes, just as a Prius parked next to the Suburban. A short Hispanic man climbed out wearing coveralls. The front had the name Diego embroidered on it. The back had a picture of a smiling industrial vacuum cleaner. Draped over one arm was an apparition of a full-size life preserver. In the crook of his opposite arm rested a scepter that would have done an Egyptian pharaoh proud.

"Is this the vehicle?" Diego asked after shaking both our hands.

"Yep."

Diego opened the back hatch. Water trickled out. A noxious cloud of wet elephant, wet elephant poop, and wet carpet followed. Diego lifted his arm to his nose and stepped back. An easy-to-interpret neon yellow hazmat suit engulfed him.

"Did you transport alpaca back here?" Diego asked. Nose clamped, he leaned in to inspect the vehicle more closely. "No. Let me guess: two-year-olds? My sister has twins from hell. Two girls, right? Look like angels. Nope. *Hijas del diablo.* They make my five boys look like saints." He shook his head and crossed himself. The hazmat suit gained a clerical collar, making it one of the more bizarre apparitions I'd seen.

"Kids can be real monsters," I agreed.

"Look. This isn't an on-site job. I need to take it back to the station, pull in our experts."

"Fine," Hudson said. "When you're done, leave the keys with anyone from EliteGuard." Hudson pointed to the intercom next to the door. "And I'd like it back today. It's a rental."

Diego's eyes grew round. "Shit, man. Those kids owe you big. This one's gonna cut into their college fund." I stared at the sequined feather headdress sprouting from Diego's plastic-shrouded head.

Hudson sighed. "Just do what you can." He handed over the keys.

"I'll do my best, but I don't do miracles."

———

I FOLLOWED Hudson and his Monopoly-piece apparitions across the parking lot, calculating how many consultations it would take to pay for everything Kyoko had destroyed. Fifty consultations? Seventy? Everything I earned for the rest of the year? I stumbled against Hudson when he stopped.

"Where's your car?" I asked.

Hudson gestured in front of him. I stepped to the side. The compact motorcycle was cherry red, with a huge round tank and low handlebars. The driver's seat wrapped around the tank. A paperback novel–size leather seat perched behind it. A helmet hung from the handlebars.

"You're kidding."

"Wait here. I think Richard has an extra helmet."

Hudson jogged back to the building and disappeared inside. I moved away from the slender machine. "He's got to be kidding."

"How far is it to Jenny's?" I asked when Hudson returned.

"From here on a bike? About ten, twenty minutes. Why? Are you afraid of motorcycles?"

He wasn't making fun of me. I appreciated that. Motorcycles weren't for everyone. They certainly weren't for me. Or at least logic said they weren't. However, a wishful part of me admired the sleek lines of the bike and envisioned the fluid freedom inherent in the machine's small frame. A hundred times while seated on sloth-like buses, I'd fantasized about switching places with motorcycle drivers, splitting the lanes and coasting ahead of all the congestion. Here was my opportunity.

I calculated the risk. Most vehicles could withstand me for twenty minutes. The Suburban had lasted almost forty. But if a motorcycle died, it could prove a lot more dangerous than if a car died.

"Have you ever ridden on a motorcycle before?" Hudson asked when I hesitated.

"Never."

"I promise to drive safely."

"Completely safely?" I asked, a little crestfallen.

"Completely."

"Oh."

"How about not recklessly?"

I reached for the helmet. Hudson laughed and handed it to me, followed by a leather jacket two sizes too big. The full-face helmet encompassed everything above my shoulders and smelled of hair gel and cologne, neither belonging to Hudson. The jacket smelled of leather and bacon.

"They're Richard's, but I figured you'd rather be safe than smell good."

Hudson shrugged on his own leather coat, then took my bag and put it over his shoulder. He started the bike and gave me a few pointers. Mainly, my job was to hold on and keep my body in line with his. Seemed simple enough.

Getting on the bike felt like climbing a pinnacle. I perched a mile above the ground and a half mile above Hudson. When I leaned forward to wrap my arms around him, I cracked my helmet against his. The seat had all the comfort of a two-by-four under my butt. Hudson turned the ignition and eased the bike forward. I cinched my arms around his waist and tightened my thighs against him. He drove around the parking lot slowly until I relaxed enough to breathe.

"Ready?" he shouted.

"Ready," I shouted back.

For the first few blocks, I watched the road streak past our knees, jolted by adrenaline each time the bike dipped left or right for a turn or a lane change. When I looked up, my breath caught. The world was in motion and I was at its center. Wind whipped against my jeans; the bike vibrated under me; the sun heated my back. The motorcycle's muffled mechanical purr blended with the wind's hiss. I tightened my arms around Hudson, savoring the feel of his solid body through his jacket.

My daydreams hadn't come close to capturing the intensity of the experience.

Hudson took a sharp right and accelerated up a curving on-ramp, the bike dipping sideways around the corner. Then we were on the freeway, a tiny scrap of metal and rubber beneath us, thousands of enormous cars surrounding us, flying across the pavement at seventy miles per hour with the rest of the traffic. It should have been terrifying.

It was utterly exhilarating.

When we dropped off the freeway after threading our way through two backlogged lanes exiting at a snail's pace, the surface streets were too tame, the turns too seldom, and the speed bumps in the neighborhoods were an affront to the pleasure of the ride.

It wasn't until Hudson backed the bike between two parked cars that I remembered the purpose of our drive. I scrambled off the bike while Hudson held it steady. My knee popped when I straightened it, and my leg muscles protested the stretch. I unstrapped the helmet and tugged it off, fluffing my hair with my free hand. Hudson turned off the motor and pulled his helmet off, still straddling the bike. I couldn't stop grinning like a fool.

"That was incredible!"

"Did I just make a motorcycle convert? Maybe when you get your license reinstated, you can take the test. You'd get a lot fewer tickets with a bike." He tapped the motorcycle's dials, a frown replacing his wide smile. "That damn curse better not have followed us."

The muscles in my cheeks gave out, and my smile deflated. "Is it broken?"

"Not broken. Just giving me weird readings. There's no way we were doing forty down this street. More like twenty-five."

Eyes downcast, I shrugged out of the leather jacket and traded Hudson the helmet for my bag. He attached the extra helmet to the back seat, then stuffed Richard's jacket inside it. Hudson unzipped his jacket but kept it on. It was a good look for him, but I turned away so he wouldn't see the defeated expression I couldn't mask. For a few minutes, I had forgotten I was me, cursed. I had been a normal woman, one for whom riding a motorcycle could be more than a once-in-a-lifetime experience. Sometimes reality sucked.

To combat a welling pity party and the accompanying tears, I distracted myself with examining the neighborhood. We stood in front of a dilapidated craftsman bungalow. Yellow paint flaked from the siding, and the trim sported more brown wood than white paint. Drapes shuttered every window, an ominous sign. A scraggly hedge and brittle, knee-high dead weeds suffocated a minuscule front yard. The slender lot squeezed between two larger homes, the boundaries defined in the front by the crisp, tidy green edges of lawns on either side and by tall wooden fences in the back.

Everything about the house, including the numbers placed at a slant down a wide porch pillar, screamed negative feng shui. I didn't need Hudson's verification to know we'd found Jenny's place.

A partially cleared pathway through the dirt and dried leaves led up the porch steps to the door. No welcome mat greeted visitors. Hudson pulled the tattered screen door aside—it shrieked loud enough to excite the next-door neighbor's dog—and pounded on the door. The sound echoed through the still house.

"I don't think she's home," I said.

He knocked again. Nothing.

"Now what?" This was our only lead on Jenny's whereabouts, and I wasn't ready to walk away empty-handed. I wriggled the handle. "We need to see inside." I pressed my face to a window, shielding the light with my hand. No shadows shifted on the other side of the curtains, and no convenient gaps revealed Jenny inside. "What if she's here and not answering?"

"Let's find out." A jaunty white captain's hat with a dark bill and a braided blue cord around the base of the brim perched on Hudson's head. A gold seagull embellished the front of the hat. Paired with the leather jacket and jeans, Hudson looked like a cruise ship captain on shore leave. Perhaps a hipster captain, since he'd also accessorized with the black frames he'd worn at breakfast.

"How're we going to do that?" I asked.

"We'll just have to try another door."

The side gate wasn't locked. Hudson reached over the top and flipped the latch. I glanced around. No curtains twitched in neighboring homes. No pedestrians walked by. Across the road, a woman sat in her car, six feet from her front door, futzing with a cell phone. I gave a mental head shake. I would never understand people's addiction to their phones. A ham sandwich rested on her ample chest, but that wasn't real. Maybe she had an addiction to ham sandwiches, too. Either way, she wasn't paying attention to us.

I followed Hudson into the backyard and he latched the gate behind us. The unforgettable smell of elephant poop assaulted my nose.

"We've definitely found the right place," Hudson said.

The backyard looked worse than the front, if that was possible. Dead vines clawed at the wooden slats of the fence, and elephant dung moldered in the churned soil.

Hudson jogged up a wheelchair ramp to the back door and jiggled the handle. Locked. He pulled a familiar packet from his jacket pocket and selected two slender tools from the flaps.

"Was lock picking part of job training?" I asked.

"No. Just something I picked up."

I shifted closer to watch him. There was no point checking the back windows; they were blockaded by drapes like all the rest. Hudson wiggled two picks into the lock at once, crouching to get a better angle.

"How can you tell what you're doing?" I whispered. Speaking softly seemed appropriate for the current crime.

"By feel." He paused and glanced over his shoulder at me. "Interested in learning?"

"Now?"

"In general."

"Why not?"

Hudson grinned. A few moments later, the lock clicked and the knob turned. Hudson tucked his tools back into his jacket and stood. Stomach fluttering, I eased into the house after him.

With the curtains closed tight, the whole house basked in a twilight ambiance. We entered through a kitchen with bare, off-white Formica counters unadorned by a single countertop appliance. One side opened to a dining room with a low center fixture, a nest of blankets, a lamp, a telephone, and a jumble of papers and pens. The hardwood floor leading to the living room was gouged in sweeping arcs on either side of the kitchen door. Shards of the door frame and splinters littered the floor.

The living room reminded me of pictures taken after a flood. Concussions pocketed the lower walls. A high-water mark of smeared dirt and scuffed paint circled the room at elbow height. Above the line, the walls were pristine white and bare. A cascade of coupon mailers and junk mail mounded near the front door beneath the mail drop slot. Several children's toys littered the empty room, most broken. A wheeled cage large enough to fit a person hunkered against one wall. Otherwise the room was bare.

There was no sign of Jenny, and our footsteps echoed in the abandoned house. Nevertheless, we tiptoed toward the single door off the living room. It led to a barren bedroom. The bathroom beyond had a bar of soap and a combination shampoo/conditioner on the edge of the tub.

Hudson crept to the closet and rolled the door open. Empty, without even a single hanger. He did one more sweep of the house before walking back to the bedroom with normal, loud strides.

"No one's here."

"I don't think she's been here for days," I said. I plucked the bottom of a curtain in the bedroom. The fabric was stapled to the wall.

This place gave me the creeps. If this was where Jenny called home, she needed some serious help—feng shui and mental.

We scoured the house for any indication of Jenny's current whereabouts. I found a hair tie in the back of one drawer, some ketchup packets in the refrigerator, and a mop in a closet. The mail proved equally unenlightening. Every credit card application, refinancing offer, ad, and coupon was addressed to "current resident." The clutter of paperwork in the dining room offered the only clues: bill receipts, lists of numbers, some torn scraps of real estate listings, plus several pages of notes scribbled in kanji on letterhead also printed in kanji. However, missing from our search was a convenient message saying, "I'm headed *here* next."

Hudson pocketed Jenny's notes. I spun in a circle in the empty house. "Where are you, Jenny Winters?" I asked.

"Not here, and I don't think she's coming back," Hudson said.

I had to agree. Frustration knotted my shoulders. "This is crap. We're no closer to finding her and getting rid of Kyoko than we were yesterday. And now, on top of elephant smuggling, I can add breaking and entering to my list of crimes."

"We'll find her." At my skeptical look, Hudson added, "Trust me, I know how to search for someone. *If* I could find a phone that works." Hudson glared at his cell phone. It was a different one than before, I thought. White instead of black. Flat instead of a flip phone. He must have picked it up from his office. And then I'd pressed against him on his bike.

The captain's hat and hipster glasses had disappeared during our search, replaced by the strange plastic and metal miniature city armor. This time I could see it wasn't a city. The taller constructions resembling skyscrapers had no windows. The lines in between the buildings looked like roads, but they were made of gold and resembled the kind of tracks driven by cars at Disneyland. It made no sense, so I ignored it.

"Maybe I can find something," I said. "I went to school with her, and that's how she remembered me. Maybe there's a clue in some of my old high school stuff. Something that will jog my memory."

"Okay. We'll go by your place first, then to my work."

Getting back on his motorcycle was less of an option than going to Hudson's work. One ride had pushed my luck. A second ride, especially before the bike had a chance to fully recover, could prove suicidal.

"Perhaps we should split up," I suggested. "We'd work faster that way."

"Good point. And I could swing by home and change my clothes."

Hudson headed for the door and I crouched by the cordless phone in the dining room, dialing Ari's number from memory. We were miles from my house and I didn't have the patience for the multiple bus transfers it would take to get me home. I needed a ride.

Hudson pounded across the kitchen and into the dining room.

"What are you doing?" he demanded.

"Calling a ride."

"Hang up!"

"No. Your phone isn't working." And this one would be dead soon, too.

"Shit. Is it ringing?"

"Yeah."

"Then it's too late."

A slender metal tie wrapped around Hudson's neck and pulled tight. Alarmed, I started to hang up when I heard Ari's voice.

"Hello?"

"Grab a pen, Ari. Pink. Midnight." I rattled off the address. Cordless phones never lasted long in my hand. Fortunately, when we were in high school, Ari and I had created a code that worked as well for notes slipped into each other's lockers as it did for short phone calls: The time indicated urgency—the closer to midnight, the greater the urgency. The color corresponded with different common scenarios. Pink represented a guy of interest. Nothing would motivate Ari more than pink right now. Plus, I didn't have a code color for "I've broken into the house of a crazy lady who gave me an elephant, and my only ride home is a motorcycle that's going to break down if I stand near it."

Static crackled through the line by the time I got to the street name. It died as Ari was saying, "What are you doing in—" No dial tone, just a dead phone.

"What's it too late for?" I asked Hudson, hanging up the phone.

"Now your friend's number is on Jenny's phone records. Whatever bad shit she's involved in, now there's a link to your friend—and you."

# SEVEN

"BUT—" Crap! I'd already involved my aunt. Now I'd entangled my best friend in this mess. "What makes you think someone's checking her phone records?"

"It's what I planned on doing."

"You can do that?"

Hudson ran his hand through his hair. A grotesque fish with a bloated body and mutant fins swam back and forth through his stomach. He paced into the kitchen and I followed him, more than ready to leave. When he spun around, I had to brace a hand on his chest to stop myself from slamming into him.

"Why'd you call someone to pick you up? I can drop you off."

"This will be faster. Besides, you said your bike was starting to have some problems. I'm beginning to think it's you who has horrible luck with vehicles." My gut twisted with guilt at the accusation.

"I didn't have bad luck until I met you."

He said it like he meant it to come out as a joke, but it didn't.

"Hey, I didn't ask you to pretend to be my boyfriend. You got yourself into this mess." I clamped my mouth shut and crossed my arms. That wasn't true. Hudson had wanted to go immediately to the police. If we'd done things his way, we'd already be free of Kyoko and Jenny.

I'd been the one to insist we play along with Jenny's demands, and he didn't even know the fear that motivated me. Nevertheless, despite several opportunities to walk away, he'd done nothing but help. I, on the other hand, had broken his phones, sabotaged his motorcycle, and made a stupid mistake, ensnaring myself more deftly in Jenny's crimes. If I was going to be angry, I should be angry with myself, not Hudson. I pushed my hair over my shoulder and reached for his arm. "Look, I'm sorry I made that call. It was stupid and I wasn't thinking. I'm grateful I'm not in this alone."

Hudson took a deep breath and released it. "I don't regret it, pretending to be your boyfriend. I mean, it would have been nice to have had drinks first like I'd planned, but this has been . . . interesting, too."

The pressure in my chest eased and I found a smile. "We can still get those drinks. Tonight. Come by my house. We can recap what we both find over a nice bottle of wine."

"It's a date." Hudson's soft smile curved his lips, and my heartbeat accelerated.

We locked the back door behind us and let ourselves out through the side gate. Hudson wanted to wait with me until Ari arrived, but I didn't want to linger near Hudson's bike. I finally convinced him to walk two blocks with me to a convenience store, where I grabbed a bag of Skittles and Hudson bought a small bag of Cheetos.

"Here." I pulled my business card from my bag and scribbled my home address on the back when we reached Hudson's bike. "It'd be best if you left before Ari arrives; otherwise, we'll be here another hour explaining everything to her. And by everything, I mean you." I eased away from his motorcycle.

Even as Hudson started to argue with me, I spotted Ari's BMW pulling around the corner three blocks away.

"See that silver car?" I pointed. "That's Ari. I'll see you tonight. Say, five-thirty?"

I trotted down the sidewalk, then zigzagged into the street to intercept Ari, not waiting for Hudson's reply. Ari slowed as she pulled up beside me. A gray kitten clung to her shoulder—not real—and her face glowed with curiosity. I popped open the passenger door and looked back toward Hudson. He waved and pushed his helmet on, then eased his bike into the street and zipped away. I watched until he turned at the corner, body leaning into the curve. With a heavy sigh, I got into the boxy car and set my bag at my feet.

"Did that hot motorcyclist just wave at you?" Ari demanded.

"Yep. His name is Hudson."

"Does Hudson by chance know where you were this morning?"

"And last night." I grinned at Ari's dropped jaw, purposely taking my time with the seat belt to make her squirm.

Ari was Italian, with olive skin and dark brown hair and eyes. She was several inches shy of my five-nine and twice as curvy. We were the same age, but Ari would always look younger: One flash of her deep dimples and she lost ten years. When faced with those dimples, teachers overlooked detention-worthy transgression, her parents turned to putty, and men of every profession and age fell over themselves to smooth the way for Ari, tearing up speeding tickets, opening doors to exclusive events, and once even holding the post office open an extra half hour.

"Details! I demand details, or this car isn't moving."

"If you don't get this car moving, we're not going to make it home."

"Oh, sure. Play the curse card." She gunned the BMW and we shot down the road after Hudson.

There was, unfortunately, a lot more to catch my best friend up on than Hudson. It didn't occur to me to keep Kyoko a secret from Ari. She was my confidant and business partner. I trusted Ari with my life, and considering I had linked her to Jenny through my hasty phone call, I owed her an explanation. Plus, Ari's help finding Jenny would be invaluable.

I found it impossible to keep my emotions in check while I recapped the last twenty-four hours, and the BMW was sputtering and coughing eight blocks before we reached my apartment. Ari executed an expert parallel park in front of a squat art deco apartment building, and we walked the last blocks. Having been my friend for over ten years, she was almost as used to electronic malfunctions as I was. Better still, she didn't complain or even appear put out by the inconvenience. All her apparitions represented concern and curiosity, not frustration.

"Jenny Winters? Did I have a class with her?" Ari asked.

"Were you in my Honors English junior year?"

"Nope. So what'd you see on Hudson?"

I was surprised Ari had waited this long to bring the conversation back to Hudson.

"Hats," I said. "Sombrero, sailor, a silver top hat from Monopoly. The silver terrier, too. A weird plastic and metal model of a city that isn't a city. A full moon. Some hipster glasses. A marble cherub. Some creepy sea creatures. A rotten banana that drips slices. And, of course, a glowing broadsword."

"Do you know what any of it means?"

"He's in hero mode when he's wearing the sword, and the Monopoly pieces always show up when he's acting suspicious or frustrated, but the rest? Not a clue."

"What did Aunt Sofie say?"

"To be open to love."

Ari's eyebrows arched high.

"Which means nothing. You know Sofie. She's always trying to play matchmaker with me."

"Hardly. Did she see something around you that indicated Hudson is special?"

"She claimed it doesn't work that way—"

"But she saw your grandma and Theo together."

"I made that point."

"I think I need to call Sofie," Ari said.

"I think Jenny and the elephant she dumped on me, not to mention the blackmail, takes precedence."

"Over a man?"

I glanced at Ari, relieved to see she was kidding.

"I didn't get a good look," she said. "I mean, he's got a hot body, I think. It's always hard to tell under leather. He's hot, right?"

"Like lava." I replayed Hudson removing his shirt and that teasing glimpse of his backside. We trudged up the stairs to my loft, and I was granted a reprieve from Ari's interrogation as she conserved her energy for breathing.

I lived in a loft at the top of a seven-story tower. No one lived beside me at the moment. The real estate company had given up on selling the next-door loft as well as the one beneath me, and a string of renters had broken their leases over the repeated electronic fritzes. I did what I could to dampen my curse when in public, but I deserved a place to relax as much as the next person. I countered my guilt by telling myself the sporadic tenants should expect some problems when they rented a unit for half the usual asking price.

If not for Sofie, I could never have afforded the beautiful loft, with its warm butterscotch-colored hardwood floors, vaulted ceilings, and second-story loft-within-a-loft bedroom. My aunt owned the loft outright, and I chipped away at payments, but in my heart, it was all mine. One look at the bones of the loft, and more specifically at the series of glass doors opening along two entire walls to a long patio, and I'd fallen in love. Sofie had let me choose every interior detail, from the smooth glass railing of the bedroom stairs to the soapstone counters in the kitchen to the oval tub in the master bath. The comfortable mix of leather library furniture and period pieces filling my living room were all me, too.

I'd lived in the loft for several years, and I still felt a thrill of possession every time I walked through the front door. Not even the hike up six flights of stairs could diminish my love for my home. The rest of the residents thought I was a glutton for fitness. They had no idea I had their safety in mind. The elevator operated at the opposite end of the tower from my loft and the stairs, protecting my neighbors from any influence I might have on the mechanics of that death box.

Ari was out of breath when we reached the top landing, and she put a hand on my arm to stop me. "I want to meet him," she said between breaths. "Bring him over tonight for dinner."

It wasn't an offer.

"Ari—"

"Don't 'Ari' me. I want to meet the man who"—pant—"has masqueraded as your boyfriend"—pant—"who has stolen an elephant with you"—pant—"and who has you breaking into houses." Pant. "He's either a terrible influence on you or a great one. And I think it should be a new rule in our relationship that I meet anyone who sees you in handcuffs."

My middle-aged neighbor, Jed, chose that moment walk by, his trash in hand. He raised his eyebrows at me. "You need to have your safeties in place if you're going to play rough, Eva," he said. "Listen to Ari."

Ari grinned. "Thank you, Jed. So you think I should meet Eva's new boyfriend, too?"

"You have a boyfriend? And I'm finding out now? Like this?" Jed gestured to the trash bag and his laundry-day house shorts and faded Hawaiian top. He peered behind us down the stairs.

"He's *not* my boyfriend," I protested. "And you don't have to worry, Jed. He's not here."

"They met yesterday," Ari told Jed. "He's in security, drives a motorcycle. Sets women's panties on fire with his smoldering-hot looks."

Jed waggled his eyebrows at me. "Wait until I tell Troy. What did you say his name is?"

"Hudson Keyes," Ari said before I could stop her.

I whirled to Jed and pointed my finger at him. "Don't even think about cyber-stalking him," I said.

"Who? Me?" Jed blinked innocently, and I pretended not to see Ari make the "call me" gesture to Jed behind my back. I didn't know how they did it, but somehow Ari, Jed, and Jed's partner, Troy, always found out information I never told them about the men I dated. I suspected Ari used her FBI agent sister-in-law Miriam to do the dirty work, but they insisted most people's basic information existed on the Internet for anyone to find. Anyone on speaking terms with electricity.

I left Ari plotting with Jed and keyed open my loft. Serenity engulfed me. I dropped my bag on the hutch inside the door and walked straight to the balcony. Large wood-framed glass doors pivoted open along the entire back and side wall, and I opened a few to let the warm April air circulate through the loft. Muted traffic noises and the rustle of palm fronds filtered in with the sweet aroma of freesias blooming on the balcony. I could feel energy returning, bringing hope and optimism with it. Somewhere in my high school memory bank, I'd find vital information about Jenny. By the end of today, Kyoko would be back in her hands and Sofie, Ari, Hudson, and I would be free of Jenny's entanglement. Then I could explore my attraction to Hudson.

"You grab the yearbooks, I'll fix us some lemonade," Ari said, shutting the front door behind her.

I stacked four yearbooks on the coffee table and accepted a glass from Ari. We plopped down side by side on the couch, propped our feet up, and made satisfied sighing sounds at the same time, which caused us to laugh. I grabbed our senior yearbook; Ari took our junior.

"She's not in here," I said after scanning the index and then the senior photos. I started thumbing through the activity pages.

"She's in here. Check this out." At the bottom of the page, listed under "Winters, Jennifer" was a black-and-white shot of Jenny, ten years younger, glaring at us from the glossy page. Her hair was slicked back, her brows furrowed, and her face half hidden behind heavy glasses that had never been in style. She must have been wearing contacts yesterday or had corrective surgery since high school, because judging by the thickness of the lenses, she would have been blind now without them.

"I wonder if she moved or transferred. Do you remember her now?" I asked.

Ari shook her head. "I don't think we shared a class. And if we did, we never talked."

"Is she anywhere else in there?"

Ari consulted the index. "Once, on page fifty-eight." She flipped to it. An action shot of a cheerleader with a vague resemblance to Jenny slanted across the bottom corner. I doubted Jenny could pull off her giddy grin.

"That was completely useless." I grabbed our sophomore yearbook and flipped to the index. Jenny was listed only once, in her school photo. She had bangs in this shot and a fledgling glare behind the same glasses. The freshman yearbook was a bust.

"How many different ways can people say 'stay cool' and 'never change'?" Ari asked, reading the comments in the margins of my junior yearbook. "Oh, listen to this winner. 'Look me up in five years, baby. I'll be the millionaire on the cover of *Forbes*.' Who's Stewart?"

"Sounds like an ass." I couldn't put a face with the name.

"Ha! 'We'll always have Maria's Bakery, love Dave.' Do I remember Dave?"

"Skinny guy, hair redder than mine. Liked to whistle."

"Oh, *Dave*. That's right. What was with Maria's Bakery?"

"I think we kissed there." I tossed my freshman yearbook back to the coffee table. "Maybe my honor's teacher would remember Jenny."

"Who was that?"

"I don't remember." I grabbed the senior yearbook again and flipped to the faculty. The teachers were listed by name but not by class. I studied their faces. I recognized one in a dozen.

"Look. Is this Jenny?" Ari asked. She pointed to a tiny photo with large font beneath identifying the group as the science club. I squinted at the half-visible face in the back row. "There's one more face than there are names in the caption," she said.

"It looks like her. Maybe." I scanned another page of teachers before a familiar smirk sparked a memory. "Mr. Hornbunkel! How could I have forgotten that name?"

Ari leaned closer to get a better look at him. "He looks like he'd quote Shakespeare to grocery store clerks when they ask him 'paper or plastic.'"

"Do you think he'd remember something useful about Jenny, because I'm at a loss. Nothing in these books has jogged a memory, and if you don't remember her, I've reached a dead end."

"Only because you don't have the Internet. And we did learn a few things. She likely was in the science club. I can hunt down the other people in the photo with her and see what they remember."

"How?"

"Facebook. LinkedIn. The alumni website. I may not be friends with any of these people, but I bet you I know someone who is. I can also look into Mr. Hornbunkel, send him an e-mail if he's still at school or find out where he is now."

"Are you sure you're not just saying what you think I want to hear?" I asked. "You can actually find all these people on the Internet?"

"Yep. Probably by the end of the day. I'll also see what the sites turn up on Jenny." A starry cloud appeared behind Ari's head, like the Milky Way condensed. Greens and reds swirled through dense solar systems, and many tiny clusters glowed too bright to look at directly. The three-dimensional galaxy could have been pulled straight out of the Hubble telescope photographs. When I'd first described the apparition to Ari, she'd explained it was how she thought of the Internet: a final frontier of unlimited possibilities. It seemed like an adequate description to me.

Of all the twentieth-century inventions I missed out on because of my curse, airplane travel and the Internet were the two I most wished I could experience.

Ari glanced at her mechanical watch, then at me.

"You're going to your consultation like that?"

"My consul— Crap!" I shot off the couch and rushed to my office. I scanned the large three-by-three-foot calendar tacked to the wall, then checked the wall clock. "I completely forgot about Max Overton! Ari, can you drive me? I've got only thirty minutes, and there's no way I'm making it to Glendon Avenue by bus in less than an hour."

"You actually forgot?" Ari asked.

"It's been a long twenty-four hours."

"Or it's the hormones addling your brain."

I stuck my tongue out at her.

———

ARI BORROWED her brother Antonio's car, and she dropped me off in front of a three-bedroom split-level house at three-thirty on the dot.

Since I wouldn't have time to change after the consultation before Hudson arrived, I'd selected an outfit that worked for business and pleasure: a summery yellow top, a black pencil skirt, and black heels. I had my satchel and I'd organized my paperwork for Mr. Overton's house on the drive, using the familiar actions to keep me calm so Antonio's car wouldn't strand Ari on the way home.

Mr. Overton opened the door after one knock. He was big—big muscles, big hands when we shook, big smile when he asked me to call him Max. His height flirted with giant status, though I was pretty sure all those stacked muscles generated an optical illusion. The only divination I got off him was a Trix cereal box dumping colorful chunks onto his feet.

He ushered me into a front room with two matching recliners, a huge television, and several framed movie posters. I counted eleven guns and three swords between four posters.

"I'm not a touchy-feely guy," Max said. "I don't want anything Chinese looking. I don't want candles or smelly dead flowers or tiny, pointless pillows. And I don't believe in chi-voodoo crap."

# EIGHT



"WHAT *DO* YOU WANT?" I asked.

"I want a woman. Not a ho, not a gold digger, and not a one-night stand. I can get all those on my own. I want a woman I can marry. My sister, Selena Bosch, said she hired you to fix her career, and two months later she met her husband. He's a good guy. Doesn't cheat at cards."

I remembered Selena. She had a two-story bungalow near the San Fernando Valley. Her house had been a simple transformation—just a matter of Selena letting go of some outdated ideas and fears that had crept into her surroundings and bringing in some new energy. Max's house wouldn't be as easy to fix. It was a masculine cliché the polar opposite of his goal.

Knots tightened my neck muscles. I needed to be focusing all my energy on finding Jenny. A consultation was the last thing I should have been doing. For the first time in my career, I was anxious to get the job over with as fast as possible.

"I've got a good job," Max said. "I work out. I'm not a troll. I'm don't understand why I'm having such a hard time finding a good woman." A duck with a cat's head waddled at his feet. I didn't attempt an interpretation.

"Let's get started."

Max ambled through the house in front of me, taking his time when I wanted to run through and rattle off a list of changes he need to make, starting with the painting of a camouflaged man sighting down a gun that was hanging at the end of the hallway, the barrel aimed straight at our chests.

"How long have you been on the hunt?" I asked, eyeing the painted face of the sniper.

"Eight miserable months. This is LA. A million women live right outside my doorstep, all of them psychos. And not the good kind."

The master bedroom was spacious, even with the enormous bed centered on one wall. Max lingered, staring at the bed and sighing. Two more bedrooms filled out the top house, both much smaller than the master. One served as a catchall storage room of clutter in his creativity and children section.

"Not much to see in there," Max said, dismissing the room that needed the most work.

The other bedroom, which comprised almost the entire relation-ship section of the house, was converted into a workout room. Mirrors covered one wall; antique weapons lined the others.

Max's house exhibited a dozen big-picture problems combating his goal for a wife. I was mentally organizing how to fix each when I real-ized that for the first time since Jenny latched on to my arm the day before, I felt normal. Confident. In control. The tight spring of fear and frustration that had coiled in my gut since Jenny handcuffed me had unwound. As always, feng shui stabilized me.

"Let me see if I get this right," I said, stepping into the workout room. I discarded my "chi-voodoo" lessons about energy movement and intentions behind decor placement and delivered my advice with blunt brutality. "All the women you date, they start out or become combative. Either they're fighting with you or they're throwing up walls. Everything starts out hot and intense, but you both get tired of the relationship too quick. When you bring up children, it becomes a clusterfuck."

He pointed at me. "That's exactly right. The nice ones dump me without explanations. The sassy ones want to fight all the time. I don't get it."

I pulled out my bagua flyer and handed it to him. "Every house has nine baguas, according to feng shui. You align the bagua like this." I turned us so the skills and knowledge, career, and helpful people and travel sections were aligned with the front of the house. "If you divide your house into nine equal squares, you can see roughly the nine sections of your life. We're standing in the relationship and love section."

We both examined the stacked weights and Bowflex machine, then the guns and swords.

"Does this room remind you of your experiences with women?"

"It's uncanny," he said, shaking his head. "I'm always doing all the heavy lifting."

"If you want to change that, we need to change a few things here."

"But I can't stop working out." He flexed an arm and winked at me. He was right: He was far from a troll. A little rough around the edges, but that was part of his charm.

"I doubt your future wife wants you to stop working out, either. But there are ways to make this room, and other parts of the house, more woman friendly."

I left Max an hour later with a list of changes, big and small. Move his weapons collection to his skills section and replace it with art representing the life he wanted. Organize the storage bedroom into a home office and bring in elements that made him either feel like a kid or think of children. Add a second nightstand in the master bedroom with a matching lamp. Rearrange his closet to make room for another person. Consider adding a couch or love seat to make a place where two people could snuggle together in the front room. Move the sniper artwork from the hall—his fame section. Women didn't like to feel hunted, and they definitely didn't like to feel stalked, which was the painting's vibe. That instruction took the most convincing, being the most "chi-voodoo" sounding.

I didn't bother with the small details, like each bagua's element, shape, or color. Max was a bold-strokes guy. I left him energized to get to work. Everything I'd told Max fell in the "common-sense feng shui" category. Everyone was more comfortable in a clean, organized house where they had adequate space to relax. Ari would do a follow-up call with him in a few weeks, and we'd see if he wanted a second consultation. Sometimes when people saw their lives start to change in response to their initial alterations, they were willing to embrace feng shui on a deeper level.

I left energized, too. The highly productive session had restored my optimism, and I looked forward to hearing what Ari and Hudson had learned about Jenny. For all I knew, Hudson had already found Jenny and she was on her way to pick up Kyoko. We could be free of this bizarre entanglement by nightfall. Then Hudson and I could have our promised date, complications-free, and I could devote the appropriate attention to the raw attraction between us.

Grinning, I strolled around the corner of the block, out of sight of Max's house, then pulled out my metro map. Clients were seldom pleased to know I traveled by bus. Some believed it meant I wasn't good enough at my job to afford a car. Others thought it made me a hippie out to save the planet, and therefore my feng shui ideas were New Age bullshit dreamed up while high. One client had thought I'd feng shuied myself out of a car and had been terrified my suggestions would cause all three of her cars to be stolen. Now I made sure none of my clients knew about my nefarious means of travel.

A green Tercel screeched to a stop at the corner. A slender, light-skinned black man jumped out. Apparitions flashed around him faster than lightning strikes, mesmerizing me. In the three steps it took him to reach the sidewalk, watches stacked up his forearm, the faces winking from gold to black to platinum and back to gold. Diamond studs sparkled in his ears, replaced by sapphires, replaced again by larger diamonds. A gigantic pink terrazzo star splayed across his chest, complete with writing: *Atlas Grant.*

Enthralled, I failed to notice the hulking driver until he grabbed my arm. Cold metal snapped around my left wrist, then my right. For a half second, I froze; then I shrieked and kicked him. My foot bounced off a calf of steel. A meaty hand clamped over my mouth, smelling like mustard. One thick arm pinned both of mine to my side and hoisted me off the ground. The skinny man opened the back door of the Tercel and my captor tossed me inside. I lunged for the opposite door, yanking on the handle, but the child locks were on, and the door didn't budge.

"Help! Let me go! Someone—"

The skinny guy hopped into the front seat and snatched his door shut. The driver hustled around the car and squeezed behind the wheel. The whole car rocked with his weight. When he shut his door, I stopped screaming. No one was going to hear me through the windows. I flopped to my side and flailed to get my feet up to the window, cursing the confines of my pencil skirt. One kick in these heels, and I thought I could shatter the glass.

"Eva! Eva, it's okay," the skinny guy said. "We're not going to harm you."

I stilled. "How do you know my name?"

"We're friends."

The driver popped the car into gear and we were rolling. My odds of escape took a nosedive.

"What do you want?"

"To talk. That's all." The skinny guy twisted in his seat to face me. He'd pulled his seat belt on, as had the driver. The normal gesture inexplicably cut through my panic.

"Talk," I demanded. I sat up and tugged my bag to the seat beside me. Miraculously, nothing had fallen out.

The skinny guy exchanged a look with the driver. I made myself ignore the flash of a halo around the skinny guy's head and the flickering watch images and really look at him. Whenever I escaped, I wanted to give the police an accurate description.

The hair on his head was trimmed the same short length as the thin mustache outlining his full lips and trailing down to a sculpted goatee. Thick lashes framed dark brown eyes. Even his eyebrows looked shaped. His clothes were hipster chic, complete with a butter-soft fawn-colored leather jacket. In a cocky, I-know-I-look-good, ladies' man sort of way, he was handsome.

The driver was too big for the car. He would have been too big for the Suburban. His skin was two shades paler than ebony, his head bald, and his shoulders double the width of the seat. He would make a great bouncer—he would fill a doorway. He had peanut brittle in his hands. It was so realistic that I didn't recognize it as a divination the first three times I looked at it.

"I'm Atlas," the skinny guy said. "This is Edmond." The terrazzo star reappeared, hanging on a gold chain against Atlas's chest. It was his own freakin' name on the star. Talk about an ego.

"Why am I handcuffed?"

"Good question." Atlas turned to Edmond. "Why'd you handcuff her?"

"That's what we always do." Edmond's voice matched his body: deep and full.

"What we *always* do?"

"It's safer this way. Haven't you seen *Cops*? They don't let hostile people ride in their cars without handcuffs, and *they* have the cage divider."

"Does she look hostile?"

"Downright scary."

Atlas turned back to me. "Okay, she looks hostile now, but she didn't earlier. Before you put the cuffs on her."

"Precautious." Edmond tapped his head.

"The only problem is," Atlas said with deliberate enunciation, his voice escalating, "we weren't supposed to grab her! We were supposed to deliver a message."

"Exactly. And she's getting the message right now."

"No, you dolt, it's not code. We're supposed to give her a message. Like talk to her. That's all. No scare tactics. We're not working for the mob. You got to stop watching those Scorsese films."

"Oh." The peanut brittle disappeared. A delicate ceramic ballerina figurine spun on his shoulder. "In my defense, that could have been more clearly communicated."

"Look, why don't you just take the cuffs off now, and we'll pretend it didn't happen," I said.

Edmond glanced at me in the rearview mirror and shook his head. "Not yet. Your eyes are all squinty. You shouldn't hold on to anger. It's not good for you. It eats you up from the inside."

"You guys just *kidnapped* me!"

"How about a cupcake? No one can be angry while eating a cupcake."

"Good idea," Atlas said. He reached for a Tupperware on the floorboard at his feet and popped the top. Chocolate and carrot cake aromas swirled through the car.

I choked on a dozen protests and finally spit out, "I don't want a cupcake! I want to know why you kidnapped me. How do you know my name?"

"You really should try a cupcake. They're delicious." Atlas selected a carrot cake cupcake with thick frosting. When I continued to glare at him, he closed the lid, then placed the Tupperware on my lap. "In case you change your mind. Ed's cupcakes are the bomb."

I checked our location. We were on West Pico Boulevard, headed deeper into the city. So far, so good. We were still in public. Public was way better than somewhere secluded.

Atlas bit into the cupcake and made a moaning sound of delight. "You're a genius with flour and sugar, Ed. When I land my first big gig, I'm going to invest it all in you and Muffin Top Bakery." Atlas ran his hand through the air in front of him like he envisioned the name in lights. Edmond beamed.

I considered using the Tupperware to bash their heads, but I didn't think I could do enough damage to make them pull over. Fortunately, getting them to stop wasn't going to require effort on my part. All I had to do was keep them talking; my curse would do the rest for me.

"Shoot, if *this* job runs a few more days, Jenny might be my final investor," Edmond said.

"Jenny? Jenny Winters?" They knew my name and Jenny's.

This was about Kyoko.

"One and the same," Atlas said. "She's hired us to keep an eye on things. Mainly you. All this over a cocktail recipe. The elephantini. I guess it'll be big." Atlas chuckled at his pun and Edmond rolled his eyes at me in the rearview mirror. "I never thought she'd become a mixologist, but Cousin Jenny's always been a little, you know, out there. Or more like in here." Atlas tapped his forehead. "Who knows what they did to her in Japan."

"Why are you watching me? Why did you kidnap me? Why am I *still handcuffed?*"

"Whoa, chill, Eva," Edmond said. "We're not kidnappers." Chocolate-drizzled éclairs lined up along the steering wheel column. Poppy seed bite-size muffins snaked across the dash. My stomach grumbled.

"We're here to make sure the people she's giving the runaround don't find you. She said it's more important than ever because the— What were her words, Ed?"

"'The retrievalist was deployed.'"

All divinations disappeared from the car and from Atlas. A gigantic needle plunged into Edmond's arm, and I flinched. Goose bumps rushed across my skin.

"What's the retrievalist?"

"Some scary dude. Like a skip tracer, but he finds anything, she said. And she used that word. *Deployed.*" When Atlas turned to face me, a giant scar bisected his face, pulling his lip askew and drooping an eyelid. I jerked back in shock. The man had freakishly vivid emotional projections. "She was real nervous. She wanted you to have your guard up, too."

"Great."

"Don't worry. We'll protect you. That's why we're here."

I had felt a good deal safer before I met them. I leaned forward and thrust my shackled hands between them. "*This* isn't protection. It's the opposite of protection. *This* is kidnapping. *This* is illegal. You put freakin' handcuffs on me like I'm a criminal or a hostage!"

"She's got a point," Atlas said, looking at Edmond. "Maybe we should—"

"Uh-uh. She's lookin' all hostile again. Eva, I know you redheads have a harder time controlling your temper, but you really got to—"

"If you tell me to relax, I'm going to brain you," I said. The terror of being kidnapped had morphed into adrenaline-fueled rage, and I fed it all my fear and confusion. I felt like I was going to vibrate out of my own skin with the emotional onslaught. Apparitions danced through the car's interior—paper-clip chains the size of anacondas writhed at our feet through waist-high drifts of meringue; Academy awards heaped in Atlas's lap, partially obscured by soft white wings and a parade of tuxedos; a black tornado spun back and forth across the dash, sucking up éclairs and cupcakes and fist-size cows. I ignored it all, wallowing in my fury and fear. With every word, I willed the car to break down, and every second it didn't pissed me off. "Jenny dumped this on me, and I'm done. I'm done playing her games. I don't want to be a part of this. So tell me where she is, or so help me, I will—"

A high, long squeak pierced the upper range of my hearing, then dove to a loud concussion. It didn't sound like a car noise; it sounded like a released horse-size balloon exploding against a nail.

"Aw, Ed." Atlas clamped a hand over his mouth and nose. "I told you not to get the club sandwich. You know what bacon does to you."

A foul odor defiled my nostrils and caught at the back of my throat. Atlas rolled down his window, and a cyclone of stench whipped through the car, rivaling the worst-smelling semi of cows.

"But I love bacon," Edmond whined. A blush stained his dark cheeks. "And she was making me nervous with all that yelling."

"Bacon does not love *you*, man. You got to cut that shit *out*. It's killing you, and it's killing me. And it's killing *her*." Atlas tossed a thumb in my direction. "You smell like raw sewage."

Yes, that was *exactly* the word I'd been looking for. I clamped my hands over my nose and mouth and breathed shallowly.

The Tercel moaned, backfired twice, and rattled to a stop. The stench settled around us.

"Damn it, Ed. Your fart's killed the car."

# NINE

"GET OUT AND PUSH," Edmond said.

"You're the one who killed it. You push."

"It wasn't my fault."

"Oh, yeah? It was working fine until you released that black cloud."

"Let me out," I said. "I'll push."

"You gonna let a woman push?" Edmond demanded.

We were on a two-lane street boxed in by blocks of stores. Edmond turned the key. The dash growled. Nothing happened under the hood. Cars horns bleated behind us.

Cussing, Atlas bounced out of the car and slammed the door shut, then stuck his head back in through the open window. "I'm not pushing your tub of lard."

"Screw you," Edmond said. He undid his seat belt and heaved himself out of the car, rocking it on its frame. After muted bickering, Atlas came around to the driver's side and leaned on the door frame, one hand on the steering wheel. Edmond braced himself behind the vehicle.

I scrambled over the center console and sprawled against the passenger seat and door. Cursing my decision to wear a pencil skirt, I flailed to right myself. I popped the door open. The car was rolling, but at a snail's pace.

"Hey," Atlas said, dipping his head to look into the car. "What are you doing?" He reached for my arm. I grabbed the Tupperware and bashed his knuckles.

"Ow! What'd you do that for?"

I stumbled out of the car and sprinted down the line of traffic backed up behind the broken-down Tercel.

"Eva! Stop!"

I glanced back through a curtain of red hair. Edmond had stopped pushing and gawked at me, dough oozing through his fingers. Atlas stood beside him, angel wings spread wide, but Edmond had his hand on his arm. The bigger man gestured at the traffic, the car, and then at me. I turned back around before I saw their decision.

"Hey, lady, are you okay?" someone shouted from the line of cars.

I didn't stop. I was not okay. I was stranded in the middle of down-town LA—not the safest place for a woman to be handcuffed—and I was carrying a Tupperware of cupcakes. I hadn't planned on bringing them with me. I simply forgot to let them go after hitting Atlas.

I cut through traffic to the other side of the road and sprinted to a taxi idling at the curb. I bent down to look in the driver's window.

"You available?" I asked.

He looked me up and down, gaze snagging on the cuffs. "Sure."

I popped open the back door, tossed the Tupperware inside, and scrambled in after it. I glanced through the rear window. I didn't see Atlas or Edmond following.

"Where to?"

I gave him my address. "But take Doheny to Burton to West Fourth."

The car eased from the curb. "You got the cash for that? I mean, if you don't, I'll take you a couple of blocks for free, but I can't afford to take you that far for nothing."

"I've got the cash." I didn't turn around in the seat until we made a right and the Tercel, Edmond, and Atlas were out of sight. Then I fought with my adrenaline, striving for tranquility. I closed my eyes for thirty seconds, counting off the time, holding my breath for five-second intervals to slow my heart and control my breathing while my body screamed for me to run. I needed to find calm if this car was going to last longer than a few blocks.

Opening my eyes, I stared down at my cuffed wrists. A tide of helplessness rose to overwhelm me, and I closed my eyes again. I should have headed to the nearest police station. I could report Atlas and Edmond, and the cops could pick them up before the tow truck arrived. But if I did that, I risked the police finding out about Kyoko—and then the world finding out about me.

I took a deep breath and concentrated on straightening my wardrobe. Hudson had gotten me out of handcuffs before; he could do it again. I settled my bag onto my lap and checked its contents, keeping an eye on our location because I didn't completely trust the taxi driver to take me home and not straight to the police. If I were in his place and someone handcuffed and running down the middle of the street hopped in my car, the police would be my first stop.

I met the driver's gaze in the rearview mirror. He was bald and tanned. His ID card said his name was Pawel Ostrowski. His accent had already identified him as a native Californian.

"You want me to call the police?" he asked.

"No. Ah, no." I scrambled for a story to clear his suspicions. "It's, well, it's a game." I looked down at my hands and then back up at the driver through my lashes. "My husband and I like to keep things interesting."

A marionette manifested on the center of the dash. Its wooden head swiveled backward to face me, squared-off mouth dropping open a little. It could have been a puppet version of a smile or of shock. Either way, it gave me the creeps. The marionette wore blue overalls and a black shirt, and it had a little cap on its wooden head. I shuddered and tugged the Tupperware back onto my lap.

Pawel nodded sagely. "My ex and I tried all kinds of things to spice it up: feathers, leather, pies, even video. But then she said she wanted to be a man. I thought she wanted to be the man in the relationship.

You know, on top, in control. Nope. She wanted a dick. What was I supposed to do with a second dick?"

If ever I'd heard a question I wasn't going to answer, that was it. Plus, *pies*?

"Maybe if I'd tried your game. We had the cuffs. Not the real ones like you've got. We had ones with leopard print, but you could jerk and get free of those. Are you under arrest? Is he going to rescue you?"

"It's, um, private."

"Yeah. I get it. Seems dangerous, though. Unless that was your husband back there."

"That was a misunderstanding."

He merged into traffic on Burton Way. The marionette stood and pantomimed a rendition of my recent escape, only it made the whole escapade look dirty.

"Is that why we're going such a convoluted route?"

"It seems safest this way."

"Look, I know it's none of my business, but you're a beautiful woman. If your man needs complicated games like this, maybe he doesn't appreciate you." He pulled up in front of my building, double-parking next to the row of parallel-parked cars. He twisted in his seat to face me. "LA's a dangerous place. A lot of people see a pretty woman helpless in handcuffs, and they're not going to think right, you know?" He held out a business card. Behind him, the marionette cloned itself into an army, and they all flexed cylindrical wooden arms. "You think you're going to 'play' this game again, you call Pawel, okay?"

I took the card. "Thank you."

"You sure you're okay to get out here?" The marionettes snapped their jaws at me.

Pawel seemed like a genuinely good guy, but his divinations made my skin crawl.

"Perfectly. There's my husband."

I pointed with my chin to Hudson, who had been leaning against the front of my building and had started our way when he saw me in the cab.

"He's got the money," I said. I stumbled out of the back of the taxi with the Tupperware, feeling loose-limbed without adrenaline. Hudson's smile turned to a scowl when he saw the silver on my wrists. The puffy cloud glowing behind his torso morphed into a great white shark tattooed with bizarre ghosts.

"No questions," I said softly. "Greet me like you've missed me, then act possessive and pay the driver. I'll pay you back." Pawel may have been nice, but I didn't need some marionette creep hanging around my apartment, thinking he'd either rescue me or find me in handcuffs again.

"Did he do this to you?" Hudson touched my wrists while leaning in to kiss my forehead.

"No. And you're my husband."

"Shouldn't I be concerned about the cuffs?"

"They were your idea."

His eyebrows rose; then he grinned, grabbed my shoulders, and yanked me to him. His lips came down on mine with possessive ferocity, and his tongue teased liquid fire across my lips before sweeping into my mouth. He shifted his grip to the back of my head, his fingers tangling in the hair at my nape, and his other arm circled me, pressing me as close to him as the Tupperware would allow.

I moaned into his open mouth, my body heating from tepid to boiling in seconds. He pulled back, and I followed, teasing his bottom lip with my tongue. I shifted to get my hands on him, only to be brought back to reality when the cuffs cut into yesterday's bruises.

Hudson eased a few inches between us.

"Something like that?" he whispered, out of breath. His eyes were dark, shuttered by thick lashes.

I licked my bottom lip and nodded. "Yeah. Perfect."

Cocky grin in place, Hudson sauntered over to pay the driver. I watched his ass until he rounded the car, then forced myself to turn toward the building. I needed a moment to recover. That kiss had been everything the chemistry between us had promised. It also had been scripted instead of spontaneous. I took a few deep breaths and tried to ignore the tingling in my lips.

"Are you okay?" Hudson asked, returning to take my arm. He wasn't talking about the way his kiss affected me. The shark had shrunk to catfish size and swam lazily through his body. A foot-tall marble angel balanced on his shoulder. Puffs of insubstantial dandelions escaped from his hair. The shark was fear, but the other apparitions remained a mystery. "What happened?"

"A little gift from Jenny."

"She cuffed you *again?*"

"Not exactly."

"Did she give you the cupcakes?" Hudson asked, peering through the clear side of the Tupperware.

"Not exactly."

"Work with me."

"Cuffs first. Do you still have your picklock toolkit?"

"You're in luck. You know, maybe you should get a set to carry with you."

"Ha-ha. Funny."

We sat at the curb, shielded between the bumper of two cars, and Hudson picked both cuff locks. I rubbed the dark bruise on my right wrist and stretched my arms.

"I'm getting pretty good at freeing you from those things. I guess practice makes perfect."

I grimaced. "Come on, we're going to Ari's for dinner. She's been tracking down info on Jenny."

Hudson helped me to my feet. While we walked to Ari's, I filled him in on my recent adventure of being "not kidnapped" and the limited information Atlas and Edmond had given me.

"None of this makes sense," I said. "Why does Jenny have Kyoko? Who 'deployed' the skip tracer that Jenny's so afraid of? And if Jenny's got cousins helping her, why didn't she leave Kyoko with them?" Okay, the last question I could answer myself, having firsthand experience with the cousins.

A flash of emptiness opened beneath Hudson's feet, like a giant hole had swallowed the sidewalk. I tripped and grabbed for his arm before my brain processed the drop-off as a vision. Hudson steadied me with his free hand, holding the Tupperware in the other. The abyss disappeared and the silver top hat appeared.

"Do you want to go to the police?" Hudson asked.

"No," I answered too quickly. Hudson cocked an eyebrow at me, the top hat growing by two feet. "I don't want to get my aunt in trouble, or you. Plus, I don't trust those guys or Jenny. They could be making up this scary retrievalist. I'm not going to trust anyone who handcuffs me."

"A sound policy."

"We can't tell Ari about my kidnapping, okay? She'll get all mother hen on me, and I don't need that."

"Mother hen?"

"It's not pretty. Promise not to tell?"

Hudson shrugged. "I promise."

"Oh, and Ari thinks you want to be my boyfriend, so you're warned."

"What gave her that idea?"

"You did when you pretended to be one and got yourself involved in this mess."

"Oh. That." He didn't look at me, but a smile curved his lips. Baby sharks still circled his midriff, but the hat disappeared and the cloud came back. I didn't warn him again. He looked confident and a trace smug, but my money was on Ari. If she was in full matchmaker mode, Hudson would be lucky to escape tonight's dinner without proposing to me and thinking it was his idea.

———

IT DIDN'T SURPRISE me to hear Antonio's voice as we approached the front door. Ari lived with her brother in his Spanish-style three-bedroom bungalow. On a Friday night, Antonio would normally have been out, so Ari must have told him about Hudson. Antonio would consider it his duty to evaluate Hudson, and he was too protective of Ari—and me—to leave us alone in the house with a strange man.

I knocked, then let myself in with my key. As a contractor, Antonio was a genius, having renovated and repaired everything in his house from the foundation to the roof. He'd also redone all the wiring and piping in my loft so everything ran off gas instead of electricity, including the lighting. But he had no eye for interior design. He'd left those details to his sister. Ari liked bold colors, lots of plants, and comfortable furniture. Their house felt like home—to me and virtually every other person who stepped past the threshold. It was feng shuied to perfection, too, if I did say so myself.

I dropped my bag into a chair and rubbed the kinks in my shoulders. Getting manhandled into a car and being handcuffed twice in two days had wreaked havoc on my shoulder muscles.

A series of trills followed by a long meow announced Chatter, Ari's cat. She trotted up to sniff our feet, talking the whole way, long tail straight up. Though she hadn't met the breed's specifications, Chatter looked Bengal to me, with a marble coat that was a mixture of tan, black, and gold. Chatter thought she was divinity itself bestowed upon us for worship.

She closed her eyes in bliss when I scratched her neck.

"Hudson, this is Chatter. Chatter, Hudson."

Chatter twined through my legs, then stood up against Hudson's thigh and tested her claws in his jeans.

"Ow." She sniffed his fingers, then accepted a rub under her chin. Seconds later, Chatter's deep purr resonated in the front room.

"You've just made a friend for life," Ari said, whisking into the room from the kitchen. Antonio propped himself against the door frame behind her and crossed his arms in front of his chest. Italian, with brown eyes, thick black hair, a square jaw, and justified confidence, Antonio delivered a powerful blast to any heterosexual woman's libido, and it was only a slight mark against him that he knew it.

At one point in time, we'd given dating a trial run. We'd flirted since high school; we'd been friends longer. Marrying him would have made me an official member of my adopted family. Ari would have died of happiness. It should have been perfect, but our hearts weren't compatible. Our breakup had been remarkably civilized, and our friendship had evolved to include the occasional benefit.

Neither of us were possessive, so Antonio's tough-guy posturing while he watched Hudson made me roll my eyes.

"I'm Ari." Ari shook Hudson's hand while Chatter head-butted her leg. "This is my brother, Antonio."

Hudson shook hands with Antonio, and Ari and I shared a laughing glance at the seriousness between the two men.

"Do you pretend to be the boyfriend of every beautiful woman you meet?" Antonio asked.

"Only the redheads," I said, answering for Hudson and giving Antonio a firm look. "What's for dinner?"

"Lasagna," Ari said. "How'd the consultation go?"

"Not bad. I've never seen so many guns in one place before."

"What?" Hudson asked.

"This is why you need a chaperone," Antonio said. It was an old argument. Antonio lived firmly in the women-should-be-treated-like-fragile-flowers camp. He believed women should be independent, but only so long as he could keep them cocooned in bubble wrap, and he didn't see a conflict between the two beliefs, either. His forceful coddling was one of the many reasons we hadn't lasted as a couple.

"Why didn't you tell me about this?" Hudson asked. "I could have gone with you."

"Don't you start," I warned.

"The man's got a point," Antonio said. He looked at Hudson with approval. I groaned.

"I'm not listening to either of you. It's been a long day. I don't want to argue." I pushed past Antonio into the kitchen. Ari followed, with Chatter on her heels. The cat sat beside the fridge and batted the handle.

"Let me get Auntie Eva something first," Ari told Chatter. "Then I'll get you some food."

Ari opened the microwave and pulled out a single piece of coffee cake on a napkin. My eyes latched on to the treat. "Homemade?"

"Would I give you anything less?"

I snatched the cake from her hand and broke off a piece. Warm brown sugar and cinnamon melted on my tongue. I relaxed my hips against the counter and closed my eyes to savor the delicious flavors. Taking another bite without opening my eyes, I could feel the day's stresses floating away on a sugar haze.

I opened my eyes when I realized the kitchen was silent. Hudson eyed me like *I* was a piece of coffee cake, Antonio watched me with fond amusement, and Ari watched Hudson, a smirk on her face.

"Coffee cake turns her into putty," she said. Hudson started and glanced at Ari. She winked at him. "That's a secret a lot don't know. You're welcome."

Hudson and I both blushed and avoided eye contact while I finished the last bite and carried my napkin to the trash. Memory of the hot kiss Hudson and I hadn't discussed set my lips tingling again.

I checked the microwave. It was empty.

"No more until after dinner, Eva." A red hen perched on Ari's shoulder. It had been only a matter of time. She was in the kitchen, at home, with family who allowed her to boss them around. The hen always appeared at times like this. Ari was content. And about to get nosy.

"I'll set the table," I volunteered. "Are we eating outside?"

"Yep," Antonio said. He grabbed plates and place mats and I selected flatware and napkins, and we both retreated to the outdoor patio.

"Hudson, could you help me with the salad?" Ari asked, effectively culling him from the herd.

Located in the back right of the house, the small outdoor patio spanned most of Ari and Antonio's love and marriage and fame sections. A one-car garage filled out their wealth section. Because their house was long and narrow, some of the back three baguas spilled over into the house, but most of the feng shui for those sections had been done outside. Which is why Ari and I had selected warm earth-toned flagstones, pink and red flowering vines to climb the stucco walls, and a variety of healthy plants to line the patio. A long pergola covered a wooden table large enough to seat six. To the side, a grouping of cushy chairs circled a movable fire pit. Looking at the area as a whole, it was no surprise Ari had a reputation as a great host and better friend, and Antonio was well liked and trusted as a contractor.

I was twitchy to rework their relationship area, but after Ari had a bad breakup a few months earlier, she had forbidden me from taking more than minimal action. She needed time to recover and had little interest in using feng shui to attract another man into her life. Antonio had been happy with the mosaic of dancing women I'd found to adorn the large gap where Ari had torn up a pear tree. He'd had no problem finding fun, unattached women to share his bed, and Ari's female relationships flourished.

I studied Antonio as he laid down the place mats. He'd dressed in faded jeans and a white V-neck undershirt that made his tanned skin glow. The shirt emphasized his wide shoulders, lean hips, and biceps that required gym work on top of his day job.

Normally I would have appreciated the view, but today I was suspicious. Antonio knew my weakness for a man in a white T-shirt and jeans, and he was playing it up.

"Why are you here?" I asked. The windows to the house were open, but the dining room separated us from the kitchen, where I could hear Ari talking with Hudson.

"I live here."

"And you didn't bother to get fully dressed when you knew company was coming over because . . . ?"

He glanced up, giving me a smoldering look through thick lashes, his grin knowing. "Just keeping an eye on Ari and you. She told me you'd gotten into some trouble." When he straightened, he flexed, and his pectoral muscles bounced.

I rolled my eyes. I wouldn't admit to enjoying the show. Hieroglyphics spiraled up both of Antonio's arms, all divinations. Carmela, Antonio and Ari's mother, would never let him hear the end of it if he got a real tattoo, and Antonio was enough of a mama's boy to care.

Ari breezed through the screen door before I could respond. She wore oven mitts and carried a lasagna large enough to feed ten. Hudson followed with a pot holder, a bowl of garlic bread, and a salad. Ari made a second trip to retrieve a bottle of wine and a pitcher of ice water, and Chatter followed her back out. After rubbing against each person, the cat flopped in the last slice of sun to groom.

While we served ourselves and ate, Ari entertained, drawing information out of Hudson with skill an interrogator would envy. We learned Hudson had dreamed of being a long-haul trucker as a child, his longest relationship had been a two-year romance in college, and he eventually wanted kids.

"You ever think about going back home?" Ari asked when he mentioned he was from Texas. I saw through her casual questions to the root of her inquiries: She was doing a background and flight-risk check on what she perceived to be a future Mr. Eva Parker. Hudson appeared oblivious.

"This is home. I'm a native Californian born in the wrong state."

When he confessed his parents were still married and he had one younger brother, I admitted to being an only child, and a bastard at that.

"That's better than having a nosy older sister and three domineering older brothers, including this one," Ari said, pointing at Antonio.

"I don't know which is worse," Hudson said. "Only children, who are always selfish and spoiled, or the babies of the family, who are always selfish and spoiled."

"Hey!" Ari and I protested.

"Being an older brother is hard work," Antonio said. "You've always got to put up with your sibling's shit, bail them out of trouble, set a good example—"

"You wouldn't know a good example if it slapped you," Ari bantered.

"The youngest have it so easy," Hudson said. "We broke in the parents, wore them down. And then they skate through on all our hard work and never appreciate it."

"Exactly," Antonio agreed. He raised his wineglass and Hudson tapped it with his own.

I forked a stray zucchini and kept my mouth shut. I'd always wanted a sibling. Even better would have been a normal family, one with two parents who stuck together and stuck around. I knew my father's identity, and I knew what he looked like in high school, because I'd seen my mom's yearbook. James Parker. My mother had given me his last name, but that hadn't been enough to make him a father. I didn't remember meeting him, though my mother said I had.

"He came to visit you a few times when you were really young," she'd said the last time I had asked about him. I'd been thirteen.

"If I was too young to remember it, it doesn't count."

"It should count for something, dear. He came to see you as much as he could. He tried. He was very young—"

"I thought that was your excuse, Annabella. You visit as much as you can, right? You're trying, right? I'm surprised I remember *you*." I'd stormed out of the room.

"Eva's not an only child," Ari said, snapping me back to the present. "She's been adopted into the da Via *famiglia*."

"We only need the paperwork to go through," I said, smiling at my best friend.

"Nope, not going to happen," Antonio said. A copyright symbol in red, white, and blue appeared over his heart. "Eva and I dated. That would be weird. And illegal. And disgusting. She can be your honorary sister."

"Eh. We all knew that was going nowhere," Ari said as if she hadn't pushed our relationship every step of the way. Antonio monitored Hudson's reaction. So did I. Hudson's eyes shot to Antonio's; then he leaned back, laid his arm across the back of my chair, and smiled at me. I stifled a giggle. Antonio had met his match for male posturing.

"So you're not a spoiled only child?"

"Of course I'm spoiled. I just know how to appear humble."

Ari snorted. Antonio barked a laugh.

"Anyway," I said, seeing Ari gearing up to regale Hudson with embarrassing tales. "Any word on the Suburban?"

Hudson glanced to Antonio and Ari. "They're up to speed? On everything?"

"Ari knows everything. Antonio?"

"Baby elephant at Aunt Fi's, Suburban trashed, crazy high school woman disappeared," Antonio recapped. "I know everything."

Hudson nodded, eyes troubled. "I got the Suburban back today and returned it. The detailers more than earned their exorbitant fee. It almost looked better than when we got it. There's no sign an elephant took a bath inside." The Scottish terrier stood by his chair, still as stone.

"Let me know how much I owe you," I said, hiding my wince. Jenny was racking up quite a bill.

"What'd you find out about Jenny?" he asked.

"Not much. We think she was in the science club in high school, and she might have transferred after junior year, since she's not in my senior yearbook."

"We *know* she was in the science club," Ari said. "I did some Facebook research and got ahold of a few of the other members. They didn't have much to say about Jenny. She was quiet, kept to herself—"

"Clear signs of a psycho in the making," I said.

"—and was obviously only in the club to put it on college applications. They all agreed she was super smart, though. Every one of them made a point of mentioning it. She went to Duke. Finished undergrad and grad in four years. I chatted with one of her college classmates, and he confirmed Jenny was like a savant. Claimed she made everyone else look bad. He didn't seem sorry that she'd graduated early. Maybe she's so smart, she snapped. You know, *A Beautiful Mind* and all that."

"She snapped and kidnapped a baby elephant?" I asked.

"Seems unlikely," Ari agreed. "I checked the news feeds again. No one's reported a missing baby elephant from any zoo or traveling show worldwide."

"What did she study at Duke?" I asked.

"Genetic biology."

"Huh," I said. It was a sentiment everyone agreed with.

"I found out where Jenny's parents lived when she was in high school," Ari said.

"Encino? Rosita Street?" Hudson asked.

"One and the same. Are they still there?"

"According to the information I found. Jenny isn't, though. She moved to Japan and works for a company called Adorable Creations."

"What's she doing here, then?" I asked. "And with an elephant? What does she do at Adorable Creations?"

"They do experiments with animals. Lab stuff," Hudson said. "They created a dog that looks like it's a puppy forever—big feet, floppy ears, stunted growth. They're right up there with the people who grow ears on the backs of mice."

We all shuddered.

"Wait. What if the elephant is part of some experiment? What do we know about Jenny?" I ticked off the points on my fingers. "She's brilliant. She studied genetic biology. She works for a company that does genetic manipulation."

"I guess Kyoko could be part of an experiment, but going from dogs to elephants is a big jump," Ari said.

When none of us had more information to share, and our speculations about Jenny's possible motives had wound down, Ari pushed back from the table. "I saw you brought some cupcakes. Let me grab them and the coffee cake. I'll be right back."

"I'll help," Antonio said, carrying the half-eaten lasagna with him.

I grabbed Hudson's arm the moment they were both inside. "We can't let them eat the cupcakes!" I hissed.

"Why not?"

"Why not?! They were made by kidnappers! We don't know what's in them. They could be drugged!"

"Didn't you say you saw one of the guys eat one?"

"Yeah, but that could have been to make me think the rest were okay."

"Didn't you also say the kidnapping seemed like a misunderstanding?"

"What are you two whispering about?" Ari asked, returning with a platter of coffee cake that had been warming in the oven. Antonio followed with the Tupperware.

"I think I'm ready to propose," Antonio said, licking a finger.

"You didn't eat one!"

"What? I had to make sure they weren't poisoned." He set the Tupperware on the table and selected a carrot cake cupcake. "The chocolate ones are pure heaven." He bit into the carrot cake and moaned. I gripped the arms of my chair, ready to launch across the table and perform the Heimlich. "I take it back. The chocolate is what's served outside the pearly gates. *This*"—he pointed at the cream cheese frosting—"is what's served on the inside."

"You're amazing, Eva. You've had the craziest couple of days, and you still thought to pick up something on your way home," Ari said.

"Maybe you shouldn't—"

Ari selected a chocolate cupcake and took a bite. She closed her eyes to savor it, then said, "Antonio is right. This is heaven. Where'd you go?"

"I . . . ah, I don't remember," I said, watching for signs of drowsiness or asphyxiation. "Like you said, it was . . . hectic."

Antonio and Ari stared at me with twin perplexed expressions.

"You know there's coffee cake on the table, right?" Ari asked. "Warm. Fresh out of the oven."

The fact that it'd been sitting in front of me for over a minute without me pouncing on it worried them. I grabbed the knife and cut myself a slice. The damage was done. If the cupcakes were poisoned, it was already in Antonio's and Ari's bloodstreams.

Hudson selected a chocolate.

"You too?" I asked, incredulous.

"I like to live dangerously," he said with a wink.

"Seriously, man, these are addictive," Antonio agreed.

"What's our next step?" I asked, pushing aside visions of all three of them rushing away in ambulances to the nearest hospital.

Barring Jenny miraculously retrieving Kyoko and disappearing from our lives, our current plan of tracking her down remained our only option. Ari would continue to contact past acquaintances via the Internet and phone—and she'd update Sofie. Hudson and I would visit Jenny's parents tomorrow. With any luck, Jenny would be holed up there, and the whole fiasco would be over by tomorrow.

Just in case, I thought it prudent to move Kyoko.

"I don't know who this retrievalist is or how he plays into everything," I told Hudson as we walked back to my place. "He could be on our side for all I know, but I don't want to take any chances with anyone finding Kyoko at Sofie's. I think we should move her tomorrow."

"Where?"

I'd already thought of this, too. "I know someone. A family friend, really. She's out of town indefinitely. Her house is more private than Sofie's. It has an alarm system. Sofie would be safer." Since this "friend" happened to be my mother, Annabella Hunt, currently in Europe shooting episodes of her treasure-hunting show, *Hunt and Seek*, I didn't even have to ask permission. Plus, adding elephant poop to my mother's life, no matter how remotely, pleased a childish part of me.

"That means transporting Kyoko again. We need another truck and trailer. One that won't crap out on us, even with Kyoko's curse." Rotten-core bananas dripped slices from his shoulders to the sidewalk, leaving a vanishing sticky trail behind us.

The drive between Sofie's home and my mother's was short enough to be feasible, but vehicle appropriation wasn't my forte. "Do you think you can find a place to rent a truck and trailer?"

"I should be able to work something out."

"Thank you." The words were inadequate, but Hudson shrugged them aside anyway. A tarnished broadsword peeked over his shoulder.

I shivered when the breeze cut through my thin top, and Hudson wrapped an arm around my shoulders and pulled me up against his warm side. My footsteps slowed as we neared my apartment. I didn't want to say good night just yet. I fantasized about how our first date would have gone had Jenny not interrupted Hudson outside the art gallery and dragged us both into her mess. Would the chemistry between us have been as tangible without the bond of our criminal escapades? Would Hudson have been as interested in me if he hadn't gotten to play the role of savior? The kiss earlier said the answer to both those questions was yes.

But shouldn't I be certain? The only way to find out would be to kiss Hudson again.

A woman had to do what a woman had to do.

"Do you want to come up?"

Hudson didn't hesitate. "Sure." He steered us into the lobby of my building and toward the elevators. "What floor?"

"The top. Seven. But, ah, I'll take the stairs and meet you up there."

Hudson stopped and took a step away from me to get a better look at my face. I missed his warmth immediately in the arctic lobby. Crossing my arms, I stifled a sigh and lined up my usual string of lies.

"Is there something I should know about the elevators?"

"Only that they're metal death boxes on tiny strings, just like every other elevator you've ever encountered."

"Hang on. Are you telling me you get irritated when you're kidnapped and frustrated when people drag you into illegal schemes, but you're *afraid* of rather ordinary elevators?"

"Shouldn't a person be irritated when they're kidnapped?"

"Sure, of course, irritated. Or perhaps *terrified* or *panicked*. Most people, when escaping said kidnappers, might get a wee bit hysterical. You invent some sex story and make a lifelong protector out of a cabbie—who threatened to cut off my balls if I ever allowed you to be endangered by our 'sex games' again, just so you know. You were cool as brass. Your best friend never suspected a thing. So, yeah, I'm a little surprised you've got a thing with elevators." He snapped his fingers. "Hang on. Are you claustrophobic?"

"Would it make it better if I got hysterical?"

Hudson ran his hand through his hair. "Maybe a little. Just enough."

"Enough for what?"

"To give me excuses." He waggled his eyebrows at me.

# TEN

HUDSON TRAILED me up six flights of stairs. Hyperconscious of his eyes on my backside the whole way, I took the stairs faster than normal. When we reached the top, we were both out of breath, but Hudson no more than me.

I flipped on the lights in my loft and waited to deliver my next lie.

"What's wrong with the lighting?"

"It's gas."

"Gas? Like what was used before electricity was invented?"

"One and the same." I had variations for the next lie: Sometimes I told men it was a feng shui thing. Sometimes I told them it was a new, greener lighting method. Some didn't even notice the lights. To Hudson I told the lie he was least likely to refute. "It was left over from a previous resident, and I got the loft cheap because of it."

"Huh." He walked to the floor-to-ceiling windows and looked out. "Nice view."

I kicked off my shoes and padded into the kitchen. "Do you like port?"

"More of a scotch kind of guy."

I filled two tumblers with a few fingers' worth and recapped the bottle. "Ice?"

"No, thanks."

I dropped two cubes in my glass. When I'd first moved in, I'd stored all my vegetables and leftovers in an ice chest, and I'd hauled up bagged ice daily. For my next birthday, Sofie gave me a propane-powered fridge that cost more than the monthly mortgage bill. For Christmas, she'd given me a gas-powered washer and dryer. It had been her idea to hire Antonio to retrograde all the electric features to gas—and I don't think she'd foreseen *that* relationship blossoming, either.

"This isn't exactly what I was expecting," Hudson said, taking his drink from me.

"Oh? How so?"

"I thought there'd be more hippie stuff." He seemed embarrassed by his words, but he didn't apologize.

"You mean New Agey stuff? Like that?" I pointed to a faceted round crystal suspended by clear fishing wire nine inches from the ceiling in the far right corner of the front room. I didn't explain it hung in the center of my love and marriage bagua and the crystal helped deflect the energy coming in through all the full-length windows. "Or that?" I pointed to the wind chime hanging above the base of my bedroom stairs, slowing the flow of chi.

"Those are . . . odd, but I was thinking more like pillows on the floor, drapey wall hangings in pastels and rainbow colors, baskets. Papasans everywhere."

"Even after Sofie's?"

Hudson shrugged.

"Fortunately for me, feng shui doesn't mean you have to live in the sixties. Though I think it's funny you went there. Most people think that since it's an ancient Chinese art, everything has to look like it's straight out of Hong Kong."

"So somehow all this stuff, arranged the way you have it, influences what happens in your life."

"Basically, yeah." I set my glass on a side table and flopped into my couch's embrace.

"It's actually rather comfortable, inviting."

"I'll take that rousing endorsement."

Hudson flushed. "I didn't mean it like that. Feng shui just seems so . . . so woo-woo. Don't pay attention to me. I sound like an ass. Your home is very nice."

"Thank you." I closed my eyes and savored the silence. His opinions about feng shui notwithstanding, I liked having Hudson in my house. Some guests simply didn't work. They sucked up all the peaceful serenity of my sanctuary and put me on edge until they left. Despite it being the sort of *woo-woo* judgment Hudson would make fun of, I didn't get those feelings from him. He strolled about the spacious great room, openly curious about me and my things, and I felt relaxed.

"Does this work?" Hudson asked, pointing to an ornate gold switch plate.

"Flip it," I said, opening my eyes.

The gas clicked twice in the fireplace, then flames illuminated the brass interior. I rose and shut off the other lights. The shiny walls backing the flames radiated a warm, cozy glow through the room. I jumped when a pair of bunnies hopped up to the glass front, then turned white tails to the warmth and snuggled against each other.

Hudson watched me with dilated eyes, and I smiled. The bunnies were a divination I could interpret. I'd known Hudson for forty-eight hours. He loved electronics, drove a motorcycle, and didn't see the value in feng shui: The con column was full to bursting. But he was also sexy as hell, dependable, honorable, a great kisser, and intelligent. In my book, that put the pro column on top.

I sashayed to his side and took the glass from his unresisting fingers, setting it on a nearby table.

"Maybe I am feeling a little vulnerable," I said softly. I stood close enough for our body heat to mingle. Tilting my head back, I dropped my lashes. Hudson sucked in a breath.

"Ah, vulnerable? That's, um . . . Right. You've been through a lot today. Maybe I should get you settled in and then . . . go." He took a step back, running a hand through his hair.

I opened my eyes fully. "You're leaving?"

"Look, Eva. I like you. Don't think I don't want this—*a lot*. But I don't take advantage of vulnerable women. I don't want—" He stopped and glared at me. "Are you laughing?"

"A little. Don't be mad. It seemed like in the lobby, you wanted me to be more emotional. But screw that." Still grinning, I reached for his neck and pulled his face close to mine. "Here's what I should have said," I breathed against his lips. "I want to kiss you. I want to start at your mouth, and I want to see what your skin tastes like everywhere from your neck to your toes. I want to know what—"

Hudson wrapped his arms around me and pulled me up against him. My breasts flattened against his hard chest, and I swallowed a moan. I slid my fingers into his hair as his mouth settled over mine, hot and wet. We didn't come up for air until my toes were curled.

I shifted in his embrace, enjoying the dual sensation of his hard body pressed against my nipples and the muscular cage of his arms. Hudson slid a hand down my spine to rest at the base of my tailbone. I wriggled against him, and he groaned. Lifting on tiptoes, I teased his deliciously firm lips with my tongue, then sank my teeth into his full bottom lip before soothing it with a gentle kiss. Hudson dipped his knees, evening our heights, and returned the kiss.

"You're absolutely gorgeous, Eva." Framing my face with his large, warm hands, Hudson stared into my eyes with the intensity of a man looking for a soul.

"You're not bad yourself, Hudson." I worked my hands under his T-shirt and up his back, running my fingers lightly along his vertebrae. Goose bumps followed my fingers back to his waistband. "Though I think I need to look at the big picture before I form an opinion."

Hudson obligingly stepped back and yanked his shirt over his head. The muscles in his stomach shifted, flexing in a clearly defined six-pack. Golden brown hair dusted his pectorals and his stomach below his belly button, disappearing under the waistband of his jeans. I moistened my lips and savored the view.

"Your turn."

I lowered the hand that had been reaching for him and smiled. I didn't try to turn taking off my shirt into something sexy; my fingers were too clumsy. I tossed my top toward the sofa, then paused with my hands behind my back on my bra's clasp. Hudson tracked me with dark, predatory eyes, and anticipation rushed hot from my bones to my skin. I forced my feet to back up, knocking into furniture as I went.

"Stay there." I spun and jogged up the stairs to my bedroom, grabbed a string of condoms from the nightstand, and trotted back down the stairs. Hudson's gaze fastened on the jiggle of my breasts above the cup of the bra, and I added a little extra bounce in my steps just to see his smile widen.

I tossed the condoms toward the coffee table and grabbed a thick blanket from within a storage ottoman. Hudson helped me spread it in front of the fireplace, but I barely noticed where the blanket fell. The golden glow of firelight against Hudson's chest and abdomen, the hunger in his blue eyes, his dimple flashing with a secretive smile—everything about him captivated me, leaving little room to concentrate on anything else. An apparition I couldn't make out shimmered around Hudson's body, drawing me to him. He met me halfway, our feet sinking into the plush blanket.

Bubbles. Tiny golden champagne bubbles floated from Hudson's skin. They rose in a continuous stream, disappearing an inch above his body, making him literally glow. I ran my hand over his taut stomach, not touching him, just the bubbles. I couldn't feel anything but the heat of him, yet the bubbles intensified in reaction to my hand, flowing brighter in an after-trail of light and effervescence.

"I believe I was promised the big picture," Hudson said. He skirted his fingertips across the tops of my shoulders, tracing the straps of my bra down to the cups. I sucked in a breath as his fingers skimmed the swell of my breasts. When I unlatched my bra and let it slide down my arms, my breasts fell into his hands. I moaned and leaned into him. Hudson rasped his thumbs across my nipples, and pleasure zinged down my body.

When I reached for him, he released my breasts and pulled me into his arms for another kiss hot enough to fuse our bodies together. The shocking pleasure of skin against skin ignited my bloodstream. With fumbling fingers, I shimmied out of my tight skirt and underwear, then helped Hudson free himself from his jeans and boxer briefs.

I slid my hand around him as he kissed my lips, my jaw, my neck. The weight of him in my palm made my breath quicken. From the moment I'd suggested tonight's date, I'd hoped we'd end up here, but I hadn't anticipated how intense or fast the spark between us would ignite, or how our urgency would spike my arousal. Curling my fingers, I squeezed him, earning a nip at the base of my neck.

I lost my grip when Hudson dipped to flick his tongue across a nipple. Gasping, I arched into him, balancing on my toes. He slid an arm around the back of my legs, another around my shoulders, and the world tilted. Hudson eased me onto the blanket and braced above me, lavishing attention on each breast. I lifted my head to stare down our bodies, feasting on the sight of him poised so close to me. Wrapping my legs around him, I tried to pull him against me.

Hudson's deep chuckle did fun things to my middle, but he wouldn't budge. Gliding a hand down my body, he traced my hips and thighs while gently nipping my breasts. The disparate sensations pinged through my body, pooling pleasure between my legs. When he teased my clitoris, I writhed and moaned, anticipation riding the cusp of frustration.

"Condom. Now," I panted.

Hudson lifted his dark gaze to mine, his bottom lip caught in his teeth.

"Oh, God, now. Please."

He shifted back to his heels to grab a foil packet, and I sat up with him, running my fingers over his body while he rolled on a condom. His pale nipples stood at attention, and when I gently tweaked them, he growled and pounced, taking me back to the floor. I shrieked, but my giggle cut off when he slid a hand over my breast. Pulling his head to me, I kissed him, relishing the returning buildup of anticipation.

Twisting, I rolled with Hudson until I lay on top of him. I guided him inside me, and every promise of chemistry and heat between us paled in comparison to the reality. My body smoldered, pleasure building in rolling waves, and when it crested, it seared through my body, burning away every moment but the present one. Hudson followed on an echo of my orgasm.

———

"I'M NEVER LOOKING at those stairs the same way again," I said, hours later, when we lay exhausted in my bed. We were both on top of the covers, bodies cooling. Hudson sprawled with his hands behind his head, eyes closed and smiling. A fluffy white cloud rested beneath his head and the bubbles were gone. I didn't see any bunnies, either.

"You were the one wriggling your heinie in my face. What'd you expect?"

"I was *walking* up the stairs in front of you."

"Exactly. Now you can appreciate my restraint earlier when we marched up the million steps to get here."

"You're a veritable monk."

He cracked his eyelids to peer at me. I was grinning like a fool, and I couldn't do a thing about it. He winked at me, and I laughed.

"I'm going to shower." I rolled out of bed and stretched gingerly, popping my toes against the carpet. Hudson shifted to watch me walk away.

"Alone?" he asked.

"I prefer not."

Hudson beat me to the shower stall.

———

"I JUST GOT this phone yesterday. Talked the rep into replacing my other phone because they know it's impossible to diagnose intermittent problems. And now this one's dead? Three phones dead in three days? What are the odds?"

Hudson wasn't really talking to me. He was talking to the useless slab of his cell phone. I rolled out of bed and padded naked to the closet. Hudson tossed his phone onto the comforter and followed me.

He wrapped an arm around me from behind and pulled me back against him, then kissed my neck. I melted into him.

"Got anything in my size?" he asked.

"I think you'd look great in that," I said, pointing to a slinky sequined spaghetti-strapped tank top.

"I don't think it'd go with my underarm hair."

He turned me around and I tilted my face up for a kiss. I could feel him getting happy against my stomach.

"I need to carry a change of clothes if I'm going to spend any time with you," he said. "This is the second morning in a row I'm going to be wearing the same clothes as the day before."

"Yeah, but you didn't have a walk of shame yesterday."

"There's definitely no shame today, either." He kissed me again and I shivered as his chest hair rasped my hard nipples. With a mischievous grin, he shimmied just to watch my reaction. I gasped when he pushed me back to arm's length. "No, you're not going to distract me," he said. "I don't care what you—"

I licked my lips.

"What you, ah, do, you won't—"

I ran my hands over my chest. His eyes glazed.

When I finished dressing forty-five minutes and another shower later, Hudson waited downstairs in my office. He handed me a glass of orange juice and chugged through his own glass's contents. The cold liquid soothed my parched throat.

"You're a little OCD, aren't you?" he asked.

"If you mean organized, yes."

I loved my office. A huge wooden desk anchored the whole room, kept company by a sleek black chair, uplifting art on the walls, a custom cabinet filled with cubbies of all sizes, and attractive filing cabinets—it had been a long and difficult quest to find filing cabinets that qualified as *attractive*. After the desk, my second-favorite feature was the giant three-by-three-foot wall calendar displaying one month at a time. Not only did the calendar keep me organized, it reminded me daily of the prosperity in my life and how blessed I was to have a successful business.

As I did every morning, I went straight to the calendar and checked the day's lineup. I had a consultation today at four, and two more tomorrow. Ari would have to reschedule all three. I also had two long-distance workups due in the next seven days.

Working for clients outside of a ten-mile radius of my loft still felt surreal. My curse denied me access to phones, Internet, and e-mail—all the easy-contact resources the world took for granted. Without Ari, my business would have remained as it started: a word-of-mouth, single-client-a-month practice funded by my aunt's generous friends.

Two years ago, when Ari had gone freelance as a graphic design artist, she had insisted on also becoming my executive assistant. The first thing she had done was build me a beautiful website—I'd seen printed screenshots. She took phone calls, booked appointments, and set up online consultations. Together we had designed templates that allowed people outside my small radius of travel to write in with their feng shui concerns, and based off pictures they sent, I was able to do written consultations for people whose homes I'd never visited. In three months, I was booking clients from across the nation and scheduling a steady stream of on-site consultations in the local LA area.

Baby elephant or no baby elephant, I decided I could finish both long-distance workups on time.

My stomach growled loud enough to turn Hudson's head. "Hey, I forgot to tell you. The kidnappers, they called Kyoko an elephantini. They thought she was an alcoholic drink. Do you think that means anything?"

"Elephantini," Hudson said, testing the word. "Does that mean she's not a real elephant, but some new kind of breed?"

"No clue."

I grabbed a sticky note and jotted down all the adjustments to the schedule I wanted Ari to make.

"Where's your computer?"

"In the shop," I said. Lie number one of the day.

"Your TV, too?"

"Nope. I don't have one."

"Is that a feng shui thing?"

"Something like that."

"You don't watch TV? At all?"

My back was to Hudson, and I closed my eyes. Never underestimate the importance of TV to men. It was the great medium of sports and explosions and porn. Plus our society entertained strange prejudices against people without TVs. Somehow, not having one made me a pariah, someone who thought herself more important and worldly than everyone else. Someone full of herself.

"Are you as hungry as I am?" I deflected.

Hudson paused before answering. "Starved."

"You do know how to work up a woman's appetite," I teased. I smiled as I turned around and kissed him. Hudson was apparition-free, and for once, I could have used a divination to give me a clue to his feelings. His expression gave nothing away. However, after a night in my electricity-free apartment, my gift had no juice. Any electricity I might have absorbed from neighboring lofts wasn't enough to fuel even a pint-size apparition.

Hudson's body language revealed as little as his face. My only option was to power through and hope he'd forget about my suspicious idiosyncrasies.

"How many donuts can you fit on your bike?"

"How many do you need?"

"Personally, at least two. Maybe five after last night. But Ari will want a few, and Antonio could eat a dozen all by himself."

"What do Ari and Antonio have to do with our breakfast?"

"Ari's my business partner and executive assistant." I waved the sticky note at him. "I need her to reschedule a few appointments for me if I'm going to be free to hunt Jenny down. And we need to make up for some lost time this morning. I thought we'd combine everything over breakfast." My stomach punctuated my words with a grumble.

"Give me a half hour. I don't want to show up at Ari's in the same clothes as yesterday."

"Doesn't matter. She'll know."

"I don't care about that. I want clean clothes."

———

I STRAIGHTENED up after Hudson left, then applied sunscreen, eyebrow darkener, light-brown mascara, and lip gloss. My bangs took a little product to get them to look naturally side swept. Satisfied I looked presentable for whatever the day held, I collected my satchel. I'd opted for practical apparel today—jeans and a lightweight T-shirt, which would make escape easier if I were kidnapped again. I didn't think too hard about the motivation behind my outfit selection, either, or I wouldn't have left my apartment.

I ran into Ari a block before her house, Chatter frolicking on a harness and leash beside her.

"Where's hunky Hudson?" Ari asked in greeting.

"He's going to meet us." Chatter planted her front legs against my thigh and flexed her claws, then belted out a meow.

"Oh, is he? And how does he know where to find you this morning? Have you developed telepathy?" Ari teased.

"We could have made plans last night." I attempted a neutral expression, but my blush gave me away. Ari opened her mouth, but I cut her off before she could pry. "Did you learn anything new after we left?"

Chatter, unimpressed by the lack of attention, twined between my legs. A wiggling blade of grass distracted her, and before I could free myself, she leapt across the sidewalk, constricting my legs in a knot with the leash. I tripped into Ari. She caught me reflexively—one hand firmly planted on my breast, the other between my legs holding the leash.

"Oof!" I straightened.

A man stared unabashedly at us from the nearby porch.

"Beautiful cat," he said, never once looking in Chatter's direction.

"Morning, Nathan," Ari called from the vicinity of my crotch as she unwound the leash from my legs.

I gave Nathan a weak wave and twisted to help Ari. "Pervert," I muttered. "Chatter, attack."

Chatter abandoned the limp piece of grass and pounced on my shoelace.

"I was hoping to have some good news for you," Ari said, "but the responses I got from a few East Coast acquaintances this morning have been curt. No one knows where Jenny is and no one cares. She didn't make any friends while at college."

"I guess we stick with the plan, then."

"Don't worry, Eva, it'll all work out. And in the meantime, you're forced to hang around with a sexy man who is fabulous in bed."

"And now *you're* psychic?"

"It doesn't take supernatural powers to interpret that silly grin you've had on your face this whole time."

I felt my cheeks with both hands and realized she was right.

"Are you going to flaunt that afterglow in front of Antonio?"

"No, no. You're right. That'd be crass." Antonio and I may not hold a candle for each other, but it seemed rude to show up at my friend-with-benefits' house with a post-sex glow *and* the man responsible.

I tried to relax my face. Ari snorted.

When we tromped inside Antonio and Ari's house, she slid the harness off Chatter, and the cat tore around the room like her tail was on fire, ending her circuit at her scratching post and ripping off shreds.

"I'll reschedule everyone at least two weeks out," Ari said. She took my sticky note and waved it at me. "You know I don't need these. I've got everything on my computer."

"Two weeks? We should be done with this by the end of today."

"Which is what you said yesterday. I'll clear this week, to be safe, and we'll see how it goes after that."

I toed off my shoes and flopped onto the couch. I couldn't afford to go long without work; I needed my good reputation and the money— now more than ever, thanks to Jenny. Being pissed off at Jenny was becoming my new normal.

A loud knock on the front door brought Antonio out of the dining room. "Hey, Eva," he said before checking the peephole. He unlocked the door and swung it wide open. "Hudson, my man, are those donuts in your hand or are you just happy to see me?"

"Oh, you went to Bee's," Ari said, pushing her brother aside to take the box from Hudson. "I haven't had their donuts in forever."

Antonio and Hudson shook hands. Hudson had dressed in jeans again, but he'd paired them with a button-up short-sleeve white shirt that made his skin look golden. I tried to quell the flutter in my stomach at the sight of him. We'd been apart thirty-odd minutes. I was acting like a teenager, because it felt like I'd missed him. I gave up my attempt to appear reserved when Hudson pulled me to him and kissed me. These stupid, out-of-proportion feelings were the whole purpose of dating.

The kiss demolished any control I'd had over my afterglow good cheer. When we pulled apart, I shot Antonio a guilty glance. A hand-size tornado slid back and forth through his torso. On anyone else, I might have been alarmed by the divination, but on Antonio, it represented his optimistic outlook: Things could be worse. I appreciated his goodwill and tried to express it with a smile. Antonio shrugged.

"He brought donuts. That's all that matters," Antonio said.

Ari rolled her eyes even as a rust-colored hen materialized on her head.

Judging by the reappearance of divinations, my ping-ponging emotions had drained a chunk of electricity from Ari and Antonio's house. Surreptitiously, I moved the gathering to the dining room, taking a moment to check out Hudson. The cowboy boots were back, along with a new divination: a windup key twisting in his stomach. It didn't look comfortable, and I hoped it had nothing to do with me.

I surveyed the open donut box. "You found a coffee cake donut?"

"It seemed like your favorite flavor," Hudson said. A furry white patch dotted his forehead and the other divinations disappeared.

Those silly, bubbly feelings came back full throttle.

It didn't take long for the four of us to demolish a dozen donuts. Hudson borrowed Ari's phone to make several calls and announced after the last one that a truck and trailer would meet us at Sofie's.

"Why chance moving her?" Ari asked.

"I want Sofie and Kyoko somewhere safe, in case Jenny's involved in something dangerous," I said. It'd do Ari no good to worry about

Jenny's cousins or the skip tracer on Jenny's tail. My gut twinged when Ari accepted my reasoning without question.

"I'll call your softball buddies to tell them you're sitting tomorrow's game out," Ari said as we left. "I really wish you could call Greta yourself, though. She's not going to be happy you're canceling last minute on tonight's Bunco."

"Tell her I'll make it up to her next time; I'll bring the fixings for Slippery Nipples."

"She's still going to yell. I hate it when little old women are mad at me. It's like inviting bad luck."

"What's Bunco?" Hudson asked as we walked down the block.

"A card game, but really more an excuse to socialize."

"And Greta is . . . your grandma?"

I snorted. The only similarity between Greta and Nana Nevie was their status as grandmothers. Greta and the other Bunco women were all members of the same senior citizen synchronized swim team that met at my gym. I'd been allowed into their club because I'd helped them out a few times with new moves for their underwater dances. In their minds, we were all the same age. "Greta is more like a sister trapped in a body sixty years older than me," I said.

Hudson stopped beside a shiny gray car and pressed a fob. The car chirped.

"What happened to the bike?"

"It's getting looked at before I let you on it again," he said. "It seemed to run fine this morning, but I want to make sure it's safe."

I swallowed my guilt and disappointment. *This is better,* I told myself. I'd been pushing my luck with one motorcycle ride. Twice would have been stupid, and it would have endangered Hudson's life, too.

The car's interior was leather and cozy. The engine purred. I didn't know makes and models of cars by sight, but I could tell when I sat in a high-end model.

"I'm going to take a convoluted route," Hudson said as he pulled away from the curb. "If we've got a tail—this retrievalist—I want to shake him. I don't want to lead him straight to Sofie's door."

"The skip tracer's after Jenny, not us." A convoluted route would not work with my curse.

"I thought the kidnappers said he's after Kyoko, the elephantini."

"True, but—"

"If Jenny thought you needed to be warned, she must suspect this retrievalist knows *you* have Kyoko."

A chilling thought, and one that, between being handcuffed, kidnapped, and some hot sex last night, had completely slipped my mind.

I monitored the side-view mirror for anyone following us, all the while repeating the mantra, *I am a still pond. I am a calm pool.* I sat next to a man who made my blood heat just looking at him, and I worried about what I'd gotten my aunt—and myself—into; calming mantras could do only so much to control my emotions.

I wasn't the least bit surprised when the car hiccupped to its death seventeen minutes later.

## ELEVEN

"WHAT THE HELL!" Hudson slammed a new burner phone against the steering wheel. "It's like I've got a curse on me that says, 'Break anything useful!' This car has run perfectly for the last two years, and *now* it breaks. Along with *another* phone?" He jerked out of the car, his back covered by a huge weird plastic city divination large enough for Chatter to play in. A silver terrier the size of a Great Dane coasted behind him on Baltic Avenue. Rapid-fire cussing echoed against the underside of the hood; then Hudson slammed it closed. I got out and slung my bag over my shoulder.

"There's nothing, *nothing* wrong with it. Just like that damn Suburban. Just like my bike." He dropped his head back to glare at the hazy blue sky. "What'd I do wrong?" he shouted. A cluster of people at the nearby bus stop turned to stare.

"Should we call a tow truck?" I asked, hoping to speed up his breakdown and get back on the road to Sofie's.

"And then what?"

"We could take the bus."

"The bus." He ran his hand through his hair and stomped back and forth in front of me. "The bus." He kicked a tire.

"I doubt the retrievalist would think to follow us on a bus."

Hudson opened and closed his mouth a few times, then threw his hands into the air. "Fine."

While Hudson talked the nearby Rite Aid manager into letting him use the store's phone to call a tow truck, I purchased water. I left Hudson alone while we waited for the tow truck. He needed space to fume; I needed space to release my guilt. There was nothing wrong with his car that time and space away from me wouldn't fix. I wasn't going to be able to convince Hudson to wait it out, though. I hoped he had a good mechanic, one who wouldn't charge him for doing nothing.

When we filed onto the bus, Hudson flopped into the seat next to me, arms crossed, a scowl on his face. After the tow truck left, he'd clammed up in a full-body sulk. I eyed the five-foot marble cherub flying at his back, gliding in and out of the bus's wall. It had a bow with an arrow notched, and its wings spanned an additional five feet. A creepy, beatific smile never altered on its enormous baby face. I couldn't make any logical leap between Hudson's obvious frustration and this child-warrior angel creature, and it was hard not to stare.

Since the bus traversed the city in a route almost as convoluted as Hudson's but twice as slow, I pulled out the long-distance consultation I had in my bag. Feng shui leveled my emotions and helped me maintain barriers around my curse, both of which were necessary if the bus was going to last the trip. If anything could take my mind off worrying about Sofie, the skip tracer on our trail, and Jenny's blackmail threat, or just being generally pissed at my curse and the limitations it forced upon my life, it was feng shui.

I caught sight of my white-knuckled grip on my ballpoint pen and forced my hand to relax. Tugging a notebook from my bag, I fanned my client's photos of each room in her home and layered them roughly into the shape of her house across my lap. When Lindsey Little had filled out my online questionnaire, she'd stated she wanted a family, but it never seemed like the right time, and she never felt financially stable enough. I wasn't surprised. The house's floor plan laid out a challenge: A huge courtyard gap carved out the children and creativity section plus pieces of her family and health section.

In addition, like a lot of people, the Little family had a lovely home to look at, but one that subtly undermined their goals. Too much water element drowned the fame section, too much wood element blockaded the career section, and too many square objects boxed in the helpful people and travel section.

I glanced up when the bus jerked to a halt, shocked to see we were almost to our stop. I'd filled two pages with notes for Ari to type up. Hudson scowled out the window, fingers drumming on his leg. He had good features for a scowl. Thick eyebrows, bright eyes. His crossed arms accentuated his excellent posture and popped out the muscles in his biceps. I leaned into him, ignoring the cherub that circled wide to stare at me, and kissed him on the cheek.

Hudson turned to me, surprised, and I kissed him on the lips, steadying myself with one hand braced on his arm. The bus rocked into motion, and my breast rubbed against his forearm. I pulled back and smiled. I kept the kiss shallow, purposely dampening my lust. Plus, we were in public, something Hudson had made hard to remember when he'd slid his tongue across my lips.

Hudson's arms slowly unfolded and the cherub vanished. A star shot from Hudson's chest, fast and bright. No, not a star. A dandelion puff. Just as quickly, it disappeared. The silver terrier appeared, complete with Marvin Gardens under its feet. It rode in a child's red wagon. A moment later, a navy poncho draped Hudson's chest. Judging by the sheer number of divinations, I needed off this bus pronto if it hoped to finish its route.

Hudson helped me pack up my project, then wove his fingers through mine and rested our joined hands on his leg. I closed my eyes and savored the peaceful moment. We were doing things out of order: handcuffs first, then kissing; sex first, then holding hands. However, I'd never been much for order in my love affairs. I liked my relationships hot and intense—and limited to a manageable length. This had all the signs of fitting my ideal relationship.

I took a deep breath and tried to clear my thoughts. I'd held men's hands before; I'd entertained the fantasy of a long-term, slow-paced relationship before. The euphoria of last night's activities predictably amplified my giddy, new-lover emotions, making this normal, couple-type moment feel more significant than it was. Which is why I side-stepped any further analysis of my disproportional bliss.

"This is us," I said when the bus stopped.

Hudson followed me to the sidewalk. The bus pulled away in a cloud of exhaust.

"I don't have a clue where we are," Hudson said.

"Follow me."

We walked along streets that grew more residential and quiet, trailed by a silent red wagon pulling an oversize Monopoly piece. I found a collapsible hat in my satchel and settled it on my head. Then I rummaged for trail mix snacks I'd added earlier. I handed Hudson his own bag.

"That thing's like Mary Poppins's bag," Hudson said. "Are you sure your cell isn't lost somewhere in its bottomless depths?"

"I'm sure."

He sighed. "No hidden laptop?"

"Nope."

"Maybe a moped?"

I laughed. "And risk getting oil in my bag? No way."

Hudson kept his own council for several blocks while the road curved steadily upward. I'd ridden this hill on my bike more times than I could count, and we had almost reached the point where I got off and walked. We were both breathing hard. Hudson offered to carry my bag, but I declined. Ari would have told me I was being too possessive of my security blanket.

"I'm sorry," Hudson said. "I shouldn't have gotten so mad earlier."

I peeked at him under the brim of my hat. He looked lost, and I could only imagine his confusion. In the last two days, he'd been dragged into a world where everything he relied on—cell phones, Internet access, vehicles—had failed him. This was my norm, but I tried to look at it from his perspective.

"It's frustrating when things break," I said. "I understand."

"It's just, *everything* has broken lately. I really do think Kyoko, or maybe Jenny, is cursed. I didn't have these problems before them."

"You didn't have them before you met me, either," I felt compelled to say.

"You're the one spot of good luck in this whole mess."

Guilt ate my stomach lining.

———

SOFIE MET us on the porch. Whether I came by foot, bike, or taxi, she was always outside waiting when I showed up. I accused her of having another gift she'd never told me about, but she called it motherly intuition. Something my real mother knew nothing about.

Dali rushed to greet us, sniffing my fingers and toes, then Hudson's, before doing a happy dance around us. On the porch, another set of canine eyes watched us, this one a familiar divination of a waist-high wolf with leopard spots. Its eyes shifted between Hudson and me, and I glanced up at Sofie. She cocked a single eyebrow at me, and I flushed. It was impossible to keep secrets from Sofie, especially not one as big as the fresh bonds of emotion-laced sex.

"Ari phoned to say you were coming," Sofie said after hugs were exchanged and we were all inside. Dali raced to the sliding glass door and I let him into the backyard. The once manicured oasis looked like it'd suffered through a tornado. Leaves and grass and floating clumps of dirt layered the pool, divots pockmarked the yard, and crushed petals wilted in the trampled flower beds. Kyoko—oblivious to her destructive nature—stood in the shallow end of the pool, tossing water with her trunk.

"Oh, I'm so sorry, Sofie!"

"Nonsense. Kyoko has been a veritable angel, and my yard could do with a makeover."

"At least we're moving her before she can totally destroy the place."

"Yes, that's what Ari said. Moving her to Annabella's." She gave me a flat look. I did my best to hold her gaze. "She's going to do far worse damage there, you know."

"That's the point."

"Eva."

"Leave it." My face contorted, and I clenched my jaw to contain the ugliness. Annabella—my mother—had that effect on me. Her betrayal was a thorn in my heart, a festering wound that never fully healed. Her greatest contribution to my life had been giving birth to me. Sixteen and unable to cope with a child *and* high school, Annabella had relied heavily on the help of Sofie, her older sister. But after high school, Annabella hadn't let a toddler slow her down or interrupt her plans. With a dozen top-tier acting schools in Los Angeles, she'd moved to New York to attend the Lee Strasberg Theatre and Film Institute. When I was between the ages of two and six, I saw her three times a year. I'd stopped looking forward to her visits when I was seven, or at least that's what I told Sofie and myself. There should be a finite number of times the same person can break your heart.

"You should get packed," I said. "Ari told you we're moving you, too, right?"

"She was vague about why."

"We don't want Kyoko to do any more damage here, and—"

"Does this have to do with two men and cupcakes?" Sofie asked.

I should have known better than to try to keep anything secret from Sofie. She simply saw too much. "Yes. Oddly, it does." I glanced at Hudson coming back from the bathroom and launched into my story as if I'd brought up the topic, explaining my bizarre kidnapping yesterday, glossing over my fear, and leaving the handcuffs out completely. "If Jenny thinks someone new and dangerous is looking for Kyoko, I want to make sure you are nowhere he can find you," I concluded.

"And you think that's Annabella's?" She looked more around me than at me. A tendril of a plant wove through her hair, growing into a crown of greenery that blossomed into wild roses. In the center of the crown sat a large Fabergé egg. Unsurprisingly, Sofie had mixed feelings about my decision. While she may have been concerned about her sister's reaction to us using her house and yard, my sole concern was keeping Sofie safe, pettiness notwithstanding. If we found Jenny today and forced her to take back Kyoko, this whole experience would be an amusing footnote to our spring. But Atlas and Edmond had spooked me. Hiding Sofie—and Kyoko—somewhere unexpected was the best option.

"No one is going to think to look at Annabella's."

"There are other places," Sofie said.

"None as perfect."

"How long are you going to keep punishing her, Eva?"

"Until we're even." I turned away and let myself outside.

———

LOADING Kyoko into a horse trailer backed up against the yard's side gate proved surprisingly easy. Dali raced in first, eager to smell everything, and Kyoko trundled after him. Hudson introduced Milo, the short, bowlegged driver in charge of the truck and trailer, as a family friend. Milo had a tanned and weathered face, and his eyes said he'd seen it all, including baby elephants in private backyards. He was all business, and though he was polite to Sofie and me, his briskness precluded conversation.

Milo's trailer made Jenny's look like a pile of junk. Thick rubber mats covered the floor of this trailer, the insides gleamed white and glossy, and the metal accents shone with polish. The outside sported an outline drawing of a stylized horse in mid-gallop, mane and tail streaming, with a windup key in its rump. The same logo repeated on the truck's front doors. The truck and trailer matched perfectly, down to the cherry red stripe bisecting the white exterior of both vehicles. This wasn't a rental.

"How do you two know each other?" I asked Milo once we were on the road. I sat in the back, Milo drove, and Hudson navigated a convoluted route, frequently checking the side mirror for a tail. Hudson's apparitions alternated between the blue, short-brimmed sombrero and the cowboy boots. The images should have belonged together, but the hat was pristine and clean, the boots old and dirty, and I'd never seen them at the same time before.

"Known Hudson since he was hock high," Milo said.

"Milo taught me how to ride."

"You know how to ride?" I had a hard time picturing Hudson on a horse, despite the cowboy boots apparition.

"Yeah." A computer monitor plopped into Hudson's lap, like one I'd seen in elementary school, with a tiny slate-green screen and a huge body.

Milo's eyes flicked to Hudson, then to me, and his eyebrows twitched. Not even Kyoko had warranted an eyebrow twitch from Milo. What was I missing here?

"And then you moved to LA, Milo?"

"No."

Slender lightning shot from the truck's ceiling, narrowly missing Hudson's elbow. Another skittered across his lap. I flinched backward, then tried to pretend I'd been reaching to scratch my back. This conversation was making Hudson . . . not nervous—that would have involved sea creatures—but tense, maybe irritated.

"My parents own horses," Hudson said after the silence had grown uncomfortable. "Milo works for them."

"Really?" I'd ridden horses a few times as a child, and I'd loved it. "What type?"

"Thoroughbreds."

"Racehorses?"

"Yep."

"That's so cool!"

"Not really."

Milo's simple divination of reins in his hands changed to a golden glow of light that shot from him, embraced Hudson, then slapped him. The marble cherub burst into existence between me and Hudson's back. Looking through the apparition was like viewing Hudson through soft stained glass. The lines of his indistinct body wavered with each pulse of the cherub's wings. I swallowed to loosen the queasy constriction of my throat, turning to look out the side window. I wanted to press for more information on his family and their racehorses—something that hadn't come up yesterday over dinner—but Hudson's body and voice had gotten tight, and lightning crackled faster around him. For whatever reason, he didn't want to talk about his family. I smothered my curiosity and spent the remainder of the drive concentrating on crushing my curse.

Annabella's and Sofie's houses fit into a lot of the same categories: both were located in Santa Monica, both had views of the ocean, and both were expensive. But Annabella's was the insecure image-obsessed version of Sofie's house. My mother's mansion poised over the driveway for a desperate, look-at-me first impression. The architect had confused *avant-garde* with *sharp*: Square windows and bony triangular columns faced the driveway, and the featureless backyard housed a rectangular pool defined by a grid work of square flagstones. With its canvas-colored stucco siding, the house had all the appeal and individuality of an emaciated runway model who had traded away her humanity in a quest to look like a mannequin.

The entire property looked as untouched as the day my mother purchased it. She hadn't added an ounce of her personality, and she'd made sure her landscapers didn't add their own style, either. The lawn was clipped to golf-course-regulation heights with a similar cross pattern, and the only trees were palm trees—just like every other home in this neighborhood.

"Are you sure your friend's going to be okay with this?" Hudson asked, staring at the spotless floor-to-ceiling glass walls along the back side of the house.

"She'll love it." I finished my lap around the lawn, making sure it hid nothing dangerous to Kyoko.

Milo tapped a blunt finger on the glass enclosing the dining room. A teapot sprang to life next to him. At least, I thought it was a teapot. It had a handle and a spout, but the middle part looked like a small, round house with a sod roof.

Dali flew out of the trailer when we opened it, danced around our legs, then tore off to explore Annabella's backyard. Kyoko bugled and trotted after him. Her attention snagged on the pool, and in less than two minutes, Dali and Kyoko were soaked. Milo jogged back to the truck and left. Hudson and I fled to the safe, dry vantage of the white-on-white living room. Since I didn't want to explain my petty reaction,

I gallantly suppressed my urge to giggle while savoring the casual destruction of Annabella's pristine yard.

"I canceled the landscaping services this week," Sofie said as I helped her unload groceries from her car. "We should be secure and visitor-free until you locate Kyoko's rightful caretaker." The Fabergé egg on her head now supported a tiny elephant ballerina. The egg appeared as one of Sofie's apparitions for Annabella. I was pretty sure the ballerina—usually human—on top represented the fragility of Sofie's relationship with her sister. From what Nana Nevie had let slip, Sofie and Annabella had been a lot closer before my birth. I'd stopped feeling guilty years ago about the rift my existence had torn between the sisters. That was Annabella's burden.

Even though this latest apparition indicated Sofie worried about Annabella's reaction to Kyoko's impromptu visit, I couldn't bring myself to feel guilty today, either. Honoring our rule—or hiding behind it—I didn't say anything about the divination. Sofie wisely said nothing about the emotions that walking through Annabella's house had stirred in me.

"I'll have Ari call you the moment we know something," I said.

———

THE RIDE back to Mid-Wilshire was uneventful. I spent it looking out the window of our taxi and envisioning what the wind flowing past the cars on the freeway looked like. The visualization served as mental white noise and prevented me from dwelling on the tornado of emotions associated with Annabella or on my growing anxiety about Kyoko. The taxi dropped us off at a mechanic's shop. I walked across the street to pick up sandwiches from a local café while Hudson talked with his mechanic. The blue coveralls said his name was Mike. I would have called him Sherlock, because according to his divinations, he'd stepped from the pages of Sir Arthur Conan Doyle's books, complete with the funny cap, century-old gentleman's smoking jacket, and pipe. The outfit might have looked good except for Mike's shaggy surfer hair tied back in a ponytail.

"There can't be nothing wrong," Hudson said. "It completely stopped working this morning. They had to winch it onto the truck."

"She must have been feeling temperamental," Mike said. An insubstantial Wookiee walked behind the mechanic and stuck his tongue out at Mike's back. Hudson's shoulders slumped.

"That damn beast *is* cursed. What do I owe you?"

"Nothing. All I did was take her for a spin. In fact, I should owe you. That car got me a date for Friday night."

Hudson circled the block in his car before he let me get in. When I did, he said, "We're driving straight to Jenny's parents'. No stops, no sidetracking. I don't care if we have a tail."

Finally.

Jenny's parents lived in a suburban sprawl in Encino. The houses were a hodgepodge of styles, the yards were meticulously maintained, and the driveways were filled with midsize commuter cars and minivans.

Harvey and Selah Winters were a mismatched couple. Harvey looked like he belonged in a beatnik club, drinking a rum and Coke and talking philosophy, not working in management at Costco like Hudson had told me. Selah had a put-together air of a woman in charge. Her cream-colored dress complemented her plump, short figure and contrasted with her ebony skin. With stylish gray hair and high cheekbones, she looked a decade younger than her husband.

They were expecting us, thanks to Hudson.

"Doing a piece on our girl for the high school alumni paper?" Harvey asked. "You won't find a more accomplished graduate."

"We always knew Jenny was going to do something big," I said. I sat on a floral-print sofa with Hudson. Harvey and Selah took the chairs opposite us. Hudson had prepared me for our cover story during the drive, and to make myself look authentic, I pulled out my notebook and a pen and poised myself to take notes.

"We'd really love to interview Jenny," Hudson said, "but we couldn't find her current location or even a phone number for her."

"Oh, that's because she's not stateside," Selah said. "We just got through explaining that to the FBI. Everyone wants to chat with our little girl lately."

"The FBI?" Hudson asked. I was very conscious of not looking at Hudson. What did the FBI know about Jenny and the elephantini she'd foisted on us?

"Jenny's a brilliant girl. A lot of people are interested in her talents," Harvey said. "But we'll tell you the same thing we told them: Jenny's in Japan. Snatched up by Adorable Creations straight out of college. She was headhunted. A couple of companies vied for her. One was American, based here in LA, but AC offered her more opportunity, so off she went. She's been there ever since."

"Except Christmases," Selah said. She lifted the platter of cookies from the coffee table between us and wouldn't set it down until we each took one. "She always makes a point of coming home for the holiday. She's so busy, you know. She's the director of the lab, or the title equivalent. If she takes too long off, the place falls to pieces."

"What exactly does she do?" I asked.

"Nothing we normal people understand," Selah said, and Harvey chuckled. "Once she gets talking about DNA, my eyes glaze over. It's not that I don't care; it just turns to gibberish in my ears."

"She works in genetics?" Hudson prompted.

"She tinkers with the fundamentals of biological structure—her words. Her work is important," Harvey said.

"Jenny always did love anything that required a microscope," Selah said.

"Our combined DNA is definitely more than the sum of its parts in that girl." Harvey and Selah shared a grin; this was a story they told often and with pride.

"If she came back to the States, do you know where she'd stay?" I asked.

"Right here. We haven't made any changes to her room."

"What about with a friend?"

For the first time, Selah lost her smile. "She's never had time to make friends. Jenny's so driven. First her studies; now her job. But that can't last forever. Eventually she'll find someone who will slow her down, help her see there's life outside a lab." A yellow diamond-shaped sign with "Baby on Board" popped into existence, hanging from a thick cord around Selah's neck.

"Eh, she's got plenty of time for all that," Harvey said, waving away his wife's concern. "She's in her career prime, making discoveries and rising through the ranks. She can make nice with strangers later." As if summoned by his wife's divination, a neon-pink Hello Kitty sign glowed in the air above Harvey.

"Do you have a number where we could reach her?" Hudson asked.

While Selah went to the kitchen to get her address book, I excused myself to go to the restroom. Instead, I took a quick peek through the house. The ranch-style, single-story home featured three bedrooms and two bathrooms. Every room was neat, like they'd been expecting an inspection. Even Jenny's preserved room looked more like a guest room than a teenager's leftovers. I learned their travel bagua needed a complete overhaul, but if Jenny was hiding in their home, she hadn't left a trace, and their pristine backyard had never housed an animal larger than a squirrel.

We left with a list of Jenny's papers and publications, her Japanese phone number, her cell phone number, and a cookie each for the road.

"I don't think they know Jenny is in LA, do you?" I asked Hudson once we were in the car.

"No."

"What do you think the FBI wanted?"

"I'd rather know how much they know."

"Do you think they suspect Jenny has an elephantini, whatever that is?"

"It's a good possibility."

Neither of us mentioned the possibility of the FBI having added us to their list of suspects in Jenny's crime. Jenny's paranoid warning to not trust the government rang in my ears. If the FBI were involved and determined I was a culprit, I might not have a choice.

"Well, that got us nowhere," Hudson said.

I nodded. Other than having a new concern to add to the pile, we'd learned nothing new. Hudson and Ari had found out more about Jenny through the Internet than her parents seemed to know. My only consolation to the otherwise wasted trip was the time we'd spent inside had given Hudson's car time to recoup.

When we checked in with Ari, she had nothing new to add, either.

"Her parents were right: Jenny doesn't have any friends, at least not from high school, and none that I could find from college. No wonder she's going around stealing elephants and dumping them on virtual strangers."

I insisted on walking home from Ari's. Hudson's car needed another break from me, and I'd take the meager pick-me-up of minimal exercise to counteract my growing dismay. We'd run into a wall. Jenny could be anywhere in LA—in the world—and everyone I cared about remained embroiled in her criminal scheme. We needed a lead.

"I'll go by my office later and see if I can't dig anything else up on Jenny," Hudson said, his thoughts in sync with mine. "Maybe her cell phone will give us some information, like her location."

I tried to take heart. He and Ari had pulled more information out of less already.

"For a woman afraid of elevators, I think it's odd that you picked the top floor," Hudson said, breathing heavily, when we reached my loft.

"Keeps me fit." I rummaged for my keys.

"That it does."

His tone made me look up. His gaze had gone smoldering and he stood close. My left hand closed on my keys, but I didn't pull them out. I reached for Hudson's shirt with my right hand and pulled him against me. Looking up at him through my lashes, I slowly wet my lips. He pounced before my tongue was back in my mouth.

Hudson walked me backward into the door, his kiss igniting embers I'd held banked all day. His hands slid up my sides, sculpting my body's curves. I arched into him, pushing against him to enjoy the firm planes of his body.

Vaguely, I remembered the keys and pulled them free. Hudson

lifted his head when he heard the jangle, then snatched the keys from my grip.

"The brass one," I said.

Hudson fumbled to get the key in the lock while kissing a hot path down my neck. I moaned, savoring the anticipation. With my hands free, I explored his chest, then slid lower to grab his ass. The door swung open, and we staggered into my loft. Hudson kicked the door shut behind us, slid my satchel from my shoulder to the floor, and reached for my shirt.

I stumbled backward, toward the living room, pulling Hudson with me by the waistband of his pants. Hudson tugged my shirt over my head and tossed it aside, then yanked me tight against him for a breathtaking kiss.

The backs of my legs slammed into something.

"Umph."

I twisted to see what it was. A chair, the green one from the front room, lay on its side in the middle of the hallway. I stared at it, trying to process the fact that an inanimate object had moved while I'd been gone.

"Oh shit," Hudson whispered.

I looked up. From the hallway, only a sliver of the front room was visible. The potted plant at the end of the hall lay in a smashed heap on the hardwood; glass shards splintered across the area rug beyond it. My upside-down couch canted against the fireplace, tufts of foam pinned beneath ripped armrests.

Ice sluiced through my veins and the blood drained from my head. "Wha—"

Hudson clamped a hand over my mouth. "Burglar," he whispered. "Could still be here."

# TWELVE

HUDSON GRABBED my shirt from the floor and tossed it to me, holding his index finger to his lips. I was rooted in place. My home, my sanctuary, had been violated.

Wrapping an arm around me, Hudson propelled me to the door. On autopilot, I grabbed my satchel. Hudson eased the door shut behind us.

"Do you know your neighbors?" he asked.

I pointed two doors down. He pulled me to Jed's door and pounded on it. I stared at my shirt.

"Unless you want to give your neighbor a show, you might want to put that on," Hudson said.

"Won't matter. Jed's gay."

"Hey." Hudson tilted my face with his hands until I stared into his eyes. "Snap out of it. I need you here."

I blinked. The door opened and I jumped behind Hudson and stuffed my arms into my shirt, yanking it down.

"Look here—" Jed started.

"Jed, someone broke into my apartment," I said.

"Eva?" Jed blinked at me, then turned a steely gaze back to Hudson.

"Call 911," Hudson said.

Jed stuck his head into the hallway and peered toward my apartment. "Are they gone?"

"I don't know."

Jed grabbed both our arms and yanked us into his apartment. Troy rushed toward us, phone in hand, looking like an avenging Latin god: thick black hair slicked back, five o'clock shadow darkening his jaw, and topless, his nut brown skin and defined abs glistening with sweat.

"I heard," Troy said. He turned his attention to the cordless phone. "Yes, I need to report a break-in."

"Are you okay?" Jed asked me, pulling me deeper into the loft and sitting me on their couch. I went willingly; I needed to get as far from the phone as possible. "You're looking a little . . . askew."

"I'm fine." I glanced down at myself. My shirt was on backward. Fighting a losing battle against a blush, I pulled my arms into the sleeves of my shirt and turned it face forward.

"You should tell your man his pants are undone," Jed said.

I whirled toward Hudson. He paced in front of Troy, who was still on the line with the 911 operator. The top button of his jeans was undone, and the zipper had slid down far enough to show the waistband of his underwear. Blue today. He'd changed them when he'd gone on his donut run a lifetime ago.

As if he felt the weight of my stare, Hudson glanced my way, then turned his back to the room and buttoned and zipped his pants.

"I love the honeymoon phase," Jed said, his eyes on Troy.

The wait for the police was interminable. It took them twelve minutes, but I spiraled through a year's worth of nightmares, all beginning and ending with Jenny. When the police arrived, they wouldn't let us into the hallway until they verified my home was unoccupied.

"The burglars must have knocked out the electricity for this floor," Troy said, gesturing to the dark bulb overhead. Nothing happened when he flicked a light switch.

"Odd," I said. I paced the entryway, listening to the cops on their radios through the door. My feeble attempt to reinstate my normal barriers couldn't counter the fear riding my thoughts.

I had my eye pressed to the peephole when the policeman gave the all clear, and I yanked the door open before his fist could make contact.

"Are you Eva Parker?" he asked. I nodded. "I'm Officer Bae. This is Officer Teague." Caucasian and tall, Bae had sandy brown hair and a baby face. Teague was shorter, Asian, and bored. He tipped his head toward me, got a nod from Bae, and walked off toward the stairs. A calculator sat on his shoulder, spewing a stream of ticker tape that undulated up his leg like a boa constrictor.

"Was there anyone inside?" Hudson asked, coming up behind me.

"And you are?"

"Hudson Keyes. Eva's boyfriend."

"Do you both reside here?"

"No, just me, Officer," I said.

Bae shifted his stance, hooking his thumbs into his belt. An enormous reporter's camera popped into existence beside him, the lens focused on Bae's face. "The perpetrators are long gone."

I tried to step into the hallway, but Bae didn't move.

"I'm sorry to tell you, ma'am, but they got all of your electronics."

"No. I—" I clamped my mouth shut. I couldn't tell my usual lies that my electronics were loaned to friends or being repaired to a police officer. Even if I wanted to, I had to match what I'd told Hudson earlier. Flustered, I tried to recall our conversation, but I kept seeing the trashed sliver of my home visible from the entrance, and all other thoughts slid away.

Bae took my hesitation as shock. "Your TVs, your computer, everything. You'll need to file a report—"

"I didn't have any," I said, thoughts scrambling.

"No computer?"

"It's in the shop," Hudson said. *That's right.*

"Your TVs?"

"I didn't have any."

"Not even one?"

"No."

"Microwave?"

I shook my head.

"Did you just move in?"

"She's a feng shui consultant," Hudson said.

Bae narrowed his eyes at me. The camera by his shoulder shifted to point at me.

"Maybe you should walk me through the place and tell me what's been taken."

Bae wouldn't let Hudson accompany us. I walked through my emotional minefield alone. The couch—the first piece of furniture I'd ever purchased—lay in shreds. My favorite reading chair had been ripped apart. Glass and ceramic shards littered the floor, remnants of art and framed memories. The middle three shelves of all four bookcases had been swept to the floor. Book spines were broken, pages ripped. Glass coated every surface.

My office suffered the brunt of the assault. The filing cabinets had been emptied across the floor, my desk overturned, my calendar torn to pieces. I stood on the threshold, hand to my mouth, and tried to hold in my tears.

"Do you see anything missing?" Bae asked.

I shook my head. It was impossible to tell. They could have taken some paperwork, a book, a picture. I wouldn't know until I'd gone through everything.

I reached to pick up the nearest piece of paper.

"Not yet," Bae said. His hand was firm on my arm. "Let's check upstairs."

I wanted to say no.

Clothes scattered down the stairs; more lay in clumps across my bedroom floor. I sidestepped the mess and opened the middle drawer of my dresser. Half the shirts had been torn out. I shoved the rest aside and stared at the back of a framed painting. I didn't flip it over. I didn't need to. It was an original early S. Sterling colored pencil drawing titled *James Parker*. The handsome teenage man with pale blond hair and a cleft chin in the portrait was crowded by overlapping images: a beagle puppy; a faded tan minivan with dark, foggy windows hinting at naked forms in the backseat; two butterflies with footballs for spots; a silver lasso; an NES video game controller; and a swath of starry night sky. My father, as Sofie had seen him twenty-six years ago. She'd given me the drawing on my eighteenth birthday. I'd buried it in my dresser the same day.

"Something missing?" Bae asked, and I jumped.

"No."

I uncurled my fist and slammed the drawer, mentally and physically, on James Parker; I had enough to deal with today. I stood at the corner of my loft and stared down at the destruction below. A hurricane in my apartment could not have caused more damage. I brushed a tear from my cheek.

A short, black woman walked into the living room, a bag clutched in one hand. "Bae? Are you in here?" she called.

"Up here." Bae trotted down the stairs, avoiding most of my clothing. "Why didn't you call up?"

"I did. Did you turn your radio off?"

Bae fiddled with the buttons on the tiny piece of electronics, looking puzzled.

I trudged after Bae. He introduced me to Officer Plunket, a one-woman crime-scene-evidence collector. She had thigh-high dominatrix boots on over her work uniform, complete with four-inch spike heels. I figured those weren't regulation boots and must be an apparition, as was the sleek panther stalking across my front room and the herd of Beanie Babies frolicking in the air between us, and shock made it easy to ignore them. At least Bae's camera had turned its lens away from me. It now focused squarely on Plunket's breasts, shooting from straight above and up close. When she pulled out her fingerprint dust, Bae motioned me toward the hallway. The camera followed us with blatant reluctance.

Hudson pulled me into his arms the moment I crossed the threshold. Jellyfish bobbed around us like live naval mines, swaying close on invisible currents. I shivered as a handful guttered through me, their poisonous eidolon stings impotent.

"Are you okay?" he asked. I shook my head.

"Can you think why anyone would want to do this?" Bae asked.

"No." I pulled free of Hudson's arms and faced the cop and his camera, ignoring the membranous horde. Only one thing had changed recently in my life, and though I'd thought about nothing else since Troy called 911, I couldn't find a connection between the destruction of my apartment and Kyoko. Even if I had, I wouldn't have said anything. I couldn't. Bae, a hardened cop, treated me with open suspicion simply because I didn't own a TV. If he knew about my curse—if anyone found out—he and everyone else would treat me like a walking plague.

I rallied my thoughts, thankful for a lifetime of lies to prompt me. "I would have told you I don't have any enemies, but . . ."

Bae studied me, then Hudson. The camera zoomed on my face. Bae's lips tightened and he narrowed his eyes at me.

"It looks like someone is trying to send you a message. Whatever you're mixed up in, I suggest you get out of it."

"I'm not—"

"This wasn't random. No one picks a penthouse loft in a building with camera security for a crime of opportunity."

"About those cameras," Hudson began.

"We'll let you know if they show us anything useful," Bae said. "But it would be helpful if we weren't working in the dark."

I didn't like his accusation, but I had to admit he had a point. When Bae excused himself to question neighbors, I spun through possible scenarios again, my mind latching on to the most unlikely connections. Like between Sofie's art being stolen and this break-in. Were those connected? Or was this the work of Atlas and Edmond? They'd said they were Jenny's cousins and working for her, but could that have been a ruse? Were they looking for information about Kyoko's whereabouts?

"Do you think it was the mysterious skip tracer?" Hudson asked.

"I don't know. Why destroy my apartment? I obviously wouldn't have Kyoko in there."

"Like the cop said, he could have been sending a message."

"If he is, I don't get it."

"'Help Jenny and I'll destroy your life'?" Hudson suggested.

I wrapped my arms around my stomach and said nothing.

It took an hour for Plunket to dust for fingerprints. She took samples of mine and Hudson's for reference, then packed up and left. Bae waited on the scene until she finished. None of my neighbors had heard anything or seen anyone suspicious.

The numbness was fading, and my fear had long since waned. Only anger was left. After the officers departed, I stomped into my apartment, grabbed the chair in the entryway, and dragged it back to the front room.

"What are you doing?" Hudson asked, trailing after me, Jed and Troy following.

"Cleaning up. Those bastards did a number on my feng shui, and I'm not leaving it like this."

"Oh, Eva!" Jed exclaimed, halting at the edge of my living room. "Is it all like this?"

"Every room."

Troy swept me into a tight hug. He'd put a shirt on at some point, and he smelled like he'd showered, too. "I'm so glad you weren't here when they did this," Troy said, not releasing me. "You could have been hurt."

"But I wasn't. I'm fine. Except for air. I need air, Troy."

Hudson returned from my office, his hands in fists. He marched upstairs. Jed followed, picking up the strewn contents of my closet as he went.

Ari arrived in a breathless rush, took one look at my loft, and pulled me into a tight hug. "Jed called. I ran the whole way." She brushed tears from my cheeks with gentle fingers. "I'm so sorry, Eva." She didn't ask if I was okay. She marched to the laundry room and returned with a broom and large plastic bags.

"Thank you," I said. I took the broom and swept piles of glass. Ari pulled her hair back into a ponytail and helped Troy straighten heavy furniture. My couch was ruined, and we bagged the destroyed cushions to take down to the Dumpster. Most of my photographs were salvageable, but only one frame survived. I cleaned methodically, anger draining with each sweep of the broom. The vases on the mantel, the ceramic lamp base, and the glass fixtures over every light and lamp all mixed together in jagged shards. Only two kitchen fixtures had been left unbroken, and until Antonio could verify the gas lines to the other lights hadn't been damaged, I didn't risk turning on any other lights.

"Come on, Eva, let's finish in the morning," Hudson said, placing his hand on my arm. I had the feeling he'd repeated himself and I hadn't noticed.

I glanced up. Daylight had bled away. Behind Hudson, Jed, Troy, and Ari waited, watching me.

"I can't leave my home like this." The negative feng shui would give me nightmares.

"We can't do much more tonight. We need to get food and rest. We'll come back tomorrow refreshed. It'll all look—"

"Don't you dare say 'better.'"

"Manageable tomorrow," Hudson finished. A round yellow disk with a piece missing from it, like a flat wheel of cheese, skimmed down Hudson's stomach. No, not cheese. The missing piece opened and closed like a mouth. *Pac-Man? What does Pac-Man have to do with anything?*

"You can stay with us tonight," Jed said. "Our spare bedroom seldom gets used—"

"Eva can stay with me." Hudson's tone made it sound like an order. Behind Hudson's back, Jed raised his eyebrows at me in silent question.

I closed my eyes. Hudson proposed disaster. If I slept at his place, not a single drop of electricity would survive. One morning waking up to a localized power outage was bizarre. The second time could be laughed off as a strange coincidence. The third time ended the relationship. I'd made superstitious men of four lovers before I'd given up alternating sleeping arrangements. Now, all men stayed with me, in a hotel, or not at all.

"You should stay with me," Ari said.

"No," Hudson said. "Eva, I want you where I know you're safe."

"You think staying at Ari's would be dangerous?" I met Ari's worried eyes.

"I think Antonio is dangerous."

My lips twitched, trying to remember how to smile.

"Don't be silly, Hudson," Ari protested. She couldn't see the tarnished broadsword hanging from Hudson's back.

My white knight had no clue he was inviting the curse into his home.

"Is Antonio home tonight?" I asked Ari.

"Yep."

"Good." I didn't want her staying alone tonight. On the slim chance the burglars spread their search to my contacts, Ari would be their next victim. I grimaced. I should never have called Ari from Jenny's abandoned house. I should never have told her about Kyoko. I'd dragged her far enough into my mess. "You'll call Sofie for me? Make sure she knows I'm okay?"

"Of course."

I turned to Hudson. "You're sure?"

"It's the only way I'm getting sleep tonight."

I packed a small duffel with clothing that looked the least touched by strangers; it gave me the willies to think of people pawing through my clothes. I added my bathroom supplies and hefted the bag. I didn't own travel-size anything, and with the weight of a full bottle of shampoo and conditioner, my face creams, and my hair product, it felt like I'd packed for a monthlong stay. Fortunately, Hudson didn't say a word about the bag's weight when he took it from me.

I locked the door behind me—a useless gesture that gave me no comfort. As we trudged down the stairs, my home's destroyed feng shui settled over me in a black cloud of bad luck.

*Doom,* my mind supplied. *This is what doom feels like.*

The evening air swirled around me, crisp and fresh, and it pushed aside some of my gloom. No one spoke on the walk back to Ari's. She gave me a lung-squeezing hug when we reached her porch. Hudson and I waited until she locked the dead bolt behind herself before we circled the block to Hudson's car.

Meditation failed me. I cataloged the broken items in my home, the memories attached to each item, and the price. The list depressed me, but I couldn't make myself stop adding to it. I'd walked away from a disaster when I should have remained. I needed to fix up my apartment. Get rid of the broken items. Clean my clothes. Straighten my office. Depression morphed to frustration the farther Hudson drove from my apartment. He was right: I couldn't do much more tonight, and it wasn't safe for me to stay in my own home. Acknowledging as much agitated the acid in my stomach, but it didn't stop me from wanting to return.

If this break-in had been about anything other than Kyoko, something would have been stolen—the art hanging on my walls, the sculptures that had been shattered, my jewelry—but nothing was missing. The burglars had been looking for something, and all signs pointed to Kyoko.

"I'm really beginning to hate Jenny," I said.

"I'm glad I'm not the only one." The car lurched and Hudson scanned the dash. It lurched again, and Hudson cussed. "Oh, no, you don't. Mike said you were fine. You *were* fine. Come on, baby. Not here." The car sputtered and the door locks buzzed. We decelerated, and the engine quieted. "Oh, come on!" Hudson shouted.

He steered the car to the curb with the last of its momentum, then set the emergency brake. We were on a dark side street. Two blocks in front of us, a major street bisected ours, and cars zipped by, mocking us.

"How much farther to your house?" I asked.

"I'm cursed." Hudson gripped the steering wheel with knuckles gone white. "The gods are pointing and laughing, and I'm the butt of their jokes. I should have guessed this would happen. I mean, why would something go my way? I can't get a cell phone that works. I can't get a car that works. It's a goddamn elephant curse. 'Here, look after this,' Jenny says. 'Oh, what is it?' 'It's the bane of all things good. I know it looks like a baby elephant, but it's evil incarnate—'"

He swung out of the car and slammed the door, cutting off his rant. A giant red wagon followed him, large enough for him to lie in. I watched him through the windshield until he lifted the hood. Sighing, I got out and shuffled to stand beside him.

"Know anything about engines?" Hudson asked.

I shook my head. *Only how to break them.*

"I know enough to know there's nothing wrong. Just like Mike said. Everything's fine. The fuses are fine; the hoses are fine. The oil and gas and fluids are fine. It must be me and this voodoo curse I've picked up. First the truck, then the Suburban, then my bike, and now my car? That elephant is a walking, breathing hunk of bad luck."

I hunched my shoulders. Hudson was a good man. He'd been supportive. He'd set his life aside to help me. He was a true gentleman. He didn't deserve to have his life dismantled by my curse. And taking me home would only feed his growing paranoia and aggravation.

"I'm sorry, Hudson. This is—"

A dark, windowless van barreled down the empty road and whipped in front of the car. The back doors snapped open, and two dark figures leapt out. They were slender and moved like gravity didn't exist beneath their feet. Both wore black—solid, unrelieved black—with ski masks covering everything but their eyes. The one on the left sprouted a hissing cobra head shimmering over his masked face. The one on the right protruded spikes like a puffer fish.

I was running before I told my feet to move. I made it two steps, then something slammed into my back and I crashed to the sidewalk. I pushed up immediately, but a sharp kick knocked my right arm askew, and I face-planted again. The weight of a small pony pounded into my kidney, and all the air burst from my lungs. Black spots danced in my vision, and when I could breathe again, my arms were pinned behind my back. The weight lifted and I sagged against the bonds. Zip ties—handcuffs by another name.

"Up."

The command came with a sharp toe to my ribs. I groaned and rolled, pulling my knees toward my chest. Two pairs of hands grabbed my arms and yanked me to my feet.

"Who are you?" I wheezed. "What do you want?"

"No talking."

The voice identified my assailant as a woman. She pushed me, and I stumbled a step forward.

"I'm not going anywh—"

I didn't see the punch that caved in my solar plexus. I doubled over, gasping for air around a knot of fiery pain. My eyes watered, and I blinked away the tears.

A barrage of cussing pinpointed Hudson. With my next prodded step, I saw him. He was sprawled facedown above an enormous abyss, hands secured in zip ties. A black-clad, snake-headed figure stood with one foot on his neck. Blood ran down his forehead.

"Let him go!"

Heavy cloth covered my face, then a drawstring cut into my neck. My head was in a bag. I screamed and tried to run. A thick bar slammed into my midriff, knocking me back a step. Hands shoved me from behind, pushing me into the bar. I folded forward on a waist-high surface. The van. I was being shoved into the van. I flopped like a fish and kicked out. Pain chopped into my calf, and my right leg went numb from knee to toe. Rough hands slid me forward. I flailed with my left leg, but all I hit was air and the van.

Hudson's cussing and yelling abruptly cut off to a wheeze. The van rocked. Something clubbed my thigh, and I cried out.

"Eva! Eva, are you there?"

"Hudson, don't—"

Pain pounded into my stomach and cut off my air supply. I gasped and curled into a ball. The back doors slammed shut. The van rocked again, the engine revved, and the van gunned into motion.

I'd been kidnapped. For real.

# THIRTEEN

I WAS SUFFOCATING. The bag clung to my mouth and nostrils, sucking flat against them with every gasp. The world diminished to my burning lungs and thundering heartbeat. Even those receded, distant. I disconnected from my body, drifting from the pain.

I was losing consciousness.

Panic flared. The bag sucked into my mouth, choking me. Unconscious, I would be helpless. I had to keep it together. In slow degrees, I calmed my breathing, forcing myself to hold each inhale a count of two, then four before releasing it. Air pulled more easily through the weave of the bag with steadier breaths.

I could hear the road beneath me now, the engine above my head. Hudson groaned. In the cab, three female voices conversed in short, terse phrases in a language I didn't know.

In the midst of congratulating myself on using my years of practice to overpower my emotions, it occurred to me I'd neutralized my one advantage: my curse.

We needed out of this van. Now. Reaching our destination would be bad. My thoughts skittered away from defining *bad*. If I could kill the van, it would buy us time. Maybe the police would investigate the broken-down vehicle.

Maybe the women would move up their plans.

Hyperventilation tightened the bag around my face. I wheezed, fighting to relax. Panic might kill the van, but it wouldn't help me. If only Hudson hadn't insisted on leaving my loft—

My loft.

Were these women responsible? I could picture them going through my place, destroying my belongings. Anger sparked. I could use anger. I had mountains of anger, volcanoes of anger, all thanks to Jenny.

I focused on my rage at being blackmailed into this horrid, terrifying situation. I pictured Jenny and fanned my fury, then pushed it out from my body. In my mind, I wrapped it around the van's engine and suffocated it.

My limbs twitched with jittery energy. My head pounded.

The van coughed and sputtered. Rapid-fire dialogue pelted between the women, the van coasted in silence, then rocked to a stop. The cab's doors opened and closed. I listened hard, but I couldn't tell if we were alone.

"Hudson," I hissed.

"Are you okay?" he asked.

"I have a bag over my head. Can you see anything?"

"Nothing. Can you move?"

"A little."

After a few muted thumps, Hudson said, "Roll over here." New distance muffled his words. "Try to get your hood near my hands. Maybe I can take it off."

I scrabbled on the cold metal floorboard, scrunching my knees to my chest to shrink my body in half. I knocked my head on a hard rod.

"Almost there. That's my forearm. A little lower."

I wriggled tighter in a ball. My calf spasmed in a charley horse and I bit my lip to keep from crying out. Any second now, the back doors would burst open and the women would pull us apart. I didn't have time to baby my throbbing leg.

Voices rose outside the van. I couldn't tell what they were saying, but they were male voices, not female. My heart lurched with hope.

*Let it be cops.* Hudson must have had the same thought, because we both started yelling and kicking at the same time.

The van rocked with our movements and our shouts echoed in the interior. A gunshot report, loud and distinct, cut through our racket. In unison, we froze. A second shot shattered the silence.

"That doesn't sound like the police," I said.

"Shh."

It was a bit late for that.

I strained to listen past the ringing in my ears. The yelling had stopped. "Quick, get this off me," I said. I wriggled back toward Hudson and stretched to align my neck and the bag's drawstring with his bound hands.

The back door of the van clicked open.

"Shit, man."

"Eva?" a second male voice asked.

I stilled, trying to place the voice. "Atlas?"

"Hang on."

The van sagged under someone's weight; then the drawstring tugged against my neck before loosening. Atlas yanked the bag off my head, taking a hunk of hair with it. I sucked in clean, crisp air and stared up into the eyes of my first kidnapper. Fanned out behind him were enormous gold-plated wings stretching beyond the van's walls.

"Are you okay?" Edmond asked. He stood at the back door, his bulk filling the opening. Floating against the palm of the hand holding the van door open hung an enormous wire whisk with a green duck for a handle. Circling his girth like a bizarre construction worker's tool belt were rolling pins and spatulas and pizza cutters and zesters.

"Get this off me," Hudson demanded. Atlas eased around me and removed Hudson's sack.

"Was that the retrievalist?" I asked.

"Nope. Those were ninjas," Edmond said. "Come on. Let's get out of here before someone calls the cops."

"I'm not going anywhere with you. Not until my hands are free."

"I don't know," Edmond said to Atlas. "She might still be holding a grudge."

"Ed, Jenny said—"

"You guys know Jenny?" Hudson demanded. He sat up in the same awkward listing, bent-knee position I huddled in. "You're the scum who kidnapped Eva yesterday? What the fu—"

"Scum?" Atlas's wings swelled and grew spikes. "You better watch your mouth, scrawny. We just rescued your ass. We can leave your ass here, too."

"Out. I want out. *Now!*" I wormed toward Edmond and kicked out. He jumped back with surprising nimbleness. I launched to my feet, then fell straight into Edmond's colossal chest when my legs collapsed.

"Easy, there," he murmured. He didn't seem to know where to hold me since my arms were pinned behind me. He settled on my shoulders, arms bent so he didn't make accidental contact with my breasts. I dropped my head forward and fought off tears. My legs hurt, my stomach hurt, my arms and shoulders and hands and wrists hurt. I'd gotten a good look around, and there was no one else nearby. No police in sight, no Good Samaritan. Just two kidnappers rescuing me from three ninjas.

"Where did they go?" I asked. I got my feet working and stepped to the side so Hudson could get out of the van.

"They ran. That way." Edmond pointed. We were close to a freeway, and the blocks were long and vacant.

"Which of you has the gun?" Hudson asked.

"That'd be me. Gangsta Boy Scout," Atlas said. "And for the lady..." He hopped from the van and brandished a hand. With a click, a blade protruded past his fingers.

"Whoa, hang on," I said.

"Turn around," Atlas said.

"No."

He blinked at me, then turned to Edmond and punched him hard in the arm. "I told you we scared her yesterday. We were only supposed to deliver a message, and you terrified her with the grab-and-go. The handcuffs were too much. Look, she doesn't trust us at all." He turned back to me. "Do we look like the kind of men who would hurt a woman?"

"Yes."

A black vortex materialized behind Edmond's linebacker shoulders, sucking his chef's tool belt and whisk into its depths, warping reality around its edges. I took a step back.

"I'm sorry, Eva," Edmond said. "I didn't mean to scare you."

Hudson gave me a level look, then turned his back to Atlas. "Cut these off me," he said. Hudson's shiny metal top hat half swallowed his head, supported in the front by empty black-rimmed glasses. Lobsters swarmed over his feet, disappeared, and returned in Day-Glo colors. The hint of a woman's face floated behind him, and the red wagon appeared with locomotive wheels. I looked away. After sucking up the electricity of two vehicles, the apparitions threatened to overwhelm me.

Atlas sawed through the zip tie with his knife. I felt foolish when I realized that had been his intent with me. When he'd freed Hudson, I turned to give Atlas my back. I held rigid, visions of the sharp blade slipping and slicing me open. When the zip tie fell to the ground, I rubbed my wrists. At this rate, the handcuff bruises were never going to heal.

I stepped away from Atlas and turned to put the cousins in my line of sight again. "Where are we?"

"That's the 405. We're near West Olympic."

"Shit," Hudson said for both of us.

I didn't know the bus routes here, and I guessed we were too far from Hudson's place to walk. I glanced up and down the street. Somewhere out there were three crazed ninja women. I didn't relish the idea of walking these deserted streets looking for a taxi with them lurking about.

"How did you find us?" I asked. "How do we know you aren't working with the ninjas?"

"Like I told you, we're following you. Jenny's orders. To keep you safe."

"Safe? Where were you when they stuffed us in there?"

"There was traffic," Edmond mumbled.

"You're a really hard person to track," Atlas said. "We lost you completely today. Had to wait around at your place for you to return. Man, I don't know who you are," Atlas said to Hudson, "but you drive like Jason Bourne. I had you this morning until you took that left on South Robertson. Then you disappeared, like, *poof*."

"I don't like this," Edmond said. "We shouldn't hang out here."

"Give me a cell phone," Hudson said, holding out his hand. "I'm calling the cops."

"No can do. That's not a good— Damn it, Ed, what'd you do that for?"

Hudson snatched Edmond's phone from his hand and pressed a button. The screen lit up, then dimmed to black. Hudson jabbed the phone a few more times. The stone cherub appeared, looming large enough to give Atlas's wings some competition. Hudson slapped the phone back into Edmond's hand.

"Hey! What'd you do to it?" Edmond prodded the flat surface. Atlas watched, then pulled out his own phone. He pressed buttons, but nothing happened. At least, not to the phone. Emotionally, his gold-plated wings turned to paper clips and cascaded to the pavement in what I decided equated to Atlas losing his savior superiority and plummeting back to the same level as us mere mortals.

"Of course," Hudson said. "Of course. Just my fucking luck. Stupid fucking elephant curse." He ran his hand through his hair, wincing when he hit the cut on his forehead, and paced in a tight circle.

"Seriously, we should go," Edmond said, eyeing the shadows—and Hudson—warily. "I don't want to be here when those ninjas come back."

For once, I agreed with him. Which was how I ended up climbing willingly into the back of my former abductors' vehicle. "I've got to be mental," I muttered.

"What was that?" Atlas asked. He scooted his seat forward a few clicks, but Hudson's knees were still squeezed to either side of the seat to fit. I squished behind Edmond, my knees propped against his canted seat, my feet dangling.

"Edmond, you better not have had any bacon today," I growled.

Edmond's eyes skittered away from mine in the rearview mirror.

"Are you okay?" Hudson asked. The marble cherub disappeared and sharks circled him, swimming through the tiny Tercel. A giant creepy fish with long, thin teeth and flat, disgusting eyes attached itself to his abdomen. I flinched and forced my gaze to Hudson's face.

"You're bleeding," I said.

Hudson dabbed at his forehead and then looked at his wet finger. "Barely." He touched the air above my nose. "Do you need a doctor?"

I assessed my body. My stomach felt bruised, the bridge of my nose raw. My hands had a rash from the sidewalk, and every muscle in my legs, arms, and back radiated abuse like I'd run a marathon without any training. But it'd take a lot more damage than this for me to consider endangering a hospital with my presence.

"No. Do you?"

Hudson shook his head.

"Where is Jenny?" I asked Atlas. "I've more than kept my end of this 'bargain.' I want out. Now—" The phantom cord of the bag tightened around my throat, cutting off my air supply. I clamped a lid on the emotions and shoved them into a padded box in my mind. I'd strand us again if I didn't get control. "I'm done, okay? She needs to take her elephant back and leave me and my family and friends alone. You tell her that for me, okay?"

"No need. You can tell her yourself."

"You know where she is?" The car's locks snapped shut in unison and the dash's lights died.

"Sure," Atlas said. "We're taking you to her now."

"We go by my car first," Hudson said.

"But—" I protested.

"My car has my keys in it and your purse. We left it with the doors wide open. Jenny can wait two minutes."

"So your car broke down, and they grabbed you, and then their car broke down? What are the odds?" Atlas said.

"Not odds. It's a curse. But at least it's not just me." Hudson sounded moderately cheered by the realization.

Hudson's car and all our belongings were untouched. The same deserted street that had made it so easy to kidnap us had also hidden the car from casual theft. I grabbed my bag from the trunk and my satchel from the backseat while Hudson tinkered under the hood and tried turning the car on. Even though it felt like hours since the ninjas attacked, it hadn't even been a half hour—far too soon to expect the car to have recovered.

I trudged to the Tercel's trunk. Fatigue, thick and cottony, cocooned me. It wasn't a physical exhaustion—aside from the panicked flailing in the ninjas' van, today had been a low-activity day for me. This had to be the emotional drain of having the contents of my home destroyed and then being kidnapped by professionals. Or it was shock. The world had receded a step, sliding a cozy blanket between me and reality.

"Open up," I said, knocking on the trunk.

Atlas whirled toward me. Golden sand dunes unfurled, sweeping over the two cars and burying Hudson and me. Atlas's skin melted, grotesquely disfiguring him. "No! Ah, no. The trunk doesn't work."

*What the hell? What is in there? No, don't think about it.* Except I couldn't not think about it, not with Atlas's terrified reaction. Was it a bomb? A body? I leaned close and sniffed. Oil. Exhaust. Dust. I rested my ear to the dirty surface and listened.

"What are you doing?" Edmond asked.

"Seeing if someone's in there." The words popped out uncensored, and I had to stifle the urge to giggle. Yep, shock. I'd run out of give-a-damn rope.

"Why would someone be in the trunk?" Edmond shuffled over, eyeing the trunk like it was going to burst open and the ninjas were going to leap out. His apparitions remained food-centered, but a stork-size needle and syringe hovered over his neck, poised to plunge into an artery.

"No one's in the trunk. The damn trunk doesn't work," Atlas said. "Remember?"

Edmond's mouth opened on a silent *"oh,"* and he visibly relaxed, the syringe disappearing and a waterfall of chocolate cascading down his chest. "Right. Don't worry, Eva. No one could have gotten in there."

I was more reassured than I should have been by his apparitions, thanks to the soft buffer of fatigue.

"Where's Jenny?" I asked Edmond.

"Hudson's house."

"What!" Hudson shot up from where he'd crouched over his engine, knocking his head on the hood. Rubbing the spot, he rounded the car and glared at Edmond. "How does she know where I live?"

Edmond shrugged.

"How do you know she's there?"

"We called her when the ninjas got you. She said she would meet us there."

"How did she know you would rescue us?" I asked.

"That's what we do," Atlas said.

"So what was the plan?" Hudson asked, rounding on Atlas. "If the van hadn't broken down, what were you going to do?"

"Pretty much the same thing. We had a gun. They had kung fu. Gun wins every time."

Hudson shook his head. The sharks still circled him, but the silver terrier stood guard at his leg now. Atlas's apparitions flickered nause-atingly, and when he mentioned the gun, a bright white halo floated above his head—false advertising, if I ever saw it.

"Let's go," Hudson said. He slammed the hood closed and locked his car; then we squeezed into the back of the Tercel again. I hugged my bag on my lap.

Edmond drove to Hudson's house without any prompting from Hudson. I clamped down on my emotions so tightly my mind numbed, but I couldn't tell if it had any effect on my curse. I'd spent more time in cars in the past three days than I had in the previous three months. I wasn't used to restraining my emotions for such long stretches, especially not under such extreme circumstances. My thoughts kept bouncing from my violated apartment to the terror of masked attackers to the panic in the back of the van, and each time a thought surfaced, I shoved it back down and replaced it with a memory of Dali playing in Sofie's yard or Chatter's crazy antics on a walk. I felt like a mental patient.

I held together pretty well until Hudson covered my hand with his. A tremor vibrated my body. The dam burst on my emotions, and I couldn't breathe through the onslaught of fear and anger and adrenaline and relief. When exhaustion swaddled me again, I welcomed it.

"We're here," he said.

I blinked. We'd parked in a minuscule driveway in front of a generic single-story house lit by a yellow porch light. Edmond and Atlas had already gotten out, and I scrambled after them.

"Where's Jenny?"

"She's inside my house, isn't she?" Hudson said. He pushed past Atlas and Edmond and marched up the short walkway. The doorknob twisted and the door opened without him unlocking it first. The sombrero topped his spiky hair, and instead of fuzzy balls hanging from the rim, tiny metal cities glinted in the porch light.

I rushed through the doorway a step behind Hudson. The lights were on in the front room, and Jenny sat on a worn sofa, a notebook open on her lap. She glanced up and smiled at me.

"Oh, good. Atlas caught up with you. I need to talk with you, Eva."

# FOURTEEN

"DO you know the *hell* we've been through because of you?" Hudson asked. He didn't raise his voice, but his neck flooded scarlet and a vein throbbed at his temple. He clenched and unclenched his hands.

The smile on Jenny's face, as if we were buddies happy to see each other, not blackmailer meeting blackmailee, sliced through the last of my cotton buffer. I'd kept my end of our fragile deal. I'd found Kyoko a hidey-hole—two, actually. I'd kept Kyoko safe; Jenny was supposed to do the same for me. She'd failed me twice in the same day.

"Please sit. I need to tell yo—"

"Sit? You want me to sit? Do you see this?" I pointed to the abrasion on my nose. "What about that?" I gestured to the blood crusted on Hudson's forehead. "We were kidnapped. By ninjas! So, no, I don't think I'll sit."

"If you would listen, there are things I need—"

"We're through with listening," Hudson said.

"There are things *you* need?" I yelled, my voice reaching a glass-shattering octave. "Someone *trashed* my house. They broke *everything*." I stomped into Jenny's personal space and shoved a finger in her face. "You're going to—"

"You didn't have information there about where you're storing Kyoko, did you?"

My jaw worked but no words formed. Clamping my mouth shut, I inhaled and exhaled noisily through my nose. Slowly, I lowered my hand and clenched it into a fist. No one spoke or moved. I started to walk away, then whirled back to face her. "What's with you and your family handcuffing me?"

"That was a misunderstanding."

"Really? In the trailer? Were you having an out-of-body experience when you cuffed me inside with an elephant?"

"Wait, there really is an elephant?" Atlas asked, coming up behind me.

"What if Hudson hadn't been there, Jenny? How was I supposed to get out?" The question had niggled my thoughts the last few days, a plus one in the Jenny-is-crazy column. "Anything could have happened to me! Then who would have hid your stupid elephant?"

"You could have called—"

"I don't *have* a cell phone."

Paper clip snakes writhed up Atlas's arms and he sidled away from me. "No cell phone?"

Jenny blinked owlish eyes at me, then racehorse blinders dropped into place on either side of her head. When she looked back down at the notebook, I couldn't see her eyes. "It all worked out."

"I don't know how you got it, and I don't care. I don't care who you're hiding it from. I want that damned cursed elephant out of our lives," Hudson said.

"Cursed, Montague? That's an . . . unexpected correlation. But, no, the elephant stays with you."

"Montague?" I repeated.

"It's my first name. That I never use." Hudson swiveled his glare from Jenny to Atlas, who covered his grin with a hand. "Which means, Jenny, you've been checking up on me."

"Of course. All my research on Eva showed her single right now."

"Research on *me?*"

"I didn't pick you at random to take care of Kyoko. Aside from your *special* assets"—she gave me a hard, warning look—"you had a variety of necessary key factors." Jenny ticked a finger for each point. "No children. Flexible job. Limited friend network. Wealthy enough to get things done but not so wealthy that you think your money can solve any problem. And most important, you're exceedingly difficult to track. I needed someone Adorable Creations could never connect back to me. And transferring Kyoko to you at the gallery was completely untraceable—until you started playing detective."

"I'm so thrilled I fit your criteria. Lucky me. Now, take her back."

Edmond ambled in, carrying my overnight bag and satchel. My hand lifted to my shoulder. I couldn't remember the last time I'd forgotten my satchel anywhere. When Edmond set the bags down, I quelled the urge to rush across the room and hug my satchel. Ari was right; it was my security blanket. If only it could offer protection against blackmail.

Edmond glanced around the tension-filled room. "What'd I miss?"

"There's a *real* elephant," Atlas stage-whispered.

"A real one? But she said it was an elephan*tini*."

"It *is* an elephantini," Jenny said. "One Eva and Montague's amateur sleuth tactics have put in danger."

"Eva and who?" Edmond asked.

"Elephant, elephantini. I don't care," I said. "She's all yours. Let's go pick her up right now. Then you won't have to worry about us endangering her anymore."

"It's not that simple. I need Adorable Creations to believe she's dead. With the ninjas in play, it's more important than ever."

"You're trying to fake the baby elephant's death? Why?" Hudson asked.

"I told you, she's not a baby elephant. She's an elephantini, the first of her kind."

"And I told you, I don't care," I said.

"That's what Adorable Creations does," Jenny continued. "They genetically modify domesticated animals to create miniature pets. They've been perfecting chromosomal alterations on cats and dogs for years, but I was brought on to work in the wildlife division. Kyoko is the result. She's a full-grown elephantini."

"You shrunk an elephant?" Hudson asked.

"I didn't shrink anything. I reset the genetic markers that control growth. She was never a big elephant. And she never will be."

"Cool," Atlas breathed.

I would have gone with *creepy* or *unnatural* or *bizarre*. Hudson wore his silver top hat again, canted at a precarious angle. The silver terrier stood on the jail square. He was as frustrated and suspicious as I was.

I paced across the room and propped myself, arms crossed, on the edge of a barstool at the high counter leading into a stark kitchen. Distance would help prevent me from throttling Jenny. "Congratulations. You stunted an elephant's growth. But I don't care how special she is—we're done watching her."

"There's more. My real job is with an American company, Evolution Solutions. I've been working for them since my junior year of college. They needed an inside eye at Adorable Creations, so I went."

"An inside eye," Hudson repeated flatly. "You're a spy. A corporate or a scientific or whatever you want to call it spy."

"Yes."

"Get out!" Atlas said. "I always thought you were just a nerd, and this whole time you've been all James Bondette."

"So give Kyoko to this American company," I said.

"I can't." Jenny's blinders disappeared, replaced by thick, dirty glasses I couldn't see through. "They need to believe she's dead and the experiment failed. Everyone does. Otherwise she and a whole lot more elephantinis will spend their whole lives isolated in labs, and that's not fair to them. Elephants are wild herd animals."

"You're not making sense," Hudson said. "Why would you take the job if you didn't want elephantinis to exist?"

Jenny ignored him, focusing on me. Her expression looked calm and her body language relaxed, but her apparitions hadn't gotten the memo. Hummingbirds buzzed back and forth through her body, and the blinders swelled in size until they blocked both sides of her face from view.

"No part of our arrangement involved you investigating me, Eva. Your job is to keep Kyoko safe and hidden. That's it."

"We don't work for you and—" Hudson began, but she cut him off without even looking at him.

"That house you so cleverly found? The house I abandoned months ago? It was being watched—by the FBI, by the ninjas, and for all I know, by the retrievalist. You don't know what you're up against, and your incompetence is endangering everything. The ninjas found you; it's only a matter of time before the FBI finds a reason to question you, too. Stop trying to find me. Stop looking into my past. You're going to contaminate everything I've done and ruin more than you can imagine."

"My bad. I didn't know you had a master plan," I said with as much sarcasm as I could muster. "There's a real easy solution here: Take the goddamn elephant back!"

Atlas and Edmond flinched back a few steps in my peripheral vision. I didn't look away from Jenny—I couldn't. A pyramid of squirming, naked newborns piled at her feet, five on the bottom row, the pinnacle baby reaching her waist. The babies writhed, one enormous fleshy pink and brown creature with a sickening number of arms and legs. I fell off the barstool and caught myself against the counter.

"The ninjas work for AC's rival, another genetic company in Japan." Only Jenny's apparitions belied her serene tone and posture. She appeared as oblivious to my outburst as Hudson's, as if she couldn't hear disagreements. "They've been hunting for Kyoko since she was just a DNA sequence, and they're ruthless. Thanks to your bumbling, they figured out you know something about Kyoko, too— hence, tonight's abduction. They'll be back, so don't be stupid. And don't screw up with the FBI; tell them nothing."

"What makes you think we're not going directly to the FBI?" Hudson demanded.

"You won't." Jenny locked eyes with me as she stood.

"Hang on. You're not going anywhere." Hudson grabbed Jenny's arm.

A metallic click froze everyone in place. I glanced past Hudson's shoulder at Atlas. He held a small black gun and aimed down his straightened arm at Hudson.

"And you wonder why I don't trust you," I said. Atlas shrugged.

"Don't breathe a word about the elephantini," Jenny said. The babies convulsed and grew by three layers, almost obscuring her.

The insane scientist eased around Hudson, who pivoted, hands raised, to get Atlas in his sights. I lunged around him, desperate to keep Jenny there. I needed off this crazy train.

Atlas shoved the gun's muzzle to my forehead. I stopped short and glared down the barrel into his wide eyes.

"Whoa. Easy." Hudson pulled me a step back and slid in front of me. I'd been too slow, anyway. Edmond had already whisked Jenny out the door, and Atlas followed, backing out, his gun centered on me until he slipped through the door. Enormous red velvet curtains pulled closed on either side of him, framing him. A bright spotlight illuminated his gun. He tossed me a wink, then shut the door just before the curtains snapped closed.

"Goddamn it!" Hudson slammed his flat hand into the wall. He stomped to the door and put his eye to the peephole, then slammed the dead bolt home. "She's full of it."

"There must have been some truth in there. But what?"

He ran his hand through his hair and released a long breath. "I don't know. A spy? It's so Hollywood."

"Her fear seemed genuine." I shuddered. The pyramid of babies topped the list of creepy apparitions. "Either way, we're stuck with Kyoko still."

I flopped onto the couch. Its worn cushions embraced me. Hudson dropped into the lone recliner. My heart twisted with worry for Sofie. The ninjas had found me; it wasn't a stretch of the imagination that they would find her house, too. Thankfully, we'd moved her this morning. If the ninjas or the mysterious skip tracer thought to check out my aunt, they wouldn't find her. No one would connect me with my mother. Annabella didn't go to great lengths to acknowledge my existence, and I returned the favor.

"I don't like this," Hudson said. "I don't trust Jenny. I want to call the police. But . . ."

"But we can't," I said.

"You're sure?"

I looked away from Hudson's probing gaze. He wasn't an idiot. He knew I had a reason for going along with Jenny's mad plan. But since I couldn't tell him the truth, I couldn't give him an explanation.

"I'm sure." My stomach growled.

Hudson sighed and pushed up from his chair. "I can at least solve one of our problems." He ordered pizza, then opened his microwave. Inside sat a bakery box. He pulled it out, grabbed two forks from a drawer, and set the box in front of me on the coffee table. "This should help."

It was coffee cake, an entire loaf.

"You had coffee cake?"

"I was optimistic this morning."

The whole world got a little brighter. I grabbed a fork, then pulled him to me for a kiss.

"Thank you."

"This isn't exactly how I pictured the evening going. I thought we'd be enjoying this after hot monkey sex."

"I'm listening." Memories of last night made my body tingle and helped me focus on something other than my sore muscles.

"Hold that thought."

Hudson went back to the kitchen to call a tow truck. I paced myself, breathing between bites of the delicious cake, letting the brown sugar and cinnamon mask my problems. When he hung up from the towing company, he placed another call.

"Matvei, I need a favor. It's personal . . . Nope, not like that. I need you to watch my place tonight."

I turned to look at Hudson over the back of the couch. The sofa wasn't positioned well. I would have shifted it to the right, moved the TV to a different wall, and opened up the room.

"I don't know who I pissed off," Hudson said after a pause, "but I need to know it's safe for me to sleep tonight. Can you keep an eye on things?"

The coffee cake in my mouth turned dry and tasteless. Tonight's sleeping arrangements had nothing to do with exploring my relationship with Hudson, no matter how much I'd prefer to pretend it did. I'd been chased from my home, hunted down on the streets, and now abandoned again by Jenny with more questions than before. Memory flashes of the ninjas leaping from the van and rushing us choked me. I set my fork down and grabbed my duffel. Doing something, anything, helped push the panic back.

Following the dark hallway toward the master bedroom, I put as much distance between myself and the phone as possible. I might luck out, and Hudson's hot water heater might run on gas, but I didn't have more than another hour or two of working lights in his house.

Like the front room and kitchen, Hudson's bedroom was minimalist. The California king had matching nightstands on either side, though only one had a lamp. The bright sky blue comforter with an enormous silver oak tree embroidered on it lay smooth across the bed. I smiled at the sight: Hudson really had been optimistic this morning. From the state of his jumbled closet, which he'd forgotten to shut the door to, he wasn't normally the kind of guy to make his bed.

I froze in horror on the threshold of the master bath. The tiny room contained a sink, a toilet—and a shower stall. The stall was square. It had a three-inch lip at the bottom with a glass door. There was no tub. How did a person survive without a tub?

I thought about my oval oversize tub and bath salts and scented candles, then about the disaster zone of my loft. If I could have driven myself, I might have left right then, ninjas or no ninjas. Sighing, I tossed my duffel bag onto the toilet lid, pulled out my shampoo and conditioner, then fiddled with the shower's knobs.

The hot water stung my wrists, where I'd abraded the flesh against the zip ties, and the bridge of my nose, which had a bright red rug burn from the sack. My ribs and stomach were mottled purple over tender tissue, but no skin was broken. I closed my eyes and leaned against the wall, losing myself in the warm spray until I heard Hudson moving in the room.

The shower door opened and closed. I turned my face up to the spray, then used my hands to slick the water off my face.

"Exquisite," Hudson said, his voice husky and his drawl pronounced. "Except for these." He brushed my side with gentle fingers.

"I could say the same of you." I shifted so the water sprayed over my shoulder and hit Hudson's abdomen. I tracked the rivulets down his stomach, bypassed Mr. Happy, and pointed to a purple bruise the size of a softball gracing his outer thigh. More bruises marred his shins, and a faint discoloring had blossomed to the right of his six-pack.

"Come here." He slid his hands around my waist and pressed against me. He kissed the tip of my nose. "Let me make things better." He kissed my right bicep and a bruise I hadn't noticed, then both my wrists.

He winced when water hit the cut on his forehead. I grabbed a washcloth he'd draped over the top of the door and sudsed it up. Then I circled him against his gentlemanly protests and forced him to stand in the spray. With gentle dabs, I cleaned the wound.

"How's it look?" Hudson asked, eyes closed as soap ran down his face.

"Not bad. Most of it was blood." A short cut and scrape remained, both fortunately shallow.

He leaned into the spray and rinsed away the soap, then turned back to me. His arms circled me, pulling me into the warm cascade of water. Dipping his head for a gentle kiss, he ran his hands softly over the curve of my waist, my butt, my hips, then back up. I traced my fingers up his back, running my nails lightly through his hair. Each tender touch, bestowed and received, mended the raw edges carved through me by tonight's violence. Caress by caress, kiss by kiss, Hudson restored my equilibrium.

When Hudson lifted his head, I opened my eyes and returned his relaxed smile.

"Much better," he said. "Now, where was I? Here?" He kissed the tip of my nose. "Or was it here?" He licked water from my neck, sparking a cascade of goose bumps down my body. He leaned back to admire my tightened nipples. "I think I was here." His lips closed around a nipple, and I moaned, arching into the heat of his mouth.

Hudson teased both nipples until my fingers curled into his scalp. Abruptly he lifted his head, leaving me gasping.

"Oh, that's right." He shifted to kiss a bruise on my ribs. "I was here, making all your bruises better."

I tightened my fingers in his hair and urged him back to my breasts. He rolled laughing eyes up to look at me. In the shower's spray, I couldn't be sure, but I thought champagne bubbles floated from his skin. I relaxed my grip and slid my hands to his shoulders as he kissed down my stomach to the vee of my legs. His hands slid around to cup my butt, lifting me toward him.

"I don't remember getting hurt there," I said. I leaned back against the shower wall and closed my eyes, curling my fingers around his biceps to anchor myself.

"We should make sure, just to be safe."

Perhaps a shower stall wasn't so bad after all.

# FIFTEEN

I WOKE to the silence of the house. With the curtains backlit by a streetlight and the clock beside the bed dead, it was impossible to determine the time. My eyes felt gritty, so I guessed it was early. Like three o'clock early.

Hudson sprawled on his back, the covers pushed to his waist. One hand rested on his stomach, the other on my thigh. I listened to the muted sounds of sporadic traffic and stared at the ceiling, waiting for sleep to return. It'd been a long time since I'd slept in an unfamiliar house. Memory of my trashed home started my pulse pounding and chased away any chance of me falling back to sleep. Easing out of the bed, I grabbed my bag and closed the bedroom door behind me. I dressed in the front room in jeans and a tank top and a loose, cowl-neck sweater.

I selected a leftover slice of pizza and meandered through the house as I ate. The pizza had been cold last night, too, when we'd finally gotten around to eating.

I peeked out the window beside the front door. The sky above the rooflines held a mix of blue with the yellow city glow. It must have been closer to five than three. Cars lined the street, and if Hudson's friend, Matvei, sat in one, I didn't see him.

I turned my back on the window, the world, and the stresses of the day awaiting me. Padding barefoot back to the kitchen, I grabbed a second slice of pizza, then roamed down the hall. Of the house's two bedrooms, I'd seen the master, complete with its sad little master bathroom and tiny walk-in closet. A half bath was squeezed between the bedrooms. Its oppressive navy tiles and stark white walls enhanced its squished-closet feel.

I cracked the door to the second bedroom, then pushed it wide, stunned. Nothing about the room matched the rest of the house. For starters, it was full. Bookcases lined one wall, overflowing with thick tomes, binders, and flotsam. A narrow table ran along another wall, buried beneath a slew of mysterious electronic paraphernalia. Where the rest of the house was neat in an almost sterile, unlived-in way, this bedroom embodied chaos. Beneath the table were two extension strips plugged into different outlets, and I counted fourteen cords leading up to doodads on the table. A desk pressed beneath the window, supporting three monitors and a filing cabinet's thrown-up last meal. A sleek chair sat behind the desk. Smaller tables held a printer and an explosion of office supplies and open-faced binders. A clear pathway led from the chair across the hardwood to the burdened table, but piles of bags and books and more electronics clogged the rest of the floor.

Gripping the door frame, I reminded myself that I had no right to make any changes to Hudson's home. If he wanted a cluttered health-hazard office, that was his prerogative. With a herculean effort, I shut the door and walked away.

I pulled out my work folder and opened it on the coffee table, but I couldn't focus on it. I tried a few yoga stretches that my jeans and injuries would allow. Moving my sore muscles felt good, but a walk or swim would have been better. I considered writing Hudson a note and going for a walk, but thoughts of ninjas lurking outside, waiting to pounce, nixed the idea. So I paced the front room and pondered last night's conversation with Jenny.

Her whole story didn't make sense. First, why steal the very thing she had been hired to create—an elephantini—the moment it was created? If she was a spy for the American company, why not pass Kyoko along to them? Why lie to both companies? I didn't believe she'd suddenly found compassion for lab animals. Plus, if Jenny's sole reason for abducting Kyoko was to ensure she didn't spend the rest of her days in a cage, why foist her off on me? For that matter, why bring her to LA at all? Why not take her to Asia and set her free with a herd or find an elephant rescue center that could take her?

I did my best to ignore the ever-present *Why me?* question. On that, Jenny's explanation had actually made sense. I *was* hard to track. I had limited online interactions—limited being *zero*—and as she'd predicted, I had enough connections to figure out a way to hide Kyoko within five hours of having her dumped on me. And, of course, she had my silence, bought by my terror of being discovered and studied.

Pushing past the snarl of anger and panic simmering behind thoughts of Jenny's blackmail, I tried to focus on solving the puzzle that was Jenny. Why was she running? Even if she convinced everyone that Kyoko had died, couldn't her Japanese company use Jenny's process to create another elephantini without her?

I needed to make a list. Maybe if I could see it all on paper, I could sort through the lies and figure out how to force Jenny to take Kyoko back and quietly leave my life forever.

I grabbed my notepad out of my satchel and jotted Jenny's name at the top of the paper, then started listing everything I knew about her and Kyoko. The pen ran out of ink three lines in. When I couldn't find a backup in my satchel, I tried the pen by the phone. It gooped ink in blobs as it wrote. I braved the office, hoping I'd find a pen lying on top of a pile. No such luck. Markers and highlighters peeked out of the desktop mound of books and papers and cords and tiny electronic parts, but no pens.

Opening the top desk drawer was a mistake. A clump of rubber bands snagged around erasers, pens, pencils, and paper clips. I lifted a pen, and a wad of office supplies came with it. I sat down in the chair. It wouldn't hurt to organize this drawer. I'd leave it better than I found it, and Hudson would have a nice surprise the next time he needed a paper clip.

I pulled the drawer out, upended it on the floor, then sat cross-legged in the small cleared pathway and sorted the items into piles. The normalcy of the activity soothed my psyche and put a halt to the endless circle of my thoughts. When I finished with the top drawer, I peeked into the next. More chaos. The silly thing was, Hudson had plenty of organization tools at his disposal. A handy plastic box made up of dozens of tiny drawers sat beside his desk. Half of the drawers were even labeled. It didn't take much effort to match the items to the correct drawers. Beneath the heap on his desk and amid the clutter on the table, I found more bins and trays, all waiting to be properly used. In no time at all, I'd lined up the bins and stacked the trays, and sorted mystery items into each of them.

"What the hell are you doing?"

I jumped. Hudson stood in the office doorway in cherry-print boxer shorts and nothing else, his hair spiked on one side from sleep. Fury pinched his mouth and furrowed his brow. A gold band encased his left ring finger, then a dozen circled it from base to tip. They retreated like a slinky back to one, then expanded thicker than before to coat his finger. Little green army men lined up on his shoulders, their tiny guns all pointed at me.

"I was looking for a pen—"

"And you thought you'd find one under my soldering gun? In my Dremel box?"

I glanced where he pointed, feeling like I was waking from a dream. Sometime after the second drawer, I'd turned off my brain and immersed myself in the uncomplicated pleasure of organization. The office included breathing room now, with a better energy flow, not to mention greater usability. The entire desktop—I could see actual wooden surface now—the overflowing bookcases, and the storage bins were now arranged for optimal efficiency. I hadn't touched the work-table cluttered with bizarre doodads and tools, but I'd cleared floor space and had been contemplating moving the desk to a better loca-tion. All without Hudson's consent.

"Normally I tell all the women who stay over to steer clear of this room, but I thought you... I can't believe..." He gestured expansively at the tidied office. "How am I supposed to find anything? You've ruined my whole system."

I folded my arms over my chest. Any part of me that might have felt apologetic for my uninvited intrusion into his private space drowned beneath a surge of anger at being lumped in with *all the women* who'd come before me.

"*Ruined* it? Because it's organized? How dreadful."

"Where's my projects book? Where's my backup flash drive?" He pawed through the neat stacks on his desk. "I'm not a client, Eva. I didn't ask for a *consultation*." He infused the word with derision. "I don't need you practicing your feng shui crap here."

"Of course not. You've got things perfectly under control, don't you? Your life must be running smooth as clockwork—"

"It was until I met you."

I snapped my mouth shut, turned on my heel—and screamed. A man loomed in the office doorway. His stocky, muscular frame filled the space. A blond buzz cut did nothing to soften his scowl or the sharp line of his jaw. Throw a fur-lined cap on him, and he'd look like he stepped straight out of a Tolstoy novel.

———

"NICE BOXERS, HUD," he said. He shifted to lean a shoulder against the doorjamb. A cartoon monkey slid down his arm and danced in the air near his knee.

Hudson ran his hand through his hair and sighed. "It's all right, Eva. This is Matvei."

I lowered my hand from my chest, where it had leapt to hold my heart.

"I heard you bellowing from outside and thought you might be in trouble. I let myself in." He made a point of looking around the office. "Looks nice in here."

Hudson glowered and shoved him aside. I listened to him stomp down the hall and the bedroom door slam.

"Is this your work?" When Matvei grinned, his menacing edges softened.

I forced my jaw to unclench. "Yep. This is the work of the devil herself, doing a little early-morning organization."

Matvei snorted. Hudson passed behind him, dressed in jeans and a black T-shirt.

"Hud's little MIA act makes sense now." Matvei raised his voice enough to be heard by Hudson in the front room. "I can't remember the last time he missed two days in a row, but if ever I saw a good reason . . ."

"Are you a coworker?" I asked.

"Yep. I've been the poor schmuck responsible for picking up all of Hud's slack."

"That's why you get paid the big bucks," Hudson shouted back.

"It seems I've overstayed my welcome, Matvei. If it wouldn't be too much to ask, could I bum a ride home from you?"

A pink ribbon slithered around Matvei's neck and tied itself into a neat bow beneath his Adam's apple.

"Ah . . ." Matvei hemmed. He backed up when I stalked toward the doorway, giving me plenty of space. I strode straight to my satchel and packed up my notebook.

Hudson accessorized with a silver top hat and a flare of army men on his shoulders. The men arrayed in a defensive formation, and one climbed the slick side of the metal top hat and took lookout from the rim. I'd seen the Monopoly pieces enough in the last forty-eight hours to know they appeared with Hudson's frustration. The connection didn't make any sense to me, but interpreting one of the less obvious divinations brought a little satisfaction.

"My landline? My fucking landline is dead?" Hudson vented a string of curses. It was actually his cordless phone that was dead, but I didn't correct him.

"He thinks he's been cursed." I made my tone express how crazy this made Hudson sound, and I didn't feel the least bit guilty.

"Five cell phones and now my landline? I don't *think* I've been cursed; I *know* I have," Hudson said.

"He's going to go on like this for at least another ten minutes," I said, speaking from experience. "I'd rather not be here for the whole show. If you can't drive me, can you point me in the direction of the nearest bus stop?"

"You're not going anywhere," Hudson said.

I straightened. "Are *you* going to attempt to stop me?"

"Damn straight, I—"

"Nobody's going anywhere," Matvei said.

We turned our glares on him. He lounged against the wall, arms crossed, watching us with undisguised amusement. The dancing monkey had been joined by the rest of his troupe.

"What do you know?" Hudson asked. He crunched the cordless phone back into its cradle.

"I know I've been sitting outside in a cold, cramped car for the last seven hours while you two were wrapped up in a nice comfy bed, and then I come in to rescue your ass from some enraged psychopath, only to find it's you. And I've gotten zero thanks."

Hudson rolled his eyes. I scooped up the bakery box containing the leftover coffee cake and a fork from a kitchen drawer, then plunked myself down in the recliner where I could see both men. No sense leaving behind good coffee cake when I left.

"Cake?" I lifted the box toward Matvei in offering.

"Is that coffee cake?"

"Yep."

He grimaced. "If there's no chocolate, it's not worth it."

And I'd trusted this man with my safety last night?

"Your point? I assume you're planning on getting to it," Hudson said.

"Yep."

"Any day now."

"I don't know. I like seeing you rattled."

"Matvei . . ."

"Killjoy," Matvei said. He pushed away from the wall, and his teasing grin vanished. "Last night was boring. Nothing interesting. But around five this morning, a teal Tercel parked at the end of the block. The two guys haven't gotten out and they seem to be watching your place. One's big, dark, and looks like a crowbar couldn't wedge him into—or out of—that tiny car. The other—"

"Looks like he thinks he's Kanye West," Hudson finished. "Yeah, we know about them. They're mostly harmless. Atlas and Edmond. Didn't catch their last names, but if you want to run the plate and see what pops up, that'd be great."

"Harmless? You weren't the one they handcuffed and kidnapped," I said.

"I think you're forgetting they helped us out last night."

"I think *you're* forgetting being held at gunpoint by our dear, harmless Atlas," I shot back. "Or perhaps you're used to it, what with your charming response to a little help—"

"You can't mess with a guy's office and not expect—"

"Him to behave like a child? Oh, did a *girl* invade your private lair? Poor *Monty*—"

"Don't call me that."

"Which one's Atlas?" Matvei asked.

Hudson didn't look away from me. I gave him a saccharine smile. I was in the wrong, and I knew it. I should never have moved anything of Hudson's without his permission, even if it would benefit him. But his criticism that I'd made things worse grated, and his accusation that *I* was the root of his problems hit too close to home. I wasn't going to back down first.

Hudson broke our staring match and ran his hand through his spiky hair.

"The skinny one," he finally answered Matvei. "But, honestly, they're not a concern. Just let me know what you find on them."

"Ooookay." Matvei glanced at me, then back at Hudson. "What about the FBI? Do you know about them, too?"

I shot Hudson a glance. A sombrero replaced the top hat, and the little green army men lined up along the rim.

"I don't know what you guys are into," Matvei said, "but the feds rolled up this morning about a half hour after the Tercel, and they haven't left yet."

Jenny's parting words surfaced in my memory. *Don't screw up with the FBI; tell them nothing.*

"Jenny," I said. "The background checks." My voice sounded hollow.

Or the FBI knew about Kyoko. My stomach chilled and I set down the coffee cake.

"Do you think they know?" I asked.

Hudson paced, tapping a finger against his chin as he thought. A Rubik's Cube twisted in the air in front of him, the grids turning and flipping, aligning and misaligning colors with each twist. The sombrero remained, but the army men disappeared. A jagged-toothed fish flickered in and out of existence, gnawing at his stomach.

"No. Not about Kyoko," Hudson said. "If they did, they wouldn't be out in their car."

I nodded in agreement. They'd either be in here arresting us, or they'd be at Annabella's. Neither of us said that aloud, though. Not with Matvei listening.

"We could tell them about the ninjas," I said.

"The ninjas?" Matvei echoed.

"How would we explain it?" Hudson asked.

"We don't have to explain anything. They're the ones who attacked us."

"Do you remember anything about them?"

"I know where their van is broken down," I said.

"It's probably gone by now. Besides, the feds will want to know why we were selected as targets."

"Random act."

"And when they start digging?"

I sighed. "What about the cousins? Can we at least tell them about Atlas and Edmond?" I knew it was wishful thinking before Hudson shook his head.

"The less we tell them, the better."

I liked law enforcers. They had a tough job, and I appreciated their dedication to keeping everyone safe. A plan that included lying to them made the coffee cake squirm in my stomach.

"Unless you want to tell them everything," Hudson said, giving me an unreadable look. I did my best to not show the whiplash of fear his words elicited. Telling the FBI everything might mean we'd reduce our sentences for our involvement with Kyoko, but it would also mean the end of my life. The moment we handed Kyoko over to the FBI, Jenny would expose my curse, and I'd be whisked off to some high-security facility for detainment and endless testing.

I shook my head and looked away from Hudson's piercing gaze. "What do you think they're waiting for?"

"Are you guys going to tell me what's going on?" Matvei asked.

"No," Hudson said.

"Then you might want to brush your teeth, because if they're waiting for something, permission or information or confirmation, the office opens in"—he checked his watch—"twenty minutes."

Cussing, Hudson stalked from the room. Matvei quirked an eyebrow at me.

"You sure you don't want to tell me?" he asked.

"Are you sure you want to know?"

Matvei glanced toward the master bedroom. "What turned our easygoing Hudson into such an ass? Yeah."

"I don't know." I raised my voice. "Perhaps you should ask *all the women* he slept with before me."

"Not going to let that one go, huh?" Matvei asked.

"You're kidding, right?"

Matvei grinned.

I grabbed my duffel rather than rooting for my toothbrush in front of Matvei, and stalked down the hall.

I rounded the corner of the bedroom and ran into Hudson. He grabbed me by the shoulders and backed me into the wall. Anger and another emotion I couldn't identify tightened the corners of his eyes and set his mouth in a hard line. When he swept in for a kiss, his lips pressed hard, almost painfully, against mine and my body responded instantly. I dropped my bag and fisted his shirt in one hand, holding tight to his shoulder with the other.

He pulled back until a few inches separated our panting breaths.

"I'm pissed as hell at you, but that doesn't mean I don't like you, and it doesn't mean I want you running off into danger, okay?" he said. "We're in this together."

"I don't go 'running off into danger.' I'm not some dim-witted damsel in distress and you're not my white knight. I'm very good at taking care of myself."

"So you don't need my help? Is that what you're saying?" His expression turned stony.

"No more than you need mine. Like you said, we're in this together. It's not 'Hudson Single-Handedly Rides to the Rescue,' okay? It's not 'Protect Eva from Harm and Herself.' And while we're clearing the air, I don't mess things up with my feng shui 'crap.' I fix things. That's my job; I make people's lives better. Open your thick head and look around, *Monty*. Your problems are obvious. You've got a stagnant career that feeds your bank account but not your heart. Women leave you because they're never fully welcome in here"—I prodded his heart—"or here." I waved toward the bedroom. "People trust you, but I bet you're having a hard time convincing your boss you're worthy of that next level of responsibility, the one that would boost your salary. The helpful people in your life—your mentors and your repairmen and the customer support people—they're hit or miss, right? And I don't even want to touch on your family. That's a tidal wave of baggage and buried emotion. You should be thanking me for what I did in your office . . . even if it wasn't my place." The half-hearted apology came out stilted.

Hudson fell back a step, and he stared at me with wide eyes.

"How did you . . ."

"It's all right here." I circled a finger in the air to indicate his whole house. His slack-jawed expression eased the last of my anger. I stood on tiptoes and kissed him gently. "Stop discounting what you don't understand." I picked up my bag and walked to the bathroom, then turned back. "And I like you, too, even when you make me so mad my hair curls."

# SIXTEEN

"HOW WELL DO you both know Ms. Winters?" FBI Agent Coutu asked. Hudson and I were settled on the couch. Coutu's partner, Agent Sevallo, had taken the recliner. Coutu remained standing, though she was short enough that if she did attempt to intimidate with her height, it wouldn't work. Then again, I was being questioned by the FBI. I was already intimidated.

"Not at all," Hudson said.

"I went to high school with her."

"What did you talk about outside Galileo Gallery three days ago? Winters seemed agitated."

My stomach went weightless, but the appearance of a ham sandwich on the folder Coutu held distracted me. I'd seen the divination before. Recently. Where had it been?

"Hang on," Hudson said. "Have you been spying on us?"

Short of vaulting the back fence, there'd been no way to avoid the FBI agents. Minutes after Matvei had left, they'd pounded on the front door and politely requested a moment of our time. We were past introductions. We were solidly in the acting phase of this conversation, where I pretended I knew nothing and suffered no guilt or nervousness. I had my fair share of lying experience, but I'd never pitted my skills against people trained to detect deceit. Already I felt like fidgeting.

Coutu's gaze never settled, always flicking back and forth between us, reading our body language and watching for clues. The agent came up to my shoulder, had soft dyed-red curls that didn't touch her suit jacket's collar, and looked to be in her late fifties. An apparition of an FBI badge clung to her gray jacket over her heart. Very literal. I could appreciate that. Literal was much easier to interpret than her ham sandwich or the rotten banana slices now dripping from Hudson's chest.

Sevallo's eyes landed on me more often than not. At least two decades younger than Coutu and almost two feet taller, he had short, thick black hair and a slight Asian cast to his Caucasian features, and when he looked at me, pink rose petals scattered across the coffee table between us. I didn't think Sevallo was having strictly professional thoughts about me. Fluffy socks draped over his arm, flickering in and out of existence with every glance my way. Finally, he scowled, and the socks disappeared along with the rose petals.

"We've been keeping an eye on Ms. Winters," Sevallo said. "Ms. Parker, please answer the question."

"She was in a hurry," I said, glancing at Hudson. "And you know how it is when you run into someone you haven't seen in years. You think there's so much to catch up on, and then you realize you actually have nothing to talk about." I cringed inwardly at not providing the whole truth, but then I thought of Jenny's threat. A few carefully worded answers were going to have to weigh on my conscience.

"Yet she left her truck with you," Coutu said. "A truck we later found off West Pico, abandoned. It looked like she'd been hauling livestock. What do you know about that?"

"The truck broke down. We had to leave it there."

"The truck works fine," Sevallo said. Hudson tensed beside me, but he didn't say anything about his elephant-curse theory. Sevallo acquired a Santa's hat. It sagged to the left, the white fluff at the tip of the hat dangling to touch his shoulder. "We think Jenny asked you to move the vehicle and dump it for her."

"No. She just wanted it moved, but then it broke down. And the trailer got a flat when we exited the freeway." All true, but even I didn't believe me. "I never imagined I'd be talking to the FBI about it. We didn't do anything illegal, did we?"

"Why did she need it moved?"

"I don't know. I was just doing her a favor. You know, good karma." God, I sounded inane.

"What about the next day? Did she ask you to break into her house?"

"I didn't break in," I protested. Again, not a lie, but I teetered on a razor's edge. Hudson had been the one to do the breaking in.

"What were you there for?"

Hudson crossed his arms over his chest. "Where is this going?"

"Just trying to put the pieces together, Mr. Keyes," Sevallo said. I couldn't look at him, not with his dunce-like Santa's cap.

"The truck," I said, pouncing on the first plausible answer. "I didn't have her number, but I wanted to let her know about the truck."

"Did you find her?"

"No."

"Do you know where she is?"

"No."

"Tell us about your phone call, Ms. Parker. To an Arianna da Via." Coutu opened the folder, its pages sliding through the sandwich. I remembered where I'd seen the ham sandwich: in the car parked near Jenny's house. It'd been Coutu, watching the house. Watching us slip into the backyard, then leave a few minutes later. Watching me get into Ari's car and drive off.

I consciously did *not* wipe my hands down my pants to dry my sweating palms. My face felt like it'd transformed to cardboard. I wanted to pat my cheeks to make sure they weren't doing something strange, but I was afraid if I moved so much as a twitch, the truth would spill out. It turned out I really sucked at lying to law enforcers. Lying about electricity I could do all day long, but this was bigger, more important, and had real and severe punishments. I wasn't cut out for this type of lying.

"'Midnight, pink,' and the address," Coutu said. "What sort of code is that?"

"A childhood one, something we came up with as teens." I couldn't have made myself look more suspicious if I tried. Coutu waited, and I added, "I don't like talking on the phone."

"You know, in our line of work, what looks fishy, is fishy," Coutu said. She shifted back on her heels and stared at me with a flat expression that missed nothing. "You're fishy, Ms. Parker. You don't have an ATM card or a credit card. You pay for everything in cash. You travel like a CIA operative. You associate with known criminals."

"I what?"

"You checked her financials? On what grounds?" Hudson demanded.

"As part of this investigation."

"This doesn't sound like a routine investigation to me," Hudson said.

"Jennifer Winters is involved in some suspicious activities. And now it looks like you both are, too."

"Like what?" Hudson demanded.

"How long have you been working with Grant and Zambo?" Coutu asked.

"Who?"

She lifted a picture from her folder and slapped it down in front of me. The shot had been taken with a zoom lens. It showed me running up a street with the Tupperware of cupcakes in my hands. The plastic container blocked the handcuffs from sight.

"I don't 'work with' Atlas and Edmond." Annoyance crept into my tone. Where had the FBI been when the cousins had stuffed me into that Tercel? "I didn't even know their last names. They gave me a ride—"

"You should never get into a vehicle with someone you don't know," Sevallo said. "Once you're in a moving car, you're captive to the driver."

"Thank you for the public safety announcement," Coutu said, shooting her partner a quelling glance. A riding crop appeared and disappeared from her right fist. I would have bet last month's profits that Coutu was breaking in the younger agent, teaching him the ropes. Her divinations were so literal! Which meant the ham sandwich probably wasn't ham; it was a bologna sandwich, as in, she wasn't believing a word out of my mouth.

"We think this was a drug deal that went south," Sevallo said.

I couldn't help it: I laughed. I heard my nerves in the sound and cut it off. "I've never been part of a drug deal in my life. That"—I pointed at the Tupperware in the picture—"is filled with cupcakes. Edmond wants to start a bakery."

"Atlas Grant has been brought up on minor possession charges twice," Coutu said. "Zambo once."

Coutu and Sevallo waited, as if expecting me to fill the silence. I stared at the picture and tried to remember if I'd seen anyone with a camera. I would have to be more alert if I was going to keep my possession of Kyoko a secret. However, I was positive now that if they knew about Kyoko, they would have mentioned her already. They were fishing. I'd simply added to their confusion.

"If everything was all hunky-dory here, and you left your friends on good terms, why are you running? Why do you look so scared?" Coutu searched my face.

"I was running because I was late. Edmond's car broke down, and I didn't have time to wait. That look—" I studied the raw fear on my expression in the photo, then made myself shrug. "I'd have to go back to that day. I had no idea I could make that face."

Coutu snorted. The bologna sandwich grew six inches. "I understand your apartment was broken into yesterday."

"Yes." My fists clenched in my lap.

"It sounds like they really trashed your place." Coutu consulted the paperwork, then pinned me with her steady brown stare. "You didn't report anything missing. Can you tell us why someone would ransack your home? From every indication in the reports, it wasn't a random crime. They were looking for something."

"I have no idea what."

"Does it seem odd to you that you did Ms. Winters a favor a few days ago, and then your apartment was tossed yesterday?" Sevallo asked.

"I guess. But I met Hudson not long ago. By that logic, the break-in could be connected to him, too."

Both agents regarded Hudson with expressionless faces, and I regretted my words.

"Do you think someone's targeting me because I helped Jenny?"

I didn't have to fake the chill my own words gave me. The ninjas were still out there, and they'd found and captured us once already. If I believed Jenny, the mysterious retrievalist had his eyes on me. And now, of course, so did the FBI.

"I sincerely hope not, but unless you cooperate, we can't guarantee your safety," Sevallo said. Pink rose petals fell through the air between us.

———

"DO you think we're being followed?" I asked Hudson an hour later as we drove to Ari's. We'd taken a taxi to Hudson's mechanic. Once again, nothing had been wrong with his car. Hudson had taken the news almost calmly.

"We're persons of interest in an FBI investigation, so, yeah, I'm pretty sure there's someone tracking us." His silver terrier perched on the dash, life-size and staring out the front windshield.

"You were quiet in there," I said.

"I don't like aiding Jenny. I don't know what she's got on you. And I don't expect you to tell me. I get it. Whatever secret is big enough for you to do this for her is probably too big to share with someone you just met, despite all we've been through together. Or, shit, maybe I don't get it. But I'm not going to push you to tell me. I just . . . I don't like lying to the feds."

I opened and closed my mouth, swallowing knee-jerk lies with a chaser of toxic guilt. The urge to tell Hudson the truth—to tell him about my curse and my fears and how Jenny was leading me around by them—almost overwhelmed me. Almost. A lifetime of self-preservation kept me from speaking.

"Whatever it is she's got, it's a well-buried secret. You seem innocent, in real life and on paper."

"You checked on me?" The question came out high.

Hudson glanced at me. His knuckles whitened around the steering wheel. Apparitions cropped up with alarming speed around him—black-frame glasses, a toddler-size marble cherub flapping in the backseat, and rotten banana slices pooling around his waist. On the dash, the terrier doubled in size atop a Chance square. "Yeah, I checked on you."

"When?"

"Yesterday morning."

After our amazing first night together and right after finding out I had no TV. I wondered if that had been the final straw to force him to turn his scrutiny on me, or if he'd planned to investigate me before he'd accepted my invitation for a nightcap.

I should have been angry, or at least felt like he'd violated my privacy, but the invisible scales in my head weighed his action against my guilt and came out balanced. "Thank you," I said softly. "For not pushing for the answer and for lying to the agents. And for helping me even when you didn't know me. And for continuing to help me now that it's gotten dangerous."

"You don't have a driver's license."

It wasn't a question, but I answered it anyway. "As embarrassing as that is to admit, no. Sorry about the parking ticket lie."

Hudson didn't speak for a block; then he said, "What Jenny has on you—is it bad?"

"It would end my life." I rubbed goose bumps from my arms. "Maybe literally."

Concern and confusion tightened Hudson's eyes. "Okay."

"So what now?"

"I'll run a check on Atlas and Edmond, now that I have their full names. But our goal is the same: Get Kyoko back into Jenny's hands. Which means we need to find Jenny. Again."

"And force her to take Kyoko back. I think that's going to be harder than finding her."

We both fell silent, pulled into our individual thoughts. Mine were chaotic and unfocused, hopscotching between gratitude that Hudson was going to continue to help me without prying and fear that the FBI would arrest us. A film of terror coated my thoughts, bristling with anger directed at Jenny. I felt helpless and adrift. I didn't know what to do next, and I couldn't see a way out of this increasingly dangerous and illegal predicament.

When we pulled up, Ari sat on her porch, worry clouding her expression, winged aluminum soda cans circling her head. I tensed at the sight. Ari had developed a fear of flying when we'd still been in high school, which was when the soda-can apparition had first appeared. Over the years, the apparition had taken root and was now associated with fears of all kinds. I expected the cans to disappear when she saw us, but instead they multiplied. A queasy feeling rolled through my middle.

I jogged up the short walkway and she rose to meet me halfway.

"Are you okay?" she asked. "I expected you hours ago. What happened to your nose?"

"We were delayed by the FBI," I said.

Ari's brown eyes rounded in her pale face. "What'd they want?" she whispered.

Hudson opened the door to the house, and I went inside, Ari on my heels. "They wanted to ask us about Jenny. They're doing some sort of investigation on her. Jenny said we tipped them off."

"You spoke with Jenny?"

I caught Ari up on our adventurous night as succinctly as possible. Ari collapsed into a chair when I described the ninjas' attack, then leapt from it when I summarized Atlas and Edmond's rescue, which necessitated confessing to my first kidnapping by the cousins. She flopped back down when I told her Jenny's brief, unsatisfactory explanation of why we needed to continue to keep Kyoko hidden for her.

"This is unacceptable," Ari said. "I wouldn't even ask something this bizarre, this . . . dangerous of you, and you're my best friend! Where does she get off on dragging you into this mess?"

"I'd like to ask her that, too, but she's disappeared on us again," Hudson said.

"Have you tried calling Sofie recently?" I asked.

"I tried." A queue of aluminum cans spun faster through Ari's midriff, phasing through the chair and back out. Every third can resembled a coffin. My heart lurched. "I've been trying every half hour for the last two hours. I was just about to head over there when you got here."

My stomach knotted. Sofie could have gotten wrapped up in a painting and not heard the phone ring, but it wasn't likely. She also could have left the house and forgotten her phone, she could have forgotten her charger, or her phone could be broken. None of those scenarios made me feel better, though.

"Can we borrow your car?"

"We don't need to borrow her car," Hudson said. "Mine's working fine."

"For now." I'd been in it for fifteen minutes. It wouldn't make the drive to Annabella's on top of that. Ari, thankfully, understood without me needing to explain.

"Here. I just filled the tank." Ari peeled her car key off a ring and handed it to Hudson. "No elephants allowed inside, okay?"

I wasn't in the frame of mind to hold up a conversation during the drive, and fortunately, Hudson wasn't feeling chatty, either. I concentrated on counting the billboards, then finding the alphabet one letter at a time in the signs we passed. When that didn't work to mask my worry, I mentally feng shuied Hudson's house.

All soothing thoughts flushed from my mind when Hudson pulled into the circular drive and Dali bounded through the open gate to the backyard, barking excitedly. I swung out of the car and suffered Dali's excited licks and wriggles. The front door to the house hung open. My skin shrank.

"Sofie!" I shouted.

Hudson rounded the car. A small shark leapt from the concrete to swallow his hand to the elbow. When he looked at me, the shark doubled in size; then Pac-Man erupted from his stomach, opened its mouth, and swallowed the tail of the shark. It kept chomping its way up Hudson's arm, devouring the shark in wedge-shaped bites, leaving Hudson's bare arm behind. If I hadn't already been freaked out, that would have done it.

"Hang on, Eva. There could still be someone here," Hudson said when I rushed to the backyard gate.

"If there was, Dali would have told us," I said.

Dali circled Hudson, licking at his fingers and feet and anywhere in between he could reach. When I pushed the gate open, Dali rushed to me, barking, then whined when I shushed him.

The backyard was a trampled mess. I'd seen the pool cleaner after weeklong fall storms. The grass looked like a pack of starved voles had been released, followed by foxes, and capped off with a herd of horses. Two heavy divots plowed from the pool to the carport. Aside from Dali's muffled woofs of disapproval, the backyard lay ominously quiet.

Kyoko was gone.

"Sofie!" I yelled. I ran to the sliding glass door and shoved it open. "Sofie!"

My voice echoed through the empty, sterile house.

# SEVENTEEN

Before I'd Smeared three muddy prints across the pristine white carpet, the power crashed. The recessed overhead lighting blackened and the stereo strangled Sofie's favorite Mozart piece. A jittery thrum sucked through my skin and vibrated against my bones. Panic.

"Sofie!" I screamed, my voice raw.

"Wait—" Hudson grabbed for me and I shrugged him aside. "Eva, someone could still be here. Let's be safe—"

I dashed from the front room to the dining room to the library, ignoring Hudson. We could be safe later. Right now Sofie could be hurt.

Upstairs suffocated in ominous silence. Empty. I pounded back downstairs and through the kitchen—

I staggered against the counter, eyes riveted on the sheet of paper and Polaroid lying on top of it. Hudson bounced off my back and grabbed me to steady us both.

The note was handwritten in kanji. I didn't need to be able to read it to know it was a ransom note. I picked up the Polaroid with shaking fingers.

Sofie, blindfolded, with duct tape slapped across her mouth and binding her wrists. A bruise stained her right jawline, and tears glistened on her cheeks. She stood in the kitchen.

I pivoted to stare at the location of the picture. Tiny black dots swirled in my vision, and a high-pitched noise resonated from my throat. My body shook inside my skin.

Hudson pushed me into a chair and stuffed my head between my legs. Bile swam in my stomach, lapping at my esophagus. I panted, staring at the wall of red hair around me, listening to the ringing in my ears.

They'd left a ransom note. *They'd left a ransom note*. It kept repeating in my head until Hudson gently removed Sofie's picture from my white-knuckle grip.

I bolted to my feet. "We need to call the police. No, the FBI! They—"

"What about Jenny's blackmail?"

"It doesn't matter." God, I'd been so selfish. I'd put my own fears of becoming a scientific experiment above Sofie's *life*. I'd been a fool. Please, please let me have a chance to make this up to Sofie.

Hudson's voice penetrated my thunderous thoughts. ". . . this translated. We need to know what it says."

"We need my aunt—"

"We'll get your aunt."

Hudson's firm tone helped me focus on his determined expression beneath a bejeweled sombrero. A Rubik's Cube engulfed around his torso and monstrous sea creatures circled around his legs.

"Jenny can tell us what this says," he said.

"We don't know where she is."

"But we know where Atlas and Edmond are."

"We do?"

"They've been following you for days. They're probably right outside."

"With the FBI!" I spun toward the front door, but Hudson grabbed my arm before I could take a step.

"And if they are? What then?"

"We have the cousins call Jenny, and then the FBI can arrest her."

"If we do that, how will we find Sofie?"

"The FBI will get Jenny to talk, to tell us where Sofie is."

"Jenny might not know where she is. And the FBI have their own agenda."

"I'm not going to stand here and do nothing!"

The doorbell rang. Hudson and I froze, staring at each other; then I pulled free and sprinted through the kitchen to the foyer.

I yanked the door open. My heart sank. It wasn't Sofie. It wasn't the FBI. It wasn't even Atlas and Edmond. It was a clown. A little person clown—a clowntini? Smears ran through her white face paint and fun-house eye and mouth makeup. Cake-smudged handprints peppered her white jumpsuit, and mystery crusty stains coated the layers of colored ruffles at her throat, waist, and cuffs. A pristine beaded breastplate layered the cotton, depicting a giant open mouth with lots and lots of teeth. The frizzy green wig sprouted a shark fin.

"Hand over the elephant."

The clown's shotgun was almost as long as she was tall, and her finger hovered over the trigger.

I latched on to the first logical thought.

"You're the retrievalist?" Jenny had been spooked by a tiny skip tracer clown?

"Listen up, animal abuser. I want that elephant. Relinquish it, rich bitch. Right. Now."

"You're *not* the retrievalist?"

"I'm going all retrieval on your ass. Hurry up. Hand it over."

A truck blocked the driveway behind Ari's car. It looked like it had spent most of its life working on a farm and had been retired to the city. Even if it could handle the weight of Kyoko, the short sides wouldn't hold her in. The clown couldn't be the feared retrievalist, not with that truck.

"Wrong house," I said, and reached for the door. We were wasting time we needed to use to rescue Sofie.

The clown jabbed me with the gun, stepping over the threshold.

"I saw the elephant." Overdue parking tickets fluttered through the air around the tiny woman and piled at her feet. "I saw you guys shove it in that tiny cage."

"Did you see a woman? Did she look okay?" I grabbed the barrel of the gun and pushed it aside to seize the clown's shoulders.

Hudson swung around the corner, grabbed the barrel in both hands, and yanked the gun from the clown.

"Hey! Get off me, crazy! Give me back my gun!"

"Tell us everything you saw," Hudson said.

"Endangered animal abuse, that's what. I've got backup coming. I'm a card-carrying member of PETA. My posse will be here any minute."

I squatted down to get on eye level with her. "Forget the elephant. Tell me about the woman. Did you see a woman? My height, auburn hair, middle-aged."

"Don't treat me like a fucking child." The clown shoved my shoulders and I toppled onto my ass. "I will mess you up, rich bitch. I will tear out your weave and feed it to your emaciated body. I'll—"

"Freeze, clown." Something ratcheted behind me.

The clown froze. I rolled my eyes up to see Hudson standing behind me like a Mexican cowboy, legs spread, wearing an insubstantial sombrero, navy poncho, and dirty cowboy boots. He held the gun aimed toward the sun. Baby sharks spewed from the hem of the poncho.

"Whoa there, tall fella," the clown said, hands shooting to the sky. "I've got a name. It's Dempsey, not 'clown,' not 'you there,' and *never* 'short stuff.' Got it?"

"Answer Eva. Tell us what you saw."

Dempsey crossed her arms over her chest. "Or what? You'll shoot me? Put me in a cage like you did that elephant? I've got rights, and so do animals."

"How many people did you see?"

"I refuse to talk to anyone threatening me with a gun."

"You just threatened us with this gun!" Hudson said.

"That's different. I'm naturally handicapped, in case you hadn't noticed. I was evening the playing field."

"There's nothing *even* about a gun."

"Enough." I pushed to my knees and took a gamble. If this woman had seen anything that would lead me to Sofie, the risk was worth it. "We had an elephant—"

"Eva—"

"I knew it! You scum-sucking rich are all the same. Think you're above God—"

"We don't have the elephant anymore. Someone stole it."

"Ha! Right. I'm supposed to believe that."

"Look for yourself. Then tell me everything you saw, because they kidnapped my aunt, too."

Dempsey narrowed her eyes at me, then shoved past Hudson into the house. A plywood sign with a cartoon pirate holding out his arm dragged a trail through the billowing parking tickets beside the clown. The pirate's arm hovered a foot above her head, and bold text proclaimed, "Arr, matey. You must be THIS tall to ride this ride."

"If this kidnapping is a trick, I will crush you under the full might of PETA. We won't rest until *you're* caged. No one harms an animal on my watch."

"Eva, do you think—"

"I don't *think*, Hudson. I want my aunt back. I'll do whatever it takes."

"Okay." Hudson cracked the gun in half and emptied the shotgun shells into the coat closet, then put the gun on the top shelf and pushed it out of sight. Two waist-high army men, their green bodies melded with green plastic stands, took point on either side of the door. A third aimed a bazooka after the clown.

I'd opened the divinations floodgate when I'd sucked in the entire house's electricity. My stampeding emotions had flattened the weak mental barriers I maintained as a buffer between me and the onslaught of apparitions. I needed to reclaim every iota of control I could muster if I was going to be any use in rescuing Sofie, but I couldn't find a crumb of calm. The elusive off switch remained as intangible as ever. My lack of control, the childhood handicap I'd never outgrown or overcome, added fuel to my frustration until the emotion howled within my head, drowning out everything else.

"Eva!" Hudson shook my shoulders. "Can you handle her?"

"Where are you going?"

"To get help."

I shuffled out to the backyard and my only link to Sofie. Dempsey jogged through the decimated yard, checking behind the bushes, muttering to herself.

"There may not be an elephant here now, but there *was*. That baby elephant's probably got separation anxiety. Where's its mother? In the garage?"

"No. We only had the baby. Now, *please*, tell me, did you see a woman? She looks like me, only twenty years older."

"I didn't see any redhead. I saw two people wedge a baby elephant into a shoe box of a cage. It was terrified." The clown marched up to me and poked my thigh with a stiff finger. "The free ride is over—"

I shoved the Polaroid into Dempsey's face. "I'm not lying to you." Through the wall of windows, I saw Hudson walk into the kitchen, followed by Atlas and Edmond. When I spotted Jenny, I snatched the photo from Dempsey's hand. "If you can't help, leave." I pointed to the side gate of the yard.

A cherry-red crest of hair superimposed over the clown's green wig. Her beaded breastplate's design morphed to enormous slanted eyes, confirming it was a divination and not part of the clown outfit. The sign and tickets disappeared, and oversize bird wings unfurled from her back. "I'm not going anywhere. Not until I have Attila back, and not until the elephant is safe."

"Attila?"

"Twin barrels of no-nonsense."

She named her shotgun? I shuffled in place. I needed to get inside. I considered picking the clown up and carrying her to her truck.

"Don't even think about it." She crossed her arms.

"What?"

"I know that look. Big people always get that look when they're thinking about using their size against me. It won't work."

I was pretty sure it would, right up until I set her down. I could carry her to her truck, but I couldn't force her to drive away.

"Fine." I turned away. I'd wasted enough time.

Jenny had the note in her hand when I threw open the sliding glass door. Her eyes scanned the page twice, and she sat down in the nearest chair.

"What's it say?" I asked.

The pyramid of naked babies piled high at her feet, leaving only her eyes visible above their silent, wailing, writhing bodies. "The ninjas have Kyoko and your aunt."

Hearing her confirm my fear sucked the air from my lungs.

"What do they want?" Hudson asked while I relearned to breathe.

"The impossible. They want to re-create Kyoko."

"Great. Problem solved," Hudson said. Everyone stared at him like he'd grown a second head. "What? I thought the whole problem was that she was a lonely herd animal. Now she'll have a whole lab of friends. Or are you ready to admit that story's a load of bull?"

Dozens of beakers shot from Jenny, lining up between her and Hudson. In unison, they shattered. "Re-creating Kyoko would be a disaster. They wouldn't keep the elephants together, Montague. They'd sell them off individually." Unexpectedly, the pyramid of babies disappeared, but more beakers materialized and shattered. "And this is Foreseeable Inc. Nothing's more important to them than the bottom line."

"Who?"

"Foreseeable. They're Adorable Creations' Japanese competitor. They've been spying on the project since its inception."

"How ironic," Hudson said, his voice flat with disbelief. "Or more accurately, unbelievable."

"Wait. Who has my aunt: the ninjas or this Foreseeable company?"

"Both. The ninjas are Foreseeable's cleanup crew."

"Stop lying, Jenny," Hudson growled.

"I wish I were making this up." Jenny dropped her gaze to reread the note, her brow furrowed. "I can't make another elephantini."

"What's an elephantini?" Dempsey asked. "Is that some snobby-ass way of saying elephant, because I know what I saw."

"Who's that?" Atlas yanked a pistol from the small of his back and aimed it at the clown. Ironically, an apparition identical to Dempsey's outfit covered him.

"Dempsey," I said. "She saw the kidnapping."

"I don't like clowns."

"I get that a lot." Dempsey eased behind me. I sidestepped out of the line of fire, then circled the front room to stand near Hudson, with the couch in front of me.

"You shouldn't wave that around," Edmond said. "What if it goes off?"

Atlas's eyes flicked toward Edmond, and Dempsey darted behind a love seat.

"Where'd she go? Shit! There's a clown on the loose." Atlas twisted left, then right, gun swinging wildly. Clown makeup smeared his face in an impossible-to-misinterpret apparition of his fear. He fired two shots into the wall at Dempsey's shadow. I dropped to the floor and covered my head with my hands. Hudson fell on top of me. Everyone was yelling, Atlas loudest of all.

"Give it back! It's still out there!"

"Shut it," Edmond bellowed, his deep voice reverberating through the house. "It's okay, guys. I have the gun."

Hudson stood and I crouched, not entirely reassured by Edmond's announcement. Edmond opened a drawer in the kitchen and dropped the gun in with the silverware. Atlas backed up against a wall, eyes wide.

"It's not okay. Clowns are not okay. They're—" Atlas squeaked when Dempsey peeked around the arm of the love seat, then marched into the open.

"Why did they take my aunt? What are their demands?" I stood up fully, arms crossed.

"They took her for leverage. They weren't able to get what they wanted out of my lab at Adorable Creations, so they're trying to get it out of me."

"And they're going to. No more games, Jenny. This is my aunt's *life*."

"I can't—"

*"What's an elephantini?"* Dempsey shouted.

Jenny pinched her lips and glared at the clown. A quiver of arrows appeared near her right hand, and one by one, they shot across the floor, just as they'd done in the trailer toward me. The final one shot through Dempsey's beaded breastplate apparition. Jenny came to the same conclusion I had: Dempsey had seen the elephantini; there was no use pretending Kyoko didn't exist. "It's a miniature elephant," she said.

"Like a miniature horse?" Dempsey asked.

"A crass correlation, but it'll do."

"Damn, you regular-sizers are obsessed with all things small and cute." Dempsey fluffed her green hair and shot Atlas a coy smile. Atlas flinched and slid behind Edmond. I drummed my fingers on my forearm. Any more delays and I'd pop out of my skin.

"Tell us what you saw," Jenny said. "What did the thieves look like?"

"Like all you regular-sizers, but with masks. You know, the bank-robber kind." We all waited for more details. Dempsey threw up her hands. "Okay. I didn't actually get a good look 'cause everyone around here is so obsessed with privacy. And they think hiring a clown is the same thing as hiring a babysitter. I'm the entertainment, folks, not your maid or your nanny or your child's servant. Anyway, I was hiding in the upstairs bathroom and I saw an elephant—excuse me, an *elephantini*—crammed into a cage by two people. I hightailed it down here as soon as the parents weren't looking. How come I've never heard of an elephantini before?"

"Jenny made it," Edmond said proudly. "Intero Europo—"

"In utero," Jenny corrected.

"She's made miniature cats and dogs and bunnies and—"

"What? Where?" Dempsey marched across the front room.

"I need to check . . . There could be . . . Tiny clown, *tiny clown!*" Atlas pushed along the wall until he cleared the front room. He made an effort to recover his dignity and slowed to a fast walk through the kitchen, but then his running footsteps echoed through the foyer and the front door slammed behind him.

"He's fun," Dempsey said with a grin made more evil by her face paint. She pointed a stubby arm at Edmond. "Tell me about the other miniature animals. Where are they? Are they crushed in cramped prisons, too?"

Edmond eyed the small finger with trepidation. Dempsey came up to his waist, and he could probably pick her up one-handed, but he backed up when she rounded the sofa. A rolling pin appeared in one of his upraised hands, a whisk in the other. Pies rained from the sky, their centers undercooked craters.

"I don't know where—"

"Don't give me the runaround. I have the backing of the entire PETA commission. All I have to do is press one on my phone, and you'll be—"

Jenny tilted her head toward the back door, and the three of us slipped out while Dempsey was distracted. I rounded on Jenny the moment we cleared the threshold. "Where. Is. My. Aunt?"

"I don't know. The note doesn't say."

"They want information, though, right? The information for Sofie. Where are you keeping it? Let's go get your notes and do the exchange."

"I think you forget—" Jenny began.

"I've forgotten nothing," I interrupted. "I'm through. You lost whatever leverage you had when they *took Sofie*. I don't care how you threaten me or if you follow through on it. I'm done. We're doing whatever it takes to get my aunt back."

Jenny's almond-shaped eyes studied me, then Hudson. "It's more complicated than that."

"There's nothing—"

"Kyoko's more than an elephantini." Jenny glanced toward the front of the house, where Atlas cowered out of sight beyond the fence. Inside, Edmond was doing a lot of open-handed arm waving, as if he were fending off blows, and Dempsey wielded her index finger like a sword. "Follow me."

Jenny marched across the pockmarked lawn to the glass-topped wall. A few feet beyond the wall, the cliff side dropped to the ocean. She peered uphill toward the house Dempsey had come from. A corner of it peeked through the cultivated flora. Farther away, several more houses rimmed the curving beach. A similar view curved in the other direction.

"The first elephantini lived two days," Jenny said. She stared out at the ocean as she spoke, eyes narrowed against the bright sun. I focused on her face and ignored her overactive apparitions. "The second lived almost a week. There were a lot more complications with elephantinis than with other species. I was hired to fix the problems. But it wasn't only the growth genetics that were flawed. Our changes had cascading effects throughout the elephantinis' molecular structures. Other systems failed almost at birth, and I realized they weren't just not working—they were aging at such an accelerated rate, it looked like they never worked at all."

"No one asked for your memoir. I want Sofie—"

"I didn't plan on making the discovery I did," Jenny said, speaking over me. "It was an accident. I was experimenting with a series of DNA strands that control cell division rates, and then . . ."

"Then?" Hudson prompted. My hands twitched to grab Jenny's shoulders and shake her.

"I created an elephantini that could live well past her twelfth decade. The average life span of a full-size Asian elephant is only seventy years."

"Naturally, that's when you decided to throw away the whole experiment," Hudson said, silver top hat glistening in the sun, half a bed-size Monopoly board spread beneath our feet.

"That's when I realized I'd created something far more valuable than Kyoko. I'd been too focused on the elephantini. I hadn't thought about why Evolution Solutions wanted me spying on *this* project in particular, a failing R and D dead end. The market for miniature elephants is minuscule." She shook her head. "I assumed they planned to sell them to the über-rich. The ultimate pet."

"Wrap it up, Jenny. What *exactly* do we need to do to get my aunt back?" Only my fear of making things worse prevented me from sprinting to the nearest neighbor's house and calling the FBI. Once I had the facts, then I'd act.

"Evolution and AC—and Foreseeable, too—they were never after the elephantini," Jenny said. She hugged her arms to her torso, and they disappeared behind a straitjacket. "It's the formula keeping her alive they want. And I created it. I created a life-lengthening formula. One adaptable to any mammal's DNA." A pyramid of naked, writhing babies piled between the three of us—Jenny's fear, swelling to fill the empty space.

"So you could make people's pets live longer?" Hudson said. "And endangered species? And . . . humans?"

"With specific modifications to an embryo's DNA, I can change a human's life span from eighty or so years to one hundred eighty."

Goose bumps washed over my scalp and shimmied down my body. The elephantini had been science fiction enough for me. We'd breached the threshold of apocalyptic thriller territory.

Jenny paced away from us, then back, for the first time showing visible agitation—to those not privy to divinations. "The moment I realized what I'd created, I destroyed everything. All my notes, incinerated. I went through all the electronic backups and changed notations. I altered the results of Kyoko's tests and switched them with different elephantinis. Everything—I did everything I could to make sure no one knew what I had made."

"If you really created a life-lengthening formula, you would be the richest person in the world. You'd get a Nobel Prize. You'd be famous. You expect us to believe that you destroyed it all?" Hudson asked. The waist-high silver terrier transposed over the pyramid of babies.

"It was the only logical solution. Think it through. Every possible outcome manifests a new nightmare. The few who could afford the life-lengthening formula would hold unreasonable power over everyone else. What if they controlled a government? Imagine a Hitler or Stalin with a two-hundred-year life span. Or if it *was* disseminated to the masses, can you imagine the impact of the next generation on the environment? On the planet's resources?"

"You'll be dead by then. What do you care?" Hudson asked.

"I've studied evolution on a micro and macro scale. As a species, we're not ready for an evolutionary jump of these proportions. As individuals, we'd self-destruct in catastrophic ways." The stacked babies disappeared with the straitjacket. A bullet train shot through Jenny and I stumbled back a step.

"If you were so intent on destroying all evidence, why is Kyoko still alive?"

Jenny pressed her lips together and released a long exhale through her nose before answering. "If I'd killed her at Adorable Creations' lab, an autopsy would have been done, and I'd have been discovered. Plus, at the time, I'd planned to take her to Evolution Solutions. While in hiding, I had time to process the ramifications of Kyoko's existence." She looked away, not meeting our eyes as she confessed, "And I grew attached to the damn creature."

"Attached?" Hudson crossed his arms.

Jenny spun back to face him, eyes blazing with intensity. "Fine. She's my greatest creation. Even if I'm the only one who ever knows. I'd sooner kill myself than destroy her!" A scalpel slid into Jenny's chest, and layers of flesh fell away to reveal a beating heart inside a crushed rib cage. I jerked to look toward the ocean, hand over my mouth.

Hudson scrutinized Jenny's expression. "Why isn't the world looking for Kyoko? An elephantini with a life-lengthening formula in her blood should warrant more than a few ninjas and a couple of FBI on your tail," Hudson said.

"There's the retrievalist, too." Jenny shuddered. "But you have to consider, no company wants to draw attention to their hunt. Right now, three companies know of Kyoko's existence and the *possibility* of a working life-lengthening formula. If any company gets too visual or vocal about searching for Kyoko, it will rouse suspicions in a lot of competitors. Currently, AC is looking for an employee who stole from them. Evolution is looking for an employee that they can't admit they hired to be a spy, so they've branded me a traitor. And Foreseeable is doing what they always do—trying to steal what they didn't have the intelligence to create. If anyone makes a fuss, the competition to find me will skyrocket. Everyone's scared. They need patents to secure their ownership of the formula. They need Kyoko and me. I can't let that happen."

"Tough." As fascinating as I was sure all of this could have been, none of it mattered while Sofie was in danger. "Hand over the formula and bring me back my aunt, or I'm heading straight to the FBI, and damn your complicated plan."

"You can't."

"Why not? You're going to stop me?" I spun and marched toward the house. I would find Sofie without Jenny's help.

"The note. It says if we involve anyone—and that means the FBI—they'll kill your aunt."

# EIGHTEEN

I STUDIED JENNY'S APPARITIONS. A straitjacket engulfed her from neck to knees, and the baby pyramid towered beside her. She was scared, but if she was lying, I couldn't tell.

"You'd better have a plan I like the sound of, or . . ." I didn't have an end to the sentence. Once again, Jenny had all the power. Only she could translate the note. For all I knew, it could have been a birthday party invitation. Or Jenny could be telling the truth, and any action on my part could endanger Sofie.

Acid burned in my throat, and I swallowed hard.

"I'll give them a formula. Not *the* formula. Something close. Something they'll think is real." Her gaze unfocused, and she marched toward the house. An endless bullet train rocketed beside her, life-size and speeding on soundless rails. The train appeared ten feet behind Jenny and disappeared ten feet in front of her. Walking next to it gave me vertigo. "This should work. We'll do the exchange in an hour."

"Is that what they said in the note? What time did they specify?" Hudson asked.

"We have twelve hours before they send the first body part."

I tripped and Hudson caught my arm.

"Where's the exchange?" Hudson asked.

"I have to call and set it up."

"Is your phone working?" My voice came out breathy and insubstantial, visions of the ninjas mutilating Sofie choking my windpipe.

Jenny pulled her cell from her pocket and frowned at it.

"And you say the elephantini isn't cursed," Hudson said.

Jenny looked from me to him. "The *elephantini* isn't."

"Is the clown gone?" Atlas yelled. He thrust his head through the open side gate to the backyard and looked both ways before easing onto the grass.

"You can't mention what I told you to my cousins," Jenny whispered. "I trust them, but not that far." She pushed open the sliding glass door and walked into my mother's house. Atlas hesitated in the doorway.

Hudson stopped me, waiting for Atlas to creep inside before speaking. "Do you believe her?"

I shook my head. It wasn't a denial. I didn't know what to think. "I know she's our best hope for rescuing Sofie."

Inside, Dempsey sat on a high barstool near the kitchen, elevating her to almost eye level. Edmond stood with his arms behind his back, looking like the front room's very own bouncer. Atlas, in full clown-wear apparition, remained pressed against the inside of the sliding glass door, and his eyes darted to Dempsey and away with a speed that had to be dizzying.

Three days ago, I hadn't known anyone in the room. Two days ago, I would have balked at the casual inclusion of another person in our secretive plans, but that had been when I'd cared about Jenny's blackmail. Now, Dempsey was just another character in the growing circus of my life, and the only one clothed appropriately for the part. I would welcome a hundred more people, a thousand more, if it guaranteed Sofie's safety.

"So, how's this go down? You give the abductors some information and they give us the elephantini?" Dempsey asked.

"They give us my aunt," I said.

"Right," Jenny said.

"And the elephantini?"

"Of course." Jenny waved Dempsey's concerns aside. I doubted the ninjas would hand over Kyoko so easily, but I didn't care. Kyoko was Jenny's problem. I only cared about Sofie.

"When do we meet these elephantini snatchers?" Dempsey pounded a tiny fist into a tiny palm.

"I need to get clear of Eva and set up the exchange," Jenny said.

"'Get clear of Eva'?" Hudson echoed.

"I can't do it with her nearby. Plus, I need to gather supplies. I'll be back." Jenny strode toward the front door, but Hudson stepped in front of her.

"I'm not going to let you disappear again."

"Eva?" Jenny waited for me to explain, her expression impatient.

I didn't like the idea of letting Jenny out of our sight, either. She hadn't done a thing to earn my trust, and if she did disappear, finding Sofie would be impossible.

But if she didn't leave, she wouldn't be able to call the ninjas to set up my aunt's rescue. I ran a shaking hand through my hair.

"You haven't been very good at keeping us informed," I said.

"Exactly." Hudson widened his stance, as if preparing to tackle the scientist. Edmond stepped around the kitchen island, but Jenny shook her head, and he stopped several feet from Hudson.

"Fine." Jenny thrummed her fingers on the back of the couch, then turned to Edmond. "Edmond and I will go to the nearest gas station to pick up new phones; then I'll send him back here, and he can park at the end of the driveway." She glanced at me for confirmation. I nodded. "I'll call Edmond once the meeting is set up. Edmond, you'll tell Eva where to go, and everyone gets to be a part of the exchange."

"Why don't we all go together?" Edmond asked.

"I've got to gather the information the ninjas demanded before we can make the exchange. It'll be faster without everyone tagging along, especially Eva."

"We're supposed to trust you?" Hudson asked.

Jenny lifted her dark eyebrows at me. Her plan worked with my curse, but it didn't mean she'd stick to it. The moment she stepped out of sight, she could disappear, taking my chance of saving Sofie with her.

"Make it somewhere close," I said, choking on the words. "Please."

She nodded. "Atlas, you're with me."

Hudson's expression turned to stone and he lifted his hands like he was being held at gunpoint. Lightning bolts struck on either side of him, and one skittered through his body. Jenny stepped around him and strode out of sight, the bullet train ricocheting along its truncated track beside her. Edmond followed her, stopping to grab the gun from the silverware drawer. Atlas took two steps after them, then spun and ran to the back door. He jogged through the backyard, swinging wide when Dempsey made a face at him through the windows.

"Where's the restroom?" Dempsey demanded. "I need to put on my war paint."

I pointed the way.

"Why'd you let her go? What if she's lying? What if she doesn't call? What if Edmond doesn't come back?" Hudson asked.

His questions mirrored my fears. I swallowed bile and held my stomach to quell my nausea. "I didn't have a choice."

Hudson scowled and opened his mouth, but before he could point out more flaws in my logic, scrabbling, scratching sounds emanated from the ceiling, followed by a long, low whine.

"Dali!"

I raced upstairs and followed the whimpers to the master bedroom closet. When I opened the door, Dali burst out, barking and whining. He sniffed my legs, then circled Hudson, sniffing and licking him, too.

"Why was he in there?" Hudson asked.

"I don't know. I must have accidentally shut him in earlier."

"Your friend isn't going to be too happy about that." Hudson pointed to the carpet shredded around the threshold. The door had its share of gouges, too.

"Aww, who's a bad doggie?" I crouched to reassure Dali, managing a faint smile. "Did you slobber on Annabella's clothes? Did you shed all over her closet?"

Dali wriggled in delight at my I-have-a-treat tone.

"Are you sure this Annabella is your friend?"

"She's like family. She'll understand."

Dempsey waited in the foyer. She'd changed and washed off her clown makeup, replacing it with tasteful eye shadow and lipstick. If not for her memorable size, I wouldn't have recognized her. Disguised under the green wig had been long, golden hair worthy of a shampoo ad. Skintight jeans and a stretchy bright blue top replaced the baggy food-stained costume, revealing a doll-like bombshell body. Had she been two feet taller, she could have been a model. She had the right face: not quite classically beautiful but still interesting.

Dali rushed her.

"Whoa!" Dempsey held up one hand like a traffic cop, and Dali slid to a stop. He sniffed and licked her fingers. His whole back end wriggled with his wagging tail, but he didn't attempt to get closer to her when she lowered her hand.

"Do you have a phone?" I asked.

"Of course."

"Where?"

"In my truck."

I breathed a sigh of relief. It might still work.

"You want me to get it?"

"Not yet."

I jogged to Ari's car and grabbed Agent Coutu's card from my bag. Edmond pulled up to the curb at the end of the driveway and waved, but he didn't get out of the car. So far so good. I hurried back to the foyer. My best chance at going anywhere involved staying as far from the Tercel as possible.

"What now?" Dempsey asked.

I curled the business card into a loop in my hand. "Now we wait." I sat on the threshold, eyes locked on Edmond. Dali flopped across my feet.

"I want Attila."

"Who?" Hudson asked.

"Her gun."

"You named a shotgun?"

"All the best weapons have names. Now hand it over."

I released a long, slow breath, picturing my body sinking into the ground. Still and calm, like the earth beneath me. "You'll get it back when we leave."

Dempsey narrowed her eyes at me. "Now."

I pinned her with the weight of my stare.

"Okay. Fine. Later." Dempsey backed away. I focused on Edmond again, waiting for him to receive Jenny's call.

One constricted breath at a time, I wound my curse back into a tight vault deep in my mind. With each inhale, I pulled the stillness from the earth into my body, sweeping my worry and fear ahead of it into the vault. With each exhale, I wedged the stillness across the vault's opening, burying my destructive emotions.

Hudson sat beside me and wrapped an arm around me. He didn't speak. He didn't attempt to offer trite assurances about Sofie's safe return. He didn't voice the hundreds of recriminations resounding in my skull.

I should have gone immediately to the police.

I should never have caved to Jenny's blackmail.

I should never have involved Sofie.

In the comfort of Hudson's quiet presence, I isolated each accusation and suffocated it with the rest of my curse.

"I don't know how you can just sit there. I've gotta move." Dempsey paced in front of us. "What if they don't show? What if they've hurt the elephantini? What if they've hurt your aunt? How do you know she's still alive?"

My breathing hitched and the vault fractured.

"Dempsey," Hudson said. "Go somewhere else."

"You can't tell me— Oh." Dempsey awkwardly patted my knee. "I'm sure she's fine. Your aunt wouldn't be much leverage if she were dead."

"Now, Dempsey," Hudson growled.

"Fine. I'm going, I'm going." She sashayed down the driveway to the Tercel in five-inch wedges. I tipped my head up to the sky, blinking when tears rolled down my cheeks. Hudson rubbed my back.

A longer hour in the history of all time has never existed. I spent it breathing. My aunt's life hung on the whim of violent ninjas pursuing potentially the most lucrative scientific advancement of all time, and the most productive activity I could undertake was breathing.

I bundled up my self-hatred and buried it with all my other emotions.

When Edmond lifted his phone to his ear, every muscle in my body tensed.

"We've got a location!" Dempsey yelled. She dashed up the driveway. Behind her, the Tercel peeled from the curb in a haze of rubber and smoke. My heart seized. Half the point of him parking at the end of the driveway was for his car to be fresh for me to ride in. I bounded to my feet and sprinted down the driveway, Dali on my heels.

"Clover Park," Dempsey shouted as she zipped past me in the other direction. I slowed. Edmond barreled through a sleepy intersection and disappeared. I spun around and ran back to the house, easily overtaking Dempsey.

"Get me Attila. It's go time!" Dempsey vaulted onto her truck's running board. I planted a hand on the driver's door, preventing her from opening it.

"Call this number." I thrust Coutu's creased business card at Dempsey. "Tell them Eva Parker says Jennifer Winters is at Clover Park. That's it. Don't tell them anything else, okay?"

"Eva, are you sure?" Hudson asked.

"Positive. We've only got Jenny's word about all this. If she's lying to us, I'm not letting her get away with it. I'm not losing my one chance at saving Sofie." If she lied about Clover Park, I'd tell the FBI everything.

"What about the elephantini?" Dempsey asked, jumping to the ground and planting her hands on her hips.

"We save my aunt, we save the elephantini." I'd promise a lot more to get a message to Agent Coutu.

"You want Attila? Make the call," Hudson said.

"Okay, okay."

I backed away so Dempsey could open the truck door and retrieve her phone. I kept my distance during the brief call.

"I'm calling on behalf of Eva Parker. She says Jennifer Winters is at Clover Park." Dempsey paused, then said, "Who am I?" She held the phone out to stare at the screen. "Who am I? I'll tell you." She tapped the screen, ending the call. "That was fun. Now hand over Attila."

Hudson retrieved the shotgun. Dempsey broke it open and looked inside the barrels.

"Where are the cartridges?"

"I must have lost them."

If it hadn't been for my curse, I might have tried to ditch Dempsey. We didn't need another person involved—not in Jenny's elephantini abduction and not in Sofie's rescue. We certainly didn't need another witness. But I didn't have the luxury of skipping out on her. Ari's car wasn't going to make it to Clover Park.

"Let's go," I said. I popped the tailgate and Dali jumped into the truck.

"Whoa. I'm not your chauffeur."

"We can take our—"

"What about the curse?" I asked, shutting Hudson down. "Come on, we're wasting time." I slid into the cab, banging my knees on the dash. The bench seat hunched as close as it could get to the dash, which meant my knees pressed against the radio knobs. Hudson climbed in next, his silver terrier disappearing into the truck's motor. He scrunched to the side and yanked the door shut, squishing us together. Dempsey climbed atop a booster seat and settled her feet on the extended pedals.

"*Now* this looks like a clown truck." Dempsey cackled as she peeled out of the driveway.

———

DEMPSEY DROVE like flames were licking the tailpipe. Under different circumstances, I would have been scared, but knowing we were racing against my curse and on our way to rescue Sofie made the succession of broken traffic laws and close calls irrelevant. After the second abrupt lane change, Dali hunkered down in the back and only whined when a sharp turn sent him sliding across the bed.

For the first time in my life, I wished my curse on Sofie. If she'd had it, she could have stalled her kidnappers and improved the odds of our rescue. Instead, I was stuck with the debilitating curse and the stupid mental block preventing me from turning it off, and my lack of control was endangering all our lives.

I blamed Annabella. My working theory was that my mother had me too young, before her gift and curse had fully developed, and she hadn't passed on the gene that would give me control of my gift. The kind of woman who abandoned her child to be raised by her sister seemed like the kind of woman who would fail to give her unborn child working DNA so she could live a normal life.

Thinking about my curse or Annabella—especially Annabella—wasn't going to help Dempsey's truck, but it was better than giving rein to the horrific images of the ninjas torturing Sofie that kept pushing to the forefront of my thoughts.

"I'm sure your aunt is okay," Hudson said, wrapping an arm around me. "They don't want to jeopardize their chance of getting Jenny's information."

His words were meant to be soothing, but they fueled the panic clawing at my skin from the inside.

"She's more than my aunt," I said, as much to distract myself as to make Hudson understand. "Sofie raised me. She's more a mom to me than my mom."

"Your mom is . . . alive?"

I snorted. "Yes. Alive. Off globe-trotting as we speak." Too busy following her dreams of travel and fame to spare a thought for me. "I was a teenage oops, one she didn't want to derail her life to deal with." It came out as bitter as I felt, but I was too wrung out to censor myself. "Sofie was supposed to be temporary assistance, helping Annabella until she graduated high school. But then there was acting school. In New York. Because LA doesn't have any good schools, right?" How had Annabella explained it to me when I was three? *All of the greats trained at the Lee Strasberg Theatre and Film Institute. You want Mommy to be great, don't you?* She hadn't liked my response, either. I'd said no, that I wanted her to be with me. But she'd already known my answer. That was her gift: The divinations Annabella saw around people showed what they wanted *right now*. It hadn't mattered; she'd gone anyway.

"Annabella? As in the name of the *family friend* whose backyard now looks like a bulldozer rampaged through it?"

"Yep. The same one who now has bullet holes in her living room and Lab hair all over her designer wardrobe." For a moment, the corners of my mouth curled up.

"Damn. I thought I had some mom issues because I wasn't allowed to date until I was sixteen," Dempsey said, barreling through a corner gas station when traffic backed up at a red light. "Boy, did that backfire. I had to make up for lost time. I dated five guys my senior year, Tom and Kevin at the same time. Take that, Ma!" She floored it through a yellow light. The engine whined and clacked ominously.

When we hit residential streets, Dempsey gunned it past stop signs, yelling, "We're coming for you, Aunt Mom!" Sharks circled through the truck, and I twisted to look at Hudson. He was pale, one hand gripping the seat back behind me, the other the handle above the door. A minivan braked ahead of us, and Dempsey swerved around them, hanging out the window to shout, "PETA elephant rescue in progress!"

We spun into the Clover Park parking lot and, brakes squealing, squeezed into a spot between a sports car and a flashy SUV. Dempsey turned the engine off, and the truck hiccupped in place, clattered as if a troupe of flamenco dancers and their castanets were trapped under the hood, and died with a long, hissing sigh.

Hudson popped open his door and half fell out of the truck, catching himself against the SUV. The car's alarm blared, and I jumped, scraping off a layer of skin on the dash. Trying to hold my ears, I squirmed out of the truck and planted my hands on the screeching SUV.

*Sofie. Please be safe.*

The alarm petered out on a whine, leaving my hands tingling. With ringing ears, I helped Dali out of the truck and jogged toward the park with the devoted Lab pacing by my side. Dali seemed to pick up on my mood and scanned the park like he knew we were looking for Sofie, completely ignoring other dogs walking by.

I was on the sidewalk before I realized what I'd done: I'd intentionally used my curse. Not like I had in the ninjas' van or Edmond's car, where I'd ramped up my emotions and waited. In that second, leaning against the blaring car, I'd pulled on the car's electricity.

That wasn't how this familial curse-gift thing worked, and I wondered what Sofie would say.

A fresh surge of anxiety bulldozed my surprise, and I focused on the busy park. Electricity from Dempsey's truck and the SUV had boosted my gift, notching the apparitions setting from intrusive to overwhelming.

"Looks like Edmond beat us," Hudson said. He pointed to the parking lot where a familiar green Tercel was parked. It was empty. "I bet Jenny's already here, too."

"What now?" a tiny medieval warrior demanded. Dempsey's beaded breastplate had grown to coat her body, now in a modified houndstooth pattern with tiny black and beige shotguns instead of teeth. A bazooka peeked over one shoulder and a bronze compass circled her feet. Hudson was no better. An abyss at his feet swam with horrors from the depths of the ocean, but he wore his tarnished knight's sword and was orbited by spinning Rubik's Cubes.

"Come on," I said. I jogged along the concrete walkway between the picnic tables and landscaping building, dismissing the teens making out under the canopy of trees and their apparitions of basketball trophies and stilettos, a yeti, and an endless waterfall of eggs cracking over their heads, yolks running down their bodies. "Check over there," I told Dempsey, pointing to a rolling grassy area and its miniature forest of trees that could be hiding a phalanx of ninjas. I skimmed over the tanned volleyball players but slowed to scan the playground. Clusters of adults chatted at the benches or hovered near their toddlers on the play set. Children darted through the jungle gym, plagued by angels and ice cream and blobs of color. A dog-size dragon swiped at kids exiting the slide, and a swarm of bees attacked a group of parents, but Jenny was nowhere in sight.

The squeal of children was dampened by the roar of an engine, pulling my gaze up. At the far end of the park, past the tailfins of private airplanes, a small plane launched off the runway of the airport beyond the fence line, and I remembered why I had stopped coming to this park. Open places were rare in LA, and I often took advantage of the low-electricity zones of parks to relax my perpetual stranglehold on my curse. At worse, I sucked up the electricity of a few cell phones and pointless gadgets normal people seemed incapable of leaving at home, or a water fountain would malfunction or lamp fail to click on at dusk. Clover Park, however, butted up to the Santa Monica Municipal Airport. No matter how slim the chances of my curse affecting the airplanes, after I'd killed my first car when I was ten, I'd refused to come back to this park.

I scrabbled with mental fingers to pull my curse in and contain it, but it was as if I were trying to collect air with my hands. Fear had demolished a lifetime of control, and I couldn't waste precious seconds grounding myself. Achieving any sense of calm was impossible.

Dempsey circled the volleyball game, huffing and puffing as she ran as easily on her five-inch wedges as I did in my flats. "Not . . . there," she said.

I fought to focus my vision and not give in to the blur of panic. The exchange was happening now, and I didn't trust Jenny to do it without me; she cared far more about Kyoko than she did my aunt.

"There!" Hudson pointed toward a two-story mesh-enclosed spiral staircase and lookout tower that resembled a child-size version of an airport control tower. An enormous misshapen wedding cake and a paper clip angel filled the top of the tower. Exiting from the bottom were three women. Jenny was impossible to miss in her familiar strait-jacket and racehorse blinders. The other two women were short, with dark hair and slim bodies. A mountain peak flowed beneath one woman's steps, and the other was adorned in jewels and snakes.

I tripped over a pile of shoes, scattering them, before I realized I was running again, Dali galloping at my side. Hudson was a half step behind us. The snake lady spotted me, said something to her companion, and they both grabbed Jenny's elbows. Jenny twisted to look over her shoulder. When her eyes met mine, a pyramid of naked babies swelled between us. She spun forward and began to run with her captors. My heart lurched, then plummeted to my toes.

"Jenny!"

They had a head start, but I might have caught them before they got to the street and the van parked at the curb if I hadn't spotted the wolf. It snarled, teeth bared beside an oblivious woman seated on the concrete bench in front of the metal control tower. The woman needed an ambulance. Deep, oozing claw marks cut across her arms and neck and disappeared under her T-shirt.

*Sofie.*

# NINETEEN

"SOFIE!" The raw scream startled me even as it burst from my lungs. I fell when I tried to turn too fast, scrambling on hands and knees until I got my feet under me again. Dali spotted Sofie and barked, racing ahead of me. Sofie didn't react. She stared somewhere between me and the escaping ninjas, body stiff, hands on her lap under a folded sweater. Unfamiliar enormous black shades covered her eyes.

"Sofie?" I grabbed her arm and she flinched, swallowing a whimper. The wounds on her arms were all apparitions, and they morphed into thorns that projected from her flesh as much as they pierced it. "It's me, Sofie. It's okay. You're safe."

She twisted away from me, and her auburn hair fell back to expose a bright orange earplug and a black strap wrapped under her hair. Tucked under the glasses was a thick mask. The ninjas had left her blind, deaf, and vulnerable in a public place.

Fury and relief made my hands shake as I gently slid my fingers through her hair. She shuddered and then stilled when I grasped the earplug. I pulled it free.

"It's me, Sofie. You're safe."

The wolf grew leopard spots, and the locket it always wore around its neck turned into a puffer fish. Rose blooms unfurled, replacing the thorns.

"Eva," she whispered, lips trembling.

"It's okay. They're gone." I reached around her and took out the other earplug, then slid the glasses off. She reached up to push the mask off, revealing hands bound by a thick plastic zip tie.

"Where are we?"

"Clover Park."

Dali, who had planted his butt in front of Sofie, wriggled forward and licked her fingers.

"Dali?" Sofie's voice broke, and tears slid down her face. She buried her face in Dali's neck and he let out a sigh of contentment. I wrapped an arm around Sofie and held her.

"Is this"—pant—"Aunt Mom?" Dempsey barreled up to the bench. Sweat gleamed on her forehead, and her warrior apparition was shackled to old-timey prisoner ball weights. "Where's the elephantini? You hide it in that thing?" Dempsey pointed toward the tower just as Atlas—the paper clip angel—trotted out. He faltered.

"Holy shit! Are you the clown?" Atlas asked.

"You think Eva rounded up a second short hottie?"

Atlas looked at me, then back at the tiny blond Barbie. "But . . . but, you're not disfigured and you don't look like a perv."

"Catch me. I'm gonna swoon," Dempsey said.

"Hey. You work as a clown. What'd you expect me to think?"

"That I like kids."

Atlas shuddered. The wings disappeared and a heavy dog collar choked him.

Sofie sat up and swiped tears from her face. Dali pressed up against her legs and rested his head on her knee. My aunt's gaze bounced from person to person, scanning their apparitions, and she clutched my hand.

"They took Jenny?" she asked.

"Yes."

A lopsided wedding cake squeezed down the stairs of the mesh tower and pried itself free of the open doorway just as Hudson jogged back across the lawn. Unlike me, he'd continued to chase Jenny and her captors—without success.

"They got away?" Wedding Cake Edmond asked.

"They got away," Hudson said.

"With the elephantini?" Dempsey hopped onto the bench beside me and raised her hand to shield her forehead like a sailor spotting land.

I scanned the grass along the street side of the park. A young couple generating their own sunset apparition walked a dog in a sweater—the sweater was real—but there was no elephantini in sight. The van had disappeared.

Hudson glanced over my head toward the parking lot. "Here come the FBI. Fast, but too late."

Atlas whirled toward him. "Why are the FBI here?"

"Because I called them," Dempsey said.

"I asked her to," I said.

"You what?" Edmond bellowed.

"Why?" Atlas loomed over me.

"Because my aunt is more important than an elephantini."

"Like hell she is! Animals have rights—equal rights!" Dempsey said.

"Jenny said no feds," Edmond said. "I can't believe you, Eva. Jenny trusted you."

"The ninjas just kidnapped Jenny. Don't you think it's time we talked to someone who could help rescue her?" I asked.

"No," Atlas said. "Jenny said no feds, so no feds. We can't let them near the elephantini."

"Why not?" Dempsey asked.

"Because they'll kill it," Atlas said.

"No, they wo—"

"Jenny said they would," Atlas cut me off. "She's my cousin. If I say we don't tell the feds anything, we don't. Got it?"

I glanced at Sofie. She tucked her bound hands back under her sweater and took a deep breath. "If that's what you want, that's what we'll do," she said.

"Are you sure? You don't have to do this. You were *kidnapped*. You have every right to talk to them. Those women need to be caught."

"Did Jenny tell you why she didn't want the FBI involved?" Sofie asked.

"Yes."

"Was it a good reason?"

"No."

Sofie arched an eyebrow.

"It wasn't a reason worth your life. It wasn't worth letting the women who did this"—I gestured toward her bruised jaw—"get away."

"Is that what Jenny would think?"

"Are you seriously going to be this calm about it?" I demanded. I felt like I was going to shake out of my skin with relief and fury and the aftershocks of panic, but Sofie, the actual kidnap victim, looked like she had spent the day reading in the park.

"We need to do what's best for Jenny *and* Kyoko."

I stared at Sofie, searching her eyes, then scanned her divinations: thorns, a flicker of gashes and a blindfold, the enormous wolf, roses blooming on the thorns. The roses were what decided me.

"Fine, but I have to tell them something. We did call them, after all."

We watched Coutu and Sevallo make a beeline for us across the park, and I wondered if Jenny now wished she hadn't told us to avoid the only people who had a chance of rescuing her from her kidnappers.

"Is this where you're going to meet Jennifer Winters?" Agent Coutu said by way of greeting.

"She's already come and gone. You just missed her."

That earned me a long, hard stare from Coutu, complete with a riding crop and a bologna sandwich. After looking our group over, Sevallo ignored us to scan the park.

"Obstructing justice is a crime. So is interfering in an ongoing investigation and wasting my time." The whip slapped rhythmically against her leg.

"That was never my intention," I swore, and it was the last honest thing I said. "We were here when Jenny called and said she wanted to meet. You made it clear that Jenny was in some trouble, and I shouldn't get involved in it, so I called you."

"Only it wasn't you who called me."

"Right. It was Dempsey. I lost my cell phone."

"Which must have made it difficult for Jenny to call you."

"I gave her Hudson's number when the truck broke down since my cell phone's been missing for a while." I thought it was a smooth save, but Coutu was a pro at detecting lies, and the bologna sandwich grew larger than most of the dogs in the park.

"Who is Dempsey?"

"Family friend," Dempsey said, giving the agent a wave. "Just hanging out here with Eva and Aunt Mom and this hunk." She tossed a thumb at Hudson.

"Let's see some ID," Sevallo said.

"Why? What is this? Pick on a little person day? What about their IDs?"

"You made the call. You're the one we'll arrest if—"

"Arrest! For what? For being little? That's sizest!" For such a small woman, she possessed the volume of a giant.

Sevallo waited, hand outstretched, until Dempsey relinquished her ID.

"Dempsey Semenchuk?" The agent guffawed.

"Not 'Semen-chuck.' It's pronounced 'Sim-ens-huk.'" Dempsey yanked her ID from his hand. "What are you, five?"

Atlas sniggered and punched Edmond in the arm. Dempsey rounded on him, but Coutu was faster.

"Mr. Grant. Mr. Zambo. Care to enlighten us about the whereabouts of your cousin?"

Edmond looked like a squirrel staring down the headlights of an SUV. Atlas's angel wings unfurled and lifted from his body, flapping into the sky and disappearing.

"I don't know, ma'am," Edmond said, jerking his gaze to his shoes.

"She left without telling us where she was going," Atlas said. He had no problem holding the agent's gaze. I wished I had his calm. I felt like my face was glowing with a fine sheen of sweat, and it was all I could do to not look at Sofie and her bound wrists hidden under the sweater.

Sofie was pale, her eyes haunted, but she was doing her best to appear relaxed. She'd swung her hair forward to hide the bruise on her jaw, and when Agent Coutu looked at her, she managed a passable smile.

Two planes departed and one landed before the agents finally gave up. I stuck to my day-in-the-park story, claimed Jenny had wanted another favor, which I'd refused, and that Edmond and Atlas, who had also been called by Jenny, had stuck around at my request so we could talk about them making cupcakes for a party Sofie was going to host. Years of lying came through for me; the cobbled-together story wasn't half bad. Not that it fooled Coutu or Sevallo, but with no reason to hold us, they eventually let us go.

We shuffled toward the parking lot in a huddle, and as soon as we were hidden from the agents' view, Atlas sawed through Sofie's plastic restraints.

"What did they do to you?" I demanded.

"They were just rough with me. They were gentler with Kyoko." She scanned Atlas and Edmond. "What happened?"

"Jenny was going to do a trade—her research for your release. We were her backup," Atlas said.

"Her research?"

In the terror of Sofie's kidnapping, I'd forgotten I hadn't had a chance to explain Jenny's full sci-fi horror story to her. I wasn't sure if Jenny's most recent explanation of a life-lengthening formula wasn't as bogus as her first "lonely herd animal" lie. Back-to-back kidnappings lent her latest story credit, but I was too emotionally exhausted to think of much beyond the fact that Sofie was safe. Since Jenny had warned us not to reveal the full truth to her cousins, I edited my answer. "Kyoko is an elephantini, a miniaturized elephant. She was genetically altered. That's what Jenny does for a living. Or did."

"Wow. Kyoko's full grown?"

"Yep. They need Jenny to make another miniature elephant, but she's scared to do it. That's why she stole Kyoko from the lab in Japan where she worked and has been on the run since," Hudson said.

"Oh, and this is Atlas and Edmond, Jenny's cousins," I said, remembering that Sofie hadn't had the misfortune of meeting them. "And this is Dempsey—"

"Protector of animal rights wherever they're wronged," Dempsey said. She puffed up and projected a gossamer cape twice as long as she was tall, blowing in an unfelt wind.

"She was snooping and saw you taken," I said.

Sofie's wide eyes bounced from person to person. A lifetime of living with me had given her the ability to adapt rapidly to changing circumstances, but being kidnapped, held hostage for ransom, and staked blindfolded and deaf in a park; lying to the FBI; and now being bombarded by all this information was taking its toll. Guilt rolled through me like a physical force, and I wrapped an arm around Sofie and held on. I longed to whisk her home, bundle her up in blankets and safety, and help her forget today ever happened, but first we had to take care of Jenny's mess.

I stiffened and didn't meet anyone's eyes. A wonderful, horrible thought had just popped up front and center in my mind: My problems were over. With Kyoko stolen, Sofie could no longer be implicated in a crime. No one was going to be following me, waiting to ambush me in hopes of getting clues about Kyoko's whereabouts. Jenny was no longer in a position to keep me buried in her mess. I could walk away clean with my aunt and Hudson.

Jenny had torn through my life like a tornado—an apt analogy since I'd be paying for the damages she wrecked for years to come: paying Hudson back for the rental and cleaning of the Suburban, purchasing new furniture to restore my loft, swallowing the hiked insurance fees that would no doubt be included in my next year's bill, and financing the landscaping to replace Sofie's yard—Annabella was on her own.

*Take Sofie, find the nearest bus, and leave,* dispassionate logic argued.

Jenny and Kyoko weren't my problem. Jenny had gotten herself into this mess, and she could get herself out.

Yet, my muscles refused to obey my logic. I couldn't abandon Jenny now, despite the fact that I hardly knew the crazy scientist and despite the hell she'd put me through. We were the only people who knew who had abducted Jenny and the only ones in the United States who knew about Kyoko. I suffered no delusions about the violence the ninjas were capable of. Abandoning Jenny to their mercy wouldn't be right, and I reluctantly admitted to myself that I wouldn't be the woman Sofie raised and was proud of if I walked away now.

That was more than enough motivation to assist any efforts to rescue Jenny, but heaped on top was the threat of the life-lengthening formula. As much as I didn't want to believe Jenny, if she was telling the truth, that formula in the wrong hands—in anyone's hands—would lead to massive problems, if not the complete devastation of the human race and, possibly, of the planet. In some inconceivable twist of reality, I had the possibility of influencing the future of humanity, and I couldn't walk away and hope for the best. Whether I wanted it or not, I was a part of Jenny's conspiracy, and I would see this through.

"How did the ninjas get Jenny?" Hudson asked. Rubik's Cubes at his fingertips, rotten banana slices falling to his feet, and jellyfish floating through his torso—Hudson appeared as conflicted as I was. He met my gaze and tried on a smile that didn't reach his eyes. Did he wish he'd never met me? In his place, my answer would have been yes. I wasn't worth this kind of insanity. Hudson, though—I wouldn't have made it through the last three days without him. I couldn't think of a single man I'd dated who would have handled an elephantini, being kidnapped, and the rescue of my aunt with such aplomb. The only possible contender was Keith, and he was a Navy SEAL.

Edmond slumped against Dempsey's truck, where we'd all clustered. "We let them. Atlas had a gun, but they had two, and they were going to shoot Sofie if we didn't let them walk away."

"Oh." Sofie patted his shoulder. "Thank you."

"What are we going to do now?" Atlas demanded.

"I can't think," Edmond said. He paced away from us, a revolving selection of cooking utensils swirling around him. "I need to bake."

"Do either of you know where they might be taking Jenny?" I asked.

"Sure. We're all meeting later for coffee."

"Not helping, Atlas," Edmond rumbled.

"Of course we don't know where they took her!"

"Do you have any idea how to find her? Any clues? Anything Jenny might have said?" I prompted. A looming clown hovered behind Atlas like a Macy's Thanksgiving Day Parade balloon. The clown had razor-sharp teeth and goat horns, with fingers that kept growing longer and longer clawlike nails. I turned to look at Edmond.

"How are we supposed to know?" Edmond asked.

"Tell us about Jenny, about what she's been having you do," Hudson said.

"She came by a couple of months ago," Edmond said. "Out of nowhere, she's on our doorstep talking nonsense and waving money in Atlas's face."

"She hired us," Atlas said. "To help her. Always insisted we meet her in public places, like she was in some spy movie. At first we did little jobs, you know? Found her a house. Bought groceries, some burner phones. Then she had us, uh, watch Eva pretty much full-time, and you know everything after that. She never talked about these ninjas until they snatched you two." Atlas pointed at me and Hudson.

"When they snatched *you*?" Sofie echoed.

I shook my head. "It was nothing. I'll tell you later."

"She didn't mention anything else when it was just you guys?" Hudson asked.

"Nope."

"She told that one person that the elephantini was dying," Edmond said. He had his eyes squeezed shut; flour and sugar and eggs dropped into an enormous bowl at his feet.

"That's right." Atlas snapped and took over Edmond's pacing. "We heard her on the phone. It was the day we picked her up outside the gallery. She told someone that she was a failure and the elephantini was dying."

"No, not that *she* was a failure. That the *experiment* had failed," Edmond said.

"That's right. The experiment failed and she'd been discovered. You know what, I bet she was talking to her spy company."

"Spy company?" Sofie echoed, her eyes wide.

"She worked as a lab spy in Japan for an American company," I explained. Sofie blinked glazed eyes, then patted my hand.

"What's Aunt Selah going to say?" Edmond moaned. "We have to find Jenny."

I glanced around at our ragtag group. We were hopeless, hapless, and running out of luck. Clearly, we weren't capable of rescuing Jenny ourselves. We had no idea how much time we had, and we had no plan for where to go from here. It was time to take matters into my own hands. The framework of a plan formed in my mind, seeded with a kernel of hope.

"It's time to go to dinner."

# TWENTY

"HOW CAN you think about food right now?" Edmond asked.

"Every minute we waste, the less likely it is we'll find Jenny," Hudson said.

Sofie tapped her nose, mouthed, *"Miriam,"* and smiled at me. It felt damn good to see that smile.

"No, no, Eva's right," Sofie said. "Where's your bag? I'll draw you some sketches of the ninjas. That should help."

"Great idea," I said.

"We don't need to know what they look like; we need to know where they are," Atlas said, speaking over me.

"We need the sketches," I said, louder. "I know someone who can use them to help. She's Ari's sister's wife, and she works for the FBI. I trust her."

"Sister's *wife?*" Edmond's eyebrows shot skyward.

"No, we agreed no FBI," Atlas said.

"We're not going to the FBI," I said. "I'm going to Miriam. She'll help, and she won't turn us in."

"How do you know?" Hudson said.

"She's family."

"She's *Ari's* family," Hudson countered.

I forgot how little Hudson knew about me. "Do you have a better idea? Does anyone? Miriam has resources and training. A fresh perspective." No one moved. "An actual chance at finding and rescuing Jenny."

Atlas and Edmond shared a look. I understood their hesitation and their muddled, panic-fogged thinking.

"Maybe we should trust her," Edmond said.

"Jenny said Eva was the key to *hiding* the elephantini. Which she did a bang-up job of. Thanks, Eva."

"No, Jenny said she was *the key*."

"Damn it, Ed. I knew watching those *Lord of the Rings* movies was going to mess with your head. This isn't some prophecy. Eva isn't destined to be the key to rescuing Jenny or to saving the elephantini. She was just good at lying low. She bought Jenny a few days."

"Don't treat me like an idiot," Edmond said, straightening from his slouch to get in Atlas's face. "Jenny's exact words were, 'Eva is the key to solving the elephantini problem.' You've been doubting Jenny since the gallery job, but everything's worked out just like she said: Eva showed up right on schedule and was so good at hiding the elephantini, we didn't even know it was a real elephant until Jenny told us. We need help, and if Jenny trusted Eva, we can, too."

Jenny didn't *trust* me; she'd *blackmailed* me. And . . . My thoughts snagged on the unique phrase *gallery job*. Not *gallery meeting* or *gallery getaway*. They weren't talking about being the getaway driver for Jenny when she'd left me handcuffed in the trailer with Kyoko. I let go of Sofie. "You? You! *You!*"

Everyone turned to stare at me with confused expressions. I jabbed a finger at Atlas. "Art thieves!"

Atlas's mouth fell open and his eyes widened until white showed all the way around his irises. Edmond hunched his shoulders, and in sync, both cousins stepped away from me.

"No, we didn't . . . I don't know what you're . . ." Atlas sprouted a paper-clip crown that fell to pieces and slithered down his body.

"Don't lie to me," I thundered, pent-up tension adding unintended volume to my statement.

"Jenny told us to steal the paintings. She wanted a way to guarantee you'd show up."

"Shut it, Ed. You're making it worse." Atlas turned to me, hands raised. "Eva, we didn't mean anything by it, I swear."

Jenny had planned the whole thing? Was I surprised? I waited a beat, and no new emotion emerged. This answered the nagging question of the coincidence of running into Jenny. She'd had the blackmail in line, the sucker all picked out to hitch to her crazy plan; all she'd needed was to find me. Since I didn't have any sort of routine in my life, she'd created a reason for me to be in a particular place at a specific time. An insane, over-the-top reason. Why not just set up a consultation with me? Or wait for me outside my loft?

I opened my mouth to ask, and then I saw Sofie's face.

"You didn't steal my paintings because you liked them?" Sofie asked in a small voice.

Everyone turned to look at her. Sofie looked like she was going to cry. I glared at Atlas.

"It was a job, just another one of Jenny's plans that didn't make any sense until later," Edmond said.

"But the paintings are beautiful," Atlas said. He slugged Edmond's arm. Edmond didn't look like he noticed Atlas's punch, but he flinched when Sofie swiped a tear from the corner of her eye.

"Oh, yeah, I really like them. All the other pieces in the storage room were bland and ugly, but yours practically begged to be stolen." Edmond was completely earnest, as if he were paying Sofie a high compliment.

"They looked like they should have been stolen?" Sofie echoed. "That's the sweetest compliment I've ever received."

I rolled my eyes, but the steel band squeezing my heart eased. Hudson's silver terrier stood at his feet, but he was smiling.

"Damn straight," Atlas said. "A bunch of stuffed shirts in some black-market auction would pay top dollar to put your art in their private collection."

"Thank you." Sofie smiled at the group at large. Paintbrushes danced around her skirt, and when the blindfold flickered over her eyes, it was detailed with a swirling design in sky blue.

I wondered if banging my head against the truck would help.

Hudson leaned close to me. "Would it be wrong if I said I was glad they stole your aunt's art, too?" he whispered as the cousins continued to heap praise upon Sofie.

I jerked my eyes to his. The light in his blue eyes reflected his soft smile, and my heart wriggled in response. He could easily have seen it the way I had been thinking, that if the artwork hadn't been stolen, I wouldn't be involved in this illegal mess. I hadn't considered I would have missed out on Hudson.

He winked before turning back to join the main conversation.

"If Jenny wanted you to trust Eva to take care of the elephantini problem, you have to trust her," Hudson said.

I wanted to protest right along with Atlas and Edmond, but I kept my mouth shut and basked in the glow of my crush on Hudson.

Atlas's golden wings deflated to a prison suit—the striped kind worn by chain gangs and not seen in California in decades—and a crown of thorns. Someone thought they were making a noble sacrifice. Edmond rained glops of runny flan, but they both finally gave me their consent. I prayed Miriam would be able to help without us all going to jail.

I turned to Sofie. "Are you ready to go to dinner?"

"I think I'm going to sit this one out, Eva. I've had all the excitement I can take." The blindfold obscured her eyes, and claw marks wounded her arms in quick succession. A fresh wave of guilt assaulted me. I should have realized she'd want to go home. I should have been going home with her, making sure she was safe and protected and that she could get to sleep without nightmares.

Sofie pulled me into her arms. "None of that," she whispered against my ear.

"What?"

"All that guilt you're spewing. Let it go, baby girl. This wasn't your fault."

Her words were meant to soothe, but they stabbed my heart. I tipped my head back, but the tears refused to be trapped, and they ran down my cheeks and dripped onto my shirt. "This *was* my fault," I whispered.

"Nonsense. You no more control those wicked women than you do me or Hudson."

"But if I hadn't—"

"There's a million alternate universes of *ifs*. Let the people living in those universes deal with them."

I dropped my head to look at Sofie. Her rich brown eyes were intent on my face; then they shifted to check the divinations swirling around me, visible only to her. She pushed a strand of hair behind my ear with fingers that trembled.

"I'm safe. Now we need to concentrate on Kyoko and Jenny. Get me some paper, and I'll do what I can."

Hudson was the only one thinking clearly enough to question how Sofie had seen the ninja's faces when they were either wearing masks or Sofie was blindfolded. Sofie fielded the question like a pro.

"I'm an artist. A ski mask can cover up only so much to the trained eye. I'll give you five sketches, my best guesses."

Sofie's sketches had nothing to do with an artist's eye or guesses and everything to do with the power of her divinations. Clearly, she'd seen the women's faces in their apparitions. Of course, there were only three women, so Sofie must not have been sure which of the five faces she'd seen were the women who had held her.

Hudson's manners forced him to accept Sofie's ridiculous explanation.

We didn't leave the park until Bernie, Sofie's boyfriend, arrived. Sofie called him from Edmond's phone, which he'd left in the Tercel and was the only working phone in the group. Bernie raced over, no explanation needed. He was a business executive and Sofie's opposite in so many ways, but he was a good guy. One of the few. Their relationship worked because Bernie gave Sofie the space she needed, and I got the impression that he was happy with whatever time she gave him. Bernie took one look at Sofie, then swept her into his arms and planted a tender kiss on her forehead. Dali swiped his fingers with an exuberant tongue.

I relaxed, knowing that Sofie was safe. She could let go of the tight control of her emotions, which was more than she would be able to do if I went home with her. For me, she thought she always had to be the strong one. With Bernie, she could be as fragile as she felt.

"I'll have Ari call you," I told Sofie as I tucked her into Bernie's car.

"Don't let them hurt Jenny or that sweet elephantini."

"I won't."

"*We* won't," Dempsey corrected me.

Sofie kissed my cheeks and hugged me tight. "Thank you for coming for me."

I squeezed her tighter. "Always."

---

EVERY SUNDAY NIGHT, the entire da Via family congregated at Ari's parents' house for dinner. Attendance wasn't mandatory, but Carmela's cooking provided enough incentive to gather the whole clan most weeks, and today was no exception.

We took a cab to Hudson's car at Ari's before driving up to the foothills, and we arrived at the da Via estate just as Antonio and Ari were getting out of Antonio's truck.

"Eva!" Ari ran to me. "Where's Sofie?"

"Safe. With Bernie."

Ari yanked me into a tight hug, and we clung to each other.

"I was so worried," she whispered into my hair.

"Me too."

"And the elephantini?" She pulled back a little. In the fading sunlight, Ari's expression was abnormally serious, her deep dimples nonexistent.

"Not so safe."

"That's why we're here," Dempsey said, pushing out of the backseat.

Ari's dark eyebrows shot upward.

"Leave the gun," I said. Bullets or no, I wasn't letting her bring a gun into Carmela's. "I mean it, Dempsey. This is a family gathering."

"She looks Italian. *He* looks Italian." Dempsey's gaze snagged on Antonio's tight jeans and scanned up to his creamy button-up shirt. With his thick hair tamed and a five o'clock shadow darkening his jawline, he looked every inch an Italian bad boy. It took Dempsey a deep breath before she corralled her thoughts. "Maybe this is a *family*, you know, mafioso. I might need protection."

"No."

"Hi, I'm Antonio." He stretched a hand to Dempsey, giving her his charming smile. She half swooned and tossed Attila into the backseat.

"Dempsey's been helping us out," I said. I gave Ari and Antonio a brief recounting of the eventful day, ending with, "We need Miriam's help. We need it to be quiet, too."

"Got it. Not a word to Ma."

"You, too, Dempsey," I said. "You can't mention anything to the family about the elephantini, Jenny, the FBI, Atlas, Edmond, Sofie being kidnapped—"

"Maybe it'd be easier if you told me what I *can* talk about," Dempsey said. She crossed her arms over her chest. "I do have a brain, you know. Smaller doesn't mean stupider."

"Fine. But if you mention something you shouldn't, I'm not rescuing you," I said.

"From what?"

"Carmela," Ari and Antonio said together.

"You guys go ahead." I ducked around the car and set my bag on the driveway. I pulled a lightweight wrinkle-resistant blouse from a zipper pocket, crouched down, and yanked my grimy T-shirt over my head.

"Nice." Hudson stood near the hood of the car, watching me.

I tugged the blouse over my head, stood, and brushed it smooth, checking to make sure it covered the bruises on my wrists that would otherwise elicit unwanted concern. I stuffed the T-shirt into my bag and examined myself in a side-view mirror. Fortunately, the scrape on my nose had healed enough to pass as a bad sunburn, but I couldn't do anything about the dark smudges under my eyes. I ran my fingers through my hair and patted my cheeks for a little extra color.

"Got a date I don't know about?"

"I want to avoid questions."

"What about another shirt in there for me?"

"Weren't you the one who said you needed to pack a spare change of clothes if you were going to hang around me?"

Hudson stepped up behind me, where I was bent to see myself in the mirror. He planted his hands on my hips, then ran them lightly up my sides. When I straightened, he turned me to face him. We were inches apart.

"I'm sorry, Eva. I shouldn't have gotten so upset with you when you straightened my office."

The apology felt like it came out of nowhere from an argument that happened a lifetime ago, not this morning. Even if I hadn't forgotten about it, I would have forgiven him for much worse: I had Sofie back; everything else was insignificant.

"I shouldn't have touched your things without your permission."

"It's not like you ruined anything. That was the first time I've seen the surface of my desk in months, years. And Sofie was right. Your feng shui skills are uncanny."

"Are you saying my assessment of your life was accurate?"

"Dead-on."

"Score one for feng shui."

"You must be damn good at what you do."

"Hmm. Flattery. I like it."

Hudson leaned down and I went up on tiptoes for a kiss. His hand slid up my back to cradle my head, and he deepened the kiss. When he pulled back, I swallowed a moan and reminded myself that I was in Carmela's driveway.

"Are you ready for this?" I asked Hudson.

"How bad can it be?"

Everyone was getting seated in the dining room, the food already on the table, when Hudson and I arrived.

"Eva!" Carmela burst from the kitchen with three extra sets of plates and silverware in her hands. She thrust everything at Antonio and swept me into a hug, kissing the air beside each cheek. She was five-five, had dyed dark brown hair that had more body than a Victoria's Secret model, and she exuded energy. "Who's this handsome stranger?" She clutched Hudson's hands and pulled his arms out to the sides so she could run her eyes over him.

I kept it simple. "This is my friend Hudson."

Carmela gave me a one-eyebrow-raised look that said she didn't believe the *friend* status; then she performed the introductions of the family.

"That's my wonderful husband, Caesar." He sat in the middle of the table tonight, not at the head. I had a special place in my heart for Caesar. Here was a man who had fathered five children and not only stuck around to raise them, but he also seemed to genuinely love them all and want to spend time with them. He had been married to Carmela for over forty years and faithful to her every single day. He was the exception to the rule: a man who could be trusted.

He stood to hug me and shake Hudson's hand.

"I'm so glad you could make it, Eva," he said.

"Me too." The da Vias were the family I'd always dreamed of having: large, boisterous, united, loving. My informal adoption into their clan was one of my proudest achievements.

Michelangelo, the oldest son, sat next to his father, along with Georgino and his wife, Helen. Their three kids, Josette, Emilio, and Desirée, were at the kids' table. Dempsey had been given a seat next to Georgino, and they were deep in discussion about the endangered El Segundo blue butterfly.

"Yes, Hudson, there'll be a quiz later," Carmela teased as she introduced Georgino's twin sister, Gianna; her wife, Miriam; and their daughter, Isra. Gianna had a tamed-down version of Ari's dimples, and they flashed now even as her serious eyes examined Hudson. Miriam was Iranian, exotic-looking even among this good-looking family, with a black bob and startlingly bright brown eyes. She smiled benignly, but when Carmela wasn't looking, she mouthed, *"We need to talk,"* to me.

I bit my lip. How much did she already know? Did she know about the FBI questioning me?

"And you know Antonio, right?" Carmela continued.

"We're familiar. You have a lovely family, Carmela."

"You say that because you know me," Ari said, coming in from the side room with two additional chairs. "Be warned: I'm the nicest and the smartest."

Michelangelo beaned her with a roll.

I sat. I ate. I chatted. Normalcy settled around me like a blanket, soothing frazzled nerves and washing away the stress of the last four days. I was home, with family. I was safe and loved. Sofie was safe. For a suspended moment in time, everything in the world was righted and everything was going to be okay. We'd find Jenny, rescue Kyoko, and save the world from Jenny's stupid life-lengthening, doomsday formula. I found my sense of humor again and teased and verbally sparred with the da Vias. I laughed for what felt like the first time in years.

When Gianna and Georgino rose to clear the table, and Dempsey was locked in a discussion with Carmela, Miriam motioned to the door and I followed her from the bright dining room to the dim family room down the hall, grabbing my bag from a hook near the door on the way. When I slung it over my shoulder, the weight of the world settled with it, and my good mood floated away.

Miriam halted near the window farthest from the doorway, looking out over the moonlit pool and patio. A steel infinity symbol twisted above her heart.

"Do you want to explain to me why there's a detail assigned to you?" Miriam asked quietly.

"You mean Coutu and Sevallo?"

Miriam cocked her head and waited.

"What do you know?" I asked.

"Why don't you tell me what you know and we'll go from there."

I licked my lips nervously. "It's about Jenny. Jennifer Winters. She dumped her crazy into my world four days ago, and everything's been shitty since." I told Miriam a heavily edited version of the last four days, never mentioning Kyoko by name or explaining what she was, just that Jenny had left me a "package." Everything else I told her was the truth: about meeting Hudson and him pretending to be my boyfriend, about delivering the "package" to Sofie and then later moving it to Annabella's. I told her about Atlas and Edmond, about the ninjas' botched kidnapping of Hudson and me, about my ransacked home. I poured out the tale of Sofie's kidnapping and the exchange gone horribly wrong. I didn't figure it was necessary to mention all the broken-down cars.

"And now what?" Miriam asked when I wound down.

"I don't know. I have sketches of the women who took her. And I found the original ransom note, not that it'll help you. It's in kanji, and a bit worse for the wear. Any DNA is gone from it." I pulled the notebook with Sofie's drawings out of my bag and handed it to Miriam. The ransom note was tucked inside the notebook. Miriam took it without looking at it.

"You've had a rough few days, haven't you?" she said.

"It's been surreal."

"Mmm." She shifted so that my face was in the light, hers in the shadows. "So your life and Hudson's were threatened, your aunt was *kidnapped*, and you still don't want to tell me what is in this mysterious package Jenny gave you? What are you asking for here, Eva? What do you want me to do?"

"I need your help. I need to know who these people are that took Jenny."

"And then what?"

"I'll . . . I don't know. Maybe then it'll be time to involve the FBI. Officially."

"Maybe?" Miriam shoved a clump of ebony hair behind her ear and leaned in closer to me. "I don't work in the same division as Coutu and Sevallo, and even I've heard all the speculation about Jennifer Winters. She was turned in by her own company, some scientific research lab funded by the government. Did you know that? They suspect her of treason—*treason*—and Coutu has been building the case. You don't want to get in the middle of that."

"I'm not here by choice."

Miriam's infinity symbol disappeared. A squirming malamute puppy in a rumpled suit and tie sat at her feet. I'd seen that puppy before, though usually when Isra was trying to pull one over on her mothers.

"Why didn't you tell Sevallo and Coutu about Sofie being kidnapped? Why are you not in their office right now with these sketches?" She waved the notebook at me.

"Because those women took the package, too," I said. I trusted Miriam to help with finding Jenny, but I couldn't bring myself to tell her about the life-lengthening formula. Not yet. Not unless I had to. I suspected Miriam would feel it necessary to tell her superiors. Once they knew, there'd be no stopping the secret from spreading, and all the cover-up Jenny had done and I had assisted in would be for nothing. Plus, I was pretty sure those treason charges would sweep me along with Jenny, straight to prison.

"Is it drugs?"

"No! Something— Oh, it's impossible to explain, but it's something we don't want falling into the wrong hands, and that includes the government's hands."

"You do realize who I work for, right?"

"Of course."

"You want me, a *government employee,* to help you find something you don't want the government to find."

"No, I want *your* help."

"My help. So long as it includes using the FBI's resources?"

"I wouldn't be asking you if I had another option. It's imperative that we find Jenny and the package."

Miriam stared at me, waiting. I listened to the grandfather clock in the hallway tick away the seconds and did my best not to squirm.

"The FBI is already looking for Jenny—"

"But they don't know she's been kidnapped by—"

"Eva."

I shut my mouth.

"I will help you, but"—Miriam paused—"but if this backfires on me, on Arianna, or even on you, I will make sure you suffer the full penalty."

"I understand," I said. "You can't break the law."

"I'm not talking about the law. If this goes sideways, I'll tell Carmela."

Carmela's wrath would shred my flesh from my bones if she discovered I'd aided a traitor to the United States. She wouldn't care about extenuating circumstances or listen to reason. After she was done picking over my carcass, she'd tell her friends what I'd done, and in days, all of LA would know. Not that it would matter. Because I'd be in jail if this backfired.

The risotto churned in my stomach, and I took my time following Miriam back to the table for dessert.

## TWENTY-ONE

DEMPSEY TOOK a taxi home after I crossed my heart and pinky-swore we would contact her if we learned anything. Then Hudson drove the two of us to his house. His car survived all but the last six blocks. He took it well, just gathered his keys, locked everything, took my hand, and with an enormous cherub flapping ahead of us and a red wagon bringing up the rear, began walking.

The two bars we passed spilled drunken people onto the sidewalk in clouds of alcohol fumes and smoke, and jazz music drifted from a coffee shop. I peered into the darkened store fronts of the strip malls and up at the bright LA night sky, content to allow the sounds of the city to fill the space between us. Hudson and I hadn't had many quiet, normal moments, and it was nice to pretend that we were walking home after a long date, not after an insane day of desperation.

Sofie had called Ari after dinner to let me know that she and Bernie were at his house with Dali, where she'd be staying until she heard from me. I breathed lighter knowing she was tucked away where all the people tracking Jenny didn't know to look.

Hudson had held his own at the da Via table. He was the first date I'd ever brought to dinner, and the da Vias had grilled him like any family members' dates. I had no idea where my relationship with

Hudson was headed, or even if we had a relationship that could survive outside this high-stress whirlwind Jenny had dumped on us, but at least I knew my family approved of him.

My footsteps were dragging by the time we reached Hudson's door. The strain of the day combined with little sleep the night before had caught up with me. While I flopped on the couch, Hudson called Matvei to watch the house. It didn't seem necessary since the ninjas had Jenny and Kyoko, but I was too tired to argue. After his brief conversation, he hit the play button on his answering machine. A woman's soft, Southern voice filled the house's silence.

"Hudson, it's me. Do you remember that buckle you won in your first 4-H show? Your dad just found it in the attic." She paused, then said, "Why don't you give us a call? It's been months since we've talked. I've been missing you."

I twisted in my seat to look at Hudson.

"That was my mom," he said. He was staring at the answering machine. "I can't remember the last time she said she missed me."

I don't think he realized how vulnerable he sounded. I walked to him and hugged him from behind.

"Sounds like you miss her, too."

"Yeah." He cleared his throat. "I haven't been back that much since college. Mom always thought I'd stay in the family business, but it wasn't me. Now I feel guilty when I go back and guilty when I stay away."

"There's not a lot of electrical engineering involved in racing horses, I take it."

Hudson twisted in my arms to face me, his eyes dark and unreadable. "No. Not much."

"This is where I tell you I told you so."

"What?" Hudson's expression turned guarded. "What are you talking about?"

"You think it's coincidence that I straightened up your family bagua and you get a call from your mom out of the blue?"

"Well . . ."

I arched a brow at him. He relaxed in my arms, a smile tugging at his lips.

"It could be a coincidence."

"Good thing I know that stubborn men make great lovers."

"We do, huh?"

"Well, the scientific experiments are ongoing. If you know of any other stubborn men I can test my theory on—"

Hudson backed me up against the wall, pinning me with his body. "You won't find anyone more stubborn than me."

"Oh? I don't know. I—"

He cut off my words with a kiss. Languid energy infused my tired limbs, and I melted against him.

"No one else," he growled.

"Mmm, are you sure?"

"Positive."

I pulled back to examine his dilated eyes, thrilled to see he was serious. Whatever this was between us, he felt its intensity, too, and was just as addicted.

"Good. The same goes for you," I said.

The next kiss left us both panting, and Hudson looked smug when he lifted his head. "Glad we got that settled."

Going on my tiptoes, I kissed along Hudson's jaw to his ear and nibbled his earlobe. He groaned and slid his hands behind my back, pulling me from the wall enough to cup my butt. I ground against him. His shoulder muscles flexed beneath my hands; then he lifted me, and I wrapped my legs around his waist, shifting for another hot kiss.

When he spun us from the wall, I tightened my arms around him, not relaxing even after he set me down on the smooth kitchen counter. Neither of us broke the kiss. The velvet of his tongue and the not-so-gentle ministrations of his lips zinged pleasure through my body, and I wriggled closer.

A soft brush of his thumbs against my stomach only emphasized all of the clothing between us, and I unfisted my hands from Hudson's shirt to wad the fabric more productively, tugging it up over his head. He leaned back to assist me, and I tightened my calves around him to keep him close. His shirt disappeared in the direction of the refrigerator while I admired his firm torso. I flattened my hands against his pectorals, then slid them down his chest, curling my fingers to lightly graze my nails across his abdomen. Hudson hissed, stomach tightening, and I glanced at him through my lashes.

"Christ, Eva." Hudson slid a hand around the nape of my neck, pulling me to him for another intoxicating kiss, and when he drew back, my bra's clasp hung undone against my back and my shirt was bunched around my ribs. Hudson circled his hands around my torso, pushing my bra and shirt aside to cup my breasts.

The heat of his palms saturated my skin, arousing and unexpectedly comforting. A rush of tenderness spiraled through my lust, and I ran my fingers across Hudson's temple and down his cheek. His blue eyes lifted to mine, obviously surprised, but whatever he saw in my expression made him smile. He leaned into my touch, teasing his thumbs in slow circles around my nipples and sending leisurely waves of pleasure pulsing to my middle. I traced his lips, then stroked my thumb across his bottom lip, watching lust darken his expression until my own pleasure pulled my eyes closed.

Hudson shifted, and I slid my fingers through his hair as he dipped toward my breast, my gentle touch turning demanding when his mouth settled over my nipple, hot and wet. His tongue flicked across the sensitive peak, and I clutched his shoulders, clinging to him as I arched to give him better access.

"Hudson, I think . . ."

He trailed kisses across my chest to my other nipple, and I lifted toward him to meet his mouth, moaning as I watched his tongue flutter over my nipple. I writhed against him, pressing our bodies as close together as our clothing would allow.

"You think what?" Hudson breathed the words against my breast, but they didn't register until he lifted his head.

"What?"

"You said you think . . ."

I stared at his kiss-swollen lips, trying to remember what I'd been saying. "I think I have too many clothes on."

"I agree." Hudson tugged my shirt and bra over my head and tossed them behind him to the floor. I reached for his pants, but he captured my hands and placed them back around his neck. "One second."

He picked me up, and I think he meant to carry me to the bedroom, but we made it only as far as the couch. In a frantic, clumsy rush, we peeled our shoes, pants, and underwear off, and from somewhere, Hudson produced a condom. I would have cheered, but I was too busy kissing a path down his body. I reached his belly button when he stopped me.

"One lick, and I'm toast," he said, his voice husky.

I arched an eyebrow and flicked my tongue over the crest of his cock.

"Eva!" Hudson stepped back, trying to give me a stern look but ruining it completely with a goofy grin. In record time, he rolled on the condom, then tipped me back onto the couch. I went willingly, reaching for him as he placed one knee between my legs. The couch was narrow, and it would be a tight fit, but I was certain we were up for the challenge.

With one foot still on the floor, Hudson captured my hands and lifted them above my head to anchor them against the armrest with one hand.

"Hey," I protested halfheartedly.

"Shh." He kissed me, a quick peck.

I lifted my eyebrows, not sure if I should object for real. Then his free hand traced down my arm, over my breast, and down my stomach, and my potential complaint evaporated. Twisting his hand so his palm brushed my clitoris and his fingers slid between my thighs, Hudson slowly delved a finger inside me. I arched into his hand, gasping with delight when he made little circles with his palm.

I reached for him, but the weight of his hand on my wrists prevented me from moving. The rhythm of his other hand against me didn't alter, building pleasure in a warm tide. I tentatively struggled, but it was like trying to move an iron bar. He had me trapped, pinned down and completely at his pleasurable mercy. And it was hot as hell.

"Hud . . . son." My breath caught on a jolt of pleasure.

His smile when he met my eyes was cocky and only heightened my arousal.

"I want you," I said. My words came out breathy and low, and Hudson's smile dissolved as his features tightened with lust. He bent closer for a long, hot kiss, slowly sliding his fingers from me so I writhed against him. Releasing my wrists, he planted his other knee on the couch, and in frustratingly slow increments, slid into me. I ran my hands up his taut forearms and biceps, straining toward him.

"You feel so good, Eva."

"Faster," I panted. "Please."

"Uh-uh. We've been doing everything fast. Let's take our time."

"Now?"

His lazy grin surprised me. "Don't think you can?"

I shook my head, my body thrumming with pleasure, my breath too fast. When he began to move—*finally*—pleasure suffused my body, tightening with each thrust. Hudson's arms trembled, but he maintained his controlled, slow, maddening rhythm. I wrapped my legs around his hips and met him, thrust for thrust, until the pressure inside me rode the cusp between pleasure and pain and unraveled in an explosive, rolling orgasm. Hudson followed me, arching over me with a shout of release.

"Slow enough?" I asked later, once Hudson had shifted so I lay on top of him.

"Mmm. No, we'll have to practice."

———

I WOKE to the first light of dawn beyond the curtains in Hudson's bedroom and the feel of Hudson's large palm spread across my breast, his body spooning mine. I stretched against him, enjoying the ache of muscles well used. Warm lips brushed my shoulder, and Hudson eased closer. Yep, he was awake and happy. Neither of us spoke, as if afraid words would let the world rush in uninvited. It was only after we'd taken turns showering that we addressed reality.

"What's the plan today?" Hudson asked as he poured two bowls of granola.

"Go home. I need to clean up." I dressed in the same jeans as the day before, and my duffel had included one final clean shirt, but even if I'd had another week's worth of clean clothes, I was ready to be back in my loft.

"I'd better bring a change of clothes," Hudson half teased.

"You're coming with me?" I'd expected Hudson to go back to work today and reclaim some normalcy. Until Miriam got back to me, there wasn't much else to do.

"Of course. Let me check with Matvei—"

The sliding glass door burst open. We both spun and I clutched at my heart. Miriam stood on Hudson's back patio with her hands on her hips, letting in a rush of crisp morning air as she graced us with a professional glare.

"What's wrong with the doorbell?" I asked.

"You didn't expect me to saunter past the surveillance team, did you?"

Shutting the door behind her, Miriam stalked to the kitchen. A steel infinity symbol twisted and looped over her heart. She was on a mission and she wasn't going to be budged from it. Water—again, an apparition—dripped nonstop from her to a puddle at her feet, and ridiculously long neon green nails tipped her real ones. I sighed. After draining the house of electricity, it was no less than I should have expected. The divinations around Hudson were overactive as well. This was another reason I preferred sleeping in my own home: no visual bombardment the next morning.

"Did you find something already?" I asked, deciding to ignore her dramatic entrance.

"Aside from the fact that you've got three parties watching your place?"

"The FBI, a blond Russian fellow, and two black guys in a crappy little Tercel?" Hudson guessed.

"No Tercel. Who's the blond guy?"

"Matvei. My useless coworker."

"Who's the third?" I asked.

"A sedan, guy's got dark hair, midthirties, Caucasian. He drove by twice, so he might not be watching, just lost. Ready to admit you're in over your head yet?"

I shook my head. "What'd you find out?"

"That you're in over your head." She flipped open a folder she'd had tucked down the front of her jacket. "Three of those sketches your aunt gave us linked to women with Interpol rap sheets a mile long, none of it petty. Miyu Shimizu, Yuuka Yamaguchi, and Nanami Sato."

"What about the other two?" I asked, curious about the extras Sofie had seen in her divinations.

"No hits. Were they part of the kidnapping?"

"I don't think so. Sofie was working from memory of faces that were covered with ski masks most of the time. I think she guessed on a couple," I said.

"Well, she was dead-on with these three. I checked out the Jennifer Winters case, too. It was pretty boring until you two showed up, acting suspicious enough to raise the radar of a dead agent. You've been sleeping somewhere different every night, dropping cars like they're stolen, associating with criminals."

"Yeah, Coutu and Sevallo told us about Atlas and Edmond," Hudson said. "I did a little checking on my own. They're small-time."

"They were also the only suspected collaborators with Winters until five days ago," Miriam said. "Now you're number one and two on the list. Plus, that charming little woman you brought to Carmela's? Dempsey Semenchuk?"

"It's pronounced 'Sim-ens-huk,'" I said, fighting a smile.

"Semen-chuk, Sim-ens-huk, either way, Dempsey's got quite the string of trespassing charges and restraining orders, with a few citations for causing a nuisance and one dropped charge for breaking and entering."

After meeting Dempsey over the business end of Attila, I had no trouble picturing her acquiring a rap sheet.

"How you got tied to Maxwell Overton and the tax evasion scheme he's got going, or what that has to do with Jennifer Winters, has the whole team thoroughly confused."

"Who?" Hudson asked.

I frowned. "I don't know a Maxwell Over— Max! He's a client. I did a consultation for him a few days ago." I rounded on Miriam. "I'm not part of any tax evasion scheme! How could you think that?"

"That's supposed to make me feel better? That you're not involved in some white-collar crime? The women holding your 'friend' have warrants for manslaughter."

The blood drained from my head. I couldn't believe I'd gotten Sofie involved in this. They could have killed her. They could still kill Jenny.

"This stops now, Eva. You're in over your head and you're lucky— damn lucky—that no one has gotten killed. Yet." Miriam's eyes drilled into me.

"But Jenny's still—"

"Leave Winters to the FBI. The sketches you gave us—I told Coutu and Sevallo it was an anonymous tip. That was plenty. Just in time, too. I don't know what happened between yesterday and this morning, but there's an entire task force dedicated to this case now, and most of them are specialists from across the country. This went from our branch's weirdest case to the agency's top priority. So, thank you. You've helped enormously. Now sit it out!" She shoved my chest, and I staggered into a chair. Then she rounded on Hudson. "You, too, security boy."

Hudson held up his hands placatingly. "Fine. We're out of it anyway."

A muscle worked in Miriam's jaw, then she took a step back and thrust her hair behind her ear. The steel infinity symbol dropped to her stomach and expanded until it looped through her abdomen. It didn't look comfortable. "Good. With the handwriting from the note being a match for Nanami Sato's, along with the sketch, we've got all we need. If Winters had brought us the note yesterday for analysis, we'd already have nabbed the kidnappers, but instead she did exactly what Sato wanted: exchanged herself for Sofie."

"Wait, the note said Jenny had to surrender?" I asked.

"Yep."

"She knew all along that she was going to be taken?" Why not just tell us, then? Why not go directly to the park, too? If she had, we wouldn't have gotten there in time to see her taken, so what had she needed time to do? Where had she been between the time she left Annabella's and when she met the ninjas at the park? I couldn't begin to guess how the crazy scientist thought, but one thing was apparent: She had never intended for us to be there when she offered herself up for the exchange. Only Dempsey's rally-racer driving skills had got us to the park in time to see Jenny taken—and Jenny had practically outrun her captors to their van when she saw us coming.

Hudson must have followed the same logic because the top hat sprouted, tall and silver, and his familiar suspicious scowl drew his brows together.

"Maybe they're in cahoots. Either way, she wasn't taken far. The trio haven't left the country, and they most likely haven't left the city. Now"—Miriam clapped her hands and I jumped—"it's time for you both to return to your regular lives. And for Pete's sake, Eva, act like you're not suspect number one! It'll be a miracle if you don't get dragged into this mess after all."

"I can't just—" I cut myself off. I couldn't tell Miriam I'd promised myself I wouldn't abandon Jenny.

*I haven't,* my subconscious argued. I'd taken the sketches to Miriam, and now the FBI knew who they were looking for. I'd colossally increased the odds of Jenny being found and rescued.

I'd also increased the chances of the life-lengthening formula—and Kyoko—falling into the government's hands, something I'd sworn to Jenny I wouldn't do.

*Something I swore under threat of blackmail,* I argued with myself. Jenny was in no position to leverage her hold over me now.

But Jenny had sacrificed herself to the ninjas to save Sofie. For that, I'd risk a lot more than I would have for blackmail.

"When will the FBI make its move?" Hudson asked.

Miriam switched her glare to Hudson. "Soon. I'm not on this case, so I don't know all the details, but Winters should be safe soon. And then"—she turned to me—"I'm getting to the bottom of this. No more 'package' crap."

*Soon* could be today or it could be five days from now. Jenny could be dead by then. Kyoko could be dissected. The formula could have been tortured out of Jenny and in the hands of some diabolical dictator bent on overthrowing the world.

Or the FBI could rescue Jenny today. They could be saving her right now.

Then Kyoko would be in their hands, Evolution Solutions would learn that Kyoko was the real deal, and everything Jenny was trying to prevent would come to pass.

I weighed my odds against homicidal ninjas. I suffered no delusions that I could best the ninjas and free Jenny and Kyoko on my own, but I also couldn't simply sit by and wait. There had to be *something* I could do, some way I could help. We just needed a little time to formulate a plan . . . without the FBI watching us.

"Okay." I tried to sound resigned. "You'll tell me the moment Jenny is safe?"

Miriam scrutinized my expression. "If you promise you're done with the insanity," she said.

"I'm not about to pit myself against murderers."

"Again," Miriam said.

"Live and learn."

A knock rattled the front door.

"Eva, so help me, if you're lying . . ." Miriam shook her head. "I won't be able to help you if you do something stupid."

"Then I won't do anything stupid."

"Too late."

Miriam stalked to the back door and gave Hudson and me a final glare. Then she slipped out and vaulted the back fence.

"For a guy who works in security, your house is very easy to break into," I said.

"I can't say it was a problem before I met you."

Another knock rattled the door.

"Do you think it's the FBI?" I asked.

"Were you serious about letting them handle everything?"

"Unless they need assistance." I batted my eyelashes at him.

"That's my Eva." Hudson brushed a kiss across my lips as he passed by to open the door.

## TWENTY-TWO

"DON'T EVEN LOOK surprised to see me," Dempsey said, barreling past Hudson and into the house. "I told you I'm not letting you out of my sight until our elephantini is safe. We compact creatures have to stick together."

"Come in," Hudson said with a sarcastic arm flourish.

Dempsey was dressed for a safari today. Her khaki pants and matching vest had more pockets than a fisherman's outfit. Her hair was slicked back into a high ponytail, and her face was made up for a film shoot. The crest of red hair rising like a faux hawk from her forehead to her ponytail almost looked like part of her outfit, as did the beaded breastplate, though I knew both were divinations. Dempsey was on a warpath.

"You planning on hunting big game today?" Hudson asked, brushing past Dempsey on his way to the phone.

"I've got Attila packed in the truck."

"That wasn't what I meant," Hudson muttered. He jabbed at the buttons on his cordless phone.

I could have told him nothing was going to happen with the phone. Just like I could have told him that the kitchen and bathroom lights were temporarily out of commission, not the lie I'd given him that I preferred to wake up without harsh fluorescent lights. Controlling my curse had been the last thing on my mind last night. Even if I hadn't blown the fuses then, six hours of sleep, followed by this morning's quickie had ensured the house's electricity was fried for at least ten hours.

Hudson slammed the phone back into the cradle.

My internal relationship countdown timer flipped on with a nauseous jolt, and sorrow washed through me. I liked Hudson. It was going to hurt to see him go, but go he would. I had no illusion on that one. He was a man of electronics and gadgets; I was a woman doomed to destroy everything he enjoyed: our relationship would inevitably crash and burn.

"The elephantini curse continues?" I asked, trying for teasing but failing.

"With a vengeance. You got a cell phone I can borrow?" Hudson asked Dempsey.

"Nope. The one I had yesterday went kaput. We must have been a victim of one of those EMP things."

I almost laughed. EMPs were electromagnetic pulses that damaged nearby electronics. Ari and I had an inside joke that Annabella had known exactly what she was doing when she named me Eva Melisande Parker—I was a walking EMP.

"Good thing you never replaced your phone, Eva," Hudson said, heading for the door.

"Where are you going?"

"Matvei will have a phone. He's not part of this elephantini business, so the curse shouldn't have affected him." He spun back around and grinned at us. "I had a stroke of brilliance this morning. We know something the FBI don't. We know about Kyoko, which means we might be able to track down the ninjas before the FBI knows where to look. Give me a minute."

He was gone before I could ask how.

"What's he talking about?" Dempsey asked.

"I don't know." The idea of rushing ahead of the FBI made the few bites of cereal I'd taken churn in my gut, but if we wanted to save

Jenny and keep Kyoko out of the government's hands, we had to be one step in front of everyone else. Maybe with the information Miriam had given us, we could be.

"I need some fresh air," I said. The silence in the house felt heavy. Dempsey shoved off the couch and followed me to the door.

"You're not going anywhere without me."

"I'm just stepping outside."

"I'm not stopping you."

I grabbed my bag and slung it over a shoulder. Outside, I spotted Hudson immediately. He stood next to a silver four-door car, hip cocked against the side panel in front of the driver's side-view mirror, talking on a phone. Matvei sat in the driver's seat, and I waved to him. He waved back, but I thought he was more curious about Dempsey than me.

Hudson talked with his hand covering his mouth, his eyes scanning the street. Matvei had the music on loud, and Hudson appeared to be talking over it, which made no sense. When Hudson saw me, he gave the blue van a half block away a pointed look. It was a nondescript van, just dirty enough to blend in, with no markings and no one in the cab.

I surveyed the rest of the street. Miriam had confirmed that the FBI were watching us. Since all the other vehicles were standard cars and trucks, and all of them were empty, that left the van.

I rocked on my feet, a plan forming. If by some miracle Hudson was able to find Jenny's location before the FBI, and if we were—out of some misguided sense of gratitude for saving Sofie or perhaps under the compulsion of idiocy—going to attempt a rescue, we wouldn't want the FBI tagging along to ruin everything. Besides, I didn't like being a suspect, and I wasn't going to make it easy on the FBI to collect data on me.

I made a beeline for the van before I could talk myself out of it. Dempsey trotted beside me.

"What're you doing?"

"Chatting," I said.

I peered in the driver's side window, but a solid partition behind the cab blocked my view of the back of the van.

"Should I get Attila?"

"No!"

"Sheesh. You're the one poking around a rapist van."

"It's not a rapist. It's the FBI."

"Maybe that's what the rapist wants you to think."

"Why would a rapist be waiting out here? Especially when the FBI have been tracking me."

"Because he's looking for easy pickin's. You and me? We're easy."

"Speak for yourself." I rapped on the back door of the van. It rocked as someone moved inside. Dempsey squealed and ran around the car parked behind the van, hiding against the side of it.

The back door of the van swung open. A lanky man with soft blond hair, rumpled slacks, and a stained white T-shirt peeked out at me. His pants were overlaid by a divination of leopard-print spandex. I'm not a fan of spandex on men, but he had the physique for it.

"Hi, I'm Eva Parker," I said, extending my hand. "I believe I'm who you're here to keep an eye on."

He shook my hand by rote, gave our clasped hands a befuddled look, and pulled free. His hand and arm were tan and freckled. I craned my head to peer behind him into the darkness of the van. Some surveillance equipment lined one side, or that's what I assumed the screens and keyboards and other wired and electronic equipment was. Two chairs were squeezed into the remaining space, and the second chair was occupied by a slightly older man, Cuban, with a shaved head and a headset over one ear. A child's drum set, complete with flailing hands-free drumsticks, clanged soundlessly around his workstation. I hazarded a guess based on the apparition that he was annoyed. With me.

I gave both men a sweet smile and amped up my own frustration levels, allowing all the selfish *why me?* feelings to overflow from their locked cage. Why had Jenny picked me to dump Kyoko on? Why had she involved me in this mess? If not for her, I would be happily performing consultations and living in my perfect loft. Instead, I was lying to the FBI, my precious loft had been ransacked, my belongings had been fondled and broken by strangers, and my relationship with a genuinely wonderful guy was on a high-speed crash course.

The last thought annoyed me the most. I would figure out a way to prove my innocence if it came to that, and my destroyed belongings could be replaced, but it had been a while since I'd found a man I wanted to spend time with, and not just physically. If I had the luxury, I'd step back, give him some space to allay his growing suspicions—or superstitions—and plan our dates strategically to optimize our time away from electronics. We'd spend a weekend at my place, go for a hike or a bike ride, and go to a museum or a play in the park. We'd do something normal, something that would give us time to get to know each other. If I played it right, I could extend a two-week relationship for months. But Jenny had ruined that. I'd be lucky if Hudson stuck around another week.

I pulled all of my frustration to the surface, haphazardly demolishing the fragile barriers around my curse. Planting a hand on the closed panel door of the van, I imagined my curse reaching out for fuel for my gift, sucking in electricity through my palm.

"I was expecting Agent Coutu," I said. "But maybe you could help me—"

"Ma'am, we're not supposed to be talking to you," the blond agent said. The leopard print on his pants rippled like a cat stretching.

"I know, but I was hoping you might have heard something. I don't feel safe—"

"We didn't hear anything, Ms. Parker. Dane, close the door," the Cuban agent said.

"You'll let me know when you do?" I stuck my torso into the door so Dane couldn't comply with his partner's order. My hand began to patter with an invisible tic, but it wasn't actually moving. Inside the van, the drum set exploded to full size and a chorus of howling dogs circled the older agent, making me thankful my apparitions didn't include sound. Dane's leopard-print pants morphed into leopard legs, transforming him into a predator faun. A gold crown circled his head, and then a pen stabbed through his hand. I jerked at the violent divination.

"I'm sure someone will contact you," Dane said.

"Uh. Thanks." I backed away from the van. Between the ethereal tapping in my hand and the troubling divinations, I decided retreat was the best option. Dane's partner launched over him and slammed the van's door. I listened to the muffled cussing inside while I stared at my hand. It looked normal. Had the tic somehow been, illogically, connected to my curse?

Dempsey sidled into view.

"Damn, girl! And here I thought you were a pushover," she hissed.

"What are you talking about?"

"The way you thumbed it to the man. Acting like nothing was going on. Classic."

I crossed the street with a strut in my step, and Hudson met us at the walkway to his house.

"What was that all about?"

"Just thanking them for their protection."

Hudson shook his head. A shark cruised around the brim of his sombrero, then submerged into air. "Come on, I might have something."

Hudson and I hitched a ride with Matvei to Hudson's car, and Dempsey followed in her truck. The van pulled out behind her, but it didn't make it three blocks before it stalled. I sat back in my seat and grinned. Before the ninjas had kidnapped us and my curse had broken down the van, I'd never thought I'd appreciate my gift's side effect. Apparently I'd been leading the wrong lifestyle to make use of it. My curse was far more suited to a life of crime. A block later I realized my brilliant plan had just cut us off from the very people capable of saving us if we actually found the ninjas, and my stomach cramped.

"What did you find out?" I asked once Hudson and I were alone in his car. "And how is it something the FBI won't know?"

"I had a coworker run the ninja van's plates after we were kidnapped, and I asked her to watch traffic cams for the vehicle. I never got a chance to check in with her yesterday."

I nodded, residual anxiety fluttering through my heart. I pushed it back down. We'd rescued Sofie, and she was safe. If we hadn't . . . No, I wouldn't even think about it.

"But this morning talking with Miriam made me realize the FBI are looking for the ninjas, Jenny, and the van. We know we're also looking for Kyoko—somewhere to hide her and something to feed her. That call was me asking my coworker to cross-check feed stores with traffic cams, looking for the van. Fortunately, there aren't a lot of stores catering to livestock owners in this city. My coworker found a cluster of hits in Mar Vista in the last three days, all within four miles of each other. I thought we'd swing by and check out the neighborhood." He grinned at me, clearly pleased with his deductions.

"I'm impressed. But how was your coworker able to get all that information?"

"I told you, security installation is only part of what EliteGuard does. We handle more complicated projects that require more sophisticated tracking information."

"That's a little scary."

Hudson shrugged.

I checked my side-view mirror as we rounded the next corner and wasn't the least bit surprised when a white car that was four vehicles behind us made the turn as well. Miriam. "Pull over at the next Starbucks," I said.

"We don't have time for a coffee break."

"This is important."

Four blocks later, Hudson pulled into the lot of a Starbucks. Dempsey followed. I bounced from the car and into the coffeehouse before either of them got their seat belts off. There wasn't a line, and I exited two minutes later with a peach Italian soda and three slices of coffee cake. Miriam idled by the curb two blocks back.

"Everyone gets one," I said to Hudson, thrusting the paper bags of coffee cake at him. Then I jogged down the street to Miriam's car.

She watched me approach, frowning. I opened the passenger door and slid in next to her, leaving the door cracked.

"What are you doing?" Miriam asked.

"I could ask the same of you."

"I'm making sure you don't do anything you might regret."

"I don't remember asking you to watch over me." I knew exactly what Miriam was doing. Miriam didn't believe I was backing off the hunt for Jenny. With good reason, but that didn't stop me from getting angry. Anger was an easy emotion these days. It simmered just beneath the surface, and it leapt eagerly to the forefront when I tugged it. I considered using the hand visualization again, but the strange spasming in my hand with the FBI van had unnerved me, so I settled for using my emotions to topple my usual mental barriers. *Curse, do your thing.*

"I'm trying to spend the first normal day with my boyfriend. Alone," I said.

"Alone? What's Dempsey doing here, then?"

I glanced back to the parking lot. Dempsey had gotten out of her truck and was standing beside Hudson's window. She was openly staring, and I suspected Hudson was watching in a mirror, too.

"We're trying to ditch her, too."

"Really." I didn't need to see the malamute puppy in the rumpled suit and tie squirming between us to read the suspicion radiating from Miriam. "I still haven't figured out how she's involved in all this."

"She's a friend of Jenny's. She thinks we can help her save Jenny, but I told her what you told me, and then I told her we were done. She's not buying it."

"Neither am I."

"That's your problem, then," I said. Blood rushed oddly soundlessly against my eardrums, accompanied by vague dizziness. Between the van and Miriam's car, I'd never intentionally drawn in so much electricity over such a short period of time, and the side effect was unexpected and freeing: More systematically than downing a series of tequila shots, the raw energy toppled my inhibitions, taking my usual deference to authority right along with my caution. So Hudson and I might not have the *best* plan, but we had *a* plan, and we were going to pursue it and save Jenny and Kyoko—ninjas, FBI, and Miriam be damned.

"You're going to have a very frustrating day, Miriam, because I don't want you to tag along with Hudson and me on our date," I said, sticking to my lie without remorse. "I appreciate what you've done for us, but I don't appreciate you interfering in my love life."

"I'm not doing anything for you that I wouldn't do for Ari and Antonio or any of the others."

"I know. So knock it off. I don't need a big sister right now; I need privacy with my hunk. The one who met the whole crazy da Via family and still wanted to hang out with me today."

Miriam narrowed her eyes and scrutinized my face.

I softened my expression and voice, honesty falling seamlessly behind the lie. "Okay, that wasn't fair. I'm sorry, Miriam. I've been really stressed the last few days, and spending a normal day with Hudson doing normal things sounds like heaven. And I don't want an audience."

Finally, Miriam smiled. The puppy curled up and put its head on its paws. "Fine. Call me if you need anything."

"Thank you." We hugged awkwardly, across the console—and through the puppy; then I slid out of the car. I smiled when I saw her phone on the dash, knowing it couldn't have survived, then tossed Miriam a wave and sauntered back to Hudson.

Of course, I knew changing Miriam's mind wouldn't be as simple as a conversation. When we pulled out of the parking lot, she followed. Her car made it two blocks before I saw her coast into a parking lot, a cloud of exhaust billowing around it. Hudson watched Miriam's car in the rearview mirror, and a Great Dane–size Scottish terrier popped into existence on his lap.

"Looks like Miriam bought my story," I said. "She must be getting breakfast. There's a really good donut shop in that center."

Hudson and the dog swiveled to look at me. I turned my attention to my slice of coffee cake and attempted to meditate on the delicious flavor.

Back at the house, looking for Jenny and her three *murderous* abductors had given me reservations. Now it seemed like a smart decision, the *only* course of action that made sense. I knew my logic was flawed by my curious lack of inhibitions, but Hudson and Dempsey weren't protesting, so I savored the brown sugar melting on my tongue and said nothing.

We drove through the Mar Vista neighborhoods where the van had been spotted, scanning cross streets and driveways with the windows down to listen for Kyoko's bugle. The longer we drove without signs of a miniature elephant, Jenny, or the ninjas, the harder it was to pretend our search was anything other than a futile attempt to make ourselves believe we were doing something productive. When Hudson's car shivered, played a discordant, clacking dirge, and died in the middle of the street, I tried not to take it as the universe telling us to give up.

"What the hell!" Hudson slammed his palm into the steering wheel.

"I'll push," I said, grateful we were on a residential street, and the traffic was light. I hopped out before Hudson could protest. I was familiar with pushing cars; it was a task I'd learned to do when I was sixteen, ironically enough. That was when I'd gained enough weight and muscle to actually be useful when leaning against the bumper of a car.

Hudson shoved out of his seat and pushed against the door frame to get the car rolling. Together we guided it to the curb. Dempsey pulled in behind the car and parked. Fire-hydrant tall skyscrapers dotted the hood of her truck. I blinked at the new divination. The red crest of hair and the beaded breastplate I got: Those were Dempsey's warrior outfits. Miniature skyscrapers made zero sense.

I retrieved my bag from the passenger seat and locked my door.

"This is ridiculous, you know," Hudson said, glaring at me over the roof of his car. "Cars don't just break down like this. Not this often. Especially not when nothing's wrong with them. But you never seem fazed by it. It's like you expect them to break down."

"What should I do? Cuss and rant and rave?"

"I've got that covered. But why don't you ever seem surprised?"

"Let's see. I was handcuffed by strangers three days in a row; I've played with a miniature elephant in my aunt's backyard; I'm helping a mad scientist who invented a formula that could destroy mankind; and I'm currently attempting to outmaneuver the FBI so I can have first crack at homicidal ninjas. I'm beyond surprise at this point. Come on."

Hudson looked like he would protest, but I didn't wait to hear it.

"Hang on. No admittance unless you promise not to do that voodoo on me," Dempsey said.

"Voodoo?" I echoed.

"I saw what you did. That FBI van, Miriam's car. You put a voodoo curse on their vehicles. That's why they broke down."

"Why would I curse Hudson's car?"

"I'm still working on that one."

"While you do that, we're wasting daylight," Hudson said. "Trust me; it's the elephantini, not Eva."

I climbed into the middle of the bench seat, my knees tucked to my chest, and didn't make eye contact. Hudson squeezed in beside me and twisted to give himself more legroom.

"Attila's got her eyes on you," Dempsey warned, "and she never blinks."

# TWENTY-THREE

WE DROVE for another twenty minutes in tense silence, widening our search. I ping-ponged between fretting over the length of time I'd been in the truck and attempting to suppress my emotions, pretending our search was an idle game.

Dempsey pulled out onto a cramped, six-lane boulevard and gunned the truck up to speed in the late morning traffic. A long string of homes and strip malls stretched in both directions, broken occasionally by a big-box center. We'd systematically woven across this boulevard four times so far in our search.

"There!" Hudson shouted. He pointed across the street, where a black van turned into a large shopping center.

"On it!" Dempsey yanked the wheel, cutting almost perpendicular through three lanes of traffic. Horns blasted and cars swerved around us, and more than one driver threw us a rude gesture. Dempsey passed up the line of cars waiting at the light to turn left, barreled into the middle of the intersection, then cut the wheel. The truck lurched toward oncoming traffic.

I screamed and braced against the dash, eyes locked on the rush of cars headed straight for us.

"Watch out! PETA rescue in progress!" Dempsey yelled,

compressing the horn and not letting up. Oncoming drivers stood on their brakes, and the squeal of tires pierced through the truck's endless horn. Dempsey swerved, missing the passing bumper of a sedan by inches; then she gunned it through the next two lanes. I stared into the shocked faces of the round-eyed drivers we cut off, my own terrified expression mirroring theirs.

"Where'd they go?" Dempsey asked.

"There." Hudson pointed to the back side of the buildings, his finger shaking as much as his voice.

The truck sputtered, and I released my death grip on the dash to pat it. The full-size shark swimming through the cab was proof I didn't need; Dempsey's stunt had guaranteed this truck wouldn't survive more than a few minutes, if that.

Dempsey slowed to an idle as we passed the end of the building, and we all turned to stare down the delivery lane running the length of the shopping center. The van had reversed into an empty loading bay, and an Asian lady with blond-streaked dark brown hair styled in an A-line bounced from the van. She was no more than five-two and thin enough to make a Hollywood actress jealous, and I recognized her from Sofie's sketch. Had Hudson and I really been taken out by that wafer? Should I be embarrassed?

The heavy horn of a semi trumpeted behind us. The ninja glanced our direction. Dempsey whipped the truck's wheel around and floored it, and we peeled out.

"I don't think she saw us," Dempsey said, barely slowing as she rounded the front side of the shopping center and barreled through the half-empty parking lot.

I thought it was unlikely the woman missed the truck leaving burn marks on the pavement.

"Should I circle around?"

"No. Let's figure out what building they were behind," I said.

That proved easy: Most of the center was taken up by a giant, out-of-business former bookstore. A taqueria sat to the right and a Great Clips to the left, but neither location required a loading ramp.

Dempsey parked and we jogged to Great Clips, then peeked into the bookstore from the relative cover where the two businesses shared a glass-front wall. Scattered panels of light illuminated a lawn of dead carpet and rows of empty freestanding bookcase tombstones symbolizing a more prosperous past. Bold lettering adorned shadowy walls: *Fiction, Music, Children's Nook.* Nothing moved inside; no shadows shifted.

"There's a door on the right," I whispered. "It must lead to the warehouse."

It was silly to whisper. The only people close enough to hear were two teenage boys loitering outside Great Clips.

By mutual silent agreement, we walked back to the truck.

"What now?" Dempsey asked. "Why are they here?"

"Best guess, because people aren't watching this bookstore as closely as they would an occupied business," Hudson said. "A place like this center would have security, but patrols probably run at predictable times."

"They have video surveillance," I said, pointing to a lamppost with a camera attached to it.

"Yep. Probably some watching the back, too. I doubt it's enough to stop these women. They've eluded police in at least two countries; they aren't dumb. They probably know how to disengage a camera or loop a video feed."

"So why are we standing here talking?" Dempsey demanded. "Let's go get 'em."

I hugged my stomach. My earlier acceptance of this plan had faded somewhere between Starbucks and Dempsey's illegal and near-suicidal dive through oncoming traffic. I didn't want to face the ninjas without trained backup.

"What are you proposing?" I asked, already dreading the answer.

"We get Kyoko out," Dempsey said.

"And Jenny," Hudson added.

"Sure. And Jenny. Then call the feds."

"We just waltz in there and, what, ask the violent ninja ladies to kindly hand over the elephantini they stole and release Jenny, then walk out?"

"Don't be ridiculous. We'll let Attila do the talking."

I glanced at Hudson. He shrugged. "I'm open to suggestions."

"We could wait for them to leave, then sneak in the back."

"What if they take Kyoko with them?" Dempsey asked, quickly adding, "Or Jenny? We could lose them forever. This could be our one chance at a rescue."

How bad would it be for the FBI to learn of Kyoko? Unbidden, I remembered Jenny's writhing pyramid of naked babies. If the FBI found Kyoko, it was only a matter of time before the government learned of the life-lengthening formula. A few more months or years before they began testing it. First on rats and bunnies, then on humans. In a generation, we could have children who outlived their parents by one hundred years. Every social problem would be amplified by time: politicians would stay in office for a century, prisons would overflow with convicts serving two-hundred-year life sentences, health care costs would skyrocket, and overtaxed resources would be exploited by generations with mutated life spans. The population would bloat, and the economy would veer toward total collapse.

Or, maybe nothing would happen. Maybe the FBI would find Kyoko, never be able to reverse-engineer the genetic mutation that had lengthened her life, and all my fears would be for naught. The last five days had warped my perspective. It was entirely conceivable that I was blowing everything out of proportion, getting swept up in Jenny's paranoia.

"We need to act fast," Dempsey said. She swung open the truck's door and half crawled into the cab to retrieve Attila.

"Hang on. I need to think."

"There's nothing to think about. I'm going to rescue that elephantini." Dempsey tucked Attila close to her body and marched toward the empty bookstore.

"Wait!" I ran in front of her and put a hand on her shoulder.

"Don't try your regular-sizer tactics on me. I know how to break your kneecaps." Dempsey angled the butt of the gun toward my knee.

"No. Just, just . . . let me think." I backed out of her range.

I didn't need to think; all my doubt crumbled beneath one simple fact: Jenny had sacrificed herself to save my aunt. What I needed to do was make sure we didn't get caught. I paced to the pole holding the camera and loosed my emotions—my disbelief that I was going to go through with this, my fear of the ninjas, my fear of being arrested, my fear of being killed—I had a lot of fear. Why had disabling the FBI van and Miriam's car seemed like such a good idea earlier? I'd cut us off from everyone who could rescue us from our own impulsive stupidity. It'd been reckless of me and out of character. I blamed my curse, and like always, my censure changed nothing.

Dempsey waited, hand on her hip. Hudson watched me with narrowed eyes. His divinations flashed between the sombrero, the silver terrier, and a yawning black abyss. He was suspicious and afraid, but the sombrero meant he wasn't going to back away from our plan. Dempsey's divinations were rock solid, the bead breastplate and the crest of flaming red hair never wavering.

"Let's go," I said. If I hadn't killed the camera with my escalating fear, nothing would. Tension knotting my stomach, I marched past Dempsey and Hudson, straight for the bookstore's doors.

"What was that all about?" Dempsey asked.

"Contemplating my priorities."

"Now?"

"Seemed important."

"Huh." She tucked Attila tighter against her side and jogged to keep up. Hudson let out a pent-up breath and stepped in stride with me.

"You guys will have to shield me while I get the lock," he said.

"Me? Shield you? I know it's PC to pretend we're all the same, but that's just stupid. I'm half your height. It's like you trying to hide an elephant behind your body—a regular elephant."

"You got a better idea?"

"I'll pick the lock. You giants shield me."

"You can pick locks, too?" I asked.

"You can't?" Dempsey looked to Hudson for confirmation. "Where'd you find this girl?"

"An art gallery."

"Oh, hoity-toity."

"I'm not hoity-toity. I'm normal." Mostly.

"What world do you live in?" Dempsey asked.

The real world. Or I used to.

"Hold this." Dempsey stopped in front of the double doors and thrust Attila into my hands. I grasped the shotgun between my thumb and forefinger, resting the butt on my toe. Dempsey snorted. "She doesn't bite."

"She—*it*—is a *gun*. It does worse than bite."

Dempsey pulled several slender metal tools from one of the pouches on her vest and bent her knees slightly to align her eye with the lock. Hudson shuffled closer to me, and we both made a miserable performance of looking nonchalant, an impossible task while holding a shotgun and shielding a burglar. It was even harder while trying to keep an eye on the parking lot and the interior of the store at the same time.

"Come on, baby. Don't resist. Show me how you like your buttons pushed," Dempsey whispered.

Hudson caught my eye, and absurdly, I had to fight off a smile. When he waggled his eyebrows at me, I giggled. Hysteria tinged the sound. I could feel it, just beneath the surface of my projected calm, and I anchored myself in Hudson's bright blue eyes. His lips quirked in a sexy half smile that I returned. His eyes dropped down my body, sliding a shiver of heat along my skin.

"Geez, down, girl. Now is *so* not the time." Dempsey snatched Attila from my hand and eased the front door open.

"Shows what you know," I whispered, and kissed Hudson hard before squeezing myself through the narrow opening. Hudson followed, but his grin disappeared the moment he crossed the threshold.

The sounds of traffic and people cut off with the closing of the door. Heavy silence and still, stale air enveloped us. I padded across the tiled entrance to the industrial carpet that ran through the rest of the store, feeling like I'd been pinned with a searchlight and everyone in the parking lot was watching, pointing, and calling the cops. When

I glanced outside, the only people in the lot were a pair of hassled parents loading four young children into a minivan, and no one looked in the direction of the vacant bookstore.

I scurried through the pyramid shelves toward the taller stands at the back of the store. *Health and Medicine* the shelf placard read. We crouched there, as far from the front door as we could get and as close to the back door as we dared go. Beyond Health and Medicine, we ran out of cover.

We all jumped when someone spoke.

The voice was muffled through the back door, which I could see now was a galley door, made to swing both directions. It had a square window about five feet up. I couldn't see anything through it but empty warehouse shelving. The door was loose-fitting, with a slender gap around the top and bottom, but what the voices filtering through those tiny openings were saying was a complete mystery since they were speaking Japanese.

"What now?" I whispered.

Jenny's voice rose above the others, also speaking Japanese. We shared wide-eyed glances. We'd found Jenny, too. The only thing that could make this better would be if—

Kyoko bugled.

Yep, the whole gang was here.

"Now we let Attila do her thing," Dempsey said.

If only we could send Attila in alone.

Hudson mimed sneaking up to the side and looking through the window. Pac-Man chomped up his jean-clad leg, then down the other, an electronic block of cheese on a mission. Dempsey pointed two fingers at her eyes, then at Hudson's eyes, then scanned the room beyond the door with them, then pointed back at her eyes. Hudson nodded. What was this, the Navy SEALs? Hudson pointed at me, then at the opposite side of the door. I nodded.

My heart thundered in my ears. Even so, the distinctive click of a gun being cocked behind us was unmistakable. We froze in unison. The hairs on the back of my neck tingled. With infinite deliberation, I lifted my hands toward my ears and twisted on a heel.

There would be no escaping criminal charges this time. We were trespassing. They could add breaking and entering to the charges, and I was pretty sure having Attila loaded and with us would make everything worse.

I was expecting the FBI. If not them, the police, and if not them, the strip mall's security officer. It took three jerky breaths for me to drag my gaze from the gun's muzzle to see the man holding it. Surprise jolted me.

It was a plainclothes stranger.

My brain hiccupped and spit out the logical answer: I was staring at the retrievalist.

———

HE WAS HUDSON'S HEIGHT, with similar lean muscles, but where Hudson looked like the boy next door, the skip tracer looked like a scrappy fighter, only one with no tattoos or scars, no distinguishing marks at all—the quintessential average-looking man, if you didn't count his cold, flat brown eyes. Those eyes didn't stop moving between the three of us, evaluating but not expressing anything. Dead eyes. The eyes of a murderer.

My gaze went back to the gun in his left hand. Then to the gun in his right hand. They were short, square guns, matte black, not a lot bigger than his hands. They should have looked unthreatening compared to Attila. But I didn't need to know a lot about guns to know that two small guns pointed at me were more threatening than one large gun pointed at the ground.

"Drop it," he said. His voice was barely a whisper, but it carried the command of a police chief.

Dempsey set Attila at her feet.

The skip tracer's left leg disappeared. It wasn't simply blocked by an apparition; it vanished. I could see the carpet behind him and the bottom shelf of the bookcase, complete with swirls of dust and grime. He didn't topple. He didn't even notice. The leg reappeared, but his torso disappeared, leaving a nauseating view straight through him to a slice of the front windows half hidden behind a bookcase. His torso solidified; then his left arm vanished. Spinning golden clockwork gears anchored each missing body part, first circling his hip, then his waist, then his shoulder. Through it all, the gun barrels never wavered.

I stared at the body parts as they disappeared and reappeared, and terror crawled up my throat. Or maybe that was my heart, trying to beat its way to freedom. This wasn't how divinations worked. Apparitions were objects with an emotional meaning to each specific individual, a symbol to express what they were feeling. They were always *something*. How could an emotion be *nothing*? Was this what it was like to encounter a sociopath? A psychopath? I always got the two confused, but I was willing to bet the retrievalist's picture would be found under both definitions in the dictionary.

"Through the door," he said in that soft, commanding voice. "You, then you, then you."

The guns reinforced the order with little ticks. Hudson, then me, then Dempsey.

With an electric eel wrapped around his torso like an anaconda and hands raised like mine, Hudson complied. I followed, watching the eel strobe in blinding flashes, and a scorpion-like stinger struck Hudson's heart with every beat. My stomach churned, Hudson's fear feeding mine.

Dempsey stumbled into line behind me, a skyscraper springing up beside her, its peaked top complete with an extra-long antenna adorned with a flashing red light. The whole construction came to Dempsey's eye level, making her look like a safari parody of Godzilla.

I followed Hudson through the door, and Dempsey was right on my heels. I knew the retrievalist stepped in line behind her, but the man moved on silent feet, and he didn't speak again. He didn't need to. As Dempsey would say, his guns were doing the talking for him.

The ninjas didn't see us right away. Four rows of industrial shelving stood between us and the loading bay where the main action was. Hudson glanced back for confirmation from our psychotic leader, then shuffled toward the women.

Beyond the shelving, the warehouse had twenty or so feet of open floor, now crowded with three ninjas, a caged elephantini, and a bound woman.

The ninjas were relaxed. One with spiky silver-tipped hair sat on a stool by a normal door just to the right of the large, closed bay door. The second stood, arms crossed, near the middle of the room. The third loomed over Jenny, her booted foot on Jenny's stomach. Yuuka, Nanami, and Miyu—I recognized them from Sofie's drawings.

A thin cord bound Jenny's ankles to her hands behind her back, and her body contorted in a painful bow. Bruises discolored her jaw, and blood smeared down her chin from her lips; Jenny's time with the ninjas had not been as comfortable as Sofie's.

Jenny and the ninjas saw us at the same time. The one in the middle of the room, Nanami, shouted and sprinted for us.

"Run! Get out!" Jenny yelled.

The crack of gunfire deafened me. I flinched and grabbed for my head—a reflexive move both too late and pointless. Blood sprayed from Nanami's leg, and she dropped between one step and the next.

Yuuka, the ninja with spiky hair by the door, jammed her hand down a boot.

The retrievalist said something in Japanese, his voice raised just enough to carry to Yuuka. She froze, then straightened, and two knives dropped from her hands to the scuffed concrete floor. Another soft command, and Miyu raised her hands high, stepping away from Jenny. She skirted her fallen comrade and sulked across the warehouse to Yuuka. Yuuka kicked the knives, and they skidded toward us.

"Move to the side," the retrievalist ordered in English. The three of us complied, lining up along the same wall as Miyu and Yuuka, though several feet separated us. "Don't move again."

He kicked the knives out of our reach, then crossed the warehouse to Kyoko's side. Those cold eyes never stopped moving, and his guns were steady, shifting immediately to aim at anyone who twitched. He stopped behind Kyoko's cage, where the elephantini provided protection for his lower body. Then he rested an arm on the cage, keeping one gun leveled on Yuuka and Miyu. The other, he pointed at Nanami.

I felt like I'd stumbled onto a movie set. This was too incredulous.

A bleeding, shot woman lay on the floor in front of me, her face pasty and her hands clenched around her leg. The bullet had gone through the meat of her thigh. It must have missed any major arteries, because blood welled from the wound and soaked her pants, but it didn't gush.

The retrievalist said something in Japanese, his voice still soft. Nanami looked up at him, and I didn't need to understand the language to translate the defiance. The words she spat at him had zero effect on his expression. His gun dipped, and he said something else. Nanami's lips tightened. She was breathing hard, like she'd been running. After a brief hesitation, she nodded.

Very slowly, she reached into her left sleeve and withdrew a knife with a long, slender blade. Just as slowly, Nanami half crawled, half dragged herself to Jenny.

It was hard to tear my eyes away from the action, but I forced myself to look around. Miyu glared at the retrievalist with a strength that should have paralyzed him, anger twisting her lips into a snarl. However, her hands stayed perfectly still, clamped behind her head as the retrievalist must have instructed. Beside her, Yuuka was stony faced. Her body language was relaxed, and her eyes revealed nothing as she watched her injured partner smear a swath of blood across the warehouse floor as she pulled herself to Jenny.

Jenny was the hardest to look at. Guilt made me want to drop my eyes. It wasn't my fault she was here, but I felt like it was. It could have been my aunt bleeding and bruised on the floor—it would have been, but Jenny exchanged herself for Sofie's safety. The fact that Jenny had gotten us all involved in her mess in the first place didn't make me feel better.

The scientist projected every scared divination I'd seen. A strait-jacket cinched her body. Tiny baseball-size naked babies formed a pyramid on her side, arms and legs flailing in a massive, mutated lump. The top babies tumbled to the floor, were replaced by new babies that welled up from within the writhing center of the pyramid, and fell again. Enormous dirt-coated Coke-bottle glasses snapped in and out of existence over Jenny's eyes whenever she looked toward the retrievalist. The ninjas scared her; the skip tracer terrified her.

Nanami sawed through the bindings on Jenny's feet, then the ones on her hands before tossing the weapon down an empty aisle. A command from the retrievalist held Jenny in place while Nanami retied the scientist's hands in front of her and fixed a cord shackle to her feet. Jenny would be able to walk, but her steps would be stunted and running would be out of the question.

My fingers tingled, and I wriggled them behind my head. Hudson shifted his feet, and the retrievalist's right gun swung to point at him. We both froze.

It took forever for Nanami to crawl back across the floor to her cohorts. After a brief exchange of words, Nanami tied Miyu and Yuuka's hands together with leftover rope from Jenny's bonds.

Kyoko twisted and turned in the tiny cage, trying to get her trunk around her side to snuffle the retrievalist. When that didn't work, she poked it up through the top to prod the gun. He shifted out of reach, and she bugled her disappointment.

The retrievalist spoke to Jenny in Japanese, then switched to another language, neither English nor Japanese, and Jenny's head jerked up and down. Another sentence and Jenny shook her head. She fumbled to her feet, shooting me hot, indecipherable glances. If she was trying to tell me something with her gaze, I needed an interpreter.

Jenny shuffled to the ninjas, where she tested and tightened their bonds. When she was done, the rope bit into their flesh, but their expressions said they felt nothing. Then the retrievalist tossed her a zip tie to bind Nanami's hands. When she was done, she stood and stumbled to the bay door, the straitjacket in place, babies tumbling around her feet. There, she used a chain to roll the door up into the roof, opening a gap no taller than Kyoko's crate. When Jenny crossed the warehouse to Kyoko and leaned against the cage to get it rolling on the tiny wheels beneath the elephantini's feet, I thought she might try something. She was close to the retrievalist, and he was watching the ninjas more than her. It would be a perfect time to catch him with his guard semi-down.

But since this wasn't a novel and Jenny wasn't suicidal, she docilely shoved Kyoko out the loading bay door and into the back of the waiting van, squeezed into the back with the elephantini, and pulled the doors shut from the inside. The retrievalist barked an order to the ninjas, and Miyu awkwardly retrieved the van's keys from her pocket and tossed them at his feet. He picked them up without looking, then backed toward the loading dock, tucked a gun into a holster at his hip, yanked the chain for the door, and ducked out before it crashed down.

At the last minute, he tossed something under the door, and the small device caused all three ninjas to shout and the two standing to whirl into crouches, while Nanami rolled and tucked. Seconds later, the device exploded with a flash, and a deafening bang slapped my eardrums. I reeled, hands clasped to my ears, my vision filled with an afterimage of the bright light. My legs sagged, and I grabbed for a shelving unit to stay upright.

Sound slowly penetrated the ringing in my ears: shouts between the ninjas checking on each other. I looked up in time to see Yuuka and Miyu stumble across the warehouse toward their knives; then Hudson grabbed my elbow.

"Come on," he said, though I read his lips more than heard him.

A child-size skyscraper darted past me. Across the warehouse, the ninjas sawed through their bindings, and once they were free, they'd come for us. I whirled and raced for the swinging door, but the world tilted beneath my feet, and my sprint turned to a stagger as I clung to the bookshelves and fought vertigo to stay upright. Hudson moved on equally clumsy feet, half falling behind me. I reached for him and we clutched each other, gaining momentum.

The galley door slammed inward, and men in head-to-toe black with enormous guns boiled through. I spun around. More men flooded the room behind us, rushing through the back door.

The lights crashed. Everyone was shouting, but I couldn't make sense of the words. In the noise and panic, someone grabbed me from behind and slammed me to the floor. My arms were wrenched behind my back, and for the fourth time in five days, I was handcuffed.

# TWENTY-FOUR

 Coutu asked.

"I already told you: I'm not hiding her." I wanted to put my head in my hands and close my eyes. I was handcuffed to a table in an interrogation chamber, where I'd been for an eternity along with my similarly shackled partners in crime. Sevallo stood with his hands braced on the table in front of me, his back to the large, one-way mirror. He wore a Santa hat, and fuzzy socks lay in front of him. I still couldn't figure out those fuzzy socks, and frankly, I was too tired to care.

Coutu was seated, a folder open in front of her. A riding crop dangled from a wrist strap on her right arm and a judge's gavel floated in her left hand. I appreciated the translucency of her apparitions: She wanted to beat the information out of me, and she was going to be the judge of everything I had to say.

Standing quietly in the corner was an unfamiliar woman who had yet to speak. Five-ten, rail thin, and dressed in the most expensive suit I'd seen outside of a Hollywood premier, she didn't look like an FBI agent. She didn't even appear interested in the interrogation. She looked like we were wasting her time. I'd have been happy to get out of her hair, but Sevallo and Coutu had just settled in to question us after leaving us shackled and alone for an endless hour, and neither agent seemed to be in a hurry.

In the chaos after the SWAT team had stormed the building, I'd lain stunned, facedown on the concrete—as instructed by a woman with a no-nonsense drill sergeant voice—overwhelmed by despair. Jenny and Kyoko had been right there, within our reach, and then they'd been taken. Again. The authorities had arrived too late. The retrievalist had disappeared, escaping all detection. Unless Hudson had some magic up his sleeve, we had zero leads and no way to track the invisible man. All the threads of information that had gotten us this far had been played out.

We'd failed.

Jenny and Kyoko would be shipped back to Japan, where they would be tortured and dissected to get the life-lengthening formula, and I was going to be arrested. My thoughts bounced between fear for humanity's future and Jenny's, and fear for my own.

I'd rested my cheek on the grimy floor and fought back tears.

It wasn't until the yelling had died down and I was in the quiet interior of the patrol car that I began to formulate a strategy. It would not do Jenny or humanity any good to keep the life-lengthening formula out of the U.S. government's hands, only to have it used by the Japanese. We'd exhausted our meager abilities, resources, and luck; it was time to bring the FBI up to speed. But maybe I could control the information and still help Jenny.

The interrogation room's lights spasmed in a seizure-inducing pattern. Coutu glanced up, then rose, flipped them off, and propped open the door. Light spilled into the room from the hallway beyond, but it made it difficult to see the agents' faces with their backs to the door.

When Coutu stood, I could see Hudson in the mirror. He looked tired, and shadows rested in the grooves around his mouth and under his eyes. He met my gaze, and I couldn't read anything there. Rotten banana slices cascaded down his chest. He thought this situation stank. I got that much. Between us, little green army men lined the edges of his pity-party red wagon. I hoped the army men meant he was still up for a fight.

On the other side of Hudson, propped in a booster seat that had been the cause of a verbal deluge of complaints and threats of a lawsuit, sat Dempsey, glowering at everything in sight. Her red crest glistened in the dim light as if it were under a spotlight, and the beaded breastplate was set in the design of a giant hand flipping off the room. I smiled a little at that. Dempsey didn't waste a lot of respect on authority.

"What were you doing in that warehouse?" Coutu directed this question, as she had all the rest, at me.

"I know my rights," Dempsey yelled, not for the first time. "Nobody speaks until we have a lawyer."

"Let me do the talking," I said.

"Don't say nothing, woman!" Dempsey ordered. She spun to face me, standing on the lip of her chair in front of the booster seat and using the bar we were all cuffed to for balance. The chair tipped forward alarmingly. "Don't you dare. Don't let them get in your head. Don't let them—"

I cut her off with a look. "Let me talk."

"But—"

*"Let me talk."*

Dempsey sat down, muttering under her breath.

"Like I told you," I began, "I don't know Jenny. She's an acquaintance from high school, and honestly, I wish I'd never agreed to help her. She needed a simple favor: move her truck and trailer from the street where it would be towed."

I flicked my gaze to Hudson's. He had leaned back in his chair as far as the cuffs allowed, and he watched me with hooded eyes. I hadn't been able to tell what he was thinking ever since we had both been shoved in the back of a police cruiser hours earlier. I half expected him to agree to tell the FBI everything if they cleared him of all charges. That would be the smart thing for him to do. Get out while he could, and without a criminal record. His career in security would be ruined with a criminal record, *especially* if breaking and entering was one of the crimes. I waited for him to decide he was done—with Kyoko, with Jenny. With me.

When he said nothing, I plowed on with half-truths, starting with revealing Sofie's kidnapping.

"Jenny must have made some powerful enemies," I said, "but you know more about that than I do. They ransacked my place and must have found out about Sofie because they kidnapped her from her sister's house yesterday."

I didn't think either believed my excuse that we hadn't mentioned the kidnapping yesterday in the park because Sofie had been exhausted and hadn't wanted to deal with questioning.

"How did you know your aunt had been kidnapped by Winters's enemies?" Coutu asked.

"The ransom note."

"You read kanji?"

"No, but I only know one person who was recently in Japan, and given your investigation into Jenny, I thought other people might be looking for her, too. And wanting something from her."

"So you called Jenny . . ." Coutu prompted.

I shook my head, avoiding the innocuous trap. I'd already told Coutu I had no way of contacting Jenny. Instead, with complete honesty, I confessed to being so distraught over my aunt's abduction that I didn't know how Jenny had been contacted, only that she'd shown up at my mother's house and set up the drop. While I spoke, Sevallo's Santa hat grew long enough for the fuzzy tip to touch his hip and Coutu's bologna sandwich stretched across the table. They weren't buying what I was saying, but as long as we got to the important part and I didn't implicate myself, Hudson, Sofie, or Dempsey in the process, I was fine with their skepticism.

"And we have your aunt to thank for the sketches 'anonymously' given to the FBI?" Coutu asked.

I nodded, mentally crossing my fingers that when the agents cross-checked my story with Sofie, she wouldn't reveal anything I hadn't.

"Why didn't you contact the authorities when your aunt was abducted?" Coutu asked.

"I was too scared at first; Jenny said the note said they'd kill her if we did. But once we had the exchange location, that's when I asked Dempsey to call you."

Coutu's lips tightened.

"Okay, let's see if you can explain how you ended up at that out-of-business bookstore today," Sevallo said. He leaned closer, Santa hat swinging forward through the table.

"With a shotgun," Coutu said.

"I have a permit for Attila. I have a right to bear arms. I—"

"We thought we saw one of the women in Sofie's sketches," I said.

"Where?"

"Going into the back of the store."

"So you were just out shopping, the three of you, and you happened across the woman your aunt identified as her kidnapper?"

I met Coutu's stare head-on. "Yes."

"Why didn't you call us? Or the cops?"

"None of us had a phone."

Coutu ran flat eyes over the three of us. Hudson raised his eyebrows. Dempsey tried to plant her hands on her hips but was brought up short by the cuffs.

"Check with Mr. Grabby Hands out there," she said. "The only thing I had on me was my purse, and he took that."

"How'd you get into the store?"

"It was open," Hudson said.

"It was open," Coutu repeated, deadpan.

"We heard Jenny in the warehouse once we were inside," I said, drawing Coutu's attention from the staring contest she and Hudson had engaged in. "She was talking in Japanese. She sounded scared. That's when the man showed up. He had two guns, and he surprised us."

"Yeah. Otherwise I woulda got the drop on him!"

"Which is why you found Dempsey's gun in the bookstore. He marched us into the warehouse, tied up the ninjas, and took off with Jenny in their van."

"After tossing a flashbang at us!" Dempsey added, slamming her hands into the table, then exploding her small fists above the surface in a fair mime of the concussive charge of the object the retrievalist had tossed under the bay door. The businesswoman in the corner jumped, then ran her hands down her suit as if she'd not been startled. Coutu lifted an eyebrow at Dempsey before turning back to me.

"It was very disorienting," I said.

"I couldn't tell my toes from my tits," Dempsey said. "Toppled right over. My ears are still ringing."

"Then you guys showed up," I finished.

Coutu leveled me with a look of open skepticism. The riding crop slapped itself against her thigh.

"What about the elephant?" The question came from the woman standing in the corner. In the time it took her to voice her question, she became pregnant, and not just-starting-to-show kind of pregnant, but enormous, hiding twins, if not sextuplets, under her thin suit.

The woman shifted, and her gigantic stomach swung through Sevallo's back. I blinked at the apparition and fought to keep my lies straight.

"Uh, what elephant?" I'd left Kyoko completely out of my story. There'd be time enough to mention her if—*when*—they tracked Jenny down. Plus, if this woman already knew about Kyoko, she most likely was from Evolution Solutions, Jenny's American employer, and was one of the people Jenny had been hiding the elephantini from, which put her at the bottom of my confession list. It also explained her presence. She must be working with the government to track down Kyoko.

I checked Sevallo's and Coutu's expressions, but they looked as stoic as always, making me think they already knew the woman's true goal and about Kyoko—or at least about an elephant. Had Evolution Solutions revealed the true nature of the elephantini to the FBI, or were they hoarding the information until they could get the patent? I shook my head to dispel my runaway paranoia.

Sevallo straightened and crossed his arms. "The three women tagged and bagged with you, they say there was an elephant. A baby elephant."

"I think I would have noticed an elephant."

"How about you guys? Notice an elephant?" Coutu asked Hudson and Dempsey.

"What is that? A crack at my size?" Dempsey demanded. She stood on her chair again, tipping forward. "You see a little person, and the first thing you think is *circus*? There's a short person; there must be an elephant around here somewhere." She mimed scanning invisible crowds.

"Please answer the question."

"No, I didn't see an elephant. Can your questions get more ridiculous? Shouldn't you be out there, after that son of a bitch who kidnapped Jenny, not wasting our time?"

"Hudson, what can you tell us about the elephant?" Coutu asked.

"Nothing. I didn't see one."

He looked as laid back as a man at a barbeque. Perhaps a little more tired, but not frazzled, like I felt. With a jolt of surprise, I realized I was the weakest link in this room. Dempsey was a pro at interrogations, and Hudson appeared to be Mr. Smooth under pressure. I wondered if the agents had been aiming the interrogation at me because they could tell I was the most likely to crack under the pressure.

It's never fun to realize you're the least competent person at a task, especially if that task is lying to federal officers.

I straightened in my seat. "That's everything I know."

"That's everything we *all* know," Dempsey said. "What now?"

They took us through three more rounds of questions, during which my answers grew increasingly curt. Hudson refused to speak. Dempsey alternated between glares and yelling. The agents tried threatening us with obstructing justice and bribing us with immunity deals, but we stuck to the story I'd created. They even started to take us to separate rooms, but Dempsey loudly demanded a lawyer, and Hudson and I echoed her, bringing the interrogation to an end. Coutu released us to work with a sketch artist, and the woman produced a quick and accurate drawing of the skip tracer.

My curse must have been successful at knocking out the camera in the vacant bookstore's parking lot; otherwise I was sure they would have pressed charges. But with no legal reason to hold us, and most likely because they hoped we'd serve as bait for the larger prize of Jenny, Sevallo and Coutu walked us to the front doors, delivered a final admonishment to come clean, complete with a promise of indemnity, and then they abandoned us on the sun-drenched sidewalk.

———

"NOW WHAT?" Dempsey asked.

"I'm going home," I said.

It took ten minutes to convince Dempsey I had no secret plans for rescuing Jenny. Hudson concurred. His voice was flat. His expression was flat. He stood with arms crossed and barely looked at me.

My heart beat heavy in my chest, and any elation I'd felt at being released sank under the weight of my bleak realization: On top of losing Jenny and Kyoko, I'd lost Hudson, too.

Dempsey took a taxi to her truck. I called Ari from a pay phone, and she arrived in full mother hen mode, complete with a bird-nest hat divination and a roost of chickens across her car's dash.

"We're okay," I said when I slid into the passenger seat. Hudson got into the back. "The FBI have nothing on us. The ninjas are in custody. The retrievalist has Jenny and Kyoko. I want to go home."

Ari studied my face, then nodded sharply. She patted my leg and I gave her hand a squeeze to thank her for not peppering me with questions. I couldn't handle any more questions. Later, I'd give her all the details, but right now, I just wanted to savor the silence.

Hot LA sun beat down on my right arm and thigh, and the hum of traffic and the road beneath the tires filled my ears with white noise. I tilted my head back against the headrest and closed my eyes.

I'd betrayed Jenny, but I'd hopefully helped save her. Guilt and relief. Cognitive dissonance at its most torturous. Back and forth, my mind ping-ponged between the emotions. Guilt and relief. Betrayal and hope. Swimming in the middle was nauseous anxiety about Hudson. What was he thinking? His divinations weren't helping me. He had on his cowboy boots and the seat around him was covered in little army men performing defensive drills. His roots were showing, and he was still feeling combative. With me? With the FBI?

"I want to get my car," he said. He gave Ari directions to where we'd abandoned it. I clenched my hands in my lap and started laying down bricks around my emotions. Men left. Men *always* left. Attachment was useless and painful; it's why I liked my relationships light and fun. Men were great for sex, for short-term companionship, and for interesting conversations. They were hell on the more delicate emotions like love and hope. Those they trampled, sometimes intentionally, sometimes not.

Maybe there were exceptions, like Ari's father, Caesar, but those exceptions were not for me. My curse burned through electricity and men with equal force and ambivalence. For me to pretend otherwise was foolhardy.

Only, in all the excitement, I'd forgotten my own rules, and I'd gotten attached to Hudson. I didn't want to see him go. Not yet. I wanted more time with him, normal time. I wanted to explore the attraction between us and find out if it could blossom into something more or if that was only wishful thinking.

In other words, I wanted the impossible.

It was time to get back to reality.

"Good-bye, Hudson," I said when we reached his car and he slid out of the backseat. My voice was a shade too raw, and I forced a smile I didn't feel.

"Don't drive off until my car starts," he said. He didn't look back.

"Are you okay?" Ari asked once he was out of earshot.

"Peachy."

# TWENTY-FIVE

"YOU SURE YOU don't want company?" Ari asked. Her car was rattling and coughing when she killed the engine in front of her house.

"I'm sure." Ari's sympathetic expression grated. "The walk will help clear my head. It's been a long day. A long couple of days. I think I'll take tomorrow off work, too. Will you call Sofie for me?"

"Of course. But your apartment . . ."

"Is trashed. I remember."

"Let me come help you fix it up."

I shook my head. "I don't know exactly what I'm going to do yet. Let me take a day and think about it." I didn't need to think about my apartment. I needed to think about Hudson and about the pain in my chest as I tried to sever all feelings I'd developed for him. I needed time alone to get my head on straight. I had no doubts that I'd rehash everything with Ari, but I needed to understand how I felt first. Or maybe I just needed to wallow alone. "I promise, I'll come by tomorrow for breakfast."

"They'll find her. I know they will."

Fresh guilt stabbed. I should have been worrying about Jenny and Kyoko, not my attachment to Hudson. "Thank you for your help and for picking me—us—up."

We hugged and then I walked away. A cluster of hens herded around my feet for half the block, then disappeared. I glanced back at Ari and waved. She waved back and went inside.

The walk did nothing to clear my head, but it felt good to stretch my legs. The FBI chairs had been hard and cold, but I had hope of my butt regaining its normal shape. I wasn't used to riding in cars as much as I had the last several days, either, and my leg muscles were stiff from lack of use. I took the long route back, stopping by a corner grocer to purchase bananas, ice cream, and a bottle of wine, then by the take-and-bake pizza place, ordering a large. Cleaning up my ransacked home was going to be a long, appetite-inducing process, and I doubted I'd be up for cooking tomorrow, either.

It was nearing sunset when I hiked up the stairs to my loft. It would be good to be home, no matter what its condition. I'd open the patio doors, let in the ocean breeze, and get my life back on track. Without Hudson.

"Hang on, Ari, I think I hear her coming now."

I pushed through the door at the top of the stairs and came face-to-face with Hudson. His blue eyes stared into mine, his expression serious. A shark fin circled his feet, bobbing up and down out of the floor as if it were water, and a fuzzy patch of white fur sat in the center of his forehead. Fear and . . . something. I hadn't seen the white fur often enough to know what it meant.

"Looks like she stopped to pick up a few things," he said into a cell phone pressed to his ear. "Including pizza." He took the cold pie from my hand without breaking eye contact. "Sorry to worry you. Thanks again. Bye."

He slid the phone into his pocket.

"Hey."

"Hey," I said. My heart fluttered, caged hope battling to be freed. I thought I'd steeled myself against Hudson, inured myself to my growing infatuation—or at least I'd started to. I couldn't afford to let my feelings for him take root. Given the preview I'd just experienced, losing Hudson was going to hurt. A lot.

If only I'd given myself this cautionary advice a few days ago.

Between the blackmail and the kidnappings, I'd missed the moment my attraction had changed to affection, but at this rate, I was in serious danger of falling in love if I didn't take a step back now.

"Do you want me to leave?" Hudson asked.

"No." It came out too weak to sound sincere.

"You don't look happy to see me. I can go."

"No," I said, stronger this time. "I'm just . . . surprised."

"Where else would I be?" he asked. "You're here. And you have pizza. It's a no-brainer." He smiled a crooked, teasing smile, and my emotional brick wall toppled.

*Oh, damn.* I was going to be miserable when this ended, but I couldn't bring myself to care.

"I thought you'd been scared off," I said.

"By what? A few guns, a few ninjas, a SWAT team, and the FBI? I'm made of sterner stuff than that. Plus, how can that compete with pizza?"

I chuckled. "Are you hungry?"

"Now that you mention it . . ."

I set my grocery bag at my feet and wrapped my arms around Hudson, lifting myself on tiptoe to kiss him. He kissed me back, sliding his free hand down to cup my butt.

"That's more like it," he said.

My apartment was exactly as I'd left it: trashed.

We ate on the patio, where it was clean and we could watch the sun set. Hudson uncorked a Cabernet. Cool evening air settled around us, and we ate listening to the muted sound of the city.

"I need a new couch—two new couches," I said. I shifted to look back into my lit apartment. I was thankful the ninjas had done no major damage to the gas lines in my walls—Antonio had given my loft a rigorous inspection earlier that day—but my gratitude was buried beneath a rubble of self-pity. "New locks, too," I added.

"I might know someone who can help you with that," Hudson said.

"Nothing electric. Just a nice solid lock. Maybe one of those bars that locks in place on both sides of the frame."

"Like on a bunker?"

"Exactly."

"You don't think that'd be overkill?"

"How about five locks up and down the door?"

"That's a lot of keys to carry."

"Good point."

"I brought a new dead bolt. Thought we might start there."

I smiled.

While Hudson replaced my old dead bolt with a new one, I swept the last of my broken mementos into a large trash bag.

"Do you want to tackle this tonight?" Hudson stood beside the kitchen, looking toward my office.

I walked to his side, and he wrapped an arm around me. I snuggled up to him.

"Not the office." I couldn't think about the office yet. Every single folder and its files were strewn across the floor, mixed with glass shards and paper clips and pens and tacks and dirt from broken potted plants. "But let's straighten the library."

"The library?" Hudson echoed.

I gestured to the built-in shelves on the right side of the short, wide hallway between the dining room and the office. "It was more impressive when the seating was intact." My oversize leather chair with matching ottoman had been gutted, and the stuffing was clumped among the book rubble. The ninjas had swept the books from the shelves by the handful.

More glass mixed in with the books and stuffing and dirt: shards from picture frames and a collection of Italian glass votive candle holders Ari had given me three Christmases earlier. I finished pulling the remaining few books from the shelves, then cleaned the swirls of dust the forensic woman had left behind when she brushed for prints. Hudson started wiping down books and setting them in a stack for me to go through.

"So where have you traveled?" he asked.

"Oh, I don't get away much."

Hudson read titles as he stacked the books. "*Italy Day by Day,*

*Discover Peru, The Rough Guide to Amsterdam, Back Roads Ireland.* You don't consider this getting away much?"

I didn't meet his gaze. "I like to read. I'm sort of an armchair traveler." Not by choice. I did my best to disguise my bitterness.

"You're the most well-traveled armchair explorer I've ever met."

I was glad when he dropped it.

Hudson swept a spot of the floor clean, then sat cross-legged and picked up another book, brushing glass shards into a growing pile. "I really hope the elephantini curse has been lifted."

"Me too," I said.

"You know, at first I thought it was just me. I mean, it was just the cars I was driving or riding in, just my cell phone that died."

"Mmm."

"But then the FBI showed up, and they started having the same problems I did."

"Maybe Jenny did more than change the length of Kyoko's life," I said, inwardly cringing at blaming an innocent animal.

"That's a stretch, though not much more than the life-lengthening formula. But it doesn't explain how the elephantini would affect—infect?—people she's never been near. Take the ninjas' van that night when they grabbed us or even the FBI van this morning. If the ninjas had been near Kyoko at that point, they wouldn't have bothered with kidnapping us. And the FBI seem to know about Kyoko, based on today's questions, but I don't think they've ever been in her presence."

"Hmm."

"Plus *everyone's* cell phone seems to have been on the fritz since Jenny showed up, including every single one of the ten thousand I've purchased in the last few days."

My gut constricted. He wasn't going to let it drop. A Rubik's Cube spun in front of his chest, the sides sliding and twisting, the colors lining up. I'd tried pretending boredom with his elephantini curse theory and I'd tried dismissing his reasoning, but it wasn't going to be enough. I needed to distract him before he reached the inevitable conclusion. His superstition and the nonstop problems had blinded him to the obvious connection between the electronic failures and me, but given a little more time to think about it, logic was going to lead him to the correct answer.

The only problem was, I couldn't make myself stop him. I could think of plenty of ways to distract him—asking a man about himself was a surefire way to change the topic and make him forget for a while. So was sex. But as curious as I was to learn more about Hudson, and as happy as I'd be to lead him upstairs and have my way with him, something stopped me.

Hudson had come through a lot with me during the past five days. He had been rock solid by my side, trusting me and supporting me the whole time. He'd passed the family test at the da Vias'. I felt closer to him than I had to any man in a long, long time. I trusted him.

In my life, I'd only trusted two men: Caesar and my grandfather Leroy Sterling. Definitely none of the men I'd dated made the cut. None of my previous lovers would have broken the law to protect me. Granted, they hadn't been given the chance, and also, breaking the law for me wasn't exactly a rousing endorsement, but I couldn't help but place Hudson in higher esteem for his actions.

Maybe this was nothing more than a textbook case of trauma-induced trust, I considered, trying to be logical. I understood the last few days had been a cocktail of extremes—stress, lust, fear, relief—and I probably wasn't thinking right. I should tackle Hudson and not let either of us form a full, coherent thought for at least twenty-four hours. After that, I could reassess my feelings more rationally.

But my usual solution didn't feel right. Hudson had placed a great deal of trust in me, and I wanted to return the favor. For the first time in my life, I *wanted* to explain my curse to a man.

A jolt of raw panic spun me on my heel, and I sprinted to the kitchen, out of Hudson's sight. I *wanted* to tell him about my curse because I wanted him to stick around. I didn't want this relationship to end before it really began. I was thinking long-term. I never thought long-term. Long-term was for other women, women who were normal. Women who had more hope and more blind faith than I did.

Women who didn't risk their lives by trusting their lovers.

If I told Hudson about my curse, I'd be handing him the very information Jenny had blackmailed me into this mess with in the first place.

I clutched the edge of the sink and took deep breaths.

"You okay?" Hudson called from the library.

"Yeah, just thirsty," I said. I turned the water on and put my wrists under the cold flow. The shock felt good.

What was it Nana Nevie told me when I'd confessed my first adult crush? *You don't walk into love, Eva, and you don't fall. You throw yourself into it. It's all or nothing.*

Nana Nevie, was the family expert on love—not because she had been married seven times, but because her gift was relationship-related prescience: She could literally see if a relationship was going to last, and for how long. Her gift was strong, and it worked on the men she fell in love with as well as it did on anyone else she saw. She'd married each husband knowing full well the exact length each relationship would last. And each and every man she'd loved with a youthful, innocent intensity.

I'd never understood Nana. I didn't understand how she could throw herself into marriage after marriage, knowing each was doomed to end, sometimes within months, sometimes after a few years. It made no sense to toss my heart out there, only to have it trampled, because the trampling was inevitable. The women in my family had no trouble attracting men; we had trouble attracting men *who stayed.* They always left. Nana's men left her amicably: She was friends with all of her former husbands, worked with several of them still, and regularly attended various events with them. Sofie's men disappeared, drifting out of her life in slow increments until one day they stopped showing up. Annabella's men abandoned her, though maybe that was what she preferred—I'd never discussed men with my mother.

Men didn't leave me. I left them. I appreciated them while I had them, and then I left before they could. It was beyond time to leave Hudson. He was hammering cracks in my emotional walls, catching glimpses of my secrets. By all rights, and by habit and logic and every self-preservation instinct I possessed, I should have been severing all ties with him. ASAP.

Yet, for the first time since I was a teenager, I didn't want to run from the risk. For the first time in my life, hope outweighed fear. I trusted Hudson. But did I trust him *enough*?

*You don't walk into love, Eva. You throw yourself into it. It's all or nothing.*

# TWENTY-SIX

"YOU SURE YOU'RE OKAY? You look a little pale," Hudson said, coming up behind me.

I turned the water off and dried my hands, then snuggled into his chest for a hug.

"I know this is tough. I'm so sorry they destroyed all your things," Hudson said. "If you want, we can go back to my place tonight."

I shook my head. "I'm good. Really. Let's finish the library. We're halfway done."

We resumed our previous positions, Hudson cleaning the books and stacking them for me to place back on the shelves in order.

My hands shook too badly for me to do anything but stand there.

"I think there's something else going on," Hudson said, falling back into his musings. "I mean, I've lost count of how many cars have broken down. Don't you think it's bizarre?"

I took a deep breath and threw myself off the cliff of certainty. "No."

"No? So you're saying all these electrical malfunctions are normal?"

"For me, yes."

Hudson looked up from the book in his hands. "What does that mean?"

I sank on weak knees to sit in front of him, thinking this might be a better conversation to have eye-to-eye.

"It means that cars typically break down when I'm in them."

"What, like you've got the world's worst car karma?"

"No. It's a fact. Why do you think Ari was so blasé about her car breaking down? It isn't her car—it's me."

Hudson was smiling, looking for the joke.

"Same with your cell phones. It's the proximity to me that keeps killing them. All those phones—okay, the really good ones—should be working fine again by now if you left them at your house. They just needed time away from me."

"That's ridiculous."

I shrugged. My heart hammered in my chest. I still had time to back out. I could burst out laughing and pretend I'd been pulling his leg. Hudson would accept it was a joke, too. He was too pragmatic not to. But the nagging suspicion would be in the back of his head. That suspicion would wedge space between us, and in a few days or a few weeks, one of us would be ending this relationship.

I ground my teeth and took deep breaths. *Oh, God, Nana, I hope I'm doing the right thing.*

"Think about the last few days. Every time a car broke down, I was in it."

"So was I," Hudson said. "Are you saying that I now kill cars?"

"You've driven places without me. Your car didn't die then. And what about Dempsey's truck? It only died when I was in it. Same with the Tercel."

"Not every time. It was random bad luck. *Really* bad luck, but random. An elephantini curse." He was backpedaling away from his reasoning now. He'd talked himself up to the threshold of making the connection between me and the curse, and now he refused to see it.

I rubbed my palms against my knees to dry them. "Forget the cars, then. What about the cell phones? Every cell phone you've had since you met me has died."

"A bad batch of microchips." He didn't sound like he believed himself.

"Your house? How often has the power gone out at your house?"

"Not often."

"Would you say it only happened when I spent the night?"

"You're saying you being in my house made all the electricity stop working?"

"Stop working, die, suspend. Something like that."

"That's—"

"Preposterous? Impossible? What about Annabella's house? When we found the ransom note, did you notice the power went out in the entire house?"

"Eva, this is crazy. You don't kill electricity. That's not possible. That's like . . . like something out of a comic book."

I hugged my stomach and pushed on through the nausea. "This loft is wired with gas for a reason, and it has nothing to do with feng shui."

Hudson's smile disappeared, replaced by a furrow between his brows. "You really believe this, don't you?"

"I do," I whispered.

He studied my eyes, and his face became a stony mask. Rotten bananas piled up at his feet. My heart squeezed and I dug my fingernails into my palms.

"This has been a really rough couple of days," he said. "Maybe we should get some rest. Everything will seem clearer tomorrow."

"No. Time won't change who I am. *What* I am." A freak of nature.

"'What' you are? Are you going to tell me that you're not human now?" Hudson rose. I pushed to my feet, but he kept his distance.

"No, I—"

"I think I've been a damn good sport, Eva. I've played along, done things I shouldn't have, because, shit, because it felt right. But this? You? Electricity?" He shoved his hand through his hair, his hard eyes scouring me.

I'd misjudged. I'd jumped without a safety net.

"Hudson—"

"Uh-uh. No. The woo-woo shit stops here. You're not cursed and neither is that elephantini." He paced away from me, only half turning when he spoke. "There's a logical explanation to this, and it's not that either one of us is crazy. I need . . . I need to think. Good-bye."

The impact of my heart against the concrete of reality shattered it into a hundred pieces. I'd been a fool to think he'd believe me. I'd been a complete besotted idiot to believe for one instant that love could conquer my curse; worse, that a few days' drama-filled crush could counter what a lifetime had taught me—I wasn't permitted long-term love.

Good. He hadn't believed me, which meant he wouldn't be a danger to me. Of all possible outcomes, Hudson's reaction hadn't been the worst conceivable.

My heart was too busy imploding to care.

A long time after the finality of the closing door had reverberated through my empty apartment, I swiped away the tears dripping from my chin, grabbed the unfinished bottle of wine, and headed for bed.

---

THE WINDOWS FRAMED a heavy navy sky when I woke. My head pounded, and I rubbed a fuzzy tongue against the dry roof of my mouth, grimacing at the foul taste. An empty Chardonnay bottle rolled against my hip, and I vaguely remembered finding it in the back of the fridge after I'd finished the Cabernet.

I threw my arm across my eyes, my thoughts swan diving back to Hudson. For the ten thousandth time, I berated myself for telling him about my curse. I should have kept my mouth shut. I should have savored the limited time left in our relationship. I should have grabbed him by his T-shirt and told him to shut up and had my way with him. I should have stopped him from leaving and proved myself to him. I should have—

*Enough.* I staggered out of bed and dressed in yoga pants and a soft T-shirt. I needed water.

I told myself the emptiness of my front room didn't look as bad this morning. I'd find furniture to fill it. It was a lot easier to fill an empty home than an empty heart.

A shape detached itself from my kitchen cabinet, and for a second the man's height and build made me think it was Hudson. Then his torso disappeared, spinning golden clockwork gears whirling above and below the impossible gap, and my surprise flashed to terror.

I opened my mouth to scream even as I spun to run, but my legs were in a different time zone, oozing into the first step when the retrievalist slammed into me. He shoved me into a wall, pinning my throat with a forearm and leaning his weight on my windpipe. The other hand jammed a cloth over my nose and mouth, and sweet fumes coated my tongue. I lashed out, shoving away from the slender man's chest, struggling to knee him.

Unfazed by my blows, he mashed against me, leaning forward to whisper in my ear, "Don't fight it, Eva."

I clawed at his arm, vainly trying to dislodge the cloth. Black spots danced in my vision. A flat white clock masked the retrievalist's face, Roman numerals circling his head and sleek black hands radiating from where his nose should have been. The clock face fell backward through his head, vanishing and revealing his true features.

Empty dark eyes held mine until the blackness in my vision swarmed, and the world disappeared.

---

AGONY JOLTED from my neck down my torso, waking me, then retreated to a dull ache in my bones and a sharp pinch at my neck. Gasping, I curled into a ball, hands reaching blindly for my neck.

"Don't touch it."

My eyes snapped open at the unfamiliar woman's voice. Lights blinded me, and tears blurred the white room and unfamiliar shapes. I scrambled to orient myself, physically and mentally. How had I gotten here?

*Don't fight it, Eva.*

Memory rushed back. I stilled, but my heart kicked up to triple-time, the pulse pounding in my head.

"Where am I?" My voice croaked and cracked. I ran a dry tongue around my parched mouth. The strange woman leaned close, filling my vision as she peered into my pupils one at a time. Asian, with dark brown eyes and black hair tied back in a neat bun, she wore a long white lab coat and held a tablet in one hand. Gold medals hung on red ribbons around her neck, remaining against her gray shirt and defying gravity as she leaned forward, proving they were apparitions. I tried to pull back, but I lay on the floor and had nowhere to go.

"It's time to work, Eva Parker," she said, straightening and stepping back.

Feet moved behind her, and I pushed myself up to sit. My fingers tingled and my arms protested. The second person wore a lab coat, too. He was slightly taller, with thick short black hair and clinical almond-shaped eyes. A thick band of sunlight speared over his head to pierce my forehead, and I blinked unhelpfully against the bright apparition.

I twisted to take in my prison, then wished I'd kept my eyes closed. Beakers and computers and microscopes and apparatus I couldn't name lined the wall and the narrow counter built against it. The opposite wall pressed close, the ceiling tight above. All the walls gleamed white and sterile, making Kyoko in a metal cage at the far end of the room completely out of place. I jerked in the opposite direction, bracing myself with a shaking hand. Jenny stood at the counter, white lab coat in place, dropping blood into little vials stacked next to a small pyramid of writhing naked babies.

She glanced up and smiled, her cut lip swollen and the bruises on her face yellow in the fluorescent light.

I whirled back toward the scientists, and the room kept spinning in my head. Panting, I fought down nausea. A laboratory coffin. I was trapped in my worst nightmare.

Clenching my jaw to prevent my teeth from chattering, I grabbed at the safeguards on my curse and shoved it tight, tight, tight into a little ball inside myself. Hide. I needed to hide. Not physically; the tiny space held no secret nooks or convenient wardrobes. I needed to conceal my curse. I needed to hide my freak of nature.

With complete ruthlessness, I smothered my emotions along with my curse until my brain hummed within a shell of numbness. For now, it would hold. It had to. It would be enough until we were rescued.

If we were rescued.

I swallowed hard. A band pressed against my throat. I raised my hand. Pain lanced through my body, tightening my muscles into cords of agony. When it faded, I lay on my side, staring at the toes of men's maroon leather shoes shaped into long points and sized for a giant. The male scientist standing in them made a tsking noise and shook his finger at me.

"Try to take the collar off, and you'll be shocked," he said. He squatted in front of me. The ends of his lab coat disappeared into the tips of the shoes. "Try to lie, and you'll be shocked. Don't work, and you'll be shocked. Stall, and you'll be shocked. Is that clear?"

I nodded when I wanted to scream.

"Why am I here?"

"To help me," Jenny said.

I swiveled to look at her. She gave me another serene smile, ruined by the scab on her bottom lip.

"I can't do this without you," she said. A dark black collar circled her neck, too.

"Don't bother lying to us, Eva," the man said. "Jennifer told us you're the key to re-creating her first success, and the traitor can't lie. Get up and get to work. You have exactly one minute to prove you're on task or"—he tapped a small object in his hand—"you'll get a reminder jolt."

My hand drifted to the shock collar around my neck.

"Ah-ah."

I lowered my hand and looked for a door. This couldn't be happening. Both ends of the long, narrow room had a floor-to-ceiling seam in the middle with no obvious handle. I was sealed in this box with three mad scientists, and one of them already knew about my curse. With the collar strapped to me, all three would know soon enough.

Sweat broke out down my entire body, chased by a shiver. I struggled to my feet, using a counter to support myself until my rubbery legs solidified. One bare foot rested where I'd lain, and the smooth floor felt shockingly warm against my sole. A quick inspection confirmed I wore yoga pants and a T-shirt, an outfit I'd chosen in a different lifetime.

The walls wavered in my vision, and I shoved my panic down deep beneath a blanket of desperation and disbelief. Jenny knew I couldn't do anything for her. All I knew about the life-lengthening formula was what she'd told me. So what was her game?

"Are you paying attention, Hiroki?" Jenny asked. "This is where you get it wrong every time. You try to force the RNA to use the wrong strands."

The man stepped to Jenny's side, peering at the computer screen where Jenny pointed.

"This is your computer station," the woman said. I stared at the keyboard and screen she indicated, afraid to touch anything. "Get to work."

"Jenny?"

Jenny's dark eyes turned to me. "Use your mutation and get us out of here. I'm re-creating everything for these Adorable Creations fools as slowly as I can, but please hurry."

I gaped at her. Beside her Hiroki laughed and pressed a button on the small device in his hand. Electricity sparked from two metal points on Jenny's collar. She stiffened. Her head fell back on a high keen, and a glass vial fell from her spasming fingers to shatter against the floor. I jumped, hand twitching toward my collar. The woman beside me huffed and grabbed a sponge to wipe up the mess. Jenny sagged into the counter, silver scissors cutting the air around her and dirty Coke-bottle glasses covering her eyes.

"I told you we need to ask more questions," the woman said.

"I know what I'm doing, Yuri." Hiroki turned to Jenny. "Tell us how she's going to get you out of here."

"She's going to kill the electricity and buy us time until the FBI finds us."

"How's she going to do that?" Hiroki's dark eyes watched me. My feet had taken root, and blood roared in my ears.

"Jenny, don't tell them," I said, speaking with oxygen-deprived lungs.

"She can do it with her mind."

"With her mind? Interesting." Both scientists studied me with identical sinister sparkles of curiosity in their eyes.

"She's insane," I said. "She's cracked under the torture. You can't believe what she's saying."

"You told us Eva Parker was the key," Hiroki said.

"She is. Without her, we all die. She's the only one who can prevent this catastrophe." Jenny gripped Hiroki's sleeve, and he shook her off.

"Why are you telling them this?" I demanded.

"Amobarbital." Jenny pointed to her arm with that sickening, serene smile. A square plastic bag filled with clear liquid was taped to her shoulder, and a slender tube ran down to a needle puncturing her arm. The needle was also taped in place, the skin around it red and puckered. "It's very freeing, really. It's a truth serum. Because otherwise, Hiroki and Yuri are too dumb to know if I'm faking the science."

Hiroki depressed the remote and Jenny convulsed.

My heart sank. I was screwed. My captors believed the words of a crazy woman, assured by science, paying no attention to logic. They should have dismissed her wild claims. Instead, both Hiroki and Yuri eyed me with predatory hunger.

"Jenny's lying. She doesn't know what she's talking about. I swear, I can't do—" A jolt of electricity speared through me, leaving me panting and clutching the counter for support when it receded. Pain fuzzed my thoughts.

Escape. I had to get out. There had to be a way. The scientists would leave eventually—for food, for a bathroom break, for sleep. I could wait, bide my time, and ignore the pain.

I heard my own lie. If I waited much longer, my curse would give itself away. The collar would die first, arousing suspicion. Then the appliances and equipment in the room would die, one by one. Then what? Would they move us again? They'd have proof or enough evidence to lock me in a new lab and begin experiments on me. There'd be more shocks. More pain.

The only element in my control was time. I could speed the whole process and openly wipe out all the electricity in this room under the keen observation of two scientists whose ethics already proved they were okay with kidnapping and torture. Either way, my secret would be out, but if I purposely drained the power, at least I would have the element of surprise.

I flashed on a memory of Hudson's angry face. I'd tried owning my curse and sharing my secret, and it'd backfired. But that had been my love life. This was my *life*. Full stop. Every minute I waited to act, Jenny gave the evil scientists more of the horrifying formula they wanted, and the more pain we both endured.

I sought out Jenny's gaze, ignoring the dirty glasses and enormous needle overlapping the one already in her arm. "You can't lie?"

Jenny shook her head.

"Are we going to die?"

"Once we finish, yes." Jenny turned back to her computer, clicking away.

"If Eva's no use in the experiment, we don't need her conscious. We'll look into this supposed electrical control later," Yuri said.

Hiroki nodded and pressed the remote controlling my collar.

# TWENTY-SEVEN

MY LEGS GAVE OUT. Pain circled my throat and dove through the nerve network of my spine until I couldn't differentiate myself from raw, unending agony. The room darkened, and I fought to keep conscious. With my last coherent impulse, I loosed my hold on my curse.

It unfurled inside me, sucking down electricity, and in gradual increments, the pain drained from my body.

It felt like hours had passed, but it couldn't have been long because everyone stood in the same spot. I sucked in a full breath and tried not to whimper on the exhale. Sweat rolled off my forehead to the floor, and the thundering of my heart interfered with my oxygen consumption. I rolled to my side and threw up.

Swiping the back of my hand against my mouth, I lifted my head and fought for a brave expression as I reached for the collar. Hiroki depressed his remote button. Nothing happened. My fingers fumbled around the strap until I found a buckle. He pushed another button on his remote, and Jenny convulsed. I clawed the strap through the buckle, and the collar fell free with two painful rips where the metal stubs tore free of my flesh.

Rage shook my insides, white-hot and consuming, a raw energy that I'd never allowed myself to feel. I screamed and threw the collar. I aimed for Hiroki's head, but he ducked, and it struck the wall with a metallic bang. The plastic battery box shattered. Kyoko's ears twitched, and she opened a groggy eye.

"How did you do that?" Hiroki demanded.

"Destroy everything," Jenny panted. Hiroki shocked her again.

I planted a hand on the computer in front of me and *pulled* on my curse. I would not be caged like an animal. I would not be a lab rat, and neither would Kyoko.

A crackly vibration shimmied beneath my skin, spiking inward from my fingertips. I'd been alarmed by the feeling when I'd done the same thing to the FBI van, but now it reassured me: I *felt* the electricity entering my body. The computer crashed. Above me, two bars of fluorescent lights popped and died, throwing the back third of the lab into shadows.

"How is she doing that?" Yuri asked. "Implants in her brain?" She lifted her tablet, pointing the tiny camera at me. Recording the freak show. Putting my curse on record.

The hairs on the back of my neck stood on end. The need to run, to stampede, shook my body. I'd severed all other options. If this didn't work . . . If I didn't escape . . .

I pried the walls around my curse wider, and the next panel of lights died. Frogs hopped around Hiroki's feet. Enormous gold coin awards draped Yuri's coat, and a samurai sword slashed through the air. Had it been real, Hiroki would have been decapitated a dozen times over.

I launched for the tablet, knocking it from Yuri's hands. It smashed to the floor, the screen cracking. I stomped my heel onto it, sucking down the meager power it contained. Hiroki grabbed my arm, shouting for Yuri to do the same. Nails scraped gouges down my arm, and an elbow knocked the air from my lungs before powerful hands yanked my arms behind my back.

Handcuffs. They were going to handcuff me. Not again. *Never again.*

A white berserker sheen fell over my vision, and I flailed, clawing and kicking blindly. My fist closed around something round, and I smashed it into the nearest body.

The glass beaker shattered over Yuri's head, and she crumpled. I jumped back in shock. Hiroki leapt over his fallen companion, hands extended to grab me, but I backpedaled, slamming against the metal doors.

A bullet train tackled Hiroki from behind.

"I am not your toy!" Jenny screamed. She kneed him in a kidney, and they both went down. Hiroki depressed the remote, and Jenny convulsed. Hiroki grunted as the electricity pulsed into him, clamping his finger onto the remote. I shoved from the door and grabbed Jenny's ankle, pulling the electricity from her, and her twitches subsided to a limp sprawl atop Hiroki. The scientist's eyes rolled back into his head, and he didn't move.

I fell back on my heels, listening to my harsh breathing. The silence ratcheted the tension in my muscles. When Jenny shifted, a startled scream strangled in my throat. She rolled from Hiroki, fingers fumbling at the collar. After a few tries, she undid the strap and yanked the collar from her neck, then popped the needle from her arm.

"Help me."

She shoved Hiroki's side, trying to roll him over. I reached across him with shaking hands and grabbed his belt, pulling him toward me. His dark eyes rolled down to rest on me before his face hit the tile. Drool slid out of his mouth.

"We need to get out of here," I said.

"We can't. Not yet." Crawling across Hiroki's body, Jenny grabbed one of his splayed arms and pulled it behind his back. I steeled myself and lifted his other wrist toward Jenny. She slid the collar around both his wrists and tightened the buckle in a makeshift handcuff.

"Kill it. Kill everything," she said. Jenny staggered to her feet and grabbed the test vials lined neatly inside a glass-fronted mini-fridge. She threw two handfuls against the wall, and glass rained to the floor, leaving smears of blood running down the walls. Her gaze landed on Yuri, and Jenny rushed the woman. In a few harsh jerks, she tugged

Yuri's white coat down her arms and used the sleeves to secure the unconscious scientist's wrists. With even less care, she rolled the woman under the counter and out of the way. Then she went back to the mini-fridge and grabbed another handful of vials.

"Get busy, Eva."

Hiroki lifted his head. I scrambled backward until I pressed against the door. A pink tutu engulfed his lab coat, and the frogs circling him began to devour his ankles.

Pushing to my feet, I scanned the floor behind Hiroki, looking for the tablet. Had I completely drained it? When I smashed it, had that destroyed the record of the video, too? I couldn't leave a scrap of evidence.

"Jenny, the tablet—"

She scooped the slender computer from the floor and brought it down hard across the lip of the counter. The device cracked and flopped into two pieces, one a flimsy screen, the other a flattened piece similar to the weird green miniature cities with gold streets that occasionally appeared in Hudson's apparitions. Jenny threw both to the floor, then dumped a beaker of liquid on top of them.

"Now get to work." Jenny circled a finger in the air like a frantic traffic cop. "Destroy everything."

I stutter-stepped to comply, brought up short by the shard-strewn floor and my bare feet. None of the remaining electronics were in reach.

Good thing I didn't need to be right next to electricity to kill it.

The thought almost made me laugh. Before Jenny had sucked me into her crazy world, I'd never thought of my curse as good in any way.

Clinging to the cold, unyielding door, I burrowed into the mental fist containing my curse. Pushing with unfamiliar muscles, I stretched its tiny container into a cavernous well hungry for more energy. The last of my hard-won and long-maintained barriers toppled. My curse burst free, unrestrained. Once out, it quested, drinking down wisps of electricity, chasing goose bumps up my body.

Emotions bubbled out of the well and crashed through me.

I stood in the foyer of Sofie's house, my stubby four-year-old fingers clinging to the handle of my mother's suitcase. "Don't go, Mommy. Please don't leave me." Sofie pulled me into a hug, and I kicked and screamed while my mother walked down the front path and got into a taxi with a wave and a blown kiss.

I rocked in a seated fetal position, chin on my knees, next to Sofie's broken-down Mercedes beside the freeway, stomach hollow with fear and self-loathing. I'd killed her car. I could have killed us both. Something in me was broken. *I* was broken and dangerous, and I knew with absolute certainty I would never, ever have a normal life.

I lay by Sofie's pool, listening to Ari's accounting of her family's summer trip to Italy, and envy ate through my thoughts, leaving tunnels filled with self-hate and bitterness.

I sat at Nana Nevie's breakfast counter the morning after a fickle teenage boy had broken my heart. While I swiped tears from my chin, she explained the impossible: that I was lovable when even my father and mother both wanted little, or nothing, to do with me.

I glared across a front room at my first lover, hands curled into fists, soured love turned bitter in my stomach, wondering if I was no better than my mother, unable to be selfless enough to make a relationship work.

The lights in the lab flickered and died, and unrelieved darkness smothered the room. My breathing cut harsh and loud through the abrupt silence, riding the edge of hyperventilation. I'd done what Jenny wanted; I'd killed it all.

A bloated pink tutu wormed on the floor, covered by monstrous frogs. Fireworks popped and towers of naked babies spilled across the tiny room. A handful of ribbons with golden disks looped around an invisible neck near the floor.

Lit by the magic within me, the apparitions shone in the pitch-black lab. Surprise bubbled through panic. Had I always been able to see apparitions in complete darkness?

I blinked and waved a hand in front of my face. Even the rapid movement was invisible in the inky room. No light filtered through a crack or seam, and no backup lights kicked in to point the way to the exit.

Hiroki screamed for help. I jerked at the sound. The baby pyramid wobbled away from me, morphing into a bullet train helmed by a pile of babies. It barreled through the lab, eight feet of its length visible as it endlessly flew along an invisible track. Abruptly, a rectangular black box obscured the center of the train, unmoving while the train's speeding cars zipped through it. Or behind it.

Kyoko's cage. Jenny was hidden behind the elephantini.

"Help! Fucking imbecile! Can't you hear me?" Hiroki screamed, banging against the floor. "You're dead, Jennifer. He'll kill you. As soon as he gets here, he'll kill you both."

I didn't need Hiroki to spell it out for me. I knew exactly who *he* referred to, and I wasn't waiting around for him to show up. I spun and slammed my hands on the metal doors. Clawing along the seam, I searched for a latch, a bar, a notch—anything I could pry or push.

The metal vibrated beneath my palm, and a muted crack resonated through the door. I jumped to the side. A panel swung outward with a suction of air, opening on an equally dark exterior. A clockwork monster stepped into the container. Gears and levers rotated around legs and torso and one extended arm and wrist. The other arm pressed against the wall, visible where it ended in an overblown Swiss Army knife. Dozens of blades fanned along its length. A giant clock face swiveled left and right, looking straight at me for one heart-stopping moment.

The retrievalist.

I didn't need light to know his extended arm held a gun. I'd had it pointed at me before, and I would take that experience to my grave.

I didn't think. I didn't hesitate. I shoved the retrievalist with every ounce of strength I had. He crashed into the wall with a curse, and I darted through the opening and out of the lab, running blind with my hands extended.

Five disorienting steps, ten. Nothing impeded my progress. Where was I? How big was this vast empty darkness? I pivoted on a step and hurled myself in a new direction.

A gunshot deafened me, and something sparked in my periphery. I tripped and collapsed. Burying my mouth in my shirt, I tried to muffle my gasps. I couldn't hear anything over the ringing in my ears, but I couldn't rely on the retrievalist being equally deaf. When no shots followed, I slowly raised my head and peeked around.

Golden gears spun around limbs I couldn't see, and the Swiss Army knife had gained a giant red lollipop. The edge of a pink tutu cut by a razor-sharp black line defined the opening of the lab's doorway. The retrievalist stood to the side, far too close to me for my comfort. The hands on his clock face spun backward; then the clock fell horizontal and shrank to a tight collar around the man's neck.

If he could see me, I'd have already been dead. I pushed to the balls of my feet, bracing myself on my hands. My finger slid into a hole in the floor and I squeaked and jerked. The clockwork monster spun in my direction, arms lifted so a dozen knives and the lollipop pointed straight at me. Barely breathing, I patted the floor. The hole was large enough for two fingers to slide in. Praying for a hatch to open in front of me, I plunged a finger into the opening. Smooth sides stretched farther than my fingertip, like a pipe opening flush with the floor. My heart plummeted. Careful investigation of the ground revealed evenly spaced holes a foot or so apart in neat lines. Each hole felt the same. Where the hell was I?

The retrievalist turned and crouched, and metal clanged on metal. He'd shut the lab. My heart tightened. Any hope of Jenny taking down the retrievalist vanished. The reverberation of sound died quickly; wherever I was, it was a lot larger than the lab. Maybe a warehouse. One with a door leading outside.

"Eva Parker. I could have told them we shouldn't have brought you in."

My muscles seized. I stood on one foot, the other inches from the ground. My heart lifted to my throat, and I willed it back into my chest. That voice—normal, not too deep, flat through the vowels— would give me nightmares if I made it out alive. *Don't fight it, Eva.* With shaky control, I lowered my foot in the next step, then stilled. My muscles twitched with suppressed energy, and it wasn't completely from my need to run. Out, out, my curse quested for new electrical sources, unchecked and free. It gathered power and poured it into the cavern where my control used to exist. It sloshed and vibrated and fed my second sight—and it gave me an advantage. Hope surged in me, mixed with something that felt a great deal like bravery. I wasn't hiding who I was. I wasn't denying pieces of myself. For the first time in my life, I was whole. It only took being kidnapped, tortured, and hunted to make it happen.

Giddy or dizzy—the difference seemed unimportant in the disorienting darkness—I reached through my curse and pulled in more electricity. I'd take out the whole building, or maybe the whole block. I'd make it as difficult as possible for whoever ran this horrific facility to operate. I was no one's lab rat.

"There's nowhere you can go. You're only making it worse for yourself."

Discordant echoes twisted the retrievalist's words. I swallowed hard and forced myself to take another step out of his crosshairs. A circular opening in the floor bit into my heel, scraping away flesh when I lifted my foot. I bit my lip and pressed on, each barefoot step whisper-quiet against the cold floor.

Since it didn't matter if I watched where I was going, I kept the retrievalist's gears and Swiss Army knife locked in my sights, making sure I moved in a diagonal line away from him. I kept my arms extended and carefully felt with each foot before taking a step. Though I wanted to flail with my arms, I kept my movements smooth and slow. If I encountered something, I couldn't chance making noise.

The retrievalist acquired a schoolboy's uniform. It popped in and out of existence on his body parts, each joint spinning with gears, enabling me to see him almost as clearly as if the lights were on. All I had to do was keep my head and I could get out of this alive.

Another step, and he disappeared altogether.

Icy dread cracked over my head and ran down my spine. I grabbed for my curse and gulped electricity through it. *Don't you dare fail me now, curse!* I couldn't get enough air, and I pressed trembling fingers to my mouth to hold in a scream, dropping to crouch in a ball. I rocked in place, drowning on panic.

"This power outage won't last forever, and if I have to hunt you down then, I won't be happy."

I lifted my head. The darkness remained empty. My thoughts slowed and took form. Fighting instinct, I turned and slunk back the direction I'd come. The retrievalist reappeared, khaki pants, white button-up, red tie, golden gears, Swiss Army knife, and all. Shifting my weight, I leaned to the side and watched the monster disappear behind a solid curtain of black.

A wall. He hadn't disappeared; he'd been blocked from view. I turned and hurried in my original direction. I had to be close. I pictured a hallway with a door at the end. Freedom. Escape. Safety.

When the retrievalist reappeared before I found a door or even an edge of this vast room, tears leaked soundlessly down my cheeks. Whatever stood between us wasn't a hallway, just an object in the vast room.

My front hand encountered something cool and solid. A wall! I groped in both directions. A metal pipe stretched both ways at waist height. It wasn't flush with the wall but suspended at least a foot from it, tunneling through evenly spaced beams. I rested a hand on the pipe, turned to put the retrievalist on my right, raised my free hand to feel in front of me, and started walking. Eventually I'd encounter a door.

Hope devoured electricity; from where, I couldn't imagine, but I could feel it flutter inside me. It felt different than before—softer, like it danced beneath my skin. Like champagne bubbles.

With my emotions wide open, the memory of Hudson in my loft flashed through my mind like a bolt of lightning, illuminating a new truth: I'd fallen in love with Hudson when I first saw the bubbles lifting from his skin, but I'd ignored my emotions and willfully misinterpreted them solely as physical attraction. Forty-eight hours I'd known the man, and I'd fallen in love. Nana Nevie would be proud.

It'd taken me days longer to act on my infatuation and confess my dark secret to Hudson, and even then, I hadn't admitted to myself that

I was in love. Now, slinking through the dark, with a murderer stalking my movements, I couldn't lie to myself. Embracing my curse had illuminated the truth—even as it had scared Hudson away.

My fear of forming a true attachment and opening myself to the painful vulnerability of love welled out of the memory of last night and Hudson's final farewell. I didn't shy from the emotion, just tucked it in with the rest of my terror and refocused on the vast emptiness around me.

The flutters of hope faded after a dozen steps in which I encountered nothing. I couldn't look away from the retrievalist, afraid he'd sneak up on me. As I tiptoed along the endless wall, irregular shapes, small and large, appeared as black objects in front of the bright apparitions highlighting the retrievalist, proving there was a lot more than the lab in this enormous building.

In my imagination, gigantic puzzle blocks dotted the room, two-dimensional and the texture of air, each a horror waiting to be touched to unfold. The holes in the floor, the box lab sequestered within this warehouse, Hiroki and Yuri and their shock collars, the retrievalist—each patch of darkness could be its own torture chamber.

"Where are you, Eva? You can't hide forever."

My heart hammered like I was sprinting rather than barely moving. Fear-soaked adrenaline pumped through my veins, setting my entire body on edge. Any second I'd run into something, make a noise, and the retrievalist would put a bullet in my back. I embraced the fear, and it splintered into a dozen forms: slipping on rocks at a cliff's edge, throwing my heart at Hudson's feet, crashing my bicycle, turning away from a life with Antonio, feeling the bag tighten around my throat as the ninjas tossed me in their van. Waking in the lab.

I savored each heart-pounding memory, piling them atop my current fear, reveling in the full sensation without the need to suppress. All my life I'd held myself back, but not now. If I was going to die— No. If I was going to survive, I would do so as a fully feeling, whole person. No more denying pieces of me, not even my curse.

With my surrender, a rush of energy filled my body, and my thoughts crystallized around my options. There were only two: I could escape and leave Jenny to her fate, or I could stop the retrievalist. There wouldn't be time to escape and return for Jenny with the police. The retrievalist would kill her first, or move her and finish forcing her to re-create the life-lengthening process, then kill her. Which meant I really had only *one* option.

I balked at my own logic, knowing it was faulty. I wasn't in any shape to rescue anyone, but maybe it wasn't the curse dampening my normal life-preserving inhibitions; maybe my emotionally unrestrained self was far braver than I gave myself credit for. Or maybe I was a fool at my core.

Either way, logic said that if the retrievalist had backup, they would have come by now or they were on their way. My best opportunity to act would be right now, when it was me against one person.

*Sure, I'll be fine. I'll just pit my feng shui skills against this skip tracer and his kidnapping, gun-wielding skills. I'm sure we're evenly matched.*

Maybe we were, because this feng shui consultant had the advantage of sight.

Sight wouldn't allow me to run up to the retrievalist and disarm him—even my electricity-addled brain saw the problems in that strategy. But if I could find something to throw, I might either fool him into wasting all his bullets on decoy sounds, or I might be able to bean him and knock him out. All of which depended on my finding something in the enormous empty space around me, and from how far I'd traveled unhindered, the stretch near the wall was swept clean.

Stepping away from the wall and any potential doorways connected to it was the hardest move I'd ever made. On jerky, hesitant steps, I walked toward the last obstacle I remembered, hoping to use whatever the mysterious object was as additional cover. I moved with my hands splayed and slowly swirling the air in front of me, and I used my toes to quest in wide sweeps for possible projectiles.

My fingers hit a corrugated wall, and it moved, screeching on unoiled hinges. The retrievalist spun, arms raised. I threw myself left, landing on my stomach as a bullet ricocheted against the metal. Sparks flashed lightning fast, illuminating nothing but leaving a false dancing light on my retina.

I scrambled to my feet and ran toward the retrievalist on an angle, slowing after a dozen steps as my hearing recovered. The retrievalist pivoted to aim behind me but too close for comfort, and I fought the urge to curl into a ball on the floor and play dead. I was too exposed. I needed cover.

Fighting a panicked need to continue running, I forced myself to resume a slow search for something to throw. Every shush of cloth against cloth, every soft scrape of my feet against the floor, every breath I exhaled, I expected to give away my position, and my legs shook under the tension.

The retrievalist fractured into a hundred pieces, and I swallowed a gasp. Black lines skewed in dozens of directions, bisecting his schoolboy uniform, but behind the lines, his shape remained intact. Cautiously, I continued to move, and my breath eased out. This wasn't a new apparition or a failure of my curse; I was seeing the retrievalist behind a holey object. With each step forward, the gaps widened in the black lines until I looked at the man trying to kill me through hand-width slats.

My fingers grazed the obstacle, encountering a sharp point, and I stopped. I'd cut the distance between us in half, putting me close enough to see the pattern on the school uniform tie. Far too close for safety. Crouching, then standing, I watched the retrievalist's apparition through the slats, and it was like viewing him through venetian blinds. Barely breathing, I leaned to one side, then the other, determining the object was hardly wider than four or five feet. If the lights came on now, I'd be exposed, and this holey thing wouldn't be much protection from bullets.

Tentatively, I reached for the object. Rough wood rasped against my flesh. Eyes so wide they hurt, I monitored the retrievalist for the slightest twitch toward me, then reached slowly into a gap. Maybe I could find something in these cracks—even something small that I could throw across the room to fool the retrievalist would help. The top and bottom of the opening were covered by slats of wood as deep as I could reach. A solid board bisected the opening, and splinters caught at my flesh, but I didn't feel anything loose. Pulling my arm free, I tested the next opening, finding exactly the same thing.

Pallets. Wooden pallets stacked—I stretched to feel—a little taller than me.

The wood creaked, and the retrievalist spun my direction, army knife extended. The gun remained invisible, but I knew exactly where it pointed—straight at my forehead.

Crouching, I shuffled a few steps back. The retrievalist stalked forward, feet silent. If I couldn't see pieces of him, I wouldn't have known he moved. With uncanny precision, he closed the gap between us, locked on my last heard location. I held my breath and listened to my pulse rattle against my eardrums.

The retrievalist halted less than five feet from me. His gun hand swung left and right, the incongruous lollipop protruding an extra two feet. His soft exhale raised the hairs on my arm. Slowly, on muscles nearly too tense to function, I straightened. The lollipop shifted to point straight at me and I froze. Three-fourths of his body disappeared, and the retrievalist eased forward two steps, disembodied gold gears churning in the black nothingness. If he stretched, he'd touch me.

I didn't blink, didn't breathe. My entire body screamed for me to run, but doing so would give me away. If I could have done so quietly, I would have lowered onto my belly and slithered away from the retrievalist. Instead, I bent double and shifted my weight, slinking to the side, away from the barrel of the gun. One step. Two—

The retrievalist jerked my direction and fired. I dropped to all fours, but anticipating the agony of being shot made me slow to move farther, and the retrievalist closed the distance between us in sure strides. I stared at a giant gear shifting and spinning at my eye level, close enough to count the golden sprockets. If he took another step, I'd get a knee to the rib cage.

Dempsey's threat to smash my knee with Attila flashed through my thoughts, reminding me that short had its advantages. I curled tight and kicked the gear with enough force to knock my arms out from under me. Beneath my heel, the retrievalist's kneecap crunched. He fell with a roar, gun firing deafeningly.

I surged to my feet and ran around the stacked pallets, expecting a bullet in my back. He fired another shot, and I hunched against the slatted wood. I should have kept running, but I couldn't tear myself from the negligible safety. Through the slats, I watched the retrievalist stagger to his feet, crouched. Cussing, he spun unerringly toward me. I threw myself against the pallets. They creaked and rocked. He fired a shot, and wood splintered. Fire speared my collarbone, but I backed up and rammed the stack again. Wood cracked, then toppled.

I ran blindly, then threw myself to the floor and covered my head with my arms. My skin crawled, waiting for the next bullet that'd end my life. Each breath sawed my throat, dangerously loud, but I couldn't quiet myself. When no shots rang out, I hazarded a peek.

Faint triangles and stripes of khaki and white cluttered a patch of floor. It took me a long moment to realize what I was seeing: the retrievalist, buried beneath the pallets.

I jerked and clamped a hand over my mouth to hold in a scream when a new apparition manifested on the floor beside the pallets. A small, elderly man knelt before a car's bumper, and a gun fired soundlessly into his chest. He toppled backward. The scene reset and the man's murder repeated. Like a movie reel stuck in a loop, the scene replayed again and again, no less horrifying for its lack of sound.

I stared, dumbfounded. Apparitions didn't work like that. They showed an emotion, not a scene.

The stack shifted.

My heart plummeted. I'd hoped I'd knocked the retrievalist unconscious. A pulse of fire ignited in my shoulder when I uncurled, and I patted my shirt. My hand came away sticky with blood, and fresh fear washed down my spine.

The floor vibrated, and a screech echoed through the enormous room. A shaft of light sliced the wall behind me. I lifted a hand to shield my eyes, thought better of it, and ran to huddle against a wall.

The diffuse light illuminated my prison, shaping it into a gargantuan rectangle large enough to make the shipping containers scattered across the holey metal floor appear small. I wasn't cowering by a wall, I realized, but by one of the freestanding containers, maybe even the one holding Jenny. The retrievalist's black-clad shape twisted in fragile angles beneath the weight of the pine pallets.

I pulled on the reserves of my physical energy, searching for a place to hide, my options as limited as my time: a few barrels, a tractor, a pile of tie-downs. The closed boxy metal shipping containers.

Footsteps pounded on metal, and deeper, the muted heavy chop of a helicopter thumped against my eardrums.

"FBI! Hands in the air!"

My knees gave out and I slid down the corrugated metal of the container.

I tried to find my voice, to comply, but I'd run out of juice. With a heavy sigh, I fumbled for my mental shields and put the lid on my curse. It slid on with the ease of flicking a switch. I hunted for a description of the sensation. Full. I was full.

I'd just turned my curse off.

## TWENTY-EIGHT

A PIRATE. A general. President Lincoln. A doctor. A horse. Wonder Woman. A two-story dragon. I'd been rescued by a costume party. They carried an arsenal of guns, bristled with knives, and a few breathed fire. They brought with them a hurricane of objects, most animated and bizarre. A baby doll crawled out of a waste-high Ming vase. Atop a flying UFO, a foot-tall Jesus smiled and waved at a man-size, machine-gun-toting robot. Twin Siamese cats played chase around an ice sculpture fruit bowl. A whale swallowed me whole and kept swimming.

Apparitions. How long had I amped my curse? How much electricity had I drained? The divinations were so strong I couldn't distinguish the real people beneath them.

"Over here!" Bright beams of flashlights sliced through the circus.

"Hands where I can see them!"

I raised shaking hands, the sticky wet fabric of my bloodied shirt pulling against my collarbone, and I winced as pain in my left shoulder halted the movement. Superman, a Roman gladiator, and She-Ra circled the buried retrievalist, ignoring me. I started to lower my hands when a light flashed across my face, blinding me; then a short woman in standard FBI SWAT gear stopped in front of me. Pinned to her Kevlar vest was a badge large enough to use as a riot shield, and a whip longer than a fly-fishing pole cracked the air beside her. I never thought I'd be so happy to see Agent Coutu.

"Eva Parker. Why am I not surprised to find you here?"

"Jenny's here. In one of these containers."

Sharp brown eyes narrowed on me. "Which one?"

"I don't know. It was dark."

"Who else is here?"

"Him." I pointed to the retrievalist. Coutu didn't turn. "And two scientists trapped in the same container with Jenny. They're dangerous."

Coutu spoke into her headset mic, then focused on me again. Behind her, a bear, a tank, a werewolf, and a gigantic gun lined up along the edge of a shipping container, and the bear undid the locks. In a rush, they threw open the doors and entered the container.

"Let me take a look at that." Coutu holstered her gun and crouched in front of me, blocking my view of the rest of the vast room. She peeled the collar of my shirt away from my neck. I hissed as fresh pain burst across my shoulder. "That scratch looks deep. You'll have a scar, but you'll live. Any other injuries?"

I released a sigh of relief, having feared a gunshot wound. On my exhale, my buffer of adrenaline ebbed away, and a dozen injuries awoke in response to Coutu's question. My feet were cut, my knees bled beneath the thin material of my pants, and scratches oozed blood on my forearms, plus a headache burst to life in the back of my skull, but I shook my head in answer to Coutu's question. I stilled almost immediately when the movement stretched my shoulder's wound. "Where am I?"

"A container ship. How did you get here?"

"A ship?"

"In Long Beach harbor."

"Long Beach?" That meant either the retrievalist had moved my unconscious body from one car to another, because a car would never normally survive the early-morning commute from my apartment to Long Beach with me as a passenger, or traveling unconscious had dampened my curse. It wasn't important now, but my brain couldn't move past the picture of being defenseless and vulnerable in the retrievalist's hands.

A chorus of shouts announced the discovery of Jenny, Hiroki, and Yuri. Coutu ordered me not to move, sicced a junior agent on me to stand watch, and jogged to the red-paneled container. The junior agent trotted to stand beside me, the person's light steps belying the sumo wrestler image I saw. A golden ladder rose beside the agent, sinking into the floor as a tiny gerbil-like creature leapt up each rung, never achieving a height above the sumo wrestler's shoulder. I closed my eyes to block out the apparition bombardment, only to snap them open a moment later when latent panic bubbled through me.

Shouts echoed through the ship's vast storage room as each shipping container was declared clear of danger. I watched as the retrievalist's gun was kicked aside, then bagged, and the pallets were lifted from his body while three agents kept him at gunpoint. He didn't move during the process, and I might have worried I'd killed him if not for his shifting apparitions. I knew the moment he regained consciousness: Gears winked out and the schoolboy's outfit clung to his body. The old man's murder on a loop solidified, as did a new looping scene of a young schoolboy sitting on a three-story tiled roof, shooting spitballs at a crowd of kids below.

I pushed back against the container wall and shoved to my feet. I couldn't face the retrievalist sitting down.

With practiced efficiency, the agents handcuffed the retrievalist and lifted him to his feet. He swung his head to look at me. Flat brown eyes bored into me with cold hate, and I fisted my hands at my sides to hide their quivering. She-Ra jerked the retrievalist around and marched him toward the ramp leading to sunlight.

"He's not a fan of yours, is he?" The high-pitched voice coming from the sumo wrestler surprised me. Beneath the apparition stood a petite woman, and if I squinted, I could make out her green eyes under a black helmet. She held a long gun across her chest with relaxed confidence, and her eyes never stopped scanning the ship.

"It's a mutual feeling," I said. Though I doubted the retrievalist would have nightmares about me.

A crowd of people rushed into the ship, pushing past the retrievalist and FBI like they didn't exist. A baker, God from Michelangelo's Sistene Chapel painting, an enormous cherry with arms, a pharaoh, the grim reaper—they each carried bags with bright green *Evolution Solutions* lettering. They stampeded past me to the container with Jenny, only slowing to let the officers leading Hiroki and Yuri in handcuffs pass.

"Bring it out, and I'll need to speak to Jennifer, too," a pregnant woman in sorcerer's robes demanded.

Scientists elbowed into the container and returned pushing Kyoko's cage. They pulled bolt cutters from a bag and snapped the lock, then opened the cage. Between the divinations and people, I couldn't see the elephantini.

I swallowed hard, but the bitterness remained. I'd endured it all for nothing. Five days of blackmail and kidnappings and crime, lying to the FBI, my ransacked apartment, Sofie's kidnapping and trauma, and today's nightmare—all was for nothing. Evolution Solutions had Kyoko. They'd gotten their life-lengthening formula, and I'd prevented nothing.

A pair of officers escorted Jenny out of the container. Her hands were cuffed in front, and behind her, a writhing heap of naked babies swelled around the shipping container. I forced my eyes to focus on Jenny's face. She looked calm and remarkably sane, and I wondered how much truth serum still muddled her thoughts.

Anger fluttered and died in my stomach. I didn't have the energy right now to be mad at Jenny's manipulations.

"I'm not getting a pulse!" someone shouted.

"She's dead," Jenny said. "The elephantini is dead."

Her words were directed at the pregnant woman giving orders, but they pressed loud against my eardrums.

"What?" A hand clamped down hard on my bicep when I started toward Jenny. The sumo wrestler had acquired brick skin, and she didn't relax her hold until I stepped back against the container wall. I strained to see through apparitions and people to catch sight of Kyoko, but the area was too cluttered.

When the pregnant woman in charge turned, I realized I knew her. She was the woman who had been in the FBI interrogation room, asking about the baby elephant. Now her belly swelled and shrank nauseatingly, but at Jenny's announcement, a gold-plated courtyard unfolded beneath her feet straight from the Inca history books, and a knot of rattlesnakes spilled from a dry fountain to repeatedly strike her feet.

"She didn't make it," Jenny continued. "She was weak. I thought she was the one. The sequencing I'd created worked, at least at first, but by the time I got it stateside, its cells were aging too fast again." She lifted bound hands to point at the destroyed lab. "None of this mess helped."

"We'll talk about it later, Jennifer," the pregnant woman said. She clapped her hands and addressed the rest of her employees. "All right. Move it back to the lab."

The scientists leapt to obey.

Jenny was serenity embodied when she met my gaze, if you discounted the swell of babies. I waited for a wink or signal from her that everything was really okay with Kyoko, but there was no subterfuge in her gaze, just pain and disappointment.

Sucker-punched by defeat, I allowed the sumo wrestler to lead me across the huge ship and up the ramp into the dying rays of the sunset, tears blurring my vision.

The dock sat so far below us that I got vertigo hobbling down the long ramp, and the riot of activity at the bottom didn't help either, but at least the long walk gave me a chance to process the chaos.

FBI, SWAT, and police vehicles and personnel cluttered the pavement, and though for the first time in my life I'd switched my curse truly off, not merely repressed or slowed it, twenty minutes later, the apparitions hadn't gotten the message. Two real helicopters circled the dockyard, alternately passing through a fake Statue of Liberty and an antennae tower covered with moss. A single-person-size tank scuttled at the civilian perimeter, holding back gawkers. The center of the action swelled with impossible beings: an overgrown troll chatted with an electric angel near a forest where two ghostly people dug a small grave; a racecar plowed harmlessly through a cluster of eagle-men; a bloated, six-foot parfait cup waded through a river of beetles; books fluttered on hardback wings, spewing black letters like rain atop a spinning tractor wheel; lightbulbs strung on elaborate wire tiers spun atop a clown's head; and running and jumping and flying and crawling and swimming around the entire lot was a menagerie of phantom animals and garage-sale items.

Portable lights illuminated the fantastical scene as the sun sank below the ocean's horizon, and beyond the chaotic pavement, the rest of the dockyard remained shadowed. Had I killed the power in the entire dockyard?

When I eventually reached solid ground, the sumo wrestler pulled me to the side of the ramp out of the way of traffic. I turned to look back at the ship. It towered over five stories above me and stretched twice the length of a football field. That fit with my imagination's re-creation of the space where I'd spent those endless dark minutes—hours?—hiding from the retrievalist.

A door slammed close by, as loud as a gunshot, and I flinched.

"We'll take her from here," someone said. A hand brushed my forearm and I flinched again. "Ms. Parker, please come with us."

I blinked into the face of Batman.

"She's in shock. Eva, can you hear me?"

I turned and the world blurred. An Amazon warrior stood beside Batman.

"Come on, let's get you taken care of," the Amazon said.

She and Batman produced a stretcher and a blanket, both real, and the fuzzy outlines of blue paramedic uniforms peeked between the seams of their apparitions. Once I was lying down—and made it clear I would *not* be belted down—they pushed me through the maze of the shipping yard. I don't think I would have made it on my own. Discounting my exhaustion, wounds, and bare feet, the apparitions would have incapacitated me. In the crush of people, divinations over-lapped in a hazy, nauseating mishmash of colors and shapes, and even lying down, the vortex of unassociated movement disoriented me. The Amazon asked me questions, but her words washed over me. Finally I gave up, closed my eyes, and wept for Kyoko.

I didn't open my eyes until the stretcher halted at the perimeter of the madness. The paramedics checked my pulse, my pupils, my feet, and my shoulder.

"You're going to need stitches, probably a tetanus shot. Don't worry; we'll be giving you a ride to the hospital any minute now," Batman said.

Normally I would have protested the hospital, but with my curse full, I wouldn't be a danger to others.

On my other side, the Amazon spoke with an unfamiliar FBI agent, and when I turned to eavesdrop, I came face-to-face with a great white shark. It swam through me, jaw agape, while I strangled my scream. Luminous jellyfish mobbed the shark, circled by deep-sea monsters.

Hudson.

He stood a few feet away, hands in fists at his sides. A sinkhole opened beneath his feet, swallowing the ground in a twenty-foot radius. I struggled to sit up, heart hammering. He didn't move closer, didn't say anything, and I couldn't read an emotion on his face either, just his montage of fear apparitions. Was he afraid for me? Or *of* me?

"Hudson." My voice came out breathy, so soft I barely heard it. I tried again. "Hudson!"

He jerked forward two steps, then stopped, not quite close enough to touch. I finally untangled myself from the blanket and sat up despite Batman's protests. I was through with waiting, through with caution.

"I love you," I said. I thought I'd used up my quota of fear for the next ten years, but my palms instantly grew clammy and my stomach took a nauseating dive into my belly. Hudson's expression didn't flicker, but the sinkhole disappeared, replaced by cowboy boots and the blue sombrero with dingly balls, both dwarfing his body. I sucked in a breath and plowed on. "I'm not normal, and I never will be. I accept it, and damn it, you're going to have to accept it, too, because I love you." Saying it the second time was easier. "You're kind and smart and resourceful and hot as hell. I want you in my life. I shouldn't have let you walk out on me. You're worth fighting for. This"—I tapped my chest, where my heart was trying to break through my rib cage—"this is worth fighting for."

Sirens wailed, people yelled, the helicopters circled, but all I heard was my heavy pulse in my ears, all I saw was Hudson's unchanged expression. He shook his head, and my heart faltered, my hand falling to my side.

"I'm an ass, Eva." Hudson stepped up to the gurney and framed my face with his hands. I forgot how to breathe. Holding me as if I might break, he brushed my lips with his. I grabbed his forearms when he tried to pull back, and his serious eyes held mine. "I think I fell in love with you the first moment I saw you."

My heart floated, lifting me with it. I slid my fingers into his hair and tugged him back for another kiss, this one infused with joy and hope and lust. I wasn't gentle. When he pulled back, a horse-fur star rested in the middle of his forehead. I jerked when something moved at eye level across his chest.

Small and doll-like, walking across the air in front of his pecs was a woman with wavy red hair in a bright purple dress with white flowers. Her skin shimmered like porcelain, flawless and sunlit despite the nighttime sky. She smiled, blue-gray eyes literally sparkling. My mouth fell open when I realized I was looking at a representation of myself. Apparition-me was cartoonish in her perfection, her full lips and big eyes an exaggeration of the real thing. Over and over again, she walked the air from the left side of his chest to the right.

I'd never seen myself in a divination before, not even on Sofie. I didn't know what it meant or why, of all Hudson's apparitions, she was the most transparent.

A flurry of dandelion puffs burst from Hudson's chest and landed on me. They should have floated through me, but they reacted as if they were as solid as me. Again, I was at a loss to explain it.

I would figure it out. Later. I slid my hands down Hudson's arms, smiling for the first time since I'd told him about my curse.

"So you believe me?"

"I should have seen it earlier, but what you do is—or should be—impossible. But, well, Occam's razor and all that. So, yeah, against all logic, I believe you. Plus, I trust you."

It was more than I'd dared hope for. "You're amazing, Hudson."

"So are you. Your special . . . gift is how they found you."

"What?"

"I had a hunch when all the power went out in a two-mile radius. The docks were the epicenter. It just took a while to convince the FBI."

"*You* convinced them?" I squeaked. *Two miles?* Holy crap.

"They suspected it was a terrorist tactic. There's been talk that Jenny was involved. She's suspected for treason, after all."

"She couldn't—"

"I know. They'll work it out. She's no longer our problem." Hudson squeezed my hands.

My euphoria faded. "Kyoko . . . Kyoko's dead," I whispered.

Hudson's face fell and he pulled me to him. I clung to his shirt as tight as my cut shoulder would allow, eyes closed, breathing in his scent.

"Maybe that's for the best," he said softly.

I nodded, though I didn't agree. I didn't think Hudson believed it, either. The tiny elephant had deserved a real life free in the wild, not shuffled from cage to cage, poked and prodded by scientists bent on self-aggrandizement.

"Come on, we need to get you to a doctor. Then I'm taking you home—my home—where I can take care of you."

"That sounds nice, but . . . two miles? Are you sure?"

"Yep, no power for two miles."

"No. About me. To your home."

Hudson peered into my eyes. "You mean, am I sure I want to take you to my house?"

I nodded.

"Eva, you don't scare me. The only thing that scared me was when you went missing. I'm not letting you out of my sight. You got that?"

I brushed tears from my cheeks. "Thank you," I said.

"For this?" He gestured to the cop cars and helicopters, SWAT team, and general mayhem operating around us. "That's all the FBI, not me."

I shook my head. "For not abandoning me."

I wanted the words back the moment I said them, hearing the little girl discarded by her mother and father in my statement. I wasn't her anymore. I was stronger. But she was still a part of me.

A new cloud of dandelion puffs shot from Hudson's chest and spiraled around us faster than a flock of hummingbirds.

"I'm not going anywhere."

# TWENTY-NINE

GALILEO GALLERY WAS BREATHING room only, the crush of well-dressed and wealthy art aficionados mingling with the casual but curious general public. S. Sterling's stolen artwork was on exhibit for the first time since its anonymous return, and the art world was abuzz. The gorgeous oil paintings had been given pride of place on the main wall, highlighted by a string of spotlights. My aunt's artwork filled the rest of the gallery, too, and from the looks of the tiny markers beside the descriptive plaques, more than half had already sold.

"Quite the turnout," Hudson said, looping an arm around me from behind and handing me a glass of champagne. He looked positively edible in tan slacks and a fitted white linen shirt. I ran my hand up his chest, savoring the heat of him against my palm.

His divination—fluffy clouds drifting past his shoulders—complemented his attire. The clouds were the only apparition around him tonight, for which I was profoundly grateful. Although it had been almost a month, I still broke out in a sweat when I recalled the visual onslaught of the night of my rescue. It had taken three days for my gift to drain the well my curse had filled. I'd spent those days holed up in my loft with Hudson, repairing the damage to my apartment and my psyche and letting my body heal. Hudson had been a tremendous help on all accounts, especially with the long soaks in my oversize oval tub.

"Eva, darling! Isn't this wonderful?" Gabriel Galileo swept through the crush of people and snatched up my hand to kiss it. The gallery owner's long dark hair was slicked back in a low ponytail, and his outfit tonight was just shy of a tuxedo. His romantic Spanish-pirate good looks were flushed with a proprietor's pride and pleasure. He pulled me close to half whisper, "I have *the* artist of the season, and the timing couldn't be better. My archnemesis just arrived. Eat your heart out, Ian Smithson!"

The last was said loud enough to draw a few glances, and Gabriel twisted to put his back to his unintended audience. He made a moue, winked, and threw his head back in laughter.

"I'm glad it all worked out," I said, smiling.

"And thanks to Mr. Keyes here, the gallery's safety rating is better than the Louvre's. No one's getting in without authorization." He leaned close. "More's the pity. Your aunt's work being stolen was the best thing that's happened to Galileo Gallery. Or, at least, them being stolen, then returned."

"I believe Sofie feels the same," Hudson said dryly.

"Yes, she's been *such* a dear through this whole ordeal. *Such* a dear. I couldn't have pulled this off without her wholehearted commitment." His effusive gesture caught a nearby patron's attention, and Gabriel rushed off to greet him.

"*Such* a dear," Hudson said, and we both laughed. Sofie had all but organized this show herself, delighted to capitalize on her moment in the spotlight.

I'd been trying to congratulate my aunt on her success for the last forty-five minutes, but every time I spotted her, the crowd swallowed her up before I got close. I finally gave up and wound through the throngs to the catered buffet.

Edmond was impossible to miss. He towered over the food table, encased in a brilliant canary-yellow chef's jacket with a matching

French cap perched on his bald head. For those of us who could see apparitions, he also wore a chain necklace of miniature cupcakes with rainbow sprinkles on yellow frosting, and a giant cream puff dangled from the center of the necklace.

The table practically groaned under a smorgasbord of sweets—bite-size pieces of brownies and fudge and cakes and pies, miniature fruit tarts, finger-size éclairs, and the pièce de résistance, tiny triangles of coffee cake.

"This looks amazing, Edmond," I said, selecting a coffee cake bite and popping it in my mouth. Brown sugar melted on my tongue, and I closed my eyes in delight.

"So do you, Eva," Edmond said. My eyes snapped open. "I mean, uh, you look very nice, uh, in that dress. Um. Eye-catching." Edmond plucked at the front of his coat, his eyes darting.

"I couldn't agree more," Hudson said.

I blushed at the suggestive look in his eyes, my blush spreading as I recalled the memorable way Hudson had greeted me in my apartment. Luckily the skirt on the blue sheath dress didn't wrinkle, and Hudson was right: my hair looked better down than it had up.

Hudson shook Edmond's hand. "Great spread. You guys outdid yourselves."

"Ms. Sterling was very understanding about—" He gestured vaguely toward the returned paintings. "This was the least we could do. And now she's going to think I'm using her, because I've already booked two other events. People apparently like my food." He said the last with awe and pride.

"Don't feel guilty," I said. "I think Sofie knew exactly what would happen when she accepted your offer to cater." I grabbed two more pieces of coffee cake and slid out of the way of the people waiting behind me.

"Atlas is working the drinks," Hudson said. "And the crowd." I glanced in the direction he indicated, easily spotting Atlas dressed all in white. An enormous gold star hung from his neck with his name printed in diamonds—an apparition only slightly less modest than the sun-bright halo shining a spotlight above him. He flirted with the women in his line and made small talk with the men, exuding the charm of a movie star. His headshot and details were in a framed stand at the side of the table, just in case an agent attended the reception. "I wouldn't be surprised if we see him in something soon," Hudson said.

"If *you* see him in something," I corrected.

"Speaking of which, we should find your aunt and get out of here soon, right?"

"Yeah. We've got another twenty minutes tops before . . ."

"Things start to fuss?"

"That's a nice way of putting it." I smiled up at Hudson. After a month of dating, Hudson was starting to understand the limitations of my curse better, and he showed no signs of being scared off by it, either. The novelty of his acceptance was an ever-present aphrodisiac.

"Hmm, I know what that look means," Hudson said. His eyes traveled down my body, and my skin tingled with anticipation. Abruptly, he rose to his tiptoes and gawked about the room. "Your aunt had better not be hiding on purpose. Aha!" He grabbed my hand and pushed into the crowd.

"Hey, where's the fire?!"

"Oh, excuse me. I didn't see—"

"The person you were trampling?" Dempsey planted her hands on her hips, but she was grinning. "What's up, hot stuff?" I squeezed in beside Hudson, and Dempsey gave me a once-over. "Whoo-ee, girl, where's an extinguisher when you need it? No wonder this lummox is trampling everything in sight."

"You look ravishing, Dempsey," I said. Her red-carpet-ready gown was shiny gold, molded to every curve, and slit to her thigh. She'd styled her blond hair in thick waves around her face, and there was nothing clownlike about her makeup.

"That's the point. I'm meeting a jockey who needs riding lessons, if you know what I mean." She waggled her eyebrows at me. "Now, where's the food? Trying to navigate in here is like hiking a forest where the trees keep moving. I can't find shit, and my sense of direction died with the feeling in my toes."

"You're close," Hudson said. "Can you see the S-curve of track lighting over there?" He pointed to the ceiling.

"Roger that."

"The food's just beyond."

"You're a good man, Hudson. Now find that fire extinguisher before Eva burns this place down." She smacked his ass and pushed through a cluster of people, shouting, "Make way for the lady!"

Hudson rubbed his butt cheek and stared after her.

"Did the wee woman hurt you?" I asked. "Maybe I should kiss it and make it better."

"Deal." Hudson grabbed my hand again and tugged me through two claustrophobic rooms to the last room in the gallery, where the crush of people thinned, and finally, I found my aunt.

"Eva!" She excused herself from the trio of men she'd been chatting with and bounced to my side, greeting me as if she hadn't seen me just six hours earlier when we'd performed the final walk-through before the opening. "Isn't this wonderful?"

"It's amazing," I agreed. Paintbrushes danced around her feet and thornless flowering rose vines twined up her arms, but the rose-tipped wand in her hand made me nervous. The rest of the apparitions reflected Sofie's overflowing happiness, and the best part was the lack of any hint of a blindfold. Sofie had recovered from her time with the ninjas with her usual grace.

"Tell me, honestly, what do you think of my latest pieces?" Sofie asked after she greeted Hudson.

We all turned to the far wall. Sofie had painted a series of small canvases with colorful, whimsical elephants playing with golden Labradors. In the large, central piece, an elephant, a leopard-printed wolf, and a silver Scottish terrier ran side by side through downtown LA. All three animals were the same height, and the elephant wore bracelets shaped in the infinity sign. The rest of the painting—more animals in a fantastical cityscape—were muted.

To those ungifted with apparitions, all the elephant—elephantini—

pictures were a break from Sofie's style, but I knew better. Sofie painted what she saw in her divinations, blending her visions with reality. When I looked at the main painting, I saw Kyoko, myself, and Hudson fleeing through the streets of LA. The pink, green, and blue tigers behind us were the ninjas. The yellow hummingbird and magpie were Edmond and Atlas; the red-backed badger was Dempsey. The window display of a pyramid of babies—these ones clothed and happy and standing on each other's shoulders like cheerleaders—was Jenny. The painting was lighthearted to anyone who didn't know what the symbols represented.

"I like that one." I pointed to a smaller painting of Kyoko spraying Dali with a fountain of water.

Hudson narrowed his eyes at the largest painting. "I can't put my finger on it, but this one makes me . . . well, it makes me tense. I prefer that one." He pointed to a smaller painting of Kyoko and Dali sunbathing. Sofie and I shared a smile.

"That one's my favorite," Sofie said, pointing to a smaller piece of a red-backed badger in a magician's garb, a huge grin lighting up its face as it gestured to a closed curtain behind it. "I knew I needed to get some of that amazing experience—the fun parts—on canvas, but it wasn't until I sketched this piece that I was inspired to paint the rest. I thought of it the day Dempsey told us her big news."

That day had been the highlight of an otherwise stellar month. Hudson had returned home from work, saying a text Dempsey had sent him, Atlas, Edmond, and Sofie had turned into an impromptu dinner party at Sofie's that night.

"What was the text?" I'd asked.

"'Success.' With about twenty exclamation points."

Confused and curious, we'd arrived at Sofie's to find our partners in crime already gathered and Sofie in tears on the porch.

"She's alive," Sofie had said, lifting sparkling eyes to mine as I rushed to her side. "Kyoko's alive!"

"How?"

The how took longer to figure out, and we pieced it together over dinner.

Jenny had remained one step ahead of everyone all along, even the retrievalist. Her years as a spy and her paranoia proved invaluable, even if she did get carried away in the execution of her secretive plans. Only Edmond believed that Jenny orchestrated *everything*. The rest of us agreed she couldn't have planned to have Kyoko stolen or my aunt kidnapped, but she used both to her advantage. Whatever Jenny's original plans were, we knew from Atlas that she set things in motion when she left my mother's house on that horrible day when Sofie was abducted.

"I didn't know what she was doing, but she had me follow her to her hidey-hole, then to a shipping company," Atlas said around a mouthful of lasagna. He washed it down with a gulp of wine, then continued. "I figured she had some secret file she was mailing somewhere for insurance. You know, like you see in movies."

In a way, it had been. One of the packages arrived at Edmond and Atlas's apartment the next morning. It contained two Evolution Solutions uniforms and the keys to a company van, along with instructions to stick to Hudson once I'd been kidnapped.

"What!" Sofie, Hudson, and I shouted at the same time.

"I'm just the messenger," Atlas said, hand raised in defense. "Jenny said she was going to have the ninjas do it, but I don't think she had a chance."

"Who thinks like that?" Hudson asked, his voice a sliver above a growl. "Where does she get off using Eva like that?"

I remembered Jenny telling the scientists in the shipping container lab that I was essential to her success. She'd probably planned to tell the ninjas the same thing, too, and they would have been my kidnappers rather than the retrievalist. It probably would have been easier to escape from the ninjas than it had been from the retrievalist, too. Either way, the only reason I'd ended up in that nightmare had been because of Jenny's say-so.

"Why?" I asked, trying to keep the quaver from my voice. I'd yet to get a full night's sleep, with every ambient sound in my loft waking me in cold sweats, and I still had to sleep with the light on. I set my utensils down on my plate, and Sofie took my hand, running her thumb soothingly across my knuckles.

"She said it would increase her odds of being rescued," Atlas said. He took in our expressions and shook his head. "Look, it wasn't my idea. I'm just telling you what she told me before she handed herself over the ninjas. Anyway, this next bit is funny, I promise. So Jenny had me drive her to the park rather than take her own car. There I am driving on the freeway, and she pulls her pants down!"

"Did she pee her pants?" Dempsey asked. "It happens, you know, when people get scared."

"No. Gross! She had two vials and a needle, and she taped them on her thigh, almost against her, you know, her *down there*. If it'd been anyone but Jenny, I would have thought it was drugs. Or, well, you know, *recreational* drugs."

"What was it?" I asked.

"Gobbledygook she might need later. Only she didn't say 'gobbledygook,'" Atlas said. "She used some long scientific word."

A word that was the name of the drug she planned to use on Kyoko before Evolution Solutions got their hands on the elephantini. She must have first planned to use it when she was rescued from the ninjas—using me as bait—but she'd had to wait when Hudson, Dempsey, and I had botched those plans.

Later, while I'd been hunted and nearly killed by the retrievalist, she must have injected Kyoko with the mystery drug hidden in her clothing, slowing the elephantini's vital signs to an undetectable level.

Caught up in my apparition nightmare and mourning Kyoko's death, I hadn't noticed Atlas or Edmond in the chaos of the parking lot. Per instructions, they'd stuck to Hudson, following him in the Evolution Solutions company van straight to the crime scene, then blending in with the other Evolution Solutions employees to slip past the police. Just as Jenny predicted, her boss had whisked Kyoko's lifeless body into their van before news crews could get wind of the real story, and all Atlas and Edmond had to do was drive away with her. Ostensibly they were returning a failed experiment to Evolution Solutions lab for dissection. Instead, they headed to my mother's house.

"I got a package, too," Dempsey said, taking over the story. "The package was on my porch when I got home from the FBI. Suckers!" Her package from Jenny had included a large metal biohazard box, an unlabeled syringe of liquid, and a cryptic note: *In exchange for a sizable donation to PETA. Try not to scare the world.* "I called Atlas the next morning, but he didn't have a clue what was going on either, so he and Edmond were just following Hudson."

"Took you long enough to realize Eva had been kidnapped," Atlas said.

"Maybe if you'd told me that was Jenny's plan—"

"Then it hit me," Dempsey said, bellowing over the burgeoning argument. "'Try not to scare the world.' It wasn't referring to the elephantini. Nothing about a miniature elephant would frighten anyone."

Hudson and I shared a look but said nothing. Dempsey, Atlas, and Edmond remained in the dark about Kyoko's life-lengthening alterations and the true danger she represented to the world.

"But you know what does scare the world? Clowns!" Dempsey feigned a lunge at Atlas, and he flinched. "And one particular world, or should I say *Atlas*, was quite scared of me when we met." She grinned evilly. "So I grabbed everything Jenny sent and drove right over to your mom's, Eva. I broke in—she really should get better locks—and found the rocket launcher. You should have seen that bad boy. It made Attila look like a peashooter. If I could have lifted it . . ."

Yep, there'd been a rocket launcher in my mother's backyard. Along with the illegal genetically modified elephant, it didn't seem worth mentioning to her. How Jenny had acquired a rocket launcher, no one knew.

Following Jenny's final instructions delivered at the dockyard while her coworkers loaded Kyoko into the van, Atlas and Edmond barreled up to my mother's house less than an hour before dawn the morning of the rescue and found Dempsey waiting, syringe ready. They'd revived Kyoko, dragged her limp, weak body into the backyard, and Atlas and Edmond fled, taking the rocket launcher and biohazard box with them.

"I peeked," Dempsey said. "I mean, it weighted a ton and said *biohazard*—of course I looked. You want to know what was inside? Elephant flesh! Sheets of it, like mutated paper, with hair and every-thing. And little squishy pink things. I think they were organs. And bones, too. It was a little kit of live elephant parts. Some assembly required." Dempsey cackled.

"Go ahead and laugh," Atlas said. "You weren't the one who had to assemble it. It was disgusting."

I gave up on finishing dinner and pushed my plate away.

"Don't even," Edmond said, his deep voice cutting through Atlas's continued complaints. "You got to shoot a rocket launcher. You said it was the best day of your life."

"I bet," Dempsey said dreamily.

Per Jenny's instructions, the cousins had layered the body parts—real, lab-grown elephantini parts—in the van where Kyoko had lain, then had blown the whole thing to smithereens with the rocket.

Dempsey didn't waste any time after Atlas and Edmond left my mother's, either. With the help of a few well-placed PETA brethren, Dempsey "emancipated" Kyoko from Annabella's backyard and rushed her to an undisclosed location.

"I can't tell you who has her or even where she is, but I have a few pictures," Dempsey said. She excused herself from the table and returned with her purse. She pulled out three photos. In the pictures, Kyoko played with a beach ball, touched trunks with a normal-size elephant, and took a bath in a natural pond. I'd cried at the sight of the happy little elephant, starting Sofie's waterworks again, too.

"How are you going to explain her size?" I asked, blotting my face with my napkin.

"I already did. I told the nice hippie people where she's staying that she was stunted from malnutrition. They have a reputation for not asking pesky questions, too, or I would have chosen somewhere else."

Knowing Kyoko was alive and safe had gone a long way toward my recovery. My only regret was that I'd never get to see her again; I'd grown fond of the elephantini during our brief interactions.

Jenny, on the other hand, I would be happy to never see again. Out of guilt or hubris, she had contacted me twice since the kidnapping, the first time in the form of an envelope stamped CONFIDENTIAL shoved under my door almost two weeks later. The envelope contained the summary of the private investigation Evolution Solutions had launched regarding the mysterious destruction of the van carting Kyoko's remains—an explosion that had received a remarkably small amount of press. The report concluded the attack originated from one of the company's competitors and had included copy of a memo that stated, "Regrettably, due to the destruction of the cadaver, irretrievable research on the suspension of cellular degeneration has been lost. All attempts to replicate the former research will be undertaken immediately." The memo was signed by Jenny, now working in the Evolution Solutions U.S. office, and sent to a list of directors and supervisors.

Considering the lengths she'd taken to ensure no company, including her own, got their hands on Kyoko, I was sure Jenny's replication efforts would perpetually fail.

I received a final envelope from Jenny the day before the art show, this one taped to the door of Sofie's pool house. It contained a wad of hundred-dollar bills that more than covered the expenses we'd incurred while caring for Kyoko. I pocketed a few thousand for new furniture and repairs to my loft, then divided the rest between Sofie and Hudson. Sofie took it upon herself to schedule new landscaping for Annabella's when she booked services for her own yard, plus she hired a carpet cleaning service and someone to do drywall repair to disguise the bullet holes in my mother's front room. I wouldn't have bothered.

The lights in the gallery flickered and surged back to life, pulling me back to the present moment.

"That's my cue," I said.

Hudson wrapped an arm around my shoulders. A piece of coffee cake floated toward me from Sofie's hand, then disappeared. Finger puppets replaced the wand, and I knew her meddling face when I saw it.

"Good night, Sofie," I said firmly.

"Your apartment is looking so lovely these days," she said out of the blue. "So charming, especially the back-right section: It's so full of possibility. What is that section of the bagua, Eva?"

It was the love and marriage section, and she knew it.

"Yes, I'm very happy with my front room," I said flatly.

"I'd say it's positively glowing." She looked significantly over my right shoulder, as if she were staring at a bagua map behind me. Maybe she was.

"As are you," Hudson said, oblivious to the undercurrents of our conversation. "I look forward to pancakes at your house this weekend, Sofie."

My aunt beamed. I gave her air kisses and hissed, "Behave." We said our good-byes before Sofie was whisked into another conversation with eager patrons.

Sofie and I hadn't yet discussed the fact that I'd drained two miles of electricity. Hudson accepted it as no more miraculous than killing a car, not knowing enough about the family curse to recognize the absurdity of my accomplishment. I think Sofie was waiting for me to bring it up. Maybe this weekend. Plus, I wanted to discuss the looping apparitions. I didn't see them as frequently as typical emotional divinations, but they hadn't gone completely away since the night of my rescue, either. If nothing else, I wanted Sofie's take on the porcelain figure of myself that strutted across Hudson's chest at the oddest times.

"You know," Hudson said, after we were in the cool, fresh air outside, "there's something called a faraday box. It can block whatever is inside from electrical pulses. I wonder if something like that would work for you."

"You want to put me in a box?"

"No. But it would be nice if I had somewhere to store a cell phone when I was at your place."

"Hmm. Planning on staying over, are you?" I asked.

"As long as you'll have me." With a gentle tug of my hand, Hudson spun me into his arms, caging me against his chest. I leaned into him, going up on my tiptoes to brush a kiss across his lips. The streetlight above us flickered.

"I might never let you go," I whispered.

"I can work with that."

I didn't notice when the streetlight died. I was too busy basking in the glow of Hudson's love.

Read on for an exciting excerpt from

# A FISTFUL OF EVIL

the first in the international bestselling
Madison Fox urban fantasy series by
Rebecca Chastain

## AVAILABLE NOW!

Madison's new job would be perfect,
if not for all the creatures trying to
eat her soul…

# A FISTFUL OF EVIL

## 1

### Don't Follow Me; I'm Lost, Too

The interview was a catastrophe. It started out fine—better than fine. Kyle, the sales manager for the bumper sticker company Illumination Studios met me in the warm confines of a nearby Starbucks, purchased me a grande green tea, and selected a table in the corner, away from the door and the cold blast of November air every customer brought in with them. Soft music, cappuccino-machine clacks and whirs, and the murmur of conversation created a cocoon of privacy.

I handed Kyle a copy of my résumé, determined to prove myself to be the mandatory employee for the boring junior sales associate position. I wasn't particularly qualified and I would normally have rather peeled hangnails than perform cold calls—which is what I strongly suspected the position entailed—but four weeks of unemployment, seven failed interviews, and escalating credit card bills proved very strong motivators.

Strong enough for me to ignore the desperate reason I'd applied for the job in the first place. *Never trust your soul-sight,* I told myself for the thousandth time. But my imminent eviction trumped mistrust of my bizarre, mutant vision.

Kyle dropped my résumé to the table without glancing at it. He scrutinized me over the top of his dry cappuccino. Kyle exuded salesman, from his maroon button-up shirt and khaki trousers to his thinning brown hair with its frosted tips. His face was pinched, as if someone had pressed his baby flesh between their hands and pulled, extending his nose and pulling his lips and eyes in tight. He couldn't have been much older than me, despite the sullen brackets around his mouth and deep grooves between his eyebrows. Maybe his expression fell into disapproving lines naturally.

"How many years' experience do you have, Madison?" Kyle asked.

"Specifically in the bumper sticker business, none, but I believe my time at Catchall Advertising will—"

"I don't care about the bumper sticker crap. I care about your experience in the field."

My weirdo radar, dulled by the overpowering mix of desperation and determination, flickered to life now.

"I honed my sales skills while working as a saleswoman at Sundage Cars. My experience there taught me how to connect with people from all walks of life." Though it hadn't taught me how to sell a car. In the six months of my employment as a used-car saleswoman, I sold a grand total of zero cars, which is why David Sundage, my cousin-in-law and owner of Sundage Cars, had fired me at the beginning of September. But I wasn't going to concern Kyle with that minor detail.

Kyle set his cappuccino down on the table and leaned back in his chair. "How old are you?" he asked.

"I'm not sure I understand the relevance—"

"What regions have you worked in before this?"

*Regions?* "I've worked mainly in Roseville since I—"

"With who? Not with Brad or Isabel." Kyle leaned forward, his dark eyes intense.

*Who?* I eased my tea to the table and ran my palms down the sides of my black knee-length skirt, telling myself it was only nerves that were making Kyle seem so volatile.

"Um, most recently with David Sundage," I said.

"Where are his headquarters?"

*Headquarters? What is this, the FBI?* Hadn't he bothered to read my résumé?

"Down Douglas," I answered, pointing vaguely west toward Douglas Boulevard and the car lot.

"Before that?"

"Also in Roseville, at Catchall—"

"Look, we can both stop playing this game. I don't care about what jobs you've had to take between IE positions." Kyle deflated into his chair with a gusty sigh. "To be honest, you're the only qualified person to apply for the job—my job. I've been ready to transfer for months now, so I'm not going to make this interview hard on you. I want you to take this job as much as you want it. I just need to make this interview look good so Brad signs my walking papers, okay?"

I nodded and tried to look like I understood more than the English words he used. I didn't know what he meant by "IE positions," and I knew I wasn't qualified for his sales manager position. I wasn't even qualified to be a junior sales associate, but who was I to argue? Managers probably didn't have to make cold calls, which automatically made the job more appealing. Plus, a management position would pay better, and I was pretty sure I could fake it until I got caught up on my bills. By then, I could find a more suitable job. Something more Indiana Jones and less Bridget Jones.

"Okay, let me make this perfectly clear," Kyle continued. "Which wardens have you worked with?"

"Wardens?" As in prison?

Kyle leaned forward, placing his hands on the table. "What's the largest evil you've ever tackled? A wraith? A pissed-off dryad?"

I cast a quick glance around for a candid camera, noting the nearest exit in case I needed to make a run for it. I'd been nervous on interviews before, but never because of a mentally unstable interviewer. Was that why Kyle had insisted we meet away from the company office? Did he even work for Illumination Studios?

I eased my hand through the strap of my purse and slid it onto my shoulder, careful not to make any sudden movements that might spook the deranged man. "I don't think I'm the right person for the job, after all," I said, and pushed away from the table.

This is why I never used my soul-sight, never followed its false leads. I shouldn't have made an exception for this job. To the marrow of my bones, I knew soul-sight was untrustworthy.

"Hang on, Madison," Kyle said, grabbing my arm as I started to stand. I froze. "You're definitely the right person for the job. You're the first enforcer to walk through that door in nearly two weeks."

"I don't even know what that means. I'm going to save us both some time and leave now." I tugged to free my arm.

"Holy crap! You're a rogue." Kyle jerked away from me, shaking his hand like I'd given him cooties. Unbalanced, I fell back into my chair.

"That explains your age," Kyle said, speaking more to himself than me. "And your job history. You haven't been playing games with me— you really don't know . . ."

I stood again as he trailed off, and his gaze snapped to focus on my face. "It was nice to meet you," I said by rote. "Good luck with—"

"One question." Kyle stood, cutting off my escape. He towered over my five-foot-ten frame by a good eight inches. Despite his wiry build, the odds weren't in my favor that I could knock him down before he could grab me.

Taking a deep breath, and reminding myself that I was in a safe public place filled with people, I said, "Okay. One more."

"Did you apply because you thought you could pretend to be qualified for a sales position or because the ad glowed?"

My breath caught. The fact that the job description in the "Help Wanted" section had glowed in soul-sight had been an inexplicable anomaly. Dead, mashed pulp couldn't glow. It wasn't alive. It didn't have a soul. But hearing that Kyle knew about the glow set my arm hairs on end. No one knew about soul-sight except my best friend, and that was only because I'd told her. Soul-sight was my own personal aberration.

Seeing my hesitation, Kyle plowed on.

"Three decades as a rogue has got to be a new record. I'm not sure why you chose to come out of hiding, but I'm not letting you get away now, not when I'm this close"—he pinched his forefinger and thumb together—"to escaping this puny region for some real action."

"I haven't been hiding. I think you're mistaken—"

"Come on. We both know you're not qualified for a sales position even if it did exist," Kyle said, flicking my résumé. The crisp white paper skittered off the table to the floor. "But if you could see the glow, you *are* qualified to be an enforcer. Hmm, let's see, how to explain this to a thirty-year-old rogue?"

"I'm twenty-five," I corrected softly, wondering why I was still standing there, why I hadn't stepped around Kyle and walked out the door.

"You have the ability to see the world differently than this 'real world,' right? Black and white? Plants and animals glow all pretty and clean. People look like they're wearing snowy-weather camouflage. Is this ringing any bells?"

There was definitely a ringing in my ears. He'd just described soul-sight. My knees wobbled and I sank disjointedly into my chair.

Kyle sat across from me, shaking his head with amazement. "I can't believe you've maintained a rogue status for so long. I mean, I understand the appeal of not having a boss, but you're also not on anyone's payroll. Why not become a real enforcer and get paid for it?"

*Paid to use soul-sight? Has he infected me with his insanity?*

"I, um—"

"Trust me, this region's not hard at all. It's a good place to cut your teeth, but it gets monotonous real fast. Still, let's see what you've got. Tell me what you see here."

"A coffee shop," I said, not quite willing to believe he and I were talking about the same thing.

"Fine. I'll go first." He twitched his long, pointy nose and grinned at me. "You've got great color. Very pure. Which is how I knew you were an enforcer. No *atrum* in sight."

I shifted in my chair, irrationally pulling my suit jacket tighter to cover myself, but Kyle had already turned away.

"Now, that guy behind the counter, he's not the honest type. Look at the way *atrum* coats his fingertips and wrists. Disgusting."

Kyle grinned at me. I tried to remember to breathe. He was truly talking about soul-sight. I wasn't the only person with the ability. All brain activity got jammed up between that thought and his statement that people—*he*—got paid to use soul-sight. Once I could formulate a complete thought, I was going to have a lot of questions.

"Go ahead, look around in Primordium. I'm going to see if I can attract us a little fun," Kyle said.

For the first time in ten years, I intentionally blinked in public.

I gripped the edges of the table for support against the wave of dizziness that broadsided me whenever I switched between visions; then I purposely examined my surroundings. The coffee shop was slate gray, all color nonexistent in this vision. From the floor (which I knew was tiled white) to the wooden tables to the chrome espresso machine, every inanimate object was shades of charcoal. The overhead lighting didn't exist in soul-sight—*in Primordium,* I corrected myself. Shadows didn't exist in Primordium, either, not traditional light-created shadows. Something worked in this vision to give depth to objects, but trying to focus on it was a recipe for a migraine. The only bright spots in the room were the people.

I forced myself to examine the man behind the cash register to verify Kyle's description, fighting against soul-sight-avoidance instincts honed over the last ten years. My fingers tightened on the table. The barista's fingertips and wrists were smeared black, like he'd had a run-in with a dirty chimney. The rest of his arms were pale gray, as was his face. I knew from experience, those dark patches repre-sented some immoral choices and actions. Light gray was normal for a human; black was pure evil. Only animals and plants were pure white in Primordium. The barista's smudged wrists meant he'd made some bad choices, but I couldn't tell what. That was only one of the flaws of soul-sight.

The only person's soul I'd ever seen that was as pure as an animal's was my own. Since I was far from perfect, I figured I couldn't see my own flaws. That was fine by me. Seeing my soul felt like looking inside myself, and it was a sure way to induce stomach-churning vertigo.

I swiveled my head to look at my companion, fully expecting him to look like a variation of every other human I'd ever seen.

Kyle, the plain-looking salesman, glowed brighter than most searchlights. I lifted my hand to shield my eyes, but it was as impractical as shining a flashlight in my eyes to shield them from the brightness of the sun.

"Aha! There are a few curious imps. Figured there would be with the traffic in here," Kyle said. He was too bright to see his facial features, almost too bright to see a solid outline. When he talked, I couldn't tell if his lips moved. It was one of the creepiest things I'd ever seen.

I had a thousand questions for this man—why had we never met before? Why did he refer to me as a rogue? Could he please dim himself?—but what came out was, "A curious what?"

"Imp." His glowing head swiveled toward me. "You have killed evil creatures before, right?"

I shook my head. "What evil creatures?"

"Amazing. Truly amazing. It's like you've been hiding under a rock, invisible to both sides." He shook his head in wonder. "You've not imploded a single imp? Not even a small one?"

"Maybe I have," I said, belatedly offended and not sure why. "What do they look like?"

Kyle laughed loud enough to draw several stares. "No shit. A rogue with zero experience." He chuckled again. "The best Brad can attract to his puny region is an untrained nobody with no clue. I'd love to see his face when—" He raised his hand to forestall my next question. "Never mind. You've got the ability; you're trainable. Brad won't turn you away, not when he's so desperate for an IE. Ah, that stands for *illuminant enforcer*, which is the job I'm leaving to you. So let me give you your first demonstration of what a true enforcer does. Watch carefully."

I tore my eyes from his shining aura. There was no after-image like with real light, which was a good thing, because I'd have been blind for a half hour after staring so hard. Logic said the bright light of Kyle should have cast shadows all over the room, but in this strange sight, logic didn't apply.

I wasn't sure where I was supposed to look, so I scanned other customers.

The coffee shop was busy but not full, with groups of two and three people scattered around the free-floating tables—mostly college students or businesspeople escaping the office. People firmly rooted in reality, not looking at dirty souls and talking about illumi-something enforcers and Primordium.

I focused on the group of four people to my right. Like everyone else in the room, they had gray dollops peeking through the V-necks of their shirts and flecks of black soot defiling their hands and wrists. I could see their features faintly through their bodies' natural light, and I flushed with embarrassment when all four turned to stare back at me. I rarely let myself use my soul-sight around people; despite my discomfort, it was heady to use it so blatantly now. Of course, to them it just looked like I was staring rudely.

"Do you see the imps?"

I swiveled back to Kyle and blinked against his brightness. Unobtrusively, I leaned against the table while the world spun back into color.

"They're the smallest of the evil creatures, little blobs of pure evil. Hardly enough brain matter to function. Just enough to recognize food and attack it."

*Not good. This is* so *not good.* I wished I were back at home with my cat, Mr. Bond, and a good book or a TV show. Something ordinary. I did not want to be talking with the only other known person with soul-sight who kept insisting there were evil creatures visible to only us. I felt like a character in a horror movie right before they slowly turn around and come face-to-face with a monster. Seeing evil on people's souls was bad enough. I didn't want to see—let alone come into contact with—something purely evil.

And yet, how could I *not* look?

I blinked, carefully focusing away from Kyle first.

I scanned the room again. Baristas. Customers. Books and CDs. Bags of coffee and insulated mugs. "What am I looking for?" Kyle didn't answer me. Movement under the nearest table caught my attention. An inky black chinchilla-like blob sat on the table's base, its glowing eyes watching me.

"What the hell is that?" Anything with life was always a version of white. Even the sullied souls of the sadistic still glowed with light undertones. Nothing living was all black—it was life that made everything glow. Furthermore, animals were never tainted by ambiguous moral choices like humans; animals were *always* white. The tiny fluff ball of blackness was darker than the inanimate objects around it. It was black—solid black. Impossibly black. Either there were varying degrees of life I'd never encountered and this was the zombie equivalent of life, or this creature—this pile of dust with bright eyes—was pure evil.

"Madison, meet your first imps," Kyle said.

The imp cocked its head at me, clearly curious. Curious meant it could think. Curious meant it was trying to puzzle me out. A thinking *evil* creature was interested in me. Abandoning my job hunt and moving back in with my parents suddenly seemed like a great idea.

The imp hopped toward me.

I lurched to my feet, sending my chair careening into the people behind me. Scrambling around the table, I put distance between myself and the creature. Its eyes tracked me. It hopped out from under the table until it was less than two feet away from me. I tensed to flee.

Kyle waved his radiant hand in front of the imp the way a matador waves a cape for a bull. Like a bull, the imp charged. I squealed. The imp disappeared.

*He'd said* imps, *right? With an* s? I spun around, looking for more.

I spied three behind Kyle's chair. Like the first one, the dark creatures were fixated on him. In a group they lunged. I jumped back, tripping over a chair. Windmilling my arms, I fought for balance while trying to keep the evil creatures in my sight, but gravity won. In a cacophony of wood and metal and flesh, I crashed to the floor. When I looked back at Kyle, the imps were gone.

"Miss? Are you okay?"

Reality popped like my ears had just unplugged. I blinked. The world swam. I rolled to my side. From my position on the gritty floor, I could see a circle of black-clad feet, and more approaching. Baristas. Everyone in the coffee shop had gone deafeningly quiet, making the cheerful jazz sound like it was blaring. I realized three things simultaneously: (1) *everyone*—from the patrons to the dishwasher—was staring at me; (2) I must look like I had gone absolutely, start-raving mad; and (3) my skirt was hiked up to my hips. *Shit. Can you die from embarrassment? Please?*

I untangled myself from the rungs of the chair I'd tripped over; stood faster than I should have, assisted by the adrenaline of embarrassment; and yanked my skirt down so that it covered me to my knees. I patted at my hair, pulling a bit of muffin out of a clump and wiping my hand on a napkin. And I assured everyone that I was fine, convincing no one.

How could I be fine? I'd just learned that I wasn't the only person with soul-sight—or the ability to see in Primordium. Worse, there were evil creatures that lived alongside us, visible only in Primordium. Creatures that gazed upon me and Kyle with the same loving look I reserved for triple chocolate fudge cake. Somehow Kyle had made them disappear, but for all I could tell, it was magic, because how did you use a sight to make something vanish? I wouldn't have believed it if I hadn't just seen it. It was the equivalent of a person using their normal sight to move an object; it just didn't happen.

Only it had.


**Continue reading; pick up your copy of *A Fistful of Evil* today!**

# ACKNOWLEDGMENTS

In 2009, I wrote 80,000 words of the first draft of this novel, read it, deemed it pure rubbish, and buried it in my "Old Stories" folder. In 2012, Eva was still pestering me to tell her story, so I took the three pieces of the original draft that I liked—Eva, Hudson, and Kyoko—and wrote an all-new 100,000-word novel. In 2013, I revised the new book, rewriting the ending as well as a 20,000-word chunk in the middle.

Then I abandoned it to focus on *A Fistful of Evil* and *Magic of the Gargoyles*, but when I started writing *A Fistful of Fire*, I was once again hearing Eva in my head. So finally in 2015, I gave this book a new chance, *another* new ending, and multiple rounds of edits, polishing it into publishing shape.

Along the way, I accrued a lengthy list of people to whom I owe a great deal of gratitude.

First, thank *you*! Thank you for taking a chance on me, and thank you for buying my novel. I hope you enjoyed it!

Second, I have the absolute best fans! I wouldn't have been able to publish this novel without your support of my previous works. Thank you for trying another of my books, especially one that is about neither Madison Fox nor gargoyles.

Kate and Jennieke, thank you for your critiques of the beginning years ago, which helped me strengthen the first chapter. The goal was always to get Kyoko into Eva's hands, but how to do so gracefully (or even believably) eluded me for far too long.

Thank you, Shaida, for pinpointing the flaws of logic in Eva's magical power. The rewrites from your feedback were extensive and painstaking, but I love the novel so much more because of it.

Ilona Andrews, your critique of my novel's cover copy was invaluable. Based on your comments, I solidified Eva's motivation, which required yet another rewrite but made the entire novel twice as strong. Thank you! (And if I find out you've read this, I'm going to have a major fan-girl freak-out.)

To my stellar beta readers: Karl, Kerri, Shandy, and Dad, you were all so helpful, and your insights changed this novel in subtle but important ways. Thank you for volunteering your time and your opinions; I'm incredibly flattered and grateful. (Dad, I'm going to continue to delude myself into believing you did *not* read the sex scenes.)

To my editors, Carrie Andrews and Amanda Zeier, thank you for taking away the worries of a plague of typos.

Sara and Mom, do you remember reading one of those earlier versions years ago? Thank you both for your gentle feedback then, and for reading the novel in its latest (and last!) permutation. I hope you both like the new ending!

For the real-life details about a police response to a break-in (which I greatly exaggerated to torture Eva), thank you again, Sara. I'm sorry you had to go through the experience, but I found it helpful. Does that mitigate the loss of your brand-new television?

Cari, thank you for scouting Clover Park for me years ago and sending me video. From the sound of the plane engines to the mesh kid's control tower, having those authentic details made Sofie's rescue scene come to life. And I couldn't resist adding in the dog in a sweater that you saw, too.

For your patience in listening to me talk about this story idea for six years, I should throw a parade in your honor, Cody. Did you know your short fiction inspired some of my favorite support characters, including Atlas, Edmond, and Dempsey? I wanted to create characters that would make you laugh. Okay, I wanted to make every reader laugh, but you were the person sitting in my head as I wrote each scene, and you're the person I'm always trying to impress. Thanks for always encouraging me to be better—and for loving me just as I am.

## ABOUT THE AUTHOR

**REBECCA CHASTAIN** is a feminist, animal advocate, and nature devotee. She believes empathy is a hero's trait and love is a motive, an inside job, and a transformative energy that shapes each person's world. She is the *USA Today* bestselling author of the Gargoyle Guardian Chronicles trilogy, the Terra Haven Chronicles series that begins with DEADLINES & DRYADS, and the Madison Fox urban fantasy series.

If given the opportunity, Rebecca will befriend your cat.

**For free stories, bonus material, updates, and so much more,
visit RebeccaChastain.com!**